WHISPER OF
Evil

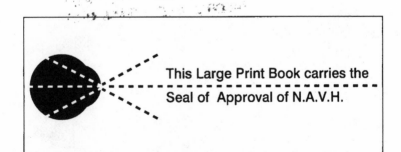

This Large Print Book carries the
Seal of Approval of N.A.V.H.

WHISPER OF
Evil

KAY HOOPER

Thorndike Press • Waterville, Maine

Published in 2002 by arrangement with Bantam Books,
an imprint of the Bantam Dell Publishing Group,
a division of Random House, Inc.

Thorndike Large Print Americana Series.

The text of this Large Print edition is unabridged.
Other aspects of the book may vary from the original edition.

Set in 16 pt. Plantin by Minnie B. Raven.

Printed in the United States on permanent paper.

Library of Congress Cataloging-in-Publication Data

Hooper, Kay.
    Whisper of evil / Kay Hooper.
      p. cm.
    ISBN 0-7862-3721-X (lg. print : hc : alk. paper)
    1. Serial murders — Fiction. 2. Psychics — Fiction.
   3. Large type books. I. Title.
PS3558.O587 W47 2002
813′.54—dc21   2002026611

This one is for Mama

PROLOGUE

She didn't know which was worse, the nausea or the terror. One threatened to choke her, while the other was a cold ache deeper than her bones.

There was so much blood.

How could one body hold so much blood?

She looked down and saw a ribbon of scarlet reaching slowly across the wooden floor for the toe of her pretty shoe. The floor was old and out of level, just enough. Just enough. That was the logical reason, of course, the mind's understanding that the blood wasn't actually reaching out for her, it was just flowing along the line of least resistance, downhill, and she happened to be in the path.

Her mind knew that.

But terror pushed aside logic and all understanding. The blood was a crimson finger curling toward her, searching for her, slow, accusing. It wanted to touch her, wanted to . . . mark her.

I did it. I did this.

The words echoed in her head as she stared at the accusing finger of blood. It was almost hypnotic, watching the blood inch toward her, waiting for it to touch her. It was almost preferable to looking at what else was in the room.

She moved before the blood reached her, stepping to one side in a slow, jerky motion. Escaping. And made herself look up, look at the room. Look at it.

The room itself was a shambles. Overturned furniture with ripped fabric and scattered cushions, ancient newspapers and musty-smelling magazines tossed about, the few rag rugs on the floor bunched up or draped absurdly across an upended table. And everywhere, crimson smears darkening and turning rusty as they dried.

There was a red, desperate handprint on the wall near where the phone was supposed to be, though that instrument had been ripped from the wall and now lay in an impotent tangle near the fireplace. The pale curtains on the front window also bore a bloody handprint, and the rod had been pulled loose at one side, obviously from the futile attempt to signal for help or even to escape.

There had been no help, no escape.

No escape.

Death hadn't come quickly. There were so many stab wounds, most of them shallow. Painful, but not fatal — at least not immediately. The once-white shirt was almost completely red, glistening here and there where the blood was still wet, darkened to a rusty crimson where it had begun to dry. And the garment was ripped and torn, like the pants, both riddled with those knife slashes of fury.

Rage. So much rage.

She heard a whimpering sound, and for an instant the hairs on the back of her neck rose in the terrifying idea that the dead could make pitiful noises like that. But then she realized the sound came from her own throat, from deep inside where there was no language, only primitive horror.

My fault. My fault. I did it.

That's what her mind kept saying, over and over, dully, like a litany, while from the depths of her soul that wordless whimper quavered like some creature lost and in pain.

She looked around almost blindly, trying not to see the blood, the rage, and the hate, and a glint of something metallic abruptly caught her eye. She focused on that. Silver. A silver chain with a heart-shaped locket lying near the body, just inches from bloodstained fingers.

It took her several long seconds to recognize and understand what she was seeing. Silver chain. Locket.

Silver chain.

Locket.

"No," she whispered.

Numbly, she looked down again and saw the finger of blood turn suddenly, curl toward her with determination, and before she could move, it touched the pale toe of her party shoe. The thin material soaked up the blood quickly, the scarlet stain spreading, wrapping her shrinking flesh.

My fault. My fault.

I did it.

She moaned and lifted shaking hands to cover her face, unable to watch an instant longer. Waiting for the blood to cover her foot and then begin to inch up her bare leg, defying gravity in its determination to swallow her.

She waited for that cold, wet sensation. But it never came. The silence closed over her, thick and curiously muffled, the way a snowy morning sounded when the earth was insulated by inches of the white stuff. She realized she was listening intently, waiting for . . . something.

It was worse, not seeing. Her imagination saw more than the blood reaching out for her, saw a bloody hand, an accusing face streaked with scarlet lifting toward her, suffering eyes filled with condemnation —

She gasped and jerked her hands away from her face.

There was no body.

No blood.

No violently disturbed room.

She stared around at a room that looked as it always did: spare and a little shabby, the floral fabrics on the couch and at the windows faded by time and the sun, the rag rugs a cheerful attempt to bring in color and hide the bad places on the old wooden floor.

She looked down to find her party shoe pristine, not marked by blood or even dirt, because she'd been so careful, so determined to look her best tonight. To be perfect.

Very slowly, she backed out of the house. She gave the undisturbed room another long look, then pulled the door closed with a hand that wouldn't stop shaking. She stood on the porch, staring at the door, and slowly the whimper deep in her throat bubbled into a laugh.

Once it started, she couldn't stop it. Like something with a life of its own, it flowed out of her, the sound of it high, so high she was sure it would fall to the hard wooden porch and break into a million pieces any second. She clapped her hand over her mouth and still the laughter bubbled out, until her throat hurt, until the sound of it frightened her almost more than the inexplicable scene she had witnessed.

Until, finally, it died away.

Her hand fell limply to her side, and she heard herself murmur hoarsely, "God help me."

MARCH . . . PRESENT DAY

It was late when George Caldwell got to bed, mostly because he'd been surfing the Internet looking for the best travel deals. He was planning a trip to Hawaii.

He was always planning something. He loved lists, loved managing details, loved making plans. Sometimes the event itself was less fun than planning it. Well, most of the time, if he was honest about it. But not this time. This was going to be the trip of a lifetime, that was the plan.

When the phone rang, he answered it from the depths of what had been a pleasant dream. "Yeah, what?"

"You'll pay."

Caldwell fumbled for the lamp on his nightstand and blinked when the light came on and nearly blinded him. It was a moment before he could focus on the clock well enough to see that it was two o'clock. In the morning.

He pushed the covers aside and sat up. "Who is this?" he demanded indignantly.

"You'll pay."

It was a low voice, a whisper really, without identifying characteristics; he couldn't even tell if he was speaking to a man or a woman.

"What are you talking about? Pay for what? Who the hell is this?"

"You'll pay," the caller breathed a final time, then hung up softly.

Caldwell held the receiver away from his ear and stared at it for a moment, then slowly hung up the phone.

Pay? Pay for what, for Christ's sake?

He wanted to laugh. Tried to. Just some stupid kid, probably, or a crank caller old enough to know better. Instead of asking if his refrigerator was running, it was just a different idiotic question, that was all it was.

That was all.

Still, Caldwell wasted a minute wondering who he'd pissed off lately. Nobody sprang immediately to mind, and he shrugged as he got back into bed and turned off the lamp.

Just some stupid kid, that's all.

That's all it was.

He put it out of his mind and eventually went back to sleep, dreaming once again about Hawaii, about tropical beaches and white sands and clear blue water.

George Caldwell had plans.

He hadn't planned on dying.

CHAPTER
ONE

TUESDAY, MARCH 21

Whoever had dubbed the town Silence must have gotten a laugh out of it, Nell thought as she closed the door of her Jeep and stood on the curb beside the vehicle. For a relatively small town, it was not what anyone would have called peaceful even on an average day; on this mild weekday in late March, at least three school groups appeared to be trying to raise money for something or other with loud and cheerful car washes in two small parking lots and a bake sale going on in the grassy town square. And there were plenty of willing customers for the kids, even with building clouds promising a storm later on.

Nell hunched her shoulders and slid her cold hands into the pockets of her jacket. Her restless gaze warily scanned the area, studying the occasional face even as she listened to snatches of conversation as people walked past her. Calm faces, innocuous talk. Nothing out of the ordinary.

15

It didn't look or sound like a town in trouble.

Nell glanced through the window of her Jeep at the newspaper folded on the passenger seat; there hadn't been much in yesterday's local daily to indicate trouble. Not much, but definitely hints, especially for anyone who knew how to read between the lines.

Not far from where she stood was a newspaper vendor selling today's edition, and she could easily make out the headline announcing the town council's decision to acquire property on which to build a new middle school. There was, as far as she could see, no mention on the front page of anything of greater importance than that.

Nell walked over to buy herself a paper and returned to stand beside her Jeep as she quickly scanned the three thin sections. She found it where she expected to find it, among the obituaries.

GEORGE THOMAS CALDWELL,
42, UNEXPECTEDLY, AT HOME.

There was more, of course. A long list of accomplishments for the relatively young man, local and state honors, business accolades. He had been very successful, George

Caldwell, and unusually well-liked for a man in his position.

But it was the *unexpectedly* Nell couldn't get past. Someone's idea of a joke in very poor taste? Or was the sheriff's department refusing to confirm media speculation of only a day or so ago about the violent cause of George Caldwell's death?

Unexpected. Oh, yeah. Murder usually was.

"Jesus. Nell."

She refolded the newspaper methodically and tucked it under her arm as she turned to face him. It was easy to keep her expression unrevealing, her voice steady. She'd had a lot of practice — and this was one meeting she had been ready for.

"Hello, Max."

Standing no more than an arm's length away, Max Tanner looked at her, she decided, rather the way he'd look at something distasteful he discovered on the bottom of his shoe. Hardly surprising, she supposed.

"What the hell are you doing here?" His voice was just uneven enough to make it obvious he couldn't sound as impersonal and indifferent as he wanted to.

"I could say I was just passing through."

"You could. What's the truth?"

Nell shrugged, keeping the gesture casual. "I imagine you can guess. The will's finally through probate, so there's a lot I have to do. Go through things, clear out the house, arrange to sell it. If that's what I end up doing, of course."

"You mean you're not sure?"

"About selling out?" Nell allowed her mouth to curve in a wry smile. "I've had a few doubts."

"Banish them," he said tightly. "You don't belong here, Nell. You never did."

She pretended that didn't hurt. "Well, we agree on that much. Still, people change, especially in — what? — a dozen years? Maybe I could learn to belong."

He laughed shortly. "Yeah? Why would you want to? What could there possibly be in this pissant little town to interest you?"

Nell had learned patience in those dozen years, and caution. So all she said in response to that harsh question was a mild "Maybe nothing. We'll see."

Max drew a breath and shoved his hands into the pockets of his leather jacket, gazing off toward the center of town as if the bake sale going on there fascinated him.

While he was deciding what to say next, Nell studied him. He hadn't changed much, she thought. Older, of course. Physically more powerful now in his mid-thirties; he probably still ran, still practiced the martial arts that had been a lifelong interest. In addition, of course, to the daily physical labors of a cattle rancher. Whatever he was doing, it was certainly keeping him in excellent shape.

His lean face was a bit more lived-in than it had been, but just as with so many really good-looking men, the almost-too-pretty features of youth were maturing with age into genuine and striking male beauty — beauty that was hardly spoiled at all by the thin, grim line of his mouth. The passage of the years had barely marked that face in any negative way. There might have been a few threads of silver in the dark hair at his temples, and she didn't remember the laugh lines at the corners of his heavy-lidded brown eyes. . . .

Bedroom eyes. He'd been known for them all through school, for bedroom eyes and a hot temper, both gifts from a Creole grandmother. Maturity had done nothing to dampen the smoldering heat lurking in those dark eyes; she wondered if it had taught him to control the temper.

It had certainly taught her to control hers.

"You've got a hell of a nerve, I'll say that for you," he said finally, that intense gaze returning to her face.

"Because I came back? You must have known I would. With Hailey gone, there was no one else to . . . take care of things."

"You didn't come back for the funeral."

"No." She offered no explanation, no defense.

His mouth tightened even more. "Most people around here said you wouldn't."

"What did you say?" She asked because she had to.

"I was a fool. I said you would."

"Sorry to disappoint you."

Max shook his head once, an almost violent negation, and his voice was hard. "You can't disappoint me, Nell. I lost ten bucks on a bet, that's all."

Nell didn't know what she would have said to that, but she was saved from replying when an astonished female voice exclaimed her name.

"Nell Gallagher? My God, is that you?"

Nell half turned and managed a faint smile for the stunning redhead hurrying toward her. "It's me, Shelby."

Shelby Theriot shook her head and repeated, "My God," as she joined them beside Nell's car. For a moment, it seemed she would throw her arms around Nell in an exuberant hug, but in the end she just grinned. "I thought you'd probably show up here eventually, what with the house and everything to take care of, but I guess I figured it'd be later, maybe summer or something, though I don't know why. Hey, Max."

"Hey, Shelby." He stood there with his hands in his pockets, expressionless now, dark eyes flicking back and forth between the two women.

Nell kept her own gaze on Shelby's glowing face. "I thought about waiting until fall or until storm season was mostly past," she said easily, "but it worked out that I had some time now before beginning a new job, so I came on down."

"Down from where?" Shelby demanded. "Last we heard, you were out west somewhere."

"Heard from Hailey?"

"Yeah. She said you were — well, I think the word she used was *entangled,* with some guy in Los Angeles. Or maybe it was Las Vegas. Anyway, out west somewhere. And that you were taking college courses at night. At least, I think that's what she said."

Rather than commenting on the information, Nell merely said, "I live in D.C. now."

"Did you ever get married? Hailey said you came close once or twice."

"No. I never married."

Shelby grimaced. "Me either. Matter of fact, half our graduating class seems to be single these days, even though most of us have hit thirty. Depressing, isn't it?"

"Maybe some of us are better off alone," Nell offered, keeping her tone light.

"I think there's something in the water," Shelby said darkly. "Honest, Nell, this is getting to be a weird place. Have you heard about the murders?"

Nell lifted an eyebrow. "Murders?"

"Yeah. Four so far, if you count George Caldwell — remember him, Nell? 'Course, the sheriff hasn't been eager to put this latest death on the list with the others, but —"

Max cut her off to say, "We've had killings here before, Shelby, just like any other town."

"Not like these," Shelby insisted. "People around here get themselves killed, the reason why is generally pretty obvious, just like who the killer is. No locked-room mysteries or other baffling whodunits, not in Silence. But these deaths? All fine, up-

22

standing men of the town with reputations the next best thing to lily-white, then they're murdered and all their nasty secrets come spilling out like a dam broke wide open."

"Secrets?" Nell asked curiously.

"I'll say. Adultery, embezzlement, gambling, pornography — you name it, we've had it. It's been a regular Peyton Place around here. We haven't heard anything about poor George's secrets so far, but it's early days yet. The other three, their secrets became public knowledge within a couple of weeks of their deaths. So I'm afraid it's just a matter of time until we find out more about George than we ever wanted to know."

"Have the killers been caught?"

"Nope. Which is another weird thing, if you ask me. Four prominent citizens killed in the last eight months, and the sheriff can't solve even one of the murders? He's going to have a hell of a time getting himself reelected."

Nell glanced at Max, who was frowning slightly but didn't offer a comment, then looked back at Shelby. "It does sound a little strange, but I'm sure the sheriff knows his job, Shelby. You always did fret too much."

Shelby shook her head but laughed as well. "Yeah, I guess I did at that. Oh, hell — is that the time? I've gotta go, I'm late. Listen, Nell, I really want to catch up — can I give you a call in a day or two, after you've settled in? We can have lunch or something."

"Sure, I'd love to."

"Great. And if you get lonesome in that big old house and want somebody to talk to in the meantime, you call me, okay? I'm still a night owl, so anytime's fine."

"Gotcha. See you later, Shelby."

With a wave to Max, the redhead rushed off, and Nell murmured, "She hasn't changed much."

"No."

Nell knew her best bet would be to get in her car and just leave, but she heard herself saying slowly, "These murders do sound pretty unusual. And to go unsolved for so long . . . Doesn't the sheriff have at least a few suspects?"

Max uttered an odd little laugh. "Oh, yeah, he has a few. One, in particular."

"One?"

"Yeah, one. Me." With another laugh, he turned on his heel and walked away.

Nell gazed after him until he disappeared around the next corner. Then she looked at the busy little town that seemed oblivious to the storm clouds moving in and, half under her breath, murmured, "Welcome home, Nell. Welcome home."

Ethan Cole stood at the window of his office and looked down on Main Street. He had an excellent view of most of the street, especially the area around the newsstand. So he saw the visibly tense encounter between Nell Gallagher and Max Tanner, saw Shelby Theriot join them for a few moments before hurrying on in a characteristic rush. Saw Max stalk away and Nell watch him until she could no longer see him.

Well, now. How about that?

Ethan had known Nell was coming back to Silence, of course. Wade Keever wasn't as closemouthed as he should have been about the legal affairs he handled, especially with a couple of drinks in him, and Ethan usually bought him a couple or three at least twice a month, just to keep on top of things. So he knew that Nell had — somewhat reluctantly, according to Wade — agreed to come home at least long enough to clear out the old house, see what family possessions she wanted to keep, do whatever else needed doing by the last blood Gallagher left with ties to this place.

Hell, maybe she'd just have a big-ass yard sale and then set a match to the ancestral home and drive back to D.C. purged of the past.

Ethan doubted she'd want to keep much, at least if all the old stories and rumors had any truth to them. And since she hadn't returned home even for family funerals in the past twelve years, it certainly looked like at least some of those stories were true.

Ethan pursed his lips unconsciously as he watched Nell get back into her very nice Grand Cherokee and drive away. He'd run the plates later, he decided, just to make sure, but he didn't expect there'd be anything he didn't already know.

He knew a lot.

Being sheriff of a small, generally close-knit community required that, of course. Good police work in Lacombe Parish, and particularly here in Silence, so often came down to what he knew about the people here long before he had a crime to solve. So he made it his business to know what most everybody was up to, whether or not it was illegal.

"Sheriff?"

He turned from the window to find one of his CID detectives, Justin Byers, standing in front of the desk. He encouraged his people to come seek him out if they needed to talk, avoiding the outdated intercom system mostly because it was outdated but also because he hated the tinny, almost eerie sounds of voices run through the things.

"What's up, Justin?"

"I'm having a little trouble running down all the financial information on George Caldwell. Nothing really suspicious, just some pretty scattered investments and a few too many details unexplained for my taste. I thought maybe if we got a warrant for his personal records —"

Ethan smiled. "I appreciate your enthusiasm, Justin, but I doubt Judge Buchanan will issue a warrant based on our uneasiness. Find out what you can, but don't push anybody, and don't call on his widow, okay?"

"Does Sue Caldwell even consider herself his widow? I mean, they'd been separated — what? — two or three years?"

"About that." Ethan shrugged. "But they were still married, and she's his legal heir. From what I hear, she's grieving. So leave her alone."

"Okay, sure. Just so you know, it's going to take a while to gather all the info you wanted —"

"Understood." Ethan's easy smile remained until the detective left the room, then faded. He didn't entirely trust Justin Byers. Then again, he didn't entirely trust at least three of the six new people he'd had to hire on since the new highway had made this a far more busy town in the last year. Ethan liked to have people he knew around him, and three of the most recent hires — including Byers — had not been born and raised in Silence.

Not a crime, that, and all had boasted fine credentials and recommendations, to say nothing of experience to spare.

Still.

Returning to his comfortable chair behind the desk, Ethan unlocked and opened the center drawer and drew out a dull brown folder. Inside were copies of three reports his office had submitted, as required, to the district-court prosecutor.

The report of the first death was straightforward enough. Peter Lynch, fifty, had died suddenly, apparently of a heart attack. Only at the insistence of a hysterical wife had an autopsy been performed, resulting in the unexpected finding of poison. Since the house hadn't been treated as the scene of a crime at the time, going back to search later had turned up nothing useful in proving what had happened, but the medical examiner believed someone might have slipped a few capsules of nitroglycerin into one of the vitamin bottles. Lynch had been known to take vitamins by the handful, and no other drugs, prescription or recreational, had been found, so there was certainly a possibility the ME was right.

The really interesting thing was that once they began seriously searching his house to find out if Lynch had kept and used any drugs, they had discovered in the bottom of his closet a concealed cubbyhole hiding a stash of truly sick porn.

Little girls dressed up and painted up to look like whores, then photographed with men who might have been their fathers. Or grandfathers. Doing things that still made Ethan's stomach churn just to think about.

"Sick bastard," he muttered under his breath.

Lynch's wife had been understandably appalled and mortified, especially when that first discovery had led to others, including evidence of trips Lynch had taken out of town that had nothing to do with business and everything to do with his abnormal pleasures. Not only had he frequently visited a house down in New Orleans that catered to men with his particular sexual proclivities, he had also kept a mistress in that city. A girl younger than his own youngest daughter.

Frowning, Ethan turned to the second report, which, again, had seemed straightforward in the beginning. Luke Ferrier, thirty-eight, had apparently committed suicide by driving his car into a bayou. Water in his lungs proved he'd drowned, and the conclusion of suicide seemed accurate enough. But a coworker insisted — loudly — that he hadn't been suicidal, so Ethan's people had taken a closer look.

Figuring money was the most likely reason a young and healthy man without many family ties would choose to kill himself, they had looked into his financial records and those of the company he worked for. Again, what they found had surprised them — not because they discovered evidence of embezzlement, but because it appeared Ferrier had repaid every penny he had "borrowed" months before his supposed suicide.

No one had suspected him, and he'd been home-free.

So why commit suicide?

The ME had allowed as how there were certainly barbiturates and muscle relaxers that didn't linger in the body; Ferrier might have been doped and his car pointed at that bayou while he was out cold, with nothing to show up in the autopsy afterward. It was possible.

But the real clincher had come when they dug a little deeper — and discovered not only an apparently chronic gambling habit but also a fat bank account in Baton Rouge and a lockbox containing, among other things, a plane ticket to the south of France dated a month after Ferrier's death. More paperwork in the box further indicated he'd been just about ready to pull up stakes and leave Silence.

So why commit suicide?

"Not suicide," Ethan said, again half under his breath. "Goddammit."

The third report concerned the death of Randal Patterson, forty-six, which had occurred just two months ago. By that point, with uneasiness in the town palpable and gossip running rampant, Ethan's deputies and detectives hadn't made the mistake of assuming anything — except the worst. Finding a relatively young, seemingly healthy adult male dead of any cause

31

would have been enough to alert them; finding said adult male electrocuted in his Jacuzzi courtesy of a live wire dropped into the tub from a nearby window sent up a huge red flag.

And the flag was fairly waved in their faces when the subsequent investigation uncovered Randal Patterson's dirty little secret: a well-equipped room in his basement containing a number of sadomasochistic apparatus and devices, and a great deal of rubber and black leather. Whips. Masks. Chains.

So far they hadn't been able to find out who Patterson had played his little games with, but it was only a matter of time.

Only a matter of time.

"Shit," Ethan muttered softly.

There was, of course, no complete report on George Caldwell as yet. It had been only a few days, after all, since he'd been found. Shot through the head, with no gun in sight. Hard to call that anything but murder.

But, so far, nothing obscene or illegal had turned up.

So far.

Ethan closed the folder and stared rather grimly across his office. He didn't like this.

He didn't like this one little bit.

Nell got out of her Jeep and stood gazing at the big white clapboard house that was set back from the road and surrounded by towering oak trees. The house sprawled without much architectural integrity, which wasn't surprising considering that the original hundred-year-old building had been remodeled and expanded several times in the past decades as the family within it had also grown.

Ironic, Nell thought, that here she stood, a century after the first Gallaghers had put down roots in this place, presumably with high hopes and determination to build a family. Here she stood. Alone. Last of the line, at least in Silence.

And stood reluctantly, at that.

Nell sighed and went around to open the Jeep's cargo hatch. The space was full, holding her suitcase and laptop case, as well as several bags of groceries she'd stopped off in town to buy. She was just about to grab a couple of the bags and head for the house when a sense other than hearing made her turn and look toward the road.

A sheriff's department cruiser was turning into the driveway.

Not really surprised, Nell leaned back

against the floor of the open hatch and waited.

The cruiser pulled up behind her Jeep, and two deputies got out. The taller of the two, unexpectedly, was the woman; she had to be close to six feet tall, Nell judged, and boasted centerfold measurements that had undoubtedly been more of a bane than a blessing in her chosen profession. She was also lovely in a darkly exotic way that spoke of a Creole heritage very common in the area.

Her older partner was probably five-nine or -ten, blond, and good-looking in a boyish way, with a wide and welcoming smile. He was one of those men who would look almost exactly the same between twenty and sixty, only then appearing to age.

"Hey, Miss Gallagher. I'm Kyle Venable, and this is Lauren Champagne."

Nell couldn't help lifting a brow at the woman, who responded with a dry, "One of my many crosses."

"Nice to meet you both," Nell said with a faint smile. "I think. Did I run a stop sign or something?"

"Oh, no, ma'am," Deputy Venable assured her hastily. "Sheriff just wanted us to come out and check the place over for you. It's stood empty awhile, you know, and

34

careful as we are to keep an eye on things, there are still vagrants about — especially out this far. If you'll let us have the key, we'll make sure everything checks out before you move in."

Nell didn't hesitate to reach into the pocket of her jacket and produce a key. "Thanks, I appreciate it," she said.

"It won't take long, ma'am," Venable said, accepting the key and touching his hat brim politely before he and his partner strode up the flagstone walkway to the front door.

Remaining where she was, Nell watched them disappear into the house. Useless to pretend even to herself that she wasn't incredibly tense; all she could do was try not to look it. She felt an all-too-familiar twinge in her left temple and massaged the area in a soothing circular motion with three fingers.

"Not now," she whispered. "Christ, not now." She rubbed harder, willing her body and mind to obey the desperate command.

It was probably no more than ten minutes before the deputies reappeared, though it seemed longer.

"Clear," Venable said cheerfully as they rejoined Nell at the vehicles. "Looks like all the windows and doors have pretty solid locks, but you might want to consider installing a good security system, Miss Gallagher. That or get yourself a big dog."

"Thanks, Deputy." She included them both in her smile and nod of gratitude as he returned the key, adding, "I probably won't be here long enough to do anything permanent, but I'll certainly keep the house locked up while I'm here."

"We'll be passing by pretty often on regular patrols, so we'll keep an eye on the place." Venable gestured toward the packed cargo area. "In the meantime, we'd be happy to help you carry some of this stuff inside."

"Oh, no, thanks, I can manage. I do appreciate the offer, though."

He touched his hat brim again, smiling. "Okay, but don't hesitate to holler if you need anything. Anything at all."

"I won't."

The two deputies got back in their cruiser, and Nell deliberately turned to unload the Jeep rather than watch them leave. By the time she reached the front porch with an armful of groceries, she was aware that the cruiser and its deputies had reached the end of the long drive and pulled out onto the road heading back toward town.

She didn't look after them.

They had left the front door standing open, guarded only by the old screen door, and for just a moment she stood there trying to brace herself both mentally and emotionally.

Another twinge in her temple urged her into the house before she was entirely ready to go, which was probably just as well. Without some sort of spur, she wasn't at all sure she would have been able to do it.

She stepped into an open foyer that was disconcertingly familiar with its polished wooden floor and round, pedestal-leg table. There should have been flowers on the table, of course, and hadn't there been a rug underneath?

Shaking off the vague musings, Nell moved purposefully past the stairs toward the kitchen, deliberately not looking through any doorways she passed. Formal dining room on one side, living room on the other, half bath under the stairs — and no need to check out any of those rooms.

Not yet. Not yet.

She put the grocery bags on the kitchen counter and spared only one quick look around the bright yellow-and-white kitchen, then immediately headed back out to the Jeep. She needed to get everything inside, and as soon as possible; the twinges in her temple had become a painful throbbing as rhythmic and inevitable as her heartbeat.

She barely made it, dumping her luggage in the foyer and locking the front door before moving unsteadily back to the kitchen. She fumbled through the bags for the few perishables that needed to go into the refrigerator, fighting the dizziness grimly even as she told herself she should at least find a chair before —

Blackness washed over her, and Nell crumpled silently to the dusty tile floor.

CHAPTER
TWO

It was a bit like meditation, he had decided. If he closed his eyes and concentrated, really concentrated, his body seemed to grow very light, almost weightless, and some part of him was able to float away for a while. Sometimes he just floated without direction, not really caring where he went, enjoying the sensations of drifting along without any ties of the flesh.

True freedom. He'd had no idea.

Sometimes, however, he focused all his energy and will on controlling his direction, concentrated on reaching a particular place, because there was someone special he had to find.

Like her. She was easy to find. The effortless connection established so long ago led him to her quickly.

She was moving about the kitchen, putting groceries away. Preoccupied, maybe even upset or unnerved by the storms rumbling all around on this restless spring night. She looked a little pale, he thought,

39

and there was a square of adhesive bandage on her forehead just above her right eyebrow.

He wondered if she had fallen. Wondered what would happen if he reached out and touched her.

He nearly did reach out but stopped himself. No. Not now. Not yet.

There were things he had to do first. A job he had to finish. He wasn't the sort of man to avoid his responsibilities, after all. That was not the way he'd been raised, and not his character. A man finished what he started.

Besides, there was plenty of time for Nell. Time to find out the truth about why she'd come home. Time to find out how much she remembered.

She walked past him, intent on placing a couple of boxes into an upper cabinet, and he was almost certain he could smell her hair, a clean scent like sunshine.

He almost reached out and touched her.

Almost.

WEDNESDAY, MARCH 22

Nell woke so abruptly that she heard the broken-off ending of her own strange, muf-

40

fled cry. She sat there in her bed, staring at the hands that were still raised and stretched out before her as though she had been reaching for something. Her hands were shaking visibly. She felt stiff, so tense her muscles protested with sharp twinges. Her fingers curled slowly, and she made herself relax her arms, lower them. Stop reaching.

The bedroom was flooded with morning light, the previous night's storms long gone, and through her slightly open window a cool, moist breeze fluttered the curtains. It smelled damp and earthy, like spring.

She didn't have to try to remember the dream. It was always the same one. Little details varied, but the basic framework of the dream had never changed. And even though it wasn't an every-night occurrence, it happened often enough to be all too familiar to Nell.

"I shouldn't have come back here," she heard herself murmur.

She had hoped that after so many years, coming back here wouldn't have made it worse. But she should have known better than that. Even driving down here she had known, had felt the wrenching sensation she had lived with for so long begin to intensify, as if a cord tied to something deep inside her were being tugged insistently.

Now the pull was steady, urgent. Impossible to ignore.

Stiffly, Nell slid from the bed and went to take a shower, allowing the hot water to beat down on her while she concentrated on shoring up her defenses. It was hard, harder than it had ever been before, but by the time she was dressed and on her way downstairs, the pull inside her was at least tolerable, pushed down and quieted so that it no longer made her feel she would be torn in half.

I shouldn't have come back here. How can I do what I have to with this inside me?

"Nell."

Halfway across the foyer, she stopped with a jerk and turned completely around, staring behind her, all around her. But there was no one there. Absolutely no one.

"I shouldn't have come back here," she murmured.

"It's a simple enough question." Ethan smiled easily as he gazed across his desk at Max Tanner. "Where were you Saturday night, Max?"

"You mean, where was I when George Caldwell was shot?" Max offered the sheriff a smile no more real than his own.

42

"I was at home, Ethan. Alone."

"No witnesses."

"And so no alibi." Max shrugged, keeping the gesture as relaxed as he could. "Sorry, didn't know I'd need one."

"Didn't you?"

"No."

Ethan nodded, mouth pursed in what was probably supposed to be thoughtful consideration. "You and George had your differences, I believe."

He *believed*. He fucking well *knew* but had to play his little games. So Max played along.

"He wanted to buy a piece of property here in town and I didn't want to sell it. He doubled his offer, I said no sale — and that was it. Hardly anything to kill a man over."

Ethan nodded again, lips still pursed. "But there was something else, wasn't there? Something about a note on that ranch of yours?"

"He called in the loan. I paid it. End of story."

"Is it? Way I heard it, you had to sell off a third of your cattle to pay that note."

"So? It left me with two-thirds of the herd and free of any debt to the bank."

"But you lost money on the deal. Prices

43

for beef were way down when you had to sell."

"The timing could have been better," Max admitted. "But it was business, Ethan, nothing more than that. George called in the note; I paid it. He was within his rights; I honored my obligations."

"You were pissed as hell, everybody knew that. Called poor George a bloodsucker, is what I heard."

Max thought grimly how easy it would be to become paranoid in a town where the sheriff "heard" a hell of a lot — including far too many private conversations. But all he said was, "I was pissed. I got over it. And that was two months ago."

Ethan frowned slightly, and Max knew he was, however reluctantly, at least half convinced that although Max might well act violently out of temper, he was unlikely to do anything rash once the anger was past.

Try as he might, the sheriff couldn't even persuade himself that he had found a motive for Max to have murdered George Caldwell, far less any evidence he might have done so. Not yet, anyway.

Still, Max didn't relax. He knew Ethan Cole.

Abruptly, the sheriff said, "So, Nell

Gallagher's back in town."

"Yeah. I saw her yesterday."

"Spoke to her too, didn't you?"

Max glanced toward the front window of Ethan's corner office and realized what a nice, clear view of Main Street it offered. "We said hello. Not much more than that."

"I guess she's home to clear out the old house, settle the family estate."

"So she said."

"Home for good?"

"I doubt it."

"She still as pretty as she was back then?"

"I'd call her gorgeous," Max replied calmly. "Just like she always was."

Reflectively, Ethan said, "Yeah, but she was a bit odd, as I remember. Not so much shy as . . . withdrawn. A loner. With that face, though, she had boys chasing after her from about the age of twelve. All those years, and none of us made much headway with her — except for you, that is."

Since it had been a statement rather than a question, Max merely said, "She wasn't easy to get close to." He wasn't about to admit that he had gotten close in the truest sense only once — and paid a very high price for it. "Considering her family's history and how they tended to isolate them-

45

selves out there, probably not so surprising."

Ethan eyed him with lifted brows. "You think that was it? Well, maybe. The family did scare at least a few would-be suitors away from those girls, that's for sure, especially that spooky old grandmother of theirs. And I remember Dad warning me not to do anything to piss off Adam Gallagher — which taking notice of either of his girls was liable to do."

Max shrugged. "He was more possessive of Hailey, I always thought. Maybe because she was older and pretty much took her mother's place after Grace ran off."

"Running off seems to be a family trait."

Knowing what was coming, Max waited.

"It was the night of Nell's senior prom, wasn't it? She packed a bag and ran off — and left you standing there all dressed up nice and fancy with no place to go."

"That's about it," Max replied.

"Rumor had it you two had a big fight."

"Rumor got it wrong, as usual."

"So what did happen?"

"Beats me."

"You really never knew why she bolted?"

"I really never knew." With another shrug, Max said, "I heard a bunch of garbled rumors afterward just like everybody else. Maybe one of them was true. Maybe her father did throw her out for some reason. Maybe there was someone she liked a lot better than me, and she ran off with him that night. Or maybe she found out where Grace was and wanted to be with her mother, and picked that night to go. Maybe one of those rumors was the truth. Or maybe not. The only person who could have told the truth was far away — and didn't bother to write, at least not to me."

"Ouch." Ethan smiled. "You should have aimed for the older sister instead. I always wondered why you didn't, considering you went through school with her."

"You were always more interested in Hailey than I was."

Dryly, Ethan said, "Everything in pants was interested in Hailey. She wasn't much to look at, but, Christ, that girl did put out some powerful signals. Hard to take your eyes off her when she walked down the street."

Max remained silent.

"Think there's any truth to the stories about her?"

"God knows. Something made her father disinherit her." Max offered the sheriff a wry smile. "I would have thought you'd know the truth about it if anybody would,

Ethan, considering how well informed you are about everything else in Silence."

"Oh, I imagine I'll get the truth of it eventually." Ethan returned the smile. "I always do."

Deciding the interview was over, Max rose to his feet. "Yeah, well, I know you have other things to think about these days. With four suspicious — and unsolved — deaths in the last eight months, we all know where your . . . attention needs to be focused."

Ethan rose as well and didn't offer to shake hands. "I don't need you to remind me what my job is." As Max turned away, he added in the same pleasant tone, "Oh — Max? I did tell you not to leave town, didn't I?"

"You told me. And you don't have to worry. I'm not going anywhere."

"Make sure you don't."

All too aware that the sheriff was determined to get the last word no matter what, Max simply nodded and left the office. He hadn't realized how tense he'd been until he was outside, around the corner, and out of sight of that office window and found himself shifting his shoulders in a half-conscious effort to relax.

Damn Ethan Cole.

Bad enough to watch a boy you'd liked

grow up into a man you didn't; give that man a badge and almost unlimited authority, not to mention a grudge, and things could get ugly in a hurry.

Trying to shake off a useless bitterness, Max walked to where he'd left his truck parked and got in. He started the engine but didn't put it in gear right away. Instead, he found himself thinking about Nell. Again.

All last night, listening to storms rumbling around and through Silence, he had tossed and turned and thought about Nell. Wondered. What sort of life had she made for herself in the last dozen years? Why had she failed to come home even for the funerals of her father and grandmother? What lay behind Hailey's odd, brittle smile whenever the subject of her younger sister had come up?

Most of all, he had wondered if any other man had managed to get close to her even once.

She had changed, that had been plain to see. Still beautiful, he hadn't lied to Ethan about that. But the incredible green eyes that he remembered with rather terrifying intensity were guarded and wary now, and there was an air of stillness, of composure, about her that had not been present years before.

She had been anything but still back then.

Max thought of the sixteen-year-old girl he had first noticed that hot summer day nearly fourteen years ago, riding a little roan mare bareback, her indecently short shorts baring most of her long, tanned legs and the white cotton blouse she wore far too sheer for his peace of mind. She had seemed wild to him, a little fey, her smile uncertain and her sudden, almost uncontrolled laughter quicksilver in the heavy, damp air. Her honey-colored hair had swung free about her shoulders, glistening in the sunlight, and her wide green eyes had stared at him with a strange look of shock, of . . . recognition.

Half eager, half fearful.

Max shook off the memory of that haunting look and grimly put the truck in gear. Enough. Enough of this. Nell Gallagher was back home just long enough to collect a few photographs and dolls from her childhood, and then she'd leave Silence for good.

He wasn't fool enough to get involved with her.

"Not this time," he heard himself mutter. "Not again."

★ ★ ★

The house roused surprisingly few memories in her, good or bad, possibly because it had been heavily redecorated since she'd last seen it. It was easy to see Hailey's preferences in the dark fabrics and patterned wallpaper most of the rooms boasted, and in fact the sense of her sister was almost overpowering.

It made Nell uncomfortable in a way she hadn't expected, and that as much as anything else eventually drove her out of the house later that morning.

The Gallagher house sat on property that had once, long ago, been a thriving sugarcane plantation. Over the years, land had been sold off, and what farming was done on the remaining family property was handled by tenant farmers, most of them raising soybeans and sweet potatoes. What family wealth still existed in the last twenty-five years had consisted of income from the tenant farmers and dividends from Adam Gallagher's highly successful ventures into the stock market.

There had almost always been enough money, and frequently more than enough, to live comfortably. She and Hailey had owned horses in childhood and, upon their seventeenth birthdays, had been presented by their father with very nice cars — their use of which had been strictly supervised to the extent of Adam holding the keys most of the time.

According to the inventory Nell had been provided by the family attorney, the horses and cars were long gone; Adam Gallagher's old Lincoln was the only vehicle left, and it was sitting on a car lot in Silence waiting to be sold.

Other things would have to be sold as well. Nell had no idea what would be left by the time debts and taxes were paid, and she didn't think much about it. She hadn't come home hoping to profit from her father's death, after all.

She walked away from the house now without looking back, allowing instinct or her subconscious to choose between one of several faint paths into the woods. There were probably fifty or so acres of forest separating the Gallagher house from the surrounding farms and ranches, the canopy of greenery high above creating a cool, dim haven where Nell had spent many childhood hours, especially during the hot and humid summers.

It didn't feel quite as peaceful now as it had then.

Even so, Nell kept walking, conscious of

a restless urge too familiar to be ignored. She stopped several times, looking around her with a searching gaze, but all she saw was the motionless green undergrowth, some of it still wet from the previous night's storms.

That realization had barely crossed her mind when Nell heard a deep, rolling rumble of thunder. She blinked, and between one second and the next the scene around her abruptly changed.

It was night, not day, and it was storming. She could feel the wind-lashed rain stinging her skin, even blinding her momentarily until she could turn her back to the force of it. She wiped the rain from her eyes and blinked, trying to see, in the strobelike flashes of lightning, what she was meant to.

A figure wearing a dark rain slicker moved along a path diverging from the one she stood upon. She thought it was a man but couldn't be sure; the slicker he wore had a hood that covered his head, and since he was moving away from her at an angle, his face wasn't visible.

The body over his shoulder was very visible.

It was a woman, Nell was sure of that. Bare arms dangled, and long, wet hair streamed down. She seemed to be wrapped in a sheet or some other pale cloth that was clinging wetly to her skin, and she was limp. Very limp.

"Nell?"

Ignoring that summons, Nell tried to move forward, to follow him and find out where he was going. Was he going to bury a murder victim? Was he carrying an unconscious woman deeper into the woods to — do whatever it was he intended to do to her? Who was he? Who was the woman?

She tried to follow, but something grabbed at her, stopped her, and when she looked down it was to see thick vines twining about her wrists, holding her still. She managed to lift her arms slightly, fingers curling into fists with the effort, but the vines held on tightly.

"Nell!"

She looked quickly through the driving rain, trying to at least see which direction the shrouded figure took through the woods. But there was so much movement of the thick, wind-blown undergrowth, and so much distortion caused by the heavy rain and brilliant flashes of lightning, that she couldn't see him now.

He was gone. . . .

"Nell!"

She blinked. The day had returned. The storm was gone. No rain, no thunder or lightning, no wind. And the vines gripping her wrists were two powerful hands.

She looked up to find Max frowning down at her, and she spared a moment to think wryly that the universe had a bizarre sense of humor. Either that, or it was out to torment her.

"I'm all right," she said, dismayed by the unsteadiness of her voice. "You can let go of me now."

"I'm not so sure." If anything, his frown deepened. "What the hell just happened, Nell? You were about a million miles away."

She was tempted to tell him she'd been farther away than miles could ever measure, but instead said, "Daydreaming, that's all." And immediately went on the defensive. "What are you doing out here?"

"I was out riding and heard something," he said, not apologizing for riding on Gallagher land rather than his own considerable spread. He seemed to realize for the first time that he was holding her wrists and abruptly released them.

"Heard what?" Nell asked, more rattled than she wanted to admit to either of them. She absently massaged her wrists as she noted the presence of a big, muscled bay gelding standing patiently ground-tied a few yards away.

"You. You cried out."

"What did I cry out?" she asked, reluctant but needing to know.

"*No.* You said it a couple more times before I got to you, then went silent. Daydreaming? Don't give me that bullshit, Nell. You sounded like something or someone was hurting you, and you were white as a sheet. Still white, if it comes to that."

Choosing her words carefully, Nell said, "I have very . . . vivid . . . daydreams. But, as you can see, no one is hurting me. No one is bothering me. I'm perfectly all right. I appreciate your concern, but I'm fine."

"Are you? What about that?" He indicated the Band-Aid above her right eyebrow.

Nell shrugged. "I'm not . . . reacquainted with the house yet, and a cabinet door caught me when I wasn't looking. It's just a scratch."

Max wasn't frowning now, but his gaze was disconcertingly steady. "It's still happening, isn't it?"

"I don't know what you mean."

"The blackouts. You blacked out, that's

how you hurt yourself."

She almost denied it but finally shrugged again and made her voice wryly dismissive. "We all have something. I pass out from time to time, that's all."

"Did you ever find out what causes it?"

"Stress, the doctors say. I guess coming back here was more stressful than I realized."

"Is that what happened here, just now?" But he shook his head before she could respond, and answered himself. "No, you weren't unconscious. Your eyes were wide open. But your pupils were dilated, and I got the feeling . . . you were somewhere else."

"Obviously I wasn't somewhere else. I was right here." Nell wasn't entirely sure why she was clinging stubbornly to the fiction that everything was fine — and normal — with her. Depending on how much he remembered, Max knew things about her that no one else in Silence knew. But as long as he didn't admit to the knowledge, she wasn't about to remind him.

He half nodded as though expecting the denial, but said, "Yeah, you were here. Why, Nell? With everything you have to do at the house, what brought you out here?"

"I wanted to go for a walk, that's all." Again, she went on the defensive. "What's with you, Max? This is still Gallagher land, and I'm perfectly entitled to walk on it. I haven't sold out to you yet."

His mouth tightened. "In case you've forgotten what Shelby told you yesterday, people have been dying around here lately. It's not especially safe for you to wander around out in the woods by yourself."

"Men have been dying, according to you and Shelby. Not women."

"So far. But there's no reason to push your luck, Nell."

"I can take care of myself."

"Can you?" He laughed shortly. "You were oblivious when I got here. Anyone could have walked up and — done any- thing at all to you."

"I'm fine, and I *can* take care of myself," she insisted, and took a step back away from him to emphasize that independence. "Don't let me keep you from your ride, Max."

For a moment, it seemed he would argue with her, but then he muttered a curse under his breath and went to remount his horse. He gathered up the reins and turned the horse back toward his own property but paused to deliver a last, flat warning before riding away.

"Be careful, Nell. Whoever killed those men seems to want to get secrets out in the open. And we both know you have plenty of secrets to protect."

She didn't move or say anything in response, just watched him ride away until the forest swallowed him up.

Was his arrival here as casual as it appeared, or more deliberate? And what about the vision he had interrupted? Had she seen the postscript of a murder here in these woods, or something every bit as evil? Who was the man, the woman?

Nell stood where she was for several minutes, looking around her, searching for some sign that might answer her questions. But the forest was peaceful and unrevealing now, and the peculiar doorway in her mind refused to open.

Great. Just great. The universe was willing to give her a glimpse, but no real help.

As usual.

Sighing, Nell looked around once again and only then realized just where she was. Twelve years had changed everything, so perhaps that was why she hadn't immediately recognized it.

The big oak tree didn't look so very different; a dozen years in the life of an oak was hardly any time at all. There were vines twining about its base that hadn't been there before, vines Nell had to pull aside in order to find the roughly carved heart and its two sets of initials.

He had caught her here on an autumn day long ago, carving her hopes into the tree with a rusty pocketknife, and after that there hadn't been much use in pretending.

Nell watched her fingers trace the *NG* and *MT,* then sighed and allowed the vines to hide it once again. And it was only then that she recognized the vines.

Poison ivy.

She had to laugh, albeit ruefully. The universe, she decided, was definitely out to torment her. She turned and made her way back through the woods toward the house, hoping to wash the plant oils off her hands before her lack of caution resulted in a rash.

A bad one.

CHAPTER
THREE

Ethan Cole looked up from his desk and only just managed not to scowl as the mayor of Silence walked into his office. Like him, she disliked intercoms; unlike him, she also disliked phones and so tended to arrive with absolutely no warning.

He could have used a little warning.

"Ethan, is there any more information about George Caldwell's death?" she asked without preamble.

Ethan made a token attempt to rise, mostly wasted since she immediately sank into one of his visitor's chairs, then he sat back down and made a show of pulling a folder off a stack in his in-box and frowning over the contents.

"Well, no, Casey, I don't see anything here you don't already know. Which I could have told you and saved you the trip if you'd called me."

Mayor Lattimore shrugged, her dark blue eyes fixed on his face. "I was coming over this way and figured I'd stop in.

Ethan, I've had a dozen calls today — and not a single answer for any of the questions I've been asked."

"What questions?"

"What you'd expect. What's going on? Why can't *we* figure out who killed George Caldwell and the others and stop him before he kills somebody else?"

Ethan stiffened. "Even assuming all four of these men were killed, who's to say they were killed by the same person?"

"Jesus, Ethan, I hope you're not suggesting we've got four separate murderers running around Silence."

"It might be the lesser of two possible evils," he said with a sigh. "All we need is for the phrase *serial killer* to start making the rounds to damned sure put this town in a panic."

"Maybe we're already in a panic," the mayor suggested. "People are scared, you can hear it in their voices."

"I know that."

"So what do I tell them?"

Irritably, Ethan said, "Tell them to lock their doors at night, be careful, and mind their own business."

"And what do I say when they ask me why we elected officials aren't doing the job we were voted in to do?"

"Say we're damned well doing our jobs. Look, Casey, I don't know what else to tell you. My people are busting their asses trying to get this thing figured out. I haven't taken a day off since January, and my overtime budget went out the window months ago. We're working the investigations — and that's all we can do. If anybody else has a practical suggestion, I'd love to hear it."

"You still don't have a suspect for even one of the murders?"

He hesitated, then said, "I'm looking at Max Tanner for the Ferrier and Patterson deaths."

She lifted an eyebrow at him. "Last I heard, you weren't even admitting Luke Ferrier's drowning was anything but suicide or an accident."

"A few things have come to light that make murder at least as likely as an accident."

"I see. And what's the connection to Max Tanner?"

Ethan was not required to explain either himself or his investigations to the mayor — not directly, at any rate — but he'd learned that when Casey Lattimore asked questions she expected answers. And she could be a royal pain in the ass

63

until she got them.

So, reluctantly, he answered. "It seems Ferrier borrowed money from Max a few weeks before he died."

"You got that from Max?"

"No. From someone who overheard Max telling Ferrier he wanted the loan repaid pronto."

The mayor frowned. "Correct me if I'm wrong, but wouldn't killing Ferrier be a stupid way to get a loan repaid?"

"Max has a temper, everybody knows that. He could have struck first and regretted it later."

"Struck by pushing Ferrier's car into a bayou? Wouldn't that theory make more sense if somebody'd beat the hell out of Ferrier rather than trying to drown him? I mean, if you suspect Max of the killing?"

Ethan hated logical women. "I said I was looking at Max, not that I considered him a solid suspect."

Without commenting on his disgruntled tone, she merely said, "And the Patterson death? What makes you suspect Max of being involved in that one?"

"We know the killer stood outside that bathroom window for a while before he dropped the electrical wire in, and we found a footprint. Style and size match up

64

with the boots Max usually wears."

"I assume you checked Max's boots?"

"Yeah."

"And?"

"And nothing. We can't prove just from the print that it was him standing outside that window."

"What else have you got?"

"Not much," Ethan admitted.

Rather than question him further on that point, she merely sighed and said, "I gather you're still against calling in outside help?"

His jaw tightened. "I am. These are grudge killings, and that means all the answers are right here in Silence. Whether there's one killer or more than one, no outsider is going to be better or quicker than we are in putting the pieces together."

"It's been eight months, Ethan."

The sheriff drew a breath and said carefully, "And the first forty-eight hours after a murder are critical. Yes, Casey, I know that. I also know that you feel qualified to comment on the investigation because you took that FBI course last year."

"That isn't —"

"I'm not saying it wasn't a smart thing for you to do. A mayor should feel qualified to oversee most aspects of town management. But law enforcement is a specialty, and one course in Criminal Investigation Techniques 101 hardly equates to fifteen years of experience on the job."

Perfectly aware that he was putting her on the defensive deliberately, Casey Lattimore nevertheless heard herself say, "I never claimed to be an expert, Ethan. And I'm certainly not trying to tell you how to do your job."

"I appreciate that, Casey."

She got to her feet, adding smoothly, "But judging by the phone calls I've been getting, the citizens of Silence want action, and they want it soon. Even so, we can't afford any mistakes. That means you'd better be damned sure of your evidence before you shine a spotlight of suspicion on anybody."

Even Max Tanner. She didn't add that last aloud. She didn't have to.

"Don't worry," the sheriff said. "I know my job."

Instead of agreeing that he did, she merely said, "Keep me advised, will you? The town council is under as much pressure as we are, Ethan; it won't look good to the voters if we all appear to be sitting on our hands."

"Meaning they might take action?"

The mayor kept her tone mild. "Elected officials can't afford to do nothing for long, you know that." She didn't wait for a response but turned toward the door, adding over her shoulder, "We'll be talking, I'm sure."

"Yeah," the sheriff agreed. "I'm sure we will."

THURSDAY, MARCH 23

What Nell discovered when she wandered around downtown Silence on Thursday morning was that most people had forgotten old scandals and questions. Most people. There were, in fact, quite a few newcomers to the area, especially since the recently completed highway had brought heavier traffic much closer to the city limits the previous year.

She counted a dozen obviously new businesses just in the downtown area, most of them the sort she would have expected, like clothing boutiques and collectibles-type stores. All were enjoying brisk foot traffic. There was also, she noticed, an unusually strong police presence in the town. She counted three different cruisers patrolling, as well as a couple of deputies on foot roaming the sidewalks.

Nell had several reasons for being in town. She had to see the family attorney to sign various papers; she paid a visit to an insurance adjuster for referrals to appraisers she could employ to look over some of the furniture and artwork at the house; and she spent some time at both the library and the courthouse.

It was after lunchtime when Nell emerged from the courthouse, and after a glance at her watch, she picked a downtown café and found herself a rather isolated booth in the rear. The waitress was blessedly incurious, the food good, and Nell enjoyed a peaceful half hour or so alone with her thoughts.

"Wade Keever says you've turned down my offer."

She looked up to find Max scowling at her. She sat back and sipped her coffee to give herself a moment, then said, "He's talking out of turn. I said I'd consider it, that's all. I just haven't made up my mind about it."

"It's a fair offer. You won't get a better offer, Nell, not for that land."

"I'm aware of that."

"Then why the hesitation?"

She glanced around, grateful that most

of the café was deserted and no one appeared to be paying attention to them. Still, she kept her voice low. "I told you. I'm not so sure I want to sell out."

Max slid into the booth, across from her. "Why not?"

Nell didn't waste time or energy commenting on his manners. "Because I'm not sure. Look, Max, I know you want that land and I know you want me gone. But maybe I'm not quite so eager to cut my last ties to this place. You don't have to worry, though — I won't sell the land to anybody else. It adjoins your property, and you'll have first chance at it. If I decide to sell."

Instead of protesting or questioning that, Max abruptly changed the subject. "Any more blackouts?"

Nell shook her head.

"What about that . . . episode in the woods? Has that happened again?"

"Nothing happened, Max."

"Don't give me that daydreaming bullshit again, Nell. Do you think I don't remember what used to happen to you? The visions?"

With an effort, she summoned a wry smile. "I was sort of hoping you had forgotten."

"It's still happening, isn't it? Just like the blackouts."

"Did you think it would go away? That I'd outgrow it eventually?" Nell had to laugh, however unamused the sound. "Curses are with you for life, Max, didn't you know that?"

"You used to call it that. The Gallagher curse."

"Most families seem to have something. Cousins that can't get along. Squabbles about property. Medical problems. A mad wife locked away in the attic. We have a curse."

"You never told me who else in your family had it."

Nell shook her head, reminding herself that it was far too easy to confide in some people. In him. "Never mind. To answer your question, yes, *it* is still happening to me. I see things that aren't there. I even hear voices sometimes. So if you want to prove I'm unfit to make decisions about the estate, you could probably at least give the judge something to think about."

His mouth tightened. "That is not what this is about, dammit."

"Isn't it?"

"No."

Nell shrugged but kept her gaze on his

face. "Well, you'll have to forgive me if I'm a bit touchy about the subject. Keever was indiscreet enough to hint that someone had questioned my fitness to inherit the estate."

"Someone? He didn't say who?"

"He wasn't quite that indiscreet."

Max frowned. "Hailey was disinherited, and from what I heard there were no loopholes in that part of the will. True?"

"True, at least from a legal standpoint. I'm the sole heir."

"Could it have been Hailey?"

"Sure."

"But you don't think it was?"

Nell shrugged again. "I think it isn't like her to lurk in the background if she wants to fight about it, but maybe she's changed in a dozen years."

"But if it isn't her, with no Gallaghers left in Silence, who would stand to benefit if you were declared unfit or barred from inheriting?"

"As far as I know . . . no one." Her tone was deliberate.

"Except someone who might want to buy land you don't want to sell? Jesus, Nell, I'd think you knew me well enough to know I don't do things that way."

"Until this week, I hadn't seen or talked

to you in twelve years, Max."

"Whose fault is that?" he demanded roughly.

For the first time, Nell avoided his dark eyes, fixing her own on the half-empty coffee cup before her. Ignoring the question hanging in the air between them, she said evenly, "How good a judge of character is any of us at seventeen? I thought I knew a lot of things then. And a lot of people. I was mostly wrong."

"Nell —"

She did not want to answer the question she knew he wanted to ask, not here and not now, so she cut him off before he could ask it. "I'll let you know about the land if and when I make up my mind. In the meantime, I don't think there's anything else we need to talk about, do you?" She made sure her voice was completely indifferent.

Max stiffened visibly, then slid from the booth without a word and stalked out of the café.

From behind Nell, a low and slightly amused voice murmured, "Looks like you still know how to push all his buttons."

She picked up her cup and sipped the nearly cold coffee, scanning the room to make sure no one noticed her talking to someone she wasn't looking at in the booth beside hers. She kept her voice as quiet as his had been. "His temper was always his Achilles' heel."

"A small but fatal weakness? Let's hope not."

"You have such a literal mind."

He chuckled. "Yeah, so I've been told. My one failing. Did you know, by the way, that Tanner's been following you around town all morning?"

"I was pretty sure he was."

"Any idea why? I mean, besides the obvious possibility?"

"Maybe he's suspicious."

"Of you? Why would he be?"

"I don't know."

"Mmm. You still sure about him?"

Nell drew a breath and let it out slowly. "I have to start with a certainty. That's my certainty."

"Okay. Then I'll stick to the plan."

"Do that. Oh — have you been out to the house, by any chance?"

"Checked out that place in the woods you told me about, but didn't find anything there. I didn't go near the house, though. Why?"

She hesitated, but only briefly. "It's probably nothing. I've just had the feeling a few times that someone was watching me." *And calling my name.*

"Inside the house?"

"Maybe through a window, I don't know."

"Shit. I don't like the sound of that."

"Look, it's probably just my imagination."

"We both know you don't imagine things."

"I've never come home before. And twelve years is a long time. It's probably just that."

"Or ghosts, maybe?"

"Oh, hell, don't even suggest ghosts. All I need is another reason not to sleep at night."

After a moment, and in an uncharacteristically kind tone, he said, "Bad enough to be dropped into the middle of a situation like this one without dragging your own baggage in as well. It can get . . . real easy to lose perspective. If this is too difficult for you, just say so."

"I'm fine."

"Be very sure of that, Nell. The stakes are high. People are dying around here, remember?"

"It's hardly something I could forget." She set her cup down, left a tip on the table for the waitress, and prepared to slide from the booth. "Just don't crowd me, okay?"

"Gotcha."

Nell didn't look back or indicate any interest whatsoever in that other rear booth, just walked up front to pay her check and then left the café.

Justin Byers hadn't had much trouble fitting in since he had come to Silence a couple of months before. He'd always liked small towns, choosing them over cities whenever there was a choice to be made, and so he felt entirely comfortable here. And his duties as a detective in the Criminal Investigation Division of the sheriff's department were both familiar and absorbing — especially these days.

But the major reason he liked this town went by the name of Lauren Champagne. *Deputy* Lauren Champagne.

Justin had never been given to fantasies — at least no more than the average male — but he'd discovered that his subconscious had a mind of its own. He was waking up virtually every morning in a tangle of sheets with his heart pounding and with the disconcerting realization that his dreams had been more than a little . . . raw.

Which made it damned hard to be cool and professional when he encountered Lauren in the course of the day.

"Hey, Justin," she offered easily when they met on the sidewalk in front of the courthouse on Thursday afternoon.

"Hey, Lauren." He hastily quashed a fleeting mental image of creamy bare flesh and strove to be professional. "Where's Kyle?"

"Inside. We had some paperwork for the clerk of court." She shrugged. "What're you up to?"

"Still trying to run down all the financial info on George Caldwell. You know, for a fine, upstanding banker, he sure had tangled finances."

Lauren smiled wryly, her dark eyes grave. "Isn't that par for the course where these killings are concerned?"

"Yeah, there always seems to be a mess left behind. Except we haven't stumbled over any of George's secret vices yet."

"You think you will?"

Quite without planning to, he heard himself say, "Well, let's just say I'm a little bothered by a few things. These scattered financial records, for one, all of which I still haven't been able to track down. As for his personal accounts at the bank where he worked, there've been some regular deposits to at least one of them with no explanation of where the income originated. It wasn't salary or bonuses, and so far it doesn't look like investment income."

"Maybe his wife knows."

"Maybe, but I'm under orders not to bother her with questions."

With a lifted brow, Lauren said, "Sheriff's orders?"

"Yeah."

"Well," she said after a moment, "I'm sure he has his reasons."

Justin was worried that the sheriff did have his reasons but reminded himself that Lauren had been here longer than he had and might well feel loyal to Ethan Cole, so all he said was, "It's making things a little difficult, that's all. Caldwell knew how to handle money, and that included how to hide it."

"To avoid paying taxes, you think?"

"Maybe. Or to squirrel some of it away in case he and Sue finally decided to divorce. What she couldn't find, he wouldn't have to share."

"Not so unusual for a man contemplating divorce."

"No," Justin agreed. "But it would be

nice to know for sure if that was his motive."

Lauren nodded but didn't comment, since her partner, Kyle Venable, joined them then to say dryly, "We have a couple of warrants to serve. Doesn't that sound like fun?"

"Loads," she agreed in the same tone. "Justin, good luck with your investigation."

"Thanks. See you, Lauren. Kyle."

"We'll be around," Kyle told him cheerfully, then followed his tall and striking partner back toward their cruiser.

Justin watched them — well, Lauren — until they got into the patrol car and left the courthouse, then continued on his way. He spent nearly an hour in the courthouse checking over property records, then paid a third visit to the bank where George Caldwell had been a VP.

By the time he came out and headed back toward the sheriff's department, he was feeling more than a little frustrated. It wasn't that he was being stonewalled, exactly; with Caldwell's death a clear murder, the judge hadn't hesitated to order the bank to make its records available to the investigators. Problem was, the bank records looked clean.

It was Caldwell's personal financial records that looked suspect, but there was nothing firm Justin could point to in order to explain why he had this itching on the back of his neck that told him to keep digging.

He just *knew*, dammit. Knew there was more to the story than he had yet discovered.

The problem was how in hell to find it.

The sheriff could have made it easier on him but instead had virtually tied his hands, and much as he wanted to it wasn't something Justin intended to complain about. He was treading carefully with the sheriff, perfectly aware that Ethan Cole didn't really trust him and equally aware that the sheriff was hiding something. Or trying to.

That was something else Justin knew but couldn't prove. And wasn't really sure he wanted to try and prove, all things considered. But he didn't have much of a choice.

Not really eager to return to the station any sooner than he had to, Justin stopped off on the way back for a cup of decent coffee at the downtown café. He sat alone at a front table and gazed broodingly out at the passing traffic.

Such a nice little town.

"Hey, Detective Byers —" One of the

young waitresses he'd spoken to maybe twice stood by his table holding an envelope. "This was left for you." She handed it over.

His name was block-printed on the front — just his name, nothing to identify him as a cop. For some reason, that bothered him.

"Who left it, Emily?"

She shrugged and popped her gum. "Dunno. Vinny just found it on the counter and told me to bring it over to you. Guess somebody figured you'd stop by. You usually do, most afternoons."

"Yeah. Thanks, Emily."

"Welcome."

As she wandered away, Justin made a mental note to stop being so goddamned predictable, then stared at the envelope, turning it in his hands. The usual number-ten business-type, treated for security so what lay inside wasn't easily visible, at least through the paper. But what lay inside clearly had shape and bulk, something like a small notebook from the feel of it.

The envelope had been handled by so many people he knew it was useless to worry about fingerprints. As for what was inside . . .

He wasted a couple of minutes trying to convince himself somebody had sent him an early birthday card — okay, maybe an early birthday booklet — sighed, and carefully pried up the lightly sealed flap.

It was indeed a small, black notebook, the sort some people carried around in their pockets or purses to jot down phone numbers or whatever. Justin handled it carefully by the edges, even though his instincts and training told him the polished surface was polished for a reason and would yield no fingerprints whatsoever. Inside, a number of the lined pages contained notes. Two initials at the top of each page, followed by what looked like a list of dates and dollar amounts.

The dates on each page were spaced no less than a month apart, with some only every three or four months, and at least one page contained only two dates, more than six months apart.

He was no expert, but the spiky handwriting — different from the block-printing on the envelope — looked familiar. It looked like George Caldwell's handwriting.

Frowning, Justin pulled out his own notebook and made a careful list of all the dates, in chronological order. What he ended up with was a date for almost every month spanning the past three years. And when he compared the dates to earlier notes he had made, he was grimly unsurprised to find that they matched the dates of the regular deposits into one of Caldwell's bank accounts.

Those unexplained deposits.

That unexplained income.

"Blackmail," Justin muttered under his breath. It was possible. Maybe more than possible. Every one of the dead men had led a double life, a secret life, their crimes and sins hidden until their deaths had exposed those dark truths.

It appeared that someone had become impatient with Justin's failure to uncover George Caldwell's nasty little secret and had decided to help the investigation himself. Or herself.

One of the blackmail victims?

The killer?

And if either, why give the book to him? Why hand evidence like this over to a detective investigating the murder of George Caldwell? To ensure justice?

Or something else?

Justin looked at the initials that headed each page. Each, presumably, represented a name. Most were unfamiliar to him, or at least suggested no one he knew. Two did suggest names that he knew, or thought he knew.

M.T. — Max Tanner?
And E.C. — Ethan Cole?
"Ah, shit," Justin muttered.

CHAPTER
FOUR

Max hadn't planned on following Nell around all day. He really hadn't. And after her cool dismissal at the café, seeking her out again should have been the last thing on his mind. But he found himself hanging around where he could watch her Jeep, and when she left town a few minutes later, he followed her at a discreet distance until she turned off into the driveway of the old Gallagher house.

It was late afternoon by then, and he had a dozen things that needed doing at the ranch, but even though he went back home and tried to concentrate on his work, he found his mind wandering again and again. An uneasy sense that he needed to be somewhere else nagged at him.

It had happened before, years ago, an urge he hadn't heeded — something he would forever regret. And it had happened again recently when he'd felt driven to saddle his horse and head toward Gallagher land, discovering Nell in the middle of the woods and in the middle of one of those "visions" of hers that left her frighteningly vulnerable.

He had almost forgotten how unsettling they were, those episodes of hers. She was physically there, eyes open, breathing — but somewhere else as well. Somewhere no one else could follow. And wherever it was, either the effort of getting there or simply what she saw left her pale and shaking.

She had told him once, hesitantly, that she had no control over what happened to her and had no idea what it was that triggered the episodes — but what she saw during them was invariably something that frightened her. When he had pressed her for details all those years ago, she had said only that "some places remember" what had happened in them — or would happen.

It had made no sense to him then. It still didn't.

But whatever he felt about her peculiar abilities, it didn't change his uneasiness and anxiety now. There was someplace he needed to be, and it wasn't here at the ranch. As a mild spring night fell, that restless urge to be somewhere else, to *do* something, was driving him crazy. He resisted as long as he could, but the feelings just kept intensifying until he couldn't ignore them any longer.

And he was only mildly surprised when his truck rounded the curve near the Gallagher driveway, to see Nell's Jeep pulling out onto the road.

Eight p.m. Where was she going?

In just a few minutes, it became obvious she was heading away from Silence; she took the new highway and headed south, in the general direction of New Orleans.

Max followed cautiously, not even bothering to find reasonable excuses for what he was doing. There weren't any. There was nothing in the least reasonable about any of this, and he damned well knew it.

Traffic wasn't especially heavy on this Thursday evening, so Max stayed back as far as he dared without losing sight of the taillights of Nell's Jeep. Which is why he nearly missed it when she took an off-ramp about a dozen miles from Silence.

Forced to close the distance between them or risk losing her in the darkness, Max followed her for several miles along a winding country road until she pulled off at a small and distinctly seedy motel where, the sign proclaimed, rooms were for rent at an hourly as well as nightly rate. Since only two cars were parked in front of two of the units, it appeared business wasn't exactly booming.

Whatever Max had expected, it wasn't this.

He cut his lights and pulled a little past the turnoff, watching as her Jeep bypassed the flickering neon sign indicating the office and went directly to the last unit at the end of the building. She parked in front, got out, and apparently used a key to let herself into unit number ten.

Max watched a dim light come on inside the room. The curtains were drawn, so it was impossible to see what was going on in there. He drummed his fingers against the steering wheel, frowning, then swore under his breath and turned his own truck back toward the motel.

He parked off to the side and crept toward the unit on foot, being very careful not to give away his approach with the slightest sound.

Not careful enough.

He heard a click he recognized and froze even before he felt the cold steel of a gun barrel against his neck.

"See, what I don't get is why you'd want to spend most of a day and night following me all over the place." Nell moved around where he could see her but kept the gun pointed at him. It was a big gun, and she held it with expert ease.

All he could think to say was, "How'd you get out here? I've been watching the door."

"Window in back." Nell took another step, then gestured with the gun toward the unit's door. "Shall we?"

Max went ahead of her, half afraid of what might await them in the room. What met his searching gaze inside was merely a cheap motel room, the one bed sagging in the middle beside a scarred nightstand, small TV bolted to the shabby dresser on the other side of the room, and the open bathroom door showing him that the tiny room was bare of any threat.

Nell shut the door behind them, then went to lean against the dresser. She still held the gun, though no longer pointed it at him. "Let's hear it, Max. Why've you been following me around all day today?"

"You going to explain that gun?"

She shrugged, smiling just a little. "A woman alone has to be careful. Your turn."

"Maybe I don't have anything better to do than follow you around."

"I remember enough about ranching to know that's a lie. You've got more than enough to do. Try again, Max."

He really didn't want to confess the truth, but something about her eyes and that little smile she wore warned him to take both her and that gun she was holding with such seeming negligence very seriously. "I was worried," he said finally. "I thought somebody should keep an eye on you."

"Why?"

"People are dying, remember?"

"Not good enough. Men are dying, four in eight months. And even if women became targets, what makes you so sure I'd be one of them? I've been gone for twelve years, only back here a few days, and only to take care of a little business before leaving again. I'm just passing through. So why would anyone want to kill me?"

"You said yourself someone had questioned your fitness to inherit the estate."

"Yeah, but nobody's challenged me legally, and the will's through probate. I inherit. And I have a will, which now takes precedence. So if anybody's after any of the property, killing me won't get it for them."

"The killer doesn't necessarily know that," Max pointed out.

"I'd think he'd make sure before getting rid of me. And since I told Wade Keever about my will today, I imagine most of Silence will know by, say, tomorrow afternoon. Sooner, if somebody buys him drinks tonight."

She paused a moment, her green eyes steady on his face, then said, "Besides, this killer doesn't seem to be acting for personal gain. No, whatever your reasons for following me around, they don't include concern about the disposition of my father's estate. So I'd like to know what those reasons are, Max. And the truth would be nice."

"I told you the truth. I was worried about you."

"Then tell me why."

He hesitated, then drew in a breath and let it out roughly. "Because you're a threat to the killer, Nell. And I'm not sure how many people know that."

Anyone who had ever lived in a small town — especially a small Southern town — would probably be quick to admit that skulking around at night for any reason wasn't the easiest thing in the world. There were lots of streetlights, for one thing, and people tended to leave their porch lights on as well.

Welcome, neighbor. Come on in and kill me.

She shook her head as she stood back from a too-lighted area at the edge of downtown Silence and warily watched the passing traffic. For a nervous town, there were sure as hell a lot of people out doing things on a weeknight.

Human nature, of course. No matter how nervous they might feel, most people simply never expected the really bad things to happen to them.

Until they did.

Hearing footsteps, she immediately withdrew deeper into the shadows and watched a young couple as they walked past her, holding hands. Oblivious to any possible threat.

Conscious of the gun tucked at the small of her back, she shifted her weight and breathed a sigh. Just because only men had been victims so far didn't mean the women of this town were safe, but none of them seemed to realize that. There needed to be a curfew at the very least —

All her senses flared suddenly, and she went perfectly still. Waiting. The traffic noises faded, and she no longer smelled exhaust fumes on the damp breeze. The harsh brightness of the streetlights seemed to dim everywhere — except a block away, where a lone man walked, shoulders hunched and hands in his pockets. As he passed beneath each streetlight, it seemed to brighten, almost as if a spotlight followed him.

She smiled unconsciously, her gaze intent on him. The damp breeze brought her now the scent of his cologne. He was wearing Polo. She could almost feel the faint tremors of the earth beneath her feet as he walked.

Or maybe that was her own heartbeat.

She watched him walk toward her. His head was bent, and he was obviously deep in thought. Oblivious. She unconsciously shook her head. Bad to be so wrapped up in thought that you left yourself vulnerable. Worse to do that when living in a town where nice, seemingly respectable men were ending up in the morgue.

She glanced around warily to make certain there was no one else in the area, and then waited until he had nearly reached her before stepping out of the shadows.

"Hey," she said.

He jumped a foot. "Jesus! You scared the hell out of me."

"Oh, sorry," she said mildly, her fingers closing around the grip of her gun as she began to draw it from the waistband of her jeans. "I certainly didn't mean to do that."

Nell didn't appear to be alarmed by

Max's warning. "Why would I be a threat to anyone?"

"Tell me something. What did you see in the woods yesterday? What did your vision show you?"

She didn't blink or look away, but it was a long moment before she finally answered. "I saw a stormy night. A man in a slicker carrying a woman over his shoulder. I don't know who he was. I don't know who she was. I don't know if she was dead or alive."

"So it could have been the killer you saw."

"Could have. Or someone else, maybe even doing something entirely innocent."

"Do you think so?"

Still without looking away from his face, Nell shook her head slowly. "Not really. Whatever he was doing . . . there was nothing innocent about it."

"Now for the big question. Did you see the past? Or the future?"

"I don't know that either."

"You still can't tell?"

"Usually, no. Not unless there's something in the vision to place it in time."

"What about other kinds of control? Can you . . . trigger . . . one of these things if you want to?"

"Not really. I can put myself in a place where one is more likely, a place where something violent happened, but it doesn't always work. There's no button I can push, Max, no switch to flip when I want to see something."

"Which makes you vulnerable as hell, whether you'll admit it or not. If you could see the killer, identify him, point the cops to him, then maybe you'd be safe. Safer, anyway. But you can't do that. And the thing is, other people don't understand your abilities, Nell. They don't understand — and yet they're talking. Speculating. Wondering just what the Gallagher curse really is. I've heard at least three people wondering out loud if this elusive killer has a chance of hiding now that our very own local witch has come home."

Quietly, she said, "So maybe he's wondering too."

"Maybe he is."

"Or maybe," she suggested, "he doesn't know a damned thing about the Gallagher curse."

"He knows about secrets, Nell, remember? Every man he's killed has had secrets, and those secrets are out or coming out. I don't know much about killers, but this one seems to have his game plan all

94

worked out, and that plan includes exposing the dark sides of people's private lives. So if you ask me, you've got a double chance of becoming a target. Because you've got a secret, and because that secret — that ability — is a threat to him."

"It's no secret if people are talking about it."

"It's something you try to hide, and that makes it a secretive thing."

"A . . . dark and secretive thing?"

"Some people would call it that. This town hasn't changed all that much, Nell, and your family never did anything to make this curse of yours something to understand and not fear. People fear what they don't understand, and some people still call psychic abilities dark. Even evil."

"Which is why they call me a witch."

"Which is why some do, yes."

She drew a breath. "And that's why you've been following me? Because you believe what I can do makes me a target?"

"That's why." He smiled faintly. "Of course, I didn't know you had a gun. I suppose you know how to use it?"

"Yeah, I know how." She turned her head slightly, looking toward the door with a faint frown. "They teach us how to do that."

"They? Who are they?"

Before Nell could answer, the door opened quietly and Casey Lattimore stepped into the room. Closing the door behind her, the mayor of Silence said dryly to Max, "*They* are the FBI. The training academy for agents is at Quantico. Right, Nell?"

"Right."

"Last year," Mayor Lattimore said from her position in the room's one armchair, "weeks after Peter Lynch died, I was feeling frustrated. Not that anybody could have been sure it was murder, not then, but nothing seemed to be *happening* in the investigation. Worse, I didn't really understand police procedure. I thought it was something I needed to understand."

"So you went up to Quantico," Max finished slowly. "Took that course for civilian authorities." He was sitting on the bed, rather gingerly.

She nodded. "And that's where I ran into Nell."

Nell, still leaning back against the dresser, said, "My unit operates out of Quantico, and sometimes we're tapped to help teach some of the courses offered. I was between assignments and ended up helping the instructor speaking to Casey's group that week. We recognized each other."

"After twelve years?" Max asked.

Casey said, "Don't forget, I taught both' of you in high school. Not to swell your head, Max, but some students really are more memorable than others. You and Nell, I remembered."

Max decided not to ask why. "Okay, so you recognized Nell. And then?"

"Well, nothing much happened then. We had lunch a couple of times. Talked, briefly, about Silence. I told Nell about my concerns, about this recent death that seemed so difficult for our sheriff and his people to resolve."

"But there wasn't much to go on," Nell continued, "especially not at a distance. So there really wasn't anything I could do, even offer anything helpful in the way of advice. Casey finished her course, and we said good-bye. Then, a couple of months ago, she called me. By then, three men were dead, and the odd little twist about their sins coming to light afterward seemed to pretty strongly indicate there was one killer. A very unusual sort of killer."

"Which attracted the interest of the Bureau?" Max lifted a brow at her.

"Which attracted the interest of my boss, the leader of the unit I belong to. He's a profiler, instinctive as well as trained. When I gave him all the information Casey had passed along to me, he was able to develop a tentative profile of the sort of person likely to be the killer."

"And?"

Nell looked at the mayor, who said, "And we immediately had a problem. According to Agent Bishop's profile, the killer was likely to be a cop."

Max whistled softly. "Which might explain why the murders are going unsolved."

"Which might explain why." Casey sighed. "Worse, what it meant was that I couldn't trust the local police — any of the police. They were all suspect, from Sheriff Cole down to his deputies, and even those not directly suspected are likely to have loyalties that could color their thinking. So I could hardly go to any of them with the information that our killer might well be a cop." She shook her head. "We needed help from investigators outside the town, outside the parish, and we had to keep it quiet because we certainly couldn't let it be known that our own sheriff's department was under suspicion."

"But the Bureau is very picky about sending in agents if the local authorities haven't asked for our help," Nell continued. "States' rights, various jurisdictions — it can get tangled and ugly in a hurry if we aren't very, very careful how we handle things. Still, Casey was in a position to ask for our help in a unique situation and to authorize us to begin investigating, so the decision was made."

"To send you in?" Max was still trying to wrap his mind around the idea that Nell — the half-wild, fey girl he remembered so vividly — was now a federal cop.

"To launch an undercover investigation," she corrected. "No agents wandering around in town flashing their badges or muscling in on the local cops. Since we knew we'd have to investigate those local cops while also working to solve this series of murders, we could hardly operate openly.

"Something much quieter and a lot more subtle was needed. Obviously. And an agent who wouldn't stand out like a sore thumb. I was chosen partly because I have a nice, innocent — and authentic — reason to be here. Settling my father's estate." She spoke without emotion. "Even the most suspicious person would be unlikely to figure me for anything other than a reluctant daughter returning home because there were things I had to take care of here. So I was perfect for the job."

Max shook his head. "They didn't send you down here alone, surely?"

"No."

He stared at her for a moment, then looked at Casey.

"Nell is my contact," she said. "I don't know the other agent — or agents — involved."

"Which is the way it stays," Nell said, looking steadily at Max. "Undercover means under cover. The safety of an agent often depends on how secure the cover is; what you don't know, you can't betray, consciously or unconsciously. If you hadn't presented a potential problem by — rather obviously — following me around today, there wouldn't have been any need to tell you this much."

"Thanks a lot," he muttered.

"Don't mention it."

Casey smiled slightly, but said, "If anybody else noticed you following Nell, Max, they'll probably chalk it up to . . . renewed interest, shall we say? Old gossip can have its uses. Since there was always a . . . mystery . . . concerning you two, people will tend to focus on that."

"Great," Max said without looking at Nell. "It's always been my ambition to look like a lovelorn jerk."

"Better than looking like a stalker or a murderer," Casey reminded him matter-of-factly.

"We all know I'm already suspected of the latter." He kept his gaze on her. "Which makes me wonder why you two decided to bring me in on this. It can't be only because I was following Nell all day. Aren't you taking quite a chance? I could be the killer, you know."

"You aren't a cop," Casey reminded him.

"No, but that profile could be wrong."

"It isn't," Nell said. "Certainly not on the major points. Bishop is very good at what he does."

Max shrugged. "Okay, but even the best make mistakes sometimes. I could still be the killer."

"You aren't," Nell said.

"You can't know that."

"Yes, I can." She waited until he reluctantly met her gaze, and added evenly, "And you know how I can."

Max was far too conscious of Casey's silent attention to say any of the things he wanted to say to Nell. He didn't know how much Casey knew but, even more, he wasn't about to open up old wounds and take the distinct risk of having Nell rub salt into them.

So all he said was, "So I'm off your suspect list. Who's on it?"

Casey said, "Just about everybody else, if you want the truth. Virtually all the men, anyway."

"You're sure the killer is male?"

Nell nodded. "Pretty sure. According to Bishop's profile, he's probably white, likely in his mid-thirties to mid-forties, and almost certainly a cop, though he could also be someone to whom cops are a hobby and his interest in them an obsession. Whichever it is, he knows police procedure, understands forensics, and has no intention of making a mistake that might get him caught."

"He doesn't want to get caught? I thought most serial killers did, at least on some level."

"This isn't a serial killer, at least not in the accepted sense. This killer isn't choosing victims at random or because he has no connection to them. This is personal to him, very personal. He's picking his victims in order to expose their secret crimes, their secret lives. Which means he

102

knows them, and probably quite well. He doesn't like secrets; somewhere in his life, maybe his childhood, a secret damaged him and somehow changed his world or his perception of himself forever."

Max frowned. "So he wants the truth to come out, no matter the cost."

"That seems to be his motivation, at least in part. We also believe that in killing these men, he's attempting to punish them for their secrets. Whoever is responsible for the secret in his own life was probably out of his reach and somehow escaped punishment for that sin or crime. Because he couldn't get justice for himself, he's trying to get it for the innocents in these men's lives — or at least that's what he believes."

Nell hesitated, frowned. "Bishop thinks there's something else too, some other piece of this guy's reasoning that would help explain either what he's doing or his choice of victims."

"That's wonderfully vague," Max noted.

Casey said, "As I understand it, profiling is mostly educated and intuitive guesswork. More of an art than a science. Bound to be some vagueness there."

Nell was still frowning. "Bishop isn't normally vague, believe me. And his pro-

103

files tend to be bull's-eyes more often than not. But something about this killer is bothering him, and I don't think even he knows why. If he hadn't been hip-deep in another tricky case himself, he'd be down here trying to solve the puzzle first-hand. As it is, I have a direct line to him and I'm under orders to keep him advised."

"But you aren't here alone," Max repeated.

"No."

"How effective can an agent be when he or she is pretending to be something else?"

"We all function quite well that way, actually. My unit is . . . peculiarly suited to undercover operations."

"Why?" Max demanded.

"Well, among other things, let's just say we're all accustomed to keeping secrets."

He frowned at her. "I thought most feds were."

"You've been watching too much television."

Casey laughed and said, "You've told him this much, Nell, might as well tell him the rest."

Nell shrugged. "It's not something the Bureau publicizes, but the Special Crimes Unit is made up mostly of agents who each have one or more . . . unorthodox investigative abilities."

"Meaning?"

"Psychic abilities, Max. I finally found something useful to do with the Gallagher curse."

CHAPTER
FIVE

Shelby Theriot had grown up in Silence, just as her parents had done. And unlike some of her friends, she hadn't even gone away to college; there was a small community college in the parish, and it had provided all the additional education Shelby could bear after finishing high school.

In high school, she had been voted Most Likely to Grace the Cover of a Magazine, which only proved that kids in high school were rotten judges of character.

Shelby didn't give a damn what she looked like, and had in fact rejected several offers that would have put her feet on the path to possible fame and fortune as a model. But she very much liked being on the other end of a camera, and over the years her pictures had begun appearing in various magazines.

It was still more of a hobby than a career, mostly because Shelby didn't really need a career, and also because she wasn't in the least ambitious. She didn't need a career because her parents had left her both a nice house and stock in a number of flourishing businesses. She wasn't ambitious because it simply wasn't in her nature to be. She took pictures because she enjoyed it and needed neither money nor approval to validate doing something that was fun and satisfying in and of itself.

All of which explained why Shelby had spent the day just wandering around with her camera, snapping pictures here and there of whatever scenery or person caught her fancy. The townspeople were too accustomed to this to protest; Shelby had formed the habit of giving away prints to her subjects, cheerfully handing over negatives as well if asked for them, and since she never used a picture without permission, no one minded even the sometimes unflattering shots she occasionally got while catching her subjects unawares.

Since the light was particularly good on this Thursday, Shelby spent virtually the entire day outside, quitting only when darkness forced her to. She stopped by the café for supper because she didn't feel like fixing anything for herself, flirted with Vinny for a few minutes afterward, and then went home.

Her small house, on the outskirts of

town, was the picture-postcard image of a white cottage, complete with a white picket fence. She loved flowers but boasted a brown thumb, so she paid a gardener to keep the front and back yards looking pretty year-round; the rest of home maintenance she took care of herself, perfectly capable of wielding both a paintbrush and a hammer with equal skill.

She drove a small, neat Honda and lived with a cat named Charlie, currently the only male fixture in her life. Despite the well-meaning attempts of friends to fix her up, Shelby had yet to meet any man who even mildly tempted her to give up her independence — or the freedom to work in her darkroom until dawn or eat cold pizza in bed while watching her favorite horror movies at midnight.

On this particular night, after a day spent happily with her camera, she intended to shut herself up in her darkroom and develop her film. She was looking forward to hours of work and was curious to see what she had captured, since there were almost always surprises.

This time, there was definitely a surprise.

"What the hell . . ." she muttered to herself, holding up the last shot of a roll she had taken around mid-afternoon.

It had amused her to notice that Max Tanner seemed to be following Nell Gallagher around town today, and at least twice Shelby had captured the image of him lurking, very intent on Nell and apparently unconscious of the fact that he wasn't exactly being subtle about it. Shelby felt she knew Max well enough to be pretty certain he hadn't been stalking with any kind of deadly intent, and that certainty had freed her to speculate as to his motives.

Had to be those abandonment issues, she'd decided. Or was it merely rejection of a particularly nasty sort when one referred to a prom date gone humiliatingly awry?

In any case, she had snapped a shot of Max skulking near one corner of the courthouse while Nell, apparently oblivious to his presence, walked down the steps toward her Jeep. That much was ordinary enough, even if interesting.

What wasn't ordinary was the odd, hazy shape just a couple of feet behind Nell.

Like any good photographer, Shelby knew a lot about shadow and light. She also had a solid familiarity with the tricks a camera could produce, some of them odd or eerie. She knew about occlusions of the lens, about double exposures, about reflections, about corrupted film.

"This is definitely weird," she muttered to herself, after silently running through possibilities and discarding them one by one. The camera was fine, the film, the paper. When she checked the negative carefully, it, too, bore the odd, shadowy shape that seemed to float behind Nell. So something had definitely *been* there, at least for the camera to see. But not the naked eye, because Shelby had seen nothing unusual when she had framed the shot.

She turned on the white lights and stood back to stare at the eight-by-ten hanging over the trays.

Every detail of the shot was clear. The building, Max, Nell. Everything just as it should be, with the light falling just so and shadows where they should have been.

But behind Nell, beginning several inches above the steps and stretching upward maybe six feet, was a shadow that had no right to be there. It was vaguely man-shaped and, though it appeared more dense than smoke, was certainly not solid.

"What the hell *is* that?" Shelby wondered aloud. No matter how carefully she studied the shot, she could find absolutely nothing solid to account for the shadow.

But that shadow was definitely there. Even more, with hardly any imagination at all it could be argued that the shadow loomed over Nell, even seemed to reach out for her.

Grasping. Threatening.

It was some time before Shelby realized that she was absently rubbing the nape of her neck because of an odd, tingly sensation, and it took a minute or so more for her to recognize what was happening.

The hair on the back of her neck was standing up.

Maybe it was nothing. Probably it was nothing. But Shelby had always listened to her instincts, and they were whispering an urgent warning now.

"Jeez." Shelby glanced at her watch, then made up her mind and left the darkroom. Too late for a visit, maybe, but not too late for a phone call.

"You don't have to do this," Nell said as Max followed her into the foyer of the Gallagher house.

"Humor me," he requested.

Nell looked at him a moment, then shrugged. "Suit yourself. But maybe I'd better remind you that I'm the one with the gun."

"I'm not likely to forget that." But he didn't bother to argue when he knew only too well he wasn't being particularly logical about this. He just went through the downstairs, turning on lights and checking windows and doors. When he was satisfied the first floor was clear, he went upstairs and checked every room up there as well.

When he came back downstairs, he found Nell in the kitchen waiting for coffee to brew.

"Happy now?" she asked dryly.

Instead of answering, Max asked a sharp question of his own. "Will you at least admit that your presence here could be a threat to this killer?"

She leaned back against the counter and gazed at him steadily for a moment, then sighed. "*If* he knows about the Gallagher curse, *if* he believes in psychic ability, and *if* he knows any specifics about my ability — maybe."

"Jesus, you're stubborn."

"I'm a cop, Max, remember? Risk comes with the territory."

"Not undue risk."

"In this situation, how do you define *undue?* I can take care of myself, you know. I'm armed. I'm trained in self-defense. And I'm here to look for a killer. It's my job."

"Is that all it is? Your job?"

"What else could it be?"

"You also came home to settle your father's estate."

Nell turned away to get out cups and silverware. "Do you take milk or sugar? I don't think I ever knew that."

"Both." He watched as she put what was needed on the counter near the coffeemaker. "Are you going to answer my question?"

"Yes, I also came home to settle my father's estate."

"Would you have come home if it hadn't also been your job?"

"I think you know the answer to that."

"You hated him, didn't you?"

Nell poured the coffee and pushed his cup across the counter to him so he could fix it the way he liked. Matter-of-factly, she said, "Yes, I hated him. And I think it's a cosmic joke that I ended up with all his property."

There were plenty of questions Max wanted to ask, but he was conscious of feeling an overwhelming caution. He was walking an emotional minefield with Nell, with a single unwary step promising destruction, and every instinct warned him not to push too hard. Not now. Not yet.

113

So all he said was, "Did he know you'd joined the FBI?"

"No. I didn't write to him either."

Max didn't rise to the bait. "What about Hailey? She talked as if she knew where you were, what you were doing."

"She didn't. I hadn't seen or spoken to Hailey since I left Silence."

He frowned. "Then she made that stuff up?"

Nell sipped her coffee, then smiled. "She always made stuff up, Max. Didn't you know?"

"You're saying she was a liar?"

"Sweet, friendly Hailey. So charming, so good-tempered. And she had a way about her, didn't she? A way of . . . getting people behind her. A way of making people believe her. Not exactly my strong suit, huh?"

"Nell —"

Abruptly, she said, "I wonder what she did to so alienate our father that he disinherited her. Do you know?"

"Supposedly . . . she ran off with Glen Sabella. He was a mechanic, and he was married. Gossip had it that your father was furious, especially since —"

"Since both his wife and his other daughter had also run off without a word."

"That was the general consensus, yes. I don't think anybody ever had the nerve to ask Adam directly, but it was common knowledge he changed his will just a couple of weeks after she left."

"Wade Keever does like to talk," Nell murmured.

"He isn't the most discreet lawyer in town. But the general feeling was also that Adam didn't give a damn who knew."

"No, he usually didn't."

"He could be mysterious about some things. The Gallagher curse, for instance."

Nell gazed at him a moment, then said, "He was mysterious about it because he didn't understand it. Any more than the rest of us did. Worse for him, though. He didn't have it."

"What? I just assumed —"

"Yeah, everybody did. Because it was the Gallagher curse, everybody figured we all had it. And he didn't do anything to discourage people from thinking that. His mother had it, and his daughter — and I think his father had it as well. Maybe he felt left out."

"Daughter. Just you? Not Hailey?"

"Not Hailey."

"She used to joke about it. Even manned the fortune-teller's tent at the school carni-

115

vals. From what I heard, she was pretty good at it."

"That sort of thing isn't hard, given a fair amount of knowledge about your neighbors and a certain . . . theatrical flair. Hailey always had both."

"But no genuine ability?"

"Not psychic ability, no."

Max thought about that for a moment. "But your psychic ability is genuine. And it's what got you into the FBI?"

"It's what got me into the Special Crimes Unit. I had to pass all the usual tests to get into the FBI."

"Wait a minute — you didn't graduate from high school."

"Yes, I did. Just not here. Went to college, too."

"On your own?"

Nell shrugged. "It took me five years instead of four, since I was working my way through, but I made it. I majored in computer science. Minored in psychology."

Max had spent so much time these last hours readjusting what had clearly been his faulty mental image of Nell that he was beginning to feel a little dizzy. "And then you joined the FBI?"

She hesitated, then shook her head. "No, then I tried to help a friend whose little sister had been abducted. There was an open-minded cop who listened to me, and they found the little girl before she could be killed."

"You'd had a vision?"

"Yes. I was living in a small town on the West Coast. The cop began coming to me from time to time with some of his more puzzling cases. Sometimes I was able to help. He's the one who introduced me to an FBI agent who was part of a new unit being put together. The Special Crimes Unit. They thought I'd fit into that unit nicely. As it turns out, I did."

"Something useful to do with the Gallagher curse?"

"Exactly. They don't treat me like a freak. They don't whisper about me or look at me nervously. They don't even think I'm the slightest bit odd. Because I'm not. I'm just one of them, another investigator with a unique tool or two to help me do my job."

"Hunting down killers?"

"Killers. Rapists. Kidnappers. Pedophiles. We usually get the real animals, because they're usually harder to catch."

After a moment, he said, "It sounds like difficult work. Emotionally difficult, I mean."

"Bishop says finding genuine psychics is never the problem. Finding genuine psychics who can handle the work consistently is. I can handle it."

"So far, you mean."

"Yeah. So far."

"So . . . you use your visions as tools? Use them to try and solve crimes?"

"To answer questions. To give me pieces of the puzzle. That's all, usually. Just a little extra help for the more conventional investigative methods."

"What about your blackouts?"

"What about them?"

"You know what I'm asking you, Nell. How do you cope with them? Prepare for them? What happens if you black out during an investigation?"

"I try to find something soft to fall on."

He set his cup down on the counter with a rather emphatic sound. "Very funny."

She was smiling faintly, but her green eyes were watchful. "It's the truth. The blackouts never come without warning. When my head starts to hurt that way, I make sure I can be alone somewhere I won't be disturbed. If I'm working with a partner, I make sure he or she is notified that I'll be . . . incapacitated for an hour or so. It's all I can do."

"And your fellow agents understand that?"

"My fellow agents tend to have baggage of their own. Our sort of abilities often come with . . . side effects. Sometimes difficult ones. We've all learned to adapt, to work within our limitations." Nell kept her voice even, casual.

"Have you?"

"Yes." The word was barely out of her mouth when the scene around her changed with stunning abruptness. It was still the kitchen, still night, but Max was no longer standing there looking at her with brooding dark eyes.

Instead, she saw her father stride in through the back door, his dark hair damp, his face like a thundercloud. She wanted to draw back, to run.

To escape.

But she could only stand there and watch numbly, listen when a dead man muttered something under his breath as he stalked through the kitchen.

"She should have told me. Goddammit, she should have *told* me. . . ."

He vanished through the doorway leading to the rest of the house, and Nell stared after him. As always, she was completely aware of having a vision, conscious of that

119

peculiar time-out-of-sync sensation that always accompanied them.

What she saw always meant something, always. What did this mean?

She turned her head to look toward the wall across from the back door, where a calendar had always hung. It was there, showing her a date of May, the previous year.

The month Adam Gallagher had died.

"Nell!"

With a start, she was back in the here and now, the dizzying out-of-sync sensation gone as abruptly as a soap bubble popping. She looked up at Max. She was only vaguely aware of his hands gripping her shoulders, but something in his face made her voice her thoughts aloud.

"He was killed too. My father was murdered."

It was raining in Chicago.

Special Agent Tony Harte stood at the window gazing out at the dreary night, sipping his coffee. He hated rainy nights as a rule. And most especially in the middle of a difficult case with nothing going right. And he wasn't the only one. The tension in the room behind him was just about thick enough to cut with a knife.

A real knife, not a metaphorical one.

On top of everything else, Bishop was always restless and uneasy whenever Miranda was out in the field without him. There was probably nobody in the world who respected Miranda's strengths and abilities more than Bishop did, but that didn't stop him from worrying about her.

Turning from the window, Tony raised a subject he hoped would occupy his boss's mind, at least for the moment. "Have you revised that profile of the killer in Silence? I mean, since we got the latest information?"

Special Agent Noah Bishop looked up from his study of photographs of bits and pieces of physical evidence and frowned slightly as he shook his head. "Nothing we've learned recently changes the profile."

"Still a cop?"

"Still probably a cop."

"How sure are you of that?"

Bishop leaned back in his chair and gazed around the sitting room of the hotel suite as if it might provide answers, his pale gray sentry eyes as sharp as always. His reply was slow. "Unofficially? Pretty damned sure. But there's always room for doubt, Tony, you know that."

"Yeah. But you tend to be awfully accurate, for all that. If you say you're pretty sure, then he's probably a cop. Tough for our people, having to keep their heads down, look for a killer, *and* police the police."

Bishop nodded, still frowning. The scar on his left cheek stood out more clearly than normal, as it always did when he was tense or upset. A useful and accurate barometer of his mood during those times when even another psychic found it difficult or impossible to read him any other way.

Not that this was one of those times.

Tony watched him. "You're still bothered by something else, aren't you? In Silence."

Since he had long ago learned the uselessness of denying thoughts or feelings another member of his team was picking up on, Bishop merely said, "There's an undercurrent I can't quite get a fix on."

"What kind of undercurrent? Emotional or psychological?"

"Both."

"With Nell? Or with the killer?"

Bishop grimaced. "Plenty of undercurrents with Nell, but we knew that going in. No, it's something about the killer I can't bring into focus. I think he has another reason for picking his victims. Not just because they have secrets he wants to expose. There's something else."

"His own history with them, maybe?"

Bishop shrugged. "Maybe. It almost feels as if . . . it's more personal for him. That maybe the sins he's punishing them for aren't just the ones exposed by their murders or the investigations. That there's something else there, if we could dig deeply enough to find it."

"So he tells himself he's killing them, punishing them, to get justice for the innocent people in their lives, but all the time it's revenge for himself?"

"At least partly for himself. But he still thinks of himself as a judge and jury. He still believes he's performing a service for society, he's convinced himself of that, by sentencing and executing these men for their secret sins."

"But also for injuring him."

Bishop ran restless fingers through his black hair, slightly disarranging the vivid white streak above the left temple. "I get the sense he despises them, all of them, and all for the same reason."

"Because they hurt him? Lied to him?"

"Maybe. Dammit, I need to be down

there. I'd have a better shot at figuring this bastard out if I was there, on the scene."

Tony said, "Well, aside from the fact that your face was plastered all over the national papers a few months ago after we cracked that kidnapping case, which would make it a little hard for you to blend into the background down there, we also have this small matter of an active serial killer here in the Windy City."

"You don't have to remind me of that, Tony."

"No, I didn't think I did," Tony murmured. "Look, maybe we can wrap things up here quickly enough that we'll be able to get down to Silence and help out."

"Yeah."

Tony watched him a moment longer, then said, "I know what you're really worried about. But Miranda's okay, you know that."

"Yes. For the moment."

It wasn't the first time Tony had wondered whether the psychic bond between Bishop and his wife was a blessing or a curse. When they were working together, concentrating on the same investigation, it was undoubtedly a blessing; together they were far more powerful and accurate, both as psychics and investigators, than either was alone. But when they were separated by necessity, as they were now, each working on a different case, then the bond often proved to be something of a problem — or at the very least a distraction.

Bishop knew Miranda was currently safe and unhurt because, even though they had closed the "doors" connecting their minds in order to keep from distracting each other, they each maintained a constant sense of the other's physical and emotional state no matter what the distance was between them. Bishop knew Miranda was safe for the moment, just as she knew he was — and also knew he was worried about her.

Tony didn't pretend to understand it, but like the other members of the unit, he was more than a little awed by it. Even among psychics accustomed to various, often extraordinary paranormal abilities, some things were still remarkable.

What must it be like to be so bonded to another person that their thoughts and feelings flowed through you as easily as your own did? To be so connected that if one was cut, the other would also bleed?

It was Tony's opinion that such incredible intimacy would require both a great deal of trust in and understanding of one's partner and an equally great degree of security and honesty in oneself. He seriously doubted that any pair of psychics who were not mates or blood siblings could have formed such a bond.

But it wasn't all good, as this situation illustrated. Bishop and Miranda had been together long enough by now that they had learned to function extraordinarily well both as a team and when separated by circumstances, but their unusual closeness literally made each in many ways incomplete without the other.

Tony had absolutely no qualms about serving with either one of them alone; even when lacking their vital other half, both Bishop and Miranda were formidable psychics and investigators, skilled and tough cops, and more than a match for most situations in which they found themselves. But he would also be the first to admit that it was far more comfortable to serve with them both, the partnership intact and the two of them functioning smoothly as if with a single mind and heart.

A hell of a lot less tension that way.

With all of that very much in his thoughts, Tony spoke carefully. "We're spread pretty thin right now, with a half-dozen separate major investigations scattered across the country all going on at once. We have to use all our resources *and* all our aces. Every team in the field has to have a dominant member, that's your rule. A lead investigator with as much experience as possible who's also the most powerful psychic available."

Bishop said, "Something else you don't need to remind me of, Tony."

"All I'm saying is that Miranda being the lead might make all the difference in her case, and you know it. Just like you being the lead here and Quentin being the lead out in California, and Isabel running the show in Boston. Besides, Miranda took care of herself for a good many years before you tracked her down and reappeared in her life."

"I know that."

"She's a black belt and a crack shot, besides being able to read at least two-thirds of the people she encounters. All of which gives her quite an edge in the survival department."

"I know that too."

"I know you know that. All of that. I also know none of it makes a damned bit of difference at the moment because you've spent way too many sleepless nights alone in bed. It's starting to show, boss."

"Look who's talking."

Tony started slightly and felt his face get warm. Damned inconvenient sometimes, he thought, working with a telepath. Especially one as powerful as Bishop. "Never mind me."

Remorselessly, Bishop said, "Nothing like getting the scare of your life to advance a relationship to the next step."

"Shit. How long have you known?"

"About you and Kendra?" Bishop smiled slightly. "Longer than you have, Tony. Long before she was shot."

Tony considered that, then shook his head. "I knew Quentin was on to us but figured that was mostly because he's usually Kendra's partner in the field. And because he so often knows things he shouldn't, damn his eyes."

Mildly curious, Bishop said, "Why even bother trying to keep it quiet?"

"I don't know. Yeah — I do know. You've said yourself there are few secrets in a unit full of psychics; sometimes it's fun to have a secret. Even if you're only fooling yourself that's what it is."

"I get that where you're concerned. It's just the sort of thing you'd like. But Kendra? She's awfully levelheaded to enjoy a secret romance."

Tony grinned. "Are you kidding? It's the levelheaded ones that go off the deep end, believe me."

"I'll take your word for it."

"Do that. I'm not nearly sure enough of her to risk having everybody openly watching us to see what happens next."

"Remember who you're talking to. In this unit, we don't have to openly watch to know what's going on."

"Yeah, but at least that way we won't feel quite so much like bugs under a microscope."

Deadpan, Bishop said, "So we should be subtle while we gleefully observe?"

"I'd appreciate it if you would," Tony responded earnestly.

Bishop lifted a brow at him. "It occurs to me that you're having a shot at that sort of subtlety now. Tony, are you trying to distract me?"

"I was working on it, yeah."

"Why?"

"You know damned well why. The tension in here. That's something you couldn't be subtle about if you tried. And you never try."

With only a mild attempt to defend himself, Bishop said, "I'm always tense during an investigation."

"No, that's a different kind of tension."

"And you'd know."

"Well, yeah."

Bishop grimaced slightly. "Okay, okay. I will do my best to stop worrying about things I can't control. In the meantime, would you care to come away from that window and do something useful? Like work?"

"I thought you'd never ask," Tony responded cheerfully, joining his boss at the conference table. But before he picked up a photograph to study, he added in a musing tone, "Getting back to Silence for just a minute — what do you think about this connection Nell has? Think it'll make things easier for her?"

"No," Bishop replied soberly. "I think it'll make things harder for her. Much harder."

Tony sighed. "And there's nothing we can do to help?"

"Some things have to happen —"

"— just the way they happen," Tony finished. "Yeah, I was afraid you were going to say that. And in some cases, boss, it really sucks."

"Tell me about it," Bishop said.

CHAPTER
SIX

"I don't know if I'll ever get used to these . . . episodes of yours," Max said, releasing her shoulders only because she moved away.

Nell nearly reminded him that he wouldn't have to since she didn't intend to remain in Silence for long, but instead heard herself say, "They're unnerving, I know. Especially for someone else. Sorry about that."

He shook his head. "Never mind. Just explain a few things, will you, please? I'm getting really tired of groping through this fog of confusion." Even though the words were flippant, his tone was anything but. "And before I try to figure out what the hell you mean by saying your father was murdered too, can you start with the basics?"

"It's getting late," she hedged, wondering if she was only talking about the lateness of the hour on this particular night or something a lot more important. She had a hunch it was the latter, and it bothered her more than she wanted to admit even to herself.

"I know. But I doubt either one of us is going to be able to sleep anytime soon. I need to understand, Nell. And I think you owe me that much."

She didn't protest, all too aware that she owed him a lot more than that. What was the going price for leaving a man in limbo? High. Maybe too high to pay. She set her coffee cup on the scarred old butcher-block table in the center of the kitchen and sat down in one of the ladder-back chairs. She waited until he sat down across from her, then spoke slowly. "Explain the visions, you mean?"

"Can you explain them?"

Nell shrugged. "I understand them a bit better than I did while I was growing up — even though what I felt instinctively way back then turned out to be pretty accurate."

"For instance?"

"What it is I actually tap into during a vision. A sociologist would say I had just experienced what they call an apparitional event. That I had seen — or at least claimed I had seen — the ghost of my father walk through this room. But that's not what I saw."

"No? What, then?"

"It was . . . a memory."

"Whose memory?"

She smiled faintly. "In the very broadest sense, it was the memory of the house."

"Are you saying this house is haunted?"

"No. I'm saying the house remembers."

"You said something like that before, years ago," Max noted. "That some places remember. But I don't understand what you mean. How can a house have a memory?"

"Any object — a house, a place — can have a memory. Life has energy, Max. Life *is* energy. Broken down into their most basic form, emotions and thoughts are energy: electrical impulses produced by the brain."

"Okay. And so?"

"And so energy can be absorbed and retained by an object or a place. By walls and a floor, by trees, even by the ground itself. Maybe certain places are more likely than others to retain energy because of factors we don't yet understand, because their physical composition lends itself to storing energy, or there are magnetic fields — or even that the energy itself is particularly powerful at a given moment and we ourselves stamp that into a place with our own

133

strength and intensity.

"However it happens, some places remember some things. Some emotions. Some events. The energy remains trapped in a place, unseen and unheard until someone with an inborn sensitivity to that particular kind of energy is able to tap into it."

"Someone like you."

"Exactly. There's nothing magical about what I do, nothing dark or evil — or inhuman. It's just an ability, as natural to me as your instincts about horses are to you. A perfectly normal talent, if you will, that not everyone has. Maybe it's genetic, like the color of our eyes or whether we're right- or left-handed; in my family it certainly seems to be, at least partly. On the other hand, there's every possibility that every human being has the capacity for some form of psychic ability, that everyone has an unused area of the brain that could perform seemingly amazing things if we only knew how to . . . turn it on."

Nell shook her head and frowned slightly as she looked down at her coffee. "We're pretty sure that some people are born with the potential to develop some kind of psychic ability, that in them the area of the brain controlling that function is at least partly or intermittently active, even if it's entirely on an unconscious level; we call them latents. They usually aren't aware of it, though another psychic often is."

Max frowned, but all he said was, "But latent abilities do sometimes become active on a conscious level?"

"They have been known to. As far as we can tell, turning a latent into a conscious, functioning psychic requires some sort of trigger. A physical or emotional trauma, usually. Like a shock to the brain, literally or figuratively. Something happens to them, an accident or an emotional jolt — and they find themselves coping with strange new abilities. Which would explain why people with head injuries or who develop certain kinds of seizures often report psychic experiences afterward."

"I had no idea," Max said.

"Not many people do. I didn't, until I joined the unit and began to learn." She shook her head again. "Anyway, in my particular case, my brain is hardwired for a sensitivity to the sort of electrical energy produced by . . . emotional or psychologically intense events. Those events leave electrical impressions behind, energy that's absorbed by the place where the events occur, and I have the knack of sensing and interpreting that electrical energy."

Max spoke carefully. "Isn't sensing electrical energy a long way from envisioning an image of a dead man?"

"Is it? The mind interprets the information it's given and translates that into some form we recognize and understand. What happened in this room *had* a form, a face, a voice — and all that survived as energy. As a memory. Just the way you recall a memory of your own, I can recall the memory of a place. Sometimes quite vividly, and sometimes only bits and pieces, images, feelings, scattered and unclear."

"Okay. Assuming I can accept all that, explain to me why that particular scene — your father walking through a kitchen he must have walked through a million times — is what this room retained. Why that? Out of everything that must have happened here in decades, all the emotional scenes and crises so common in every kitchen everywhere, why was that very normal scene important enough to retain?"

"Because it wasn't normal. What my father was feeling when he walked through this kitchen then was . . . incredibly intense. He was emotionally devastated."

Max frowned. "You felt that?"

"Sensed it — some of it, at least. It was difficult to get a fix on his emotions,

136

simply because he was overwhelmed by them himself. But I know he was distraught, in shock, that he'd just discovered something he could hardly believe was true."

"Something *she* should have told him, isn't that what you heard him say?"

"Yes. Given the calendar I saw, that must have been when he found out whatever it was that made him disinherit Hailey. He died in late May, and he'd changed his will just a few weeks before that, not long after she left."

Still frowning, Max said, "So why do you believe he was murdered? No one suspected it was anything other than a heart attack."

"Yes, but there was no one here *to* suspect, no one to question. All the rest of the family was gone, not on the scene to wonder. He had no close friends. It looked like a heart attack; he was the right age for one and had been warned by his doctor that his habits and temperament put him into the high-risk category. And with no other unexplained deaths before then to put anyone on guard . . ."

"I understand why no one here would have suspected a murder, but how can *you* be so sure he was killed? Did he think he was going to be, fearing for his life in that scene you envisioned?"

For the first time, realizing, Nell felt a chill. "No, he had no idea," she said slowly. "No fear or worry. His mind was entirely focused on the shock he'd had, but he wasn't in the least afraid or concerned for himself. It was . . . I must have picked up on something else. Sensed something else."

"Like maybe the killer?"

She drew a breath. "Like maybe the killer."

Nate McCurry was scared.

He hadn't been at first. Hell, he'd barely paid attention when Peter Lynch had died, and as for Luke Ferrier, well, Nate had always expected something bad to happen to him.

But when Randal Patterson's death had exposed his S&M leanings, Nate had started to get nervous. Because he had something in common with Randal. And, he was beginning to think, with the others as well.

Not that Nate had any big *secret*, not like those other guys. He hadn't broken the law, and he didn't have any whips or chains in his basement or skeletons in his closet.

But sometimes a man had things he wanted to keep to himself; that was perfectly natural. Perfectly normal.

Unless there was a madman running around punishing men for their sins, that is.

He was nervous enough to install a security system in his house, paying double to have it done quickly when, the installation guy had told him, the company was backed up on work because so many orders had come in.

So he wasn't the only nervous man in Silence.

And at least he could claim it was just good business to protect oneself. After all, he sold insurance. And everybody knew insurance companies were very big on reducing risk.

That's what Nate was doing, reducing risk.

But he was still scared.

It didn't help that he lived alone. Creepy to be alone when you were scared. He kept the television on for background noise, because every rattle of a tree branch or sudden hoot of an owl out there made him jump. But even with the background noise, he found himself going from window to window and door to door, checking the locks. Making sure.

Watching the night creep slowly along.

He didn't sleep.

He had stopped sleeping days ago.

"Nell, are we talking about the same killer? Are you saying your father was his first victim?"

She hesitated, then shrugged. "I don't know. Maybe. Maybe that was the start of his little execution plan."

"And he was here in this house."

Again, she hesitated. "There's no way for me to be sure, Max. But it makes sense. My father was found here in the house, right?"

"Yeah."

"Nobody suspected the body had been moved."

"Not that I ever heard. But since it looked like a heart attack, I doubt anyone even considered the idea."

That was true enough, and Nell nodded.

Max watched her broodingly. "Even if he was moved, what you picked up was right here, in this room — so the killer was probably here at some point."

Perfectly aware of what was bothering him about that, Nell tried to avoid discussing it. "It would be nice if I could peek back into that scene and try to get a better fix on the killer, but it doesn't seem to work that way. Or it never has. I never see the same scene twice."

"Do you ever see a second scene in the same place?"

"So far, no. It's as if, once I've tapped into the energy of a place, I've drained some of it away, eased the pressure somehow. Like the way you can be shocked by static electricity when you first touch something but not when you touch it a second time."

"The same thing can shock you a second time if you go away for a while and then touch it again later," Max pointed out. "Once the static has a chance to build back up."

"Yes, but so far I haven't figured out the time frame, if there is one, for this kind of energy. Maybe I could go back a week or a month or a year later and see something, but I haven't been able to yet. Different places may have different time frames depending on the intensity of the energies absorbed. Or this particular type of energy may dissipate completely once someone is able to tap into it. I just don't know."

"Nobody in this unit of yours has figured it out yet?"

Nell smiled slightly. "Well, aside from a pretty full load of cases to occupy most of our time, between us we also have a very wide range of paranormal abilities to deal with and try to understand. We're learning, slowly and mostly through bitter experience as we live each day and investigate cases, what our ranges and limits are, but that's an individual thing."

"And no help from science."

"No. As far as today's science goes, psychic abilities can't be validated in any acceptable sense. Oh, there are still people scattered around trying to do research, but our feeling is that today's technology and scientific methodology just isn't capable of effectively measuring or analyzing the paranormal. Not yet."

It was Max's turn to smile, albeit briefly. "That sounds just a bit like the company line."

"It is, more or less. One of the reasons I wanted to join the SCU was because I thought Bishop and his people had a very reasonable way of looking at the paranormal. They don't discount anything just because science can't explain it yet. And I have never heard any member of the team use the word *impossible* when referring to any aspect of the paranormal."

"Sounds like a pretty good way to live."

A little surprised, Nell said, "Coming from a hardheaded rancher, that's unexpected."

Max dropped his gaze to his mostly empty coffee cup and said slowly, "Maybe once you're touched by the paranormal, it changes your thinking about a lot of things."

Nell was very tempted to follow that path and find out where it would lead them but shied away. Not now. Not yet. The slightly sick feeling in the pit of her stomach told her she wasn't yet ready to face the truth of how badly she had messed up Max's life. So she reached for professionalism, for the safety net of why she was supposed to be here. She reminded herself that there was a dangerous killer on the loose. Which was more than enough reason to concentrate on her job and push everything else aside.

At least for now.

So all she said was, "One thing it doesn't change, in essence, is how a murder or series of murders is investigated. The next step for me is to try to gain access to the crime scenes. All of them. And I can't do that by openly waving my badge."

Max's smile twisted faintly, showing his

recognition of a path not taken, but he didn't protest. "I think we're finally coming to the real reason why you and the mayor took me into your confidence. You need me, don't you, Nell?"

The statement sent an odd little shock through her, and Nell had to remind herself that he meant she needed him professionally. Of course he meant that.

She chose her words carefully. "The information we've been able to gather pointed to you as the insider most likely to be helpful to me. You knew all the victims fairly well. The people here are entirely aware of the sheriff's dislike and distrust of you and so wouldn't be surprised if you were found to be . . . investigating things on your own in order to clear yourself. Owning your own ranch makes it possible for you to arrange flexible working hours without arousing any undue suspicion. And you have the habit of riding around the countryside, beyond the bounds of your ranch, making use of back trails and old dirt roads, so you have a strong familiarity with the area, and the sort of mobility I could find useful."

"And," he finished, "nobody would be surprised or suspicious to see us together."

"And that."

"Was it your idea, Nell?"

She almost denied it, wanted to, but finally said, "It made . . . a certain amount of sense. With everything added together and my certainty that you weren't the killer —"

"Was it your idea?"

She waited a beat, too conscious of things left unsaid and unanswered. This was even harder than she had expected it to be. "It was my suggestion."

He drew a breath. "I'm not so sure I like being used."

Nell made sure she didn't sound angry or defensive when she said, "It's to your advantage to do what you can to help uncover the truth, we both know that. Left to his own devices, the sheriff is more likely to arrest you than clear you. At least by helping me — us — you're assured of an impartial investigation completely focused on finding the real killer. And we don't intend to stop working until we do find him."

"And you consider it your duty to . . . suffer my company for the duration?"

Again, Nell replied carefully, uneasily aware of the ironic truth that Max was the one person here in Silence capable of seeing through her pretense. And it was liable to be sooner rather than later. "We're both adults, Max. And twelve years is a long time. The past is done, over. Right now, in this time and place, what we both want is to find the truth of what's happening here in Silence. That's all. That's enough."

But even as the careful lies were spoken, she knew that she was doing nothing more than postponing the inevitable. Sooner or later, Max would demand the truth.

She only hoped she was strong enough to give it to him.

"Is it enough?" he asked.

"It's my job. It's why I'm here."

Max nodded slowly, his dark gaze fixed on her face with an intensity she could feel under her skin. "And it's the only reason you're here. That's what I'm supposed to believe."

"I didn't come back until I had to. You made that point yourself."

"You didn't come back . . . until you had a reason to. A nice . . . safe . . . professional reason."

Sooner indeed.

"Like I said. It's my job." She nearly held her breath, afraid he'd keep pushing. More afraid he wouldn't.

Abruptly, Max shoved his chair back and

146

got to his feet. "Okay," he said, face expressionless. "I'll think about it."

Nell felt that sick sensation in the pit of her stomach again, but this time it was accompanied by a stab of pain. Hiding that, she said, "I'll be here tomorrow. There's enough to keep me busy here in the house. But don't take too long, Max. If you decide to pass, I'll have to figure out something else, some other way of gaining access to the crime scenes. And time is an issue."

She knew she sounded like a pro. Matter-of-fact and disinterested. Professional all the way.

He nodded, still expressionless. "There's one thing about your visions you haven't explained, you know."

She knew. "Yes."

"You've told me that sometimes what you see is something that hasn't happened yet. The future. But how can that be, if it's memories you're tapping into?"

"I don't know."

"Could it be a second, completely different ability? Precognition?"

"Bishop says not, and the others agree." She shrugged, conscious of the tension in her shoulders. "The experience is essentially the same, whether I'm seeing past or future. The same sensations, emotions, the same time-out-of-sync awareness. So it's the same ability. The flip side of it maybe, but the same."

"How can a place hold the impression, the *memory*, of an event that hasn't yet occurred?"

"I don't know. We don't know. Maybe time is more flexible than we can possibly imagine, not linear at all but a loop, or a series of loops. Maybe different time lines occupy the same physical world but in alternate dimensions, dimensions I'm somehow able to tap into because they contain another kind of energy I'm sensitive to. Or maybe it's a question of fate, of the physical world holding the energy of future events because those events *will* happen, are destined to happen — in a sense have already happened."

Max shook his head. "That's a little too metaphysical for me."

"You asked." She smiled slightly, wondering if she could have done this, handled this, if she hadn't been able to lean on duty and professionalism. No. Definitely not. "The simple truth is, I don't know how it works. I only know that it does."

He seemed about to say something else, but finally shook his head again. "Well, I guess I have to accept that. For now, anyway."

Nell was tempted to ask if he expected anything to change later but once again shied away from probing too deeply. She rose to her feet and walked with him to the front door.

"I'll let you know something tomorrow," he said.

"All right." She looked at him gravely, wondering if he was putting her off for the sake of appearances or for some other reason. He'd danced awfully close to guessing her true motivation in coming here, and from there it was only a step to also guess she was involving him in the investigation for reasons other than the flimsy ones she had stated.

Did he know? And if he did, would he use the knowledge for a little payback?

Abruptly, Max said, "That scene you saw out in the woods. A man carrying the body of a woman."

"Maybe a body. She might not have been dead."

"Either way, it could be something that hasn't happened yet."

Nell made her voice matter-of-fact. "There's no way to be sure. I've checked records of dead or missing women in the

149

county, and nothing seems to fit what I saw. No female murder victims in years, at least none found in the woods. So maybe it hasn't happened yet."

"And if it hasn't happened yet . . . it could be you. It could be a vision of your own future you saw."

"I never see my own future."

"You mean you never have before."

"I can take care of myself, Max."

Max's hands lifted slightly, as if he wanted to grab her and shake her, but in the end they curled into fists at his sides and he said tightly, "You're here investigating a series of murders, you're a threat to the killer, and you've seen something that could mean a confrontation with him that you'll lose."

There was no way she could reassure him of her safety, since it would have been a lie. So Nell didn't even make the attempt. "Whatever I saw changes nothing, and if that's how it ends, then that's how it ends. I'm here to do a job, Max, and I intend to do it." She paused, but not long enough to give him the chance to argue with her. "Don't bother telling me to lock the door behind you. I will."

"Have you got a death wish, Nell, is that it?"

"No. Good night, Max."

They stared at each other for a moment, then Max swore beneath his breath and went out the door, closing it with a distinct click behind him.

Nell threw the dead bolt with the same emphatic sound, then stood there for a moment watching her hands shake. She had thought she was ready for this, but hours spent in Max's company had proved her wrong. She wasn't ready for this. She would never be ready for this.

But there was no going back. Not now.

Nell sighed, wondering if there had ever been a point when she could have turned back. Probably not. The universe was about balance and about dealing with the past.

Sooner or later.

As for Max, all things considered, his display of concern for her safety was definitely unexpected, and she wasn't quite sure how she felt about it. Scared mostly, because retribution wasn't nearly as effective if it wasn't preceded by an interlude of unsuspecting happiness.

She looked at her hands again and willed them to stop shaking, not surprised when it only half worked. She was tired. And worried. And afraid. And for just an instant, she was tempted to open the door and call Max back, because being alone in this house tonight was almost more than she could bear.

Her hand even reached out for the door-knob, but Nell forced it to fall to her side.

I can do this. I can take care of myself. I have to.

She walked across the foyer toward the kitchen, pausing at the side table beside the stairs where the phone and answering machine were. The answering-machine light was blinking. When Nell pushed the button, the message she heard was brief.

"Nell, it's Shelby. Listen, when I was taking some pictures today I got something . . . unexpected. I think you should see it. I can bring it to your place tomorrow, first thing, if that's okay. I may be out late to-night, but you can leave a message on the machine and let me know what time."

Nell glanced at her watch, then reached for the phone.

It was still a bit before midnight when he did his meditation thing and sent his dream self off to visit Nell. It was, he'd decided, the best way to keep an eye on her without being too obvious about it. The connection took him to her even faster than before, and it pleased him to be able to so easily follow the well-worn path.

Some things seemed unaffected by the passage of time.

Not surprisingly, she was in bed, asleep, and for a time he hovered near and just looked down at her. Fascinating to be so close to her when she was entirely unaware of it. To be able to stare at her unabashedly.

She was a beautiful woman, even in the dark. The night stole color, so the hair spread out over her pillow was shimmering darkness and her skin was pale, smooth, her relaxed features the picture of delicate femininity. The covers were drawn up to her shoulders, so all he could see of her sleepwear was that there was nothing frilly or sexy about it, maybe just a T-shirt or something like that, colorless and shapeless.

While he watched, she stirred restlessly, and a shaft of moonlight streaming in the window fell on her face and allowed him to see a fleeting, uneasy frown.

It caught him off guard for an instant, even shook him.

Was she simply disturbed by being in this house again after so many years? Was that what disrupted her sleep on this quiet, peaceful night? Or was her sleeping mind somehow aware of him? Could she sense him?

Hear him?

He felt a moment of uneasiness, even fear, but then the possibilities occurred to him, and they were too fascinating and seductive to ignore.

He focused his concentration and gathered enough energy to whisper her name, watching intently to gauge her reaction. He was almost certain there was a reaction, that another frown flitted across her face and there was a break in the evenness of her breathing.

Ah.

How receptive would she be?

How far could he go?

After considering briefly, he whispered again, this time telling Nell to turn over in bed. He repeated the command, soft but insistent, willing her to obey. There was another catch in her breathing, another brief frown, and then she turned over.

A very minor success, he thought, but a good indication of control. A good beginning. Another tool he could no doubt find a use for. Yes, definitely.

He was going to have to think about this.

Practice a bit more until his control over her improved.

Smiling, he left Nell to her disturbed dreams.

CHAPTER
SEVEN

FRIDAY, MARCH 24

Ethan Cole closed the file folder and scowled across his desk at the small group assembled uncomfortably in several straight-backed visitor's chairs. "So what're you telling me?"

Justin Byers glanced at the other two CID detectives — strictly speaking, only the three of them made up the entire Criminal Investigation Division for the Lacombe Parish sheriff's department, though the uniformed deputies helped out when necessary — and realized glumly that he was still expected to be spokesman. Whether he liked it or not.

"We're telling you that we don't have much more this week than we had last week," he replied matter-of-factly. "We know all four of the victims received a phone call the night before they were killed, the calls placed from different pay phones around town. So far, we haven't

156

been able to find any witnesses who noticed anyone placing the calls. Other than that, there's nothing new to report."

If anything, the sheriff's scowl deepened. "Any of George Caldwell's secrets come to light yet?"

Lying without a blink, Justin said, "Not so far."

"Shit. I hate waiting for that."

The lone female detective, Kelly Rankin, offered, "Like waiting for the other shoe to drop. Unnerving." She shook her head and absently pushed a wayward strand of pale hair off her face.

Ethan half nodded in agreement. "I'll say. Look, do we have any idea at all whether this bastard is finished with his little rampage?"

Justin said, "There's just no way to know that. Maybe he had only four names on his hit list, or maybe he's got a dozen. So far, we haven't found the common denominator — not a single person with any kind of a grudge that we can connect to all four men."

Kelly spoke up again, saying, "Granted, we haven't yet sifted through the victims' secret lives thoroughly enough to find everything there is to find; these guys kept their secret sins *very* well hidden. And

157

those sins are all so . . . varied. I mean, we've got pornography, gambling, embezzlement — and God only knows what Caldwell's secret will be."

"All different," Ethan mused.

She nodded, her blue eyes intent. "Yeah. So maybe we're wasting time combing through the secrets looking for a common denominator, one enemy they all made."

Justin said, "Maybe the secrets *are* the common denominator."

The third CID detective, Matthew Thorton, agreed with a nod. He looked tired, which wasn't really surprising, his gray eyes bloodshot and graying dark hair somewhat rumpled. "That really is the only thing we're sure of so far — that at least the first three victims led some kind of a secret life. So maybe what we've got here is a killer whose only goal is to expose secrets. Maybe none of them did anything to him personally. Maybe he just plain doesn't like people pretending to be something they aren't."

"Which, if true, is not going to make our jobs any easier," Justin finished with a sigh. "Forget even trying to figure out who the next victim might be. And if this guy doesn't have a tangible connection to the victims, if there's no trail there for us to find, then we've got about zero chance of catching him, unless he makes a mistake."

The sheriff eyed him somewhat grimly. "That's a pretty defeatist attitude."

"Realistic. Serial killers with no connection to their victims get caught when they fuck up. Period." Catching himself belatedly, he added in a much more diffident tone, "At least everything I've read on the subject says so."

After a long moment, Ethan leaned his chair back until it creaked, and shook his head. "I'm still not convinced we've only got one killer here. For one thing, we've got four distinctly different causes of death: poison, drowning, electrocution, and gunshot. How often does a single killer vary his methods over that wide a range?"

"Not often," Justin admitted. "But it happens. Especially if one of his goals is to throw off the police."

"Maybe. But unless you people can uncover George Caldwell's secret life — assuming he had one — or discover some other connection to the first three victims, then I'm inclined to consider his murder as a single crime separate from the other three."

That surprised Justin somewhat. If Ethan Cole was indeed one of Caldwell's blackmail victims, would he be prodding his investigators to look for a motive specific only to that murder? Or was he convinced such a motive would both implicate someone else *and* surface before anyone could find evidence of Caldwell's secret vice?

Or was Justin totally wrong about the sheriff, seeing reluctance or interference in an investigation when none was actually there?

Kelly said, "He got a phone call from a pay phone just like the others the night before he was killed, that's certain." It wasn't quite an objection, merely a very careful reminder.

"People get calls from pay phones. It happens."

Justin exchanged glances with the other two, then said, "Well, we're bound to find the truth if we dig deep enough. In any case, there is one thing that sets Caldwell's murder apart from the others. He's the only one of the four who we can be reasonably sure saw his killer."

Obviously musing aloud, Kelly said, "I wonder if that means something. *If* the Caldwell murder is part of the series, then why was he killed so . . . directly? Face-to-face, I mean."

Justin said, "We're assuming that Luke Ferrier was either rendered unconscious by some drug while he was driving, and so accidentally drove into the water, or else was rendered unconscious beforehand, put into his car, and the car pointed at that bayou, right? That he probably had no opportunity to see his killer."

Kelly frowned at him. "Well, I'm assuming. There was no sign of a struggle, nothing to indicate that Ferrier put up any kind of a fight. So it only makes sense that either it was suicide or else he was out cold and couldn't struggle. And since he'd clearly been making plans to leave Silence, I'm not buying the suicide theory."

Justin nodded. "Okay. But if we assume the killer was there with Ferrier even if he wasn't seen, that he put the man in his car and pointed it at the bayou, then the only murder of the four that really sticks out in terms of how it was executed is the first one — the murder of Peter Lynch."

"The killer didn't see him die," Ethan realized. "If, that is, the poison was mixed in with his vitamins at some earlier point so there was no telling when he'd get to those particular pills."

"Not that we're certain it was." Justin sighed. "We're not certain of a hell of a lot."

Kelly shook her head. "Is anybody else getting the feeling this guy is just playing with us?"

"I've got that feeling," Matt said, dispirited.

"A direct challenge to us?" Justin considered, then shrugged. "Maybe. But it feels to me like he's got his game plan all laid out and means to stick to it, no matter what we do. Like each murder is designed as part of the victim's punishment. Peter Lynch, the health nut, is poisoned; Luke Ferrier, so proud of his college swimming trophies, is drowned; Randal Patterson, famous for his personal vanity, is electrocuted in his tub; and George Caldwell, who did community ads and school presentations on gun safety and owned an extensive collection of firearms, is shot in the head."

Kelly blinked at him. "Jesus, you're right. I never thought about it that way, but . . . it all fits."

Ethan was also eyeing him, and very thoughtfully.

As offhandedly as possible, Justin said, "It may fit, but it's just another theory and it doesn't help us a damned bit as far as I can see. We're still no closer to being able to either I.D. this guy or predict his next move *or* his next victim."

"But you think he's not done," Ethan said.

"I think it would be a mistake for us to assume that. Because even if his personal hit list had only four names on it, the truth is, he's getting away with murder — so far, at least. And whatever his reasons were for starting all this, success can only encourage him. If he's bent on punishing the wicked, the fact that we haven't been able to stop him is bound to encourage him to keep right on doing it. He might even decide he's been chosen by God to do just that. And we all know that if you look for wickedness, even in a nice little town like Silence, you're bound to find it."

"Shit," Ethan said. He sighed. "Okay, people — whether Caldwell's murder is part of the rest or not is something we need to know, and pronto. Find out."

Carefully neutral, Justin said, "It might be a good idea to talk to his widow. I know the timing's lousy, but —"

The sheriff swore again, but under his breath. "Do it. Talk to anybody you need to talk to, but find the truth."

"No matter what that is?" Justin asked.

"No matter what."

"You see what I mean?" Shelby indicated

the photo she'd just placed on the butcher-block table in Nell's kitchen. "I got a couple of other shots of you, but this was the only one where something I couldn't explain showed up. Definitely what I'd call weird."

Nell bent over the picture, frowning. The word she would have picked to describe it was *unsettling*. To see herself walking down the courthouse steps, completely unaware of the shadow looming over her . . . She felt a little chill crawl slowly up her spine. The sense she'd had of being watched was beginning to feel like a lot more than nerves at being back home again.

She said, "And there's nothing you can find to account for it? It isn't just a shadow of something, some object, outside the frame, or a problem with the lens, or —"

Shelby shook her head, bright-eyed. "Nope. I've considered every possibility that might account for it, and none of them fits. That shadow was not visible to the naked eye — only the eye of the camera. And it is definitely there. So unless you believe in ghosts . . . Do you, by the way?"

Nell smiled slightly without looking up. "As a matter of fact, I do. But according to everything I've heard on the subject, it's rare to find photographic evidence of a ghost outside in the open. Not unheard of, mind you, but rare."

"The scale's wrong too," Shelby said. "I mean, if we're talking the ghost of your average human being. My estimate is that the shadow is about seven feet tall. Or long. Whatever."

Nell traced that threatening shape with a finger, then sat back with a sigh, trying not to make it obvious that the slow chill was leaving icy tracks up and down her spine as if it meant to stay awhile. "And it's on the negative too?"

"Yeah." Shelby sipped her coffee, watching the other woman with those bright, speculative eyes. "This happened to be the only shot I took of you yesterday, so I have no way of knowing if the shadow was . . . following you around. Like Max was."

"Max I can handle," Nell said lightly.

"Can you?"

"You don't think so?"

Slowly now, Shelby said, "I think you and Max have a lot of history between you. And probably quite a few unanswered questions. But, Nell, what can be excused, even forgiven, of a seventeen-year-old girl isn't so easy to overlook in a woman pushing thirty. And Max isn't twenty-two anymore, forced by a very young girlfriend and her . . . unusual family to keep his distance and maybe not ask too many questions."

More briskly, Shelby added, "Of course, there were things he had to ask when you ran off. And since you weren't around for him to ask . . . From what I heard, he confronted your father that night. Did you know?"

"No." Nell refused to ask for more information about that, and a part of her hoped Shelby wouldn't offer it. But that was hardly Shelby's style.

"Max has never been one to complain publicly or tell his business to other people, we both know that. So everything I heard was second- or thirdhand. But my own father told my mother that Adam Gallagher bragged about how he'd kicked Max Tanner down his front steps. Literally."

Nell winced.

Watching her, Shelby said, "My own feeling is that Max wouldn't have fought back, not against your father, not if he couldn't be sure what had made you run away like that. He might have a hell of a temper, but Max doesn't strike out blindly. Maybe he even thought it was his fault, that he'd done something to drive you away. I know your father always claimed he didn't know why you'd run and blamed Max for it."

"It wasn't Max."

"No. I never thought it was. But some did, Nell. There were lots of theories, everything from date rape or an unplanned pregnancy to the idea that you found yourself caught between two domineering men and couldn't take it anymore."

Rather than answer the implied question of what had actually happened, Nell merely said, "It sounds like Max has . . . every right to be bitter."

"Yeah. But there he is." Shelby tapped the photograph with a finger, smiling faintly. "Couple of days after you're back in town, he's following you, maybe even watching over you. I guess he's the forgiving sort."

Again, Nell didn't answer the implied question of why Max might believe she could be in any kind of danger. "I guess he is. Or maybe he just wants a few answers."

"Maybe. And maybe you can handle him — at least this time around. But I'd be careful if I were you, Nell. Like I said, he isn't twenty-two anymore. And whatever he was twelve years ago, I don't think he's a man to be left behind now."

"He never was," Nell murmured. "Some things stay with you no matter how far you run." Before Shelby could pounce on that, she added in a stronger voice, "So maybe this . . . shadow . . . is following me, or maybe I just happened to pass by it yesterday. An old courthouse like this one is at least as likely as any other old building to house ghosts, I'd say."

"And the jail used to be in the basement," Shelby reminded her, accepting the change of subject without a blink. "I seem to recall at least one old story about an unjustly accused man committing suicide there. Aren't wrongful deaths supposed to be more likely to — inspire? create? — spirits?"

Nell dredged through the bits of knowledge and information her mind had absorbed in recent years. "Wrongful deaths. Sudden or violent deaths. Or people with some kind of unfinished work they desperately want to complete. At least, I think those are the most likely candidates to stay and make their presence felt rather than move on."

Shelby pursed her lips thoughtfully. "So

this is just a ghost hanging around the courthouse, is that what we're saying?"

"Could be."

"Mmm. And are ghosts like that prone to loom over passersby in a threatening manner?"

"I'm not an expert, Shelby."

"Aren't you?"

"No."

"You don't have a crystal ball?"

"I'm afraid not."

"No tarot cards?"

Beginning to smile, Nell answered, "Sorry."

"Well," Shelby said in mock disgust, "of all the disappointments. And here I was expecting wild and mystical things of our returning witch."

"Yeah, Max told me that was the general attitude."

Shelby grinned at her. "Don't tell me you thought this town might have changed. Oh, no. Still narrow-minded and frightened of anything perceived to be too different, that's Silence. Or most of Silence, anyway."

"I'm surprised you choose to stay here," Nell offered.

"Are you? It's not so surprising, really. I'm perceived to be different — but not *too* different to present a threat. I like it here, all things considered." She cocked her head to one side like an inquisitive bird. "What about you? Any yearnings to stay put now that you're back home?"

"I've thought about it once or twice." Nell shrugged. "But I don't much like knowing I frighten people. Even ignorant people, afraid I'll put a curse on them or something."

"But you are psychic," Shelby said matter-of-factly.

In the same tone, Nell said, "Lots of people are psychic."

"I'm not."

Nell laughed under her breath. "Has it occurred to you that this shadow being visible might have had nothing to do with me and everything to do with you?"

Shelby frowned briefly, then shook her head. "No, because if that were so, I'd have seen something like it show up in my pictures long before now."

"Maybe. But psychic ability isn't always obvious from childhood, you know. Sometimes it . . . appears . . . fully blown in adulthood."

"Really?"

"So I've heard."

"Appears out of nowhere?"

Nell hesitated, then said, "Well, there's usually a trigger. A shock or some other kind of trauma."

"I haven't had anything like that," Shelby said, more disappointment than relief evident in her voice. "I've had a pretty boring and uneventful life, on the whole. And since this hasn't happened before, I think we can safely assume this shadow appeared on the picture because you were in it, not because I took it."

Giving in, Nell said, "Well, if we assume that, the question becomes — why? Why did this particular shadow appear in this particular shot on this particular day? Am I being haunted? Because I never have been before. Is it the courthouse being haunted? If that were true, it's at least possible you would have seen a shadow on other pictures before now. You have photographed the courthouse before?"

"Lots of times. With and without people. But I've never gotten a shadow like this one before."

Nell studied the photograph, trying to see some identifiable shape without imposing one created by her uneasy imagination. The shape was vaguely manlike but elongated somehow, distorted. And Shelby

171

was right, it did almost seem to . . . loom over her.

A charitable soul might say the shadow curved over her almost as though sheltering her.

Nell thought it looked more threatening than protective.

"It gives me a bad feeling," Shelby said.

Hearing the seriousness in that statement and sharing the sentiment, Nell nevertheless said, "A shadow can't hurt me."

"If that's what it is. But there's nothing there to *cast* a shadow, Nell. Nothing with a physical presence, that is. So maybe it's something else. And maybe it can hurt you." She frowned. "I didn't want to say anything before, but you're looking a little . . . brittle today."

"I didn't sleep well, that's all."

"Just last night, or since you got home?"

Nell shrugged, the gesture itself an answer.

Grave, Shelby said, "Is that why you believe in ghosts? Because if so, I have a very comfortable guest room you're welcome to."

"No, this house isn't haunted." Nell grimaced slightly. "No footsteps on the stairs or chains rattling in the night or unexplained cold spots. I haven't seen or heard anything — out of the ordinary." She wasn't about to mention the vision of her father here in this room or admit that several times she could have sworn someone had whispered her name; there were no ghosts in this house, she was sure of that.

Besides which, though Shelby had been the closest thing to a female friend she'd had as a kid, her own secretive nature had prevented her from confiding much at all of her life or her abilities, and she wasn't willing to go into any of that now.

Still grave, Shelby said, "Then maybe it's emotional ghosts disturbing your sleep. Coming home after so many years can't be easy."

Nell shied away from the tacit invitation to talk about whatever might be bothering her, wondering grimly if it was the discretion recently learned because of her job or the old reluctance to open up that kept her silent.

Whichever it was, she heard herself say, "I never sleep well the first few nights in a strange bed. It'll pass. And this place really doesn't feel like home, you know. Far as I can tell, Hailey changed just about everything from the rugs to the wallpaper; I don't even recognize half the furniture."

"She liked to shop," Shelby observed with a grin.

"No kidding."

"The word in town was that with only one of his girls left, your father sort of went overboard trying to keep her here. Gave her anything she wanted, pretty much."

Nell could have said that her sister had always been good at turning circumstances to her benefit, but all she said was, "I'm not surprised."

"It seemed to work too. I mean, she seemed pretty happy. Until there were a few whispers about her and Glen Sabella, and the next thing we all knew the two of them ran off."

"Our father was always . . . very unforgiving. If she had done anything to disappoint him, he wouldn't have hesitated to let her know how he felt about it."

"And disowned her?" Shelby shook her head. "Jeez, talk about being hard-nosed. He didn't disown you, though."

"I didn't run off with another — I didn't run off with a man." Nell saw Shelby's eyes narrow, and added quickly, "Anyway, like I said, this doesn't really feel like home. But I do have a lot on my mind, so it's not surprising I haven't slept well."

Shelby looked at her a moment, then

tapped one finger on the photo still lying between them on the table. "And this?"

"I don't know how to explain this," Nell confessed. "Maybe we're both . . . making too much of it. We may not be able to explain it, but that doesn't mean it isn't . . . just a shadow."

"And if it's something more?"

"Then I have no idea what that would be. But — I may know someone who could figure it out for us. Do you mind if I keep this?"

"No, of course not. I made myself a print to brood over, but this one's yours." Shelby rummaged in her shoulder bag and produced a manila envelope. "I even brought you the negative. Hey, you will tell me if this expert of yours figures it out, won't you?"

"Sure." Nell slid the photo into the envelope with its negative, her gaze on the other woman. She debated for a silent moment, but since it was something she'd been considering ever since the day she'd arrived and spoken to Shelby, she abruptly decided to follow her instincts. "Shelby . . . these murders. They interest you, don't they?"

"I've always loved mysteries, you know that." Shelby grinned. "The more murky the better. And this one's about as murky as they come. Why?"

Nell drew a breath and let it out slowly. "Because I have a favor to ask. And a story to tell."

Business was slow on this Friday, so Nate McCurry left his secretary in the office doing paperwork and went off toward town on the pretext of calling on a few customers. What he actually did was stop in at the café for a cup of coffee and the opportunity to listen in on the latest about the investigation.

He wasn't the only one doing that either. The place was unusually busy on this weekday morning roughly halfway between the breakfast and lunch rush hours, with most of the customers having coffee like Nate or some sort of light snack they could pretend was brunch.

Other than that, however, nobody was trying to pretend.

"I heard the cops found all kinds of shit George Caldwell had stashed away," one customer announced, sitting at the lunch counter with his back to it so he could see everyone else.

"Like what?" another demanded.

"Porn is what I heard. Really nasty stuff too."

"Naw, I heard it was diamonds."

Somebody laughed, and another man, older and heavyset, said incredulously, "You saying poor old George was a jewel thief? Setting aside the fact that he was about as light on his feet as I am, I wouldn't say there'd be much to interest a jewel thief around here."

"Plenty of people put their money in gold or jewels, Ben. You might be surprised at just how many."

Ben Hancock shook his head and said, "Wasn't jewels. Or porn. I'd be surprised if they'd found anything at all. Yet, anyway."

"Okay, but what do you think he was into? He must've been into something, Ben, or he wouldn't have got his head blown off."

With a shrug, Ben replied, "If I had to guess, I'd say George's biggest problem was that he was nosy. Always poking into things that didn't concern him. Always writing things down and making those lists of his."

"But why'd somebody want to kill him for that?"

"I'm just saying, he might've found something that somebody didn't want him to find, that's all. This whole thing's about secrets, isn't it? So maybe it wasn't

177

George's secret that got him killed. Maybe it was somebody else's."

"Like whose?"

"Hell, I don't know. The killer's, maybe?"

Someone else said, in a hopeful tone, "Maybe it's not about secrets. Maybe it's just about something usual. Like money."

Nate McCurry spoke up then, making sure his voice sounded only mildly interested. "If you believe the newspapers, people get killed because of money every day. But there are other reasons too. And if you look at the other three dead men, two of them had secrets that had nothing to do with money."

"That's true enough," Ben allowed. "And George had been separated from Sue for a long time, so you know the marriage had been in trouble — for whatever reason. Maybe it was just a midlife crisis, the way she kept saying, or maybe it was something else."

One of the few women in the café said, "I heard there was another woman, but if there was, he sure didn't show her off around here."

"Married," Ben guessed. "Either that or he didn't want to give Sue any ammunition to use in court."

Obviously speaking from bitter experience, another man said, "The judge does tend to award the wife a bigger settlement if the husband has been screwing around, especially if he's doing it so that everybody *knows* he's doing it."

Patiently, Nate said, "Yeah, but would cheating on a wife he'd already left and hadn't lived with for two or three years make George a target for this killer? Is that a big enough secret — or a big enough sin — to make this killer want to punish him?"

Ben grimaced. "Jesus, how many of us can say we don't have at least a little secret or two and a few minor sins laying around? If that's the yardstick this guy is using, then nobody is safe."

Trying not to sound as desperate as he felt, Nate said, "The police haven't found any other connection between the men except that they all had secrets?"

"We don't know about George yet," Ben reminded.

"Yeah, but the others?"

"According to the papers there's no other connection. Of course, we don't know that the police are making all their information public. Maybe Ethan and his people know something they aren't telling."

"I don't think they know squat," somebody else muttered loudly. "Running around chasing their own tails, if you ask me."

They were still pondering that when a tall man rose from a shadowed booth at the back and came to the front to pay his bill. He had a pleasant word with Emily when she emerged from the kitchen to take his money, then saluted the others with a cheerful, "Have a nice day, folks," as he left the café.

The bell on the door jingled, the waitress returned to the kitchen, and the customers were left staring at each other.

"Was he here the whole time?" someone asked uneasily.

"The whole time," Ben confirmed. "Didn't you see him back there?"

"No, Ben, I didn't see him back there. Jesus."

Somebody else muttered, "They ought to make them all wear uniforms, even the detectives."

"Guilty conscience?"

"Hell, no. But he shouldn't eavesdrop."

"Part of his job," Ben pointed out, obviously enjoying the chagrin all around him.

"Shit."

Nate McCurry looked out the window

beside his table to watch Detective Justin
Byers strolling away.

He was scared.

He was really scared.

CHAPTER
EIGHT

"I think I can handle it," Shelby said.

"I know you can. But be careful, okay?"

"I will if you will."

Nell smiled. "I'll be careful."

"I'm glad to hear it. And, listen — you have a standing offer to come use my guest room, so don't hesitate. If nothing else, you just might want some company."

The words were barely out of her mouth when they both heard through the open kitchen window a sharp whistle from out back and Max's voice calling Nell's name.

"Or maybe that won't be a problem," Shelby murmured, amused.

Glancing down at the envelope holding a photograph that in addition to a threatening shadow also showed Max lurking and watching her very intently, Nell said, "I suppose it would be useless to pretend this is just a casual visit to offer a neighborly good morning."

"Entirely useless," Shelby responded with a grin as she got to her feet. "I'll be in touch if and when I have something. But for now, I'm going away. Don't bother showing me out, just tell Max I said hi, okay?"

Nell took Shelby at her word and didn't walk with her through to the front of the house. Instead, she put the envelope safely away in a drawer, then shrugged into the light jacket hanging ready by the back door. She went out to find Max, as she'd expected, riding his bay gelding and leading a saddled pinto.

"I thought we might as well get an early start," he said in lieu of a good morning.

"Shelby said hello," Nell responded in a wry voice.

They both heard Shelby's little car roar to life out front, then the cheerful tattoo of its horn as she headed back to town.

Max grimaced. "I should have called first."

Determinedly offhand, Nell said, "Like the mayor said, if people see us together, they'll likely focus on past history instead of making any connection to the murders. Shelby certainly did. I can stand it if you can."

He handed over the pinto's reins. "I'd put up with just about anything to find out who killed those men."

Nell decided not to examine that sharp

remark too closely. She patted the horse, then paused before mounting to say, "For all you know, I might not have been near a horse in twelve years."

"If so, it'll come back to you quickly. Natural riders never lose their abilities."

Nell swung up easily and settled into the saddle. "Well, as a matter of fact, I still ride every chance I get."

"Are there many chances in D.C.?"

"A few. And I work quite a bit outside D.C., you know." She barely paused. "I gather you've decided to help and that you feel approaching at least some of the crime scenes by horseback is the way to go."

"Didn't I say so?"

She wasted a moment wondering how long he would carry the chip on his shoulder, then reminded herself that he wasn't likely to improve in temperament, at least as long as she continued to hold him at a distance.

It didn't help much, knowing that. In fact, it didn't help at all.

Pleasantly, she said, "Probably a good idea, at least for the first two murders. The bayou where Luke Ferrier drowned is closest, isn't it?"

"Yeah."

"Lead the way."

Silently, he turned the bay and set off through the woods.

Nell followed, trying to focus completely on familiarizing herself with the pinto's smooth gait, with enjoying the mild warmth of the morning and the clean scents of spring. She wanted her mind occupied with trivialities rather than open and receptive; her restless night had left her feeling raw and unsettled, a state not helped at all by Shelby's eerie photograph — or by Max and his silent insistence that she answer questions she was not yet ready to face.

It was hardly the best condition in which to go looking for evidence — psychic or physical. In fact, it was the worst possible condition. Not for the first time, she wondered if she was being unprofessional in not telling Bishop she was too close to this situation to do her job effectively. But the answer she arrived at was the same one she had reached every time she had asked herself the question before: Doing that would only confirm that she was a coward, so afraid of facing her past she was willing to allow it to ruin her present and her future.

She couldn't do that, could she?

Could she?

No. She had to deal with this, no matter

185

what it cost her. It was impossible to move forward until she stopped looking back, she knew that only too well. And she needed to move forward. For Max's sake as well as her own.

She fixed her gaze on the uncommunicative expanse of his leather jacket and stifled a sigh that only the pinto's turned-back ear could have caught.

Why did everything have to be so goddamned hard?

Max stopped at a fork in the trail they were following and turned in the saddle to look back at her and say briefly, "I guess they told you about your grandmother's house?"

"Yeah, they told me." Nell stopped her own horse, gazing along the south trail that all during her childhood had led her to an old house at the edge of a plowed field where her grandmother had chosen to live alone. "It burned down."

"It had been standing empty since she died," Max reported. "I rode out this way pretty regularly and never saw anybody around or any sign of vandalism. Far as I could tell, your father and Hailey never went there once they'd cleared the place out, and nobody from town would have — except maybe some kid on a dare."

186

Well aware that her grandmother's house had long been considered by the local children to be a spooky, haunted place to be approached only when proving one's bravery, Nell merely nodded in understanding.

"It must have been a couple of years later that it caught fire and burned to the ground before anybody could get to it. The fire chief figured it was a lightning strike."

Dryly, Nell said, "And nobody was much surprised, right? That God finally struck down the wicked?"

He grimaced. "I did hear one or two people calling it a judgment. She went out of her way to make people afraid of her, Nell, you know that."

"She was an eccentric old woman who kept to herself because the visions she lived with terrified her." Surprised at her own ferocity, Nell made an effort to hold her voice even. "Some people never adjust. She didn't. She saw tragedies she couldn't change and tried to hide from them. It's not her fault that other people didn't understand."

After a long moment, Max said, "You're right. I'm sorry. Look, this path is the shortest way to the bayou, but if you'd rather ride out past your grandmother's place first —"

"No, thanks. I'd just as soon go directly to the bayou."

"Okay. This way, then."

Nell followed him as he took the alternate trail, sparing the other one only a brief glance. Sooner or later, she'd have to go there, of course, force herself to stand and look at that burned-out shell of a place. And remember. But she preferred to do that alone.

She had to do it alone.

"Did he have what?" Sue Caldwell stared at Justin with bewildered eyes. "A secret place?"

"Well, did he have a place he liked to keep just to . . . store things he didn't want to show other people, let's say." Justin made his voice even, soothing.

Her pale face flushing suddenly, Sue said, "If you mean did he have some horrible little hiding place like Peter Lynch had, the answer is *no*. My husband did not have any dirty secrets, Detective Byers."

Highly conscious of the little black notebook he was still carrying around with him, Justin nevertheless quickly assured her that he'd intended to imply no such thing. "But even the best of men have things they don't want to be . . . public

188

knowledge. A stash of old magazines, maybe — something like that."

Stiffly now, Sue said, "I wouldn't know about that, Detective. He certainly never had that sort of thing when he lived here with me."

Since he knew they stood a snowball's chance of getting a warrant to search the house George Caldwell had moved out of nearly three years before his death, Justin hadn't even bothered to ask. Plus, he figured any man with a secret blackmail game going would have made damned sure he had his evidence close by — not hidden away in a house with his estranged wife.

And after having spent more than half an hour talking to her, Justin was also convinced that Sue Caldwell hadn't known her husband at all. She struck him as one of those unimaginative people who took everything at face value, a discarded wife still honestly bewildered as to why her husband would have left her and virtually certain he would have come home eventually.

Blunt now, Justin said, "Forgive me, but is it true that your marriage broke up over another woman?"

"No, it is not," she said flatly, eyes bright with indignation. "George was having a midlife crisis, that's all. He bought that little red car, started taking trips all over the place and wearing flashy clothes, just the sort of thing you'd expect. He was about to turn forty and he couldn't stand the thought of losing his youth. But there was no other woman. I would have known if there had been."

Justin wondered, but didn't challenge her assertion. "I see. And you can't think of any enemies he might have made either during your marriage or after he moved out?"

"Certainly not. George was a fine man, everyone said so." She sniffed suddenly. "A fine man. It had to be that maniac everybody's talking about, the one who killed those other men. Because there was no reason, just no reason, to kill George."

Justin knew denial when he heard it; no way was Sue Caldwell willing or even able to believe her husband might have had a nasty little secret that could have gotten him killed. She could lump his death in with those of the other men only because some "maniac" was doing the killing, murdering without rhyme or reason, and the fact that the other victims had led secret lives did not, of course, mean that George had as well.

Figuring he wasn't going to get anything

else from the widow Caldwell, Justin made soothing noises once again and began to take his leave.

Fifteen minutes later, he pulled his car into the parking lot of the apartment building where Caldwell had lived, and sat there for a few moments, brooding. They had searched the apartment. Questioned the neighbors. Gone over his little red sports car with a fine-tooth comb. Searched his office at the bank, the lockbox he'd kept there.

Nothing.

But if George Caldwell had been a blackmailer, then somewhere there had to be the evidence of it. He had to have kept some kind of proof against his victims, whatever it was he had held over their heads to induce them to pay him.

Justin was still uncertain as to whether he believed the killer himself had sent the notebook to him. It seemed most likely. Which would logically mean, he thought, that the killer was not among the blackmail victims; why provide the police with evidence that would furnish a motive for murder?

Then again, it might be a dandy little diversion. With several blackmail victims to choose from, the killer might have decided he'd be lost in the crowd and draw no more attention from the police than any of the others. A hide-in-plain-sight choice. That made a certain amount of sense.

Of course, it could also be true that exposing Caldwell's sins might have been more important to him than protecting his own ass, and sending the notebook to one of the cops was the only way he could accomplish that. Which certainly argued an obsession amounting to mania.

Justin pulled the little black notebook from an inner pocket and thumbed through it slowly. There had been, of course, no fingerprints whatsoever. He'd used his own latent kit to dust every goddamned page, without getting so much as a smudge. Which certainly screamed "planted evidence." Or else a man who was very, very careful.

He wasn't absolutely positive the handwriting was George Caldwell's, so that was still a question mark. And since he had to consider the whole blackmail scheme a possibility rather than a probability, the only way he could justify continuing to explore the theory was by telling himself that knowing why George Caldwell died would tell him more than the death of any of the other victims had.

He really believed that. So he kept pushing onward and kept studying the damned notebook.

Now that he'd had time to consider, he could name at least two possible matches for nearly every set of initials and sometimes three or four, but the only way to be certain who had been blackmailed — assuming anyone had — was to find the evidence Caldwell would have had to use against his victims.

And Justin had to search carefully, because he didn't dare risk Sheriff Cole finding out what he was looking for; so far, Ethan Cole was the only match Justin had been able to come up with for the initials E.C. Which meant he couldn't tell the sheriff about this little black book. Not yet, anyway, not until he was able to rule out Cole as a possible blackmail victim.

And a possible murderer.

He looked up again to study the apartment building where George Caldwell had lived, then flipped a mental coin, sighed, and got out of his car. If Caldwell had been a blackmailer, somewhere there would be evidence of it. There had to be.

If Justin could only find it.

"It was last September," Max reminded

Nell as they stood some yards from one of the few bayous in the immediate area, studying very faint marks on a patch of sandy ground. "To their credit, the cops pulled the car out on the other side and tried to be careful not to disturb any possible evidence here, but I'm surprised you can still see anything after all this time."

She knelt down and traced the sharp edge of one tire track with her finger. "This is what's left of the tracks? No other vehicle has been here?"

"I doubt it, given how hard it is to get a vehicle in here, but there's no way to be absolutely positive. For what it's worth, I came out here the next day, and as far as I can tell these are the original tire tracks from Luke Ferrier's car."

"According to the report, the initial conclusion was suicide, right?"

"Right."

"Then later it was decided that Ferrier might have been drugged and the car deliberately pointed at the water."

"Yeah."

Nell half closed her eyes, trying to bring what she was feeling into focus. She expected it to be difficult with Max so near, and it was, but even so there was something . . . off. It felt strange, different from what she was accustomed to, from what it should have been. Almost as though she were trying to sense through a veil. Whatever lay on the other side was so dim and vague it was like the whisper of an echo, and groping toward it tentatively was frustrating.

"Nell?"

"Wait. There's something. . . ." She concentrated for what felt like hours, then finally rose with a sigh. "Dammit."

"What?"

"It's too vague to get hold of. Whatever happened out here happened fast, too fast to leave much of an energy signature." She frowned down at the tire track. "But that track tells me he was probably trying to stop the car before it went into the water, otherwise the marks wouldn't have lasted this long or been this deep."

"Then it wasn't suicide — and he wasn't unconscious when the car went in."

"That idea always bothered me a bit, that the killer made sure Ferrier was out cold before he killed him," Nell confessed. "Doesn't really match up with the other three victims. In fact, if you assume Caldwell saw his killer and knew he was about to be shot, then you can argue that all four suffered either physically or emotionally just before they died."

"You're not including your father in the group?"

Nell shook her head. "For now, no. Whatever certainties I feel, the fact is that there's no evidence my father's death was anything but natural, much less that this killer was also his murderer. Unless and until I can find that evidence, I have to consider his death as separate from the others." She shrugged. "Maybe he just pissed somebody off and paid for that with his life. He was . . . very good at pissing people off."

Max's eyes narrowed, but he didn't question the comment about her father just then. "But the other four deaths were planned, and in detail. And all of them suffered. Part of the punishment?"

"It would make sense. It also might explain why the first of them, Peter Lynch, was the only one who probably wasn't in the killer's presence when he died. Killing by remote control, at a distance, might have been a kind of failed experiment. Maybe the killer thought it would be safer, I don't know. But despite the physical agony that Lynch went through being poisoned, it obviously wasn't enough for the killer. Wasn't a satisfying enough punishment. He wanted to be there. He wanted to watch."

"Christ." His mouth twisting slightly, Max added, "Like some kind of ghoul."

"He's killed at least four men, Max, and possibly five. I'd say death was unquestionably one of his . . . interests."

"And you still say he's a cop?"

"Bishop says it's likely. I agree." Without waiting for him to comment on that, Nell moved away and began to study the area with a critical eye. Remote: There wasn't a house or even a pasture fence to be seen. Nearly inaccessible: The car had been driven from the highway through what were basically a few clearings in the woods strung together to form the suggestion of a roadway, so horseback was indeed the best way to get to this side of the bayou.

This section of the bayou wasn't even visible from the highway, and in fact Ferrier's car had been discovered only because of a couple of teenagers riding by on horseback.

"What signs point to the killer being a cop?" Max demanded. He stood without moving, hands in his pockets, frowning very slightly as he watched her.

Nell could feel him watching her but tried to make her voice detached and impersonal when she answered him. "The biggest red flag is how careful he's been to vary his killings. There's been nothing impulsive about these four murders, nothing spur-of-the-moment, so it's clear he's planning every step. The fact that he's been careful not to establish any kind of pattern that might help the police I.D. him says he knows and understands police procedure. Even more, he's pitting his skills and intelligence against the adversary he knows best — other cops."

"Catch me if you can," Max said slowly. "Catch me if you're good enough."

"Exactly. He's testing their mettle. And there's a personal edge to that, a sense that part of his plan is to . . . humiliate the police. Make them look bad in their inability to catch him. I wouldn't be surprised if a future victim — assuming we don't stop him — turned out to be a cop. I think he has a personal grudge against someone in the sheriff's department."

"That your idea, or Bishop's?"

Nell thought there was a personal edge to that question, but all she said was, "It's a feeling I've had since I came back here. There's nothing concrete to base it on."

"Just a feeling you trust."

She nodded. "Just a feeling I trust. A lot

of what I do is based on that sort of thing."

"Hunches. Intuition."

"You know it's more than that."

He nodded, but said, "Still, it sounds like you're doing a bit of profiling on your own. FBI training?"

"We've all spent a little time in Behavioral Sciences, and most of us have some kind of psychology training under our belts. It's like with any other kind of hunting; you have to understand your quarry if you intend to catch him." Nell shrugged, then moved back toward the woods where their horses were tied. "In any case, there's nothing here I can tap into. What about Ferrier's house? Isn't it still standing empty?"

"Yeah. It was a rental, but nobody's been interested in living there since he was killed." Max followed her to the horses. "The owners packed up his personal stuff and put it into storage, since no relative had shown up to claim anything. You think you might be able to pick up something there?"

"Won't know until I try." Nell mounted the pinto.

Max followed suit, swinging aboard the bay and gathering the reins. "His place was a couple miles from here as the crow flies.

We'll attract less attention if we ride."

"Lead on."

He did, and for ten minutes or so they rode in silence. Fairly tense silence, really; Nell could feel it in herself and see it in the set of Max's shoulders. Then he chose to direct them along the edge of a plowed field where they could ride abreast, and as soon as she came up beside him he said abruptly, "Didn't you tell me once that you'd been psychic since you were very young?"

"I may have. The first vision I can clearly remember happened when I was about eight. Why?"

"Something you were born with? Or something that was triggered?"

Nell sent him a quick glance. "Born with. It runs in my family, remember? I probably had visions when I was younger but didn't understand what was happening and can't now remember them. That's fairly typical of most born psychics."

"What about the blackouts?"

"What about them?"

Unusually patient even if his voice still sounded a bit edgy, Max said, "How old were you the first time you had a blackout?"

"As far as I remember, about the same

age, I suppose. Nobody ever told me I had them when I was younger, but I may have."

"So they're connected. The blackouts and your visions."

"Maybe. One theory is that certain kinds of psychic experiences are triggered or intensified by excess electrical energy in the brain. It's at least theoretically possible that a buildup of that sort of energy might . . . overload the brain and cause periodic blackouts as a side effect. Other types of physical side effects have been reported."

Max turned his head to look at her steadily. "So it isn't stress at all."

She managed a smile. "Let's call it stress of a certain kind. Not emotional, just . . . brain chemistry."

"And if that happens too long or too often? Won't it damage the brain?"

"It hasn't so far."

Max swore under his breath. "But it might?"

Nell reined her horse to a stop when he did. "I don't know. Nobody knows. Maybe." She was feeling more raw by the moment, and angry at him for pushing.

He looked more than a little angry himself. "Then how in hell can you justify deliberately putting yourself into situations where your abilities are likely to be triggered? Jesus Christ, Nell, it's playing Russian roulette with your life."

"It's *my* life," she reminded him tightly. "Besides, it's all theoretical. We don't know what's going on in my brain, Max, not for sure. Nobody knows. Medically, a CAT scan and other tests show increased electrical activity even in parts of the brain normally considered inactive, which seems to be true for every psychic we've tested so far. But whatever is going on doesn't seem to be harming any of us; having periodic medical tests to determine that is one of the requirements for the psychic members of our unit. Maybe our brains adapt to the excess energy, I don't know. All I do know is that there's no sign of any organic damage."

"Yet."

She drew a breath. "All right — there's no damage yet. Maybe there never will be. Or maybe I'll wake up one day with my brain fried. Is that what you want me to say?"

"I want you to tell me why you're going out of your way to trigger experiences that may kill you, Nell."

She said steadily, "I can do my best to use my abilities in the most positive way I

can think of, or I can hide from them —
and from the world. Is that what you'd
prefer, Max, that I end up like my grandmother? That I hide myself away in a little
house back in the woods, keeping everyone
at a distance while I live in terror of experiences I have absolutely no control over?"

"No, of course not. But there must be a
middle ground."

"*This* is my middle ground. I work with
people who are doing their best to understand and master psychic abilities, people
who take care of and watch out for each
other. And I use my abilities deliberately,
trying to have more control so I'm not
blindsided every goddamned time it happens to me. Can you understand that?"

After a long moment, Max nodded.
"Yeah. Yeah, I can understand that." He
lifted his reins, and the horses moved forward again. "But it's a dangerous choice,
Nell."

He had no idea just how dangerous, she
thought as she followed him. No idea at
all.

CHAPTER
NINE

It was easy to see why the house hadn't roused any interest in would-be renters in the months since Ferrier's death. No doubt originally constructed to house a tenant farmer or migrant workers who would toil in the nearby fields, it was a small place at the end of a long dirt road that would be unbearably dusty in summer, and though it looked in decent repair there was nothing in the least inviting in its drab appearance.

They tied their horses at the edge of the woods out of sight of the road and walked across the weed-infested backyard.

"I doubt anyone would see us if we went to the front," Max said, "but there are a couple of neighbors down the road who might notice if we make ourselves too obvious."

"Were the neighbors questioned?" Nell asked as they stepped up onto the rear porch. She reached into the pocket of her jacket and produced a small, zippered leather case.

"I think Ethan sent a couple of his people out here — belatedly. Far as I know, nobody reported seeing or hearing anything suspicious, though you'd know more about the police report than I would." He eyed the small case she was opening, and added, "Is that what I think it is?"

"Probably." She selected one of the small tools and bent to begin working on the door lock.

"Burglar's tools?"

"Let's call them tools to unlock doors and leave it at that, shall we?"

"Did my tax dollars pay for those?" he wondered dryly.

"No. Do you happen to know how long it's been since anybody was in this house?"

"Not offhand, no. Did the Bureau send you to burglar's school?"

"Bishop taught us. He thought the skill might come in handy. He was right."

"He was a burglar before he joined the FBI?"

"Actually, I think he was studying criminal psychology and law when the FBI came calling. I have no idea where he picked up his more . . . esoteric skills."

"He has a lot of those?"

"A few."

Max frowned down at her as a soft click

announced her success with the lock. "This is breaking and entering, isn't it?"

"Do you care?" Nell retorted, straightening and pushing open the door.

"Not really." Max followed her inside the house. "But if Ethan or any of his people catch us out here, my ass is in serious trouble."

"Umm. He's convinced you killed Ferrier, isn't he?"

"Wants to be convinced. There's a difference."

"So you two are still at odds?"

With mock surprise, Max said, "Didn't Wade Keever fill you in on that?"

She smiled slightly. "As a matter of fact, he did."

"Yeah, I thought so. Telephone, telegraph, tell Wade. Fastest way short of a billboard to make anything public." Max shrugged. "Ethan and I haven't been close for a long time, you know that. And you know why."

Nell sent him a look, then turned her gaze to their rather musty surroundings. The small house was furnished, though there was certainly nothing to shout about in its worn and threadbare offerings. The tiny kitchen held the bare essentials in the way of appliances, the small living room boasted only a sagging couch and one faded chair, and through the doorway to the bedroom she could see an ancient brass bed.

"Ferrier certainly didn't live beyond his means, did he?" she said.

"Apparently he was stashing all his ill-gotten gains away to finance his planned move to the south of France. At least, so I heard."

Nell frowned slightly and went toward the bedroom, choosing that room automatically because it tended to be the most personal in a house.

The instant she crossed the threshold, she got a flash of something — movement, color, the faint echo of a breathless laugh, the scent of perfume — and she stopped just two paces inside the room, closing her eyes and concentrating. Behind her, Max stood in the doorway and watched her, silent.

The jumble of impressions was all noise and colors in her mind for a moment or two, and then the energy of the most intense activity this room had contained surged to the surface of her awareness, and Nell opened her eyes with a start to find the bare little space drastically changed.

Instead of stark sunlight streaming

through the uncurtained windows, it was nighttime, and candles burned all around the room, casting a golden glow over the tumbled covers of the old brass bed.

And the two people in it.

Nell recognized the man from the photos she had seen, a dark, heavy-shouldered man with a handsome, cruel face. He lay on his back on the bed, grinning up at the naked woman crouched astride his naked body.

The woman, dark hair streaming down her back, rode him with a fierce, greedy insistence, her throaty moans and cries erupting at last into a wild sound of release that was a laugh of pure triumph. Her head turned, bright, mocking eyes seeming to fix on Nell as she laughed again.

Victory. Conquest.

I win. I win again.

"Jesus." Her own voice brought Nell out of it, and she stared, shaken, at the bare, stained mattress on the ancient bed. There was no one there. No tumbled covers. No candles scattered around the room providing an intimate glow. No mocking laughter. "Jesus," she repeated softly.

"Nell?"

She turned slowly to face Max.

"What did you see?"

"Hailey. I saw Hailey."

Shelby paused before leaving her house to take one more look at her copy of the photograph of Nell leaving the courthouse, and frowned as she considered it. Nothing new occurred to her, except that she was probably going to regret what she was about to do. Probably.

She gathered up her cameras and headed toward town. This had to look casual, and as Shelby well knew, there was a trick to looking casual when you were anything but.

The first step was for her to wander around with her cameras taking pictures of whatever caught her fancy. She did that most days anyway, so nobody'd be surprised by it.

And she wasn't terribly surprised to find virtually everyone she encountered over the next half hour or so eager to discuss the murders. She was even less surprised to find there was another topic of conversation.

Nell.

At least four people stopped Shelby as she made her way casually through the downtown area, and all of them wanted to talk about Nell.

"Did you hear? Nell Gallagher's been

around all this time, just not in town, and you know all this killing started back after her father died. . . ."

"I heard she came back because she *knows* who the killer is, just the way those Gallaghers always knew things. . . ."

"Did you hear? Nell Gallagher didn't come home just to settle her father's estate, it was because she's afraid Hailey will show up and fight her for it. . . ."

"I heard the sheriff asked her to come back, that's what I heard, so she can give him a reading and tell him who the murderer is. . . ."

Shelby offered no theories of her own but merely listened and smiled and nodded and wondered how people managed to build around the grain of truth that was Nell's homecoming such a range of possibilities. It was fascinating, in a horrifying sort of way.

You didn't have to be psychic to pick up on the feelings of the townspeople. Everybody was scared. They were scared and they were searching for answers. Unfortunately, all too soon, they'd forgo answers and just look for somebody — anybody — to blame for disrupting the town. And with a faceless murderer roaming about apparently beyond the reach of the law and retribution, Nell looked like the odds-on favorite to be that target.

Which made Shelby more determined than ever to find the truth.

"Shelby, you know Nell Gallagher, don't you?"

Shelby snapped a picture to prove she had a reason for loitering around the courthouse and then turned to smile at Sheriff Cole. "Sure, Ethan, I know her. Why?"

He grimaced slightly. "Know where she's been the last dozen years? What she's been doing?"

"Not really. I've heard things, of course, just like you must have, mostly from Hailey before she left, but nothing directly from Nell." This time, her question was more insistent. "Why?"

"I was just curious." He smiled. "Character flaw, you know that."

"I would have thought all your curiosity would be wrapped up in this murder investigation."

Ethan's smile turned wry. "Hell, I'm only human. Nell comes back to town, still gorgeous, apparently still single — and still an enigma. At least, I always thought so. Natural enough for me to be curious."

Shelby raised her eyebrows. "Then why

don't you ask *her* what she's been doing these last years?"

"And feed the gossip?" His voice was as wry as his smile. "People are already talking about Max following her around like a besotted idiot; all I have to do is appear to be even a little interested, and everybody'll have us in some kind of love triangle before you can say soap opera."

"And that would be a wrong impression. Of course."

His eyes narrowed. "Of course."

Shelby decided it was time to change the subject. "I heard you guys haven't made much headway investigating George Caldwell's murder."

"We don't publicize all our findings, Shelby."

"I didn't say I *read* it, Ethan, I said I *heard* it. Gossip, you know. Which, in Silence, we have a lot of. I always thought whoever named our town had a real sense of humor."

Frowning, the sheriff said, "Are you saying my people have been talking out of turn?"

Shelby shrugged. "They're frustrated, I suppose. Bound to be. And probably defensive whenever somebody demands to know what the sheriff's department is doing to catch this killer, so it's natural they'd talk at least a bit. But if it makes you feel better, I haven't heard any specifics about the investigation. Just a general sense of failure."

"Great. That's just great."

"Well, it's pretty obvious, you know. It's not like somebody's sitting in your jail charged with four murders."

Flatly, Ethan said, "We have no hard evidence that Luke Ferrier's drowning was anything other than accidental or suicide."

"Accidental? Ethan, everybody knows which side of the bayou that car went into, and from what I hear there's no way a car could have gone that far off the road unless it had been driven carefully and deliberately."

"That doesn't rule out suicide, Shelby."

"Except that a healthy bank account and tickets out of the country came to light after he died, I hear. Sounds more like he meant to take a plane when he left. And isn't it a bit coincidental for a man with secrets like that to die by his own hand when other men are being murdered apparently because of their secrets?"

Ethan's frown deepened. "So that's common knowledge, huh?"

"You mean has anyone else been connecting the secrets to the killings? Oh, yeah. These are pretty damned big secrets, Ethan. They sort of stick out in this quiet little town. And judging by what I've been hearing, every man in Silence between the ages of eighteen and sixty is examining his past and his conscience, wondering if he's done anything to paint a big bull's-eye target on his back."

"Shit."

"No open panic yet. But it's coming." Shelby hesitated, then said slowly, "Have you considered asking for help?"

"I'm not calling in outsiders," he said emphatically. "This is our problem, and we'll handle it."

"Not outsiders. Nell."

"You mean because she's supposed to be psychic? I don't believe in that shit."

"You don't necessarily have to believe in it to use any tool that might possibly help, do you? Cops have been known to use psychics, even if they don't want to admit it publicly. What harm could it do to ask her? Ethan, people are already talking about her."

"Yeah, I know."

"What if the killer hears that and gets worried?"

"You think he'd be less worried if I call

her into the station to talk to her?"

"Don't call her in. Make it more casual than that."

"I don't think so."

Deliberately, Shelby said, "So you're so unwilling to have people think you're chasing after her like Max that you won't even ask her if she can help? My mama used to call that cutting off your nose to spite your face."

His mouth tightened. "And did she ever warn you about poking your nose in where it wasn't wanted?"

"Frequently."

"You should have listened to her, Shelby." The sheriff turned and walked away, the stiff set of his shoulders belying his casual air.

Shelby absently took a picture of him when he paused at the curb, making sure her own face remained pleasantly un-revealing. Or at least she hoped that was how she looked.

Tricky, this business of not letting on that she knew more than she was saying. And she had a hunch it was going to get even more tricky as time passed.

She had a feeling she was going to enjoy herself very much.

Not that this wasn't a serious matter, she

knew that. Even a deadly matter. But that reminder did nothing to dim Shelby's lively interest.

She watched Ethan Cole stalk away, then turned her own footsteps in a different direction.

Anyway, the first task had been easy. She doubted the next task would be.

Max drew his horse to a stop and sat there for a moment gazing silently toward the Gallagher family home. Then he turned his head and looked at Nell. "I never heard a whisper about Hailey being involved with Luke Ferrier. He was single, so was she. Why keep it quiet?"

Since she knew that answer, Nell merely said, "What I want to find out is whether she had been involved with any of the other men."

"You think she was the connection between them?"

"I don't know what to think. But these men were being punished for their secrets, and Luke Ferrier at least had an apparently secret affair with my sister."

Max frowned. "Everybody knows — now — that Peter Lynch kept a mistress in New Orleans and collected porn of a particularly sick nature, but if he was involved with anybody local, I never heard about it."

Nell turned her gaze toward the house and frowned herself. "I'd say he was most likely, though, given that his secret was of a sexual nature. And maybe Randal Patterson; he was the one with all the sadomasochistic gear in his basement, right?"

"Right. Far as I know, nobody's been able to find out who he played his little games with." He shook his head slightly. "You seriously believe it might have been Hailey?"

It was a question Nell wasn't eager to answer, but she knew there was little choice in the matter. So she merely drew a breath and said, "Let's find out. Isn't Patterson's place within riding distance?"

"Yeah. But are you sure you're up to it?"

"What do you mean?"

"I don't have to be psychic myself to see what it takes out of you to . . . tap into one of these visions of yours. Maybe we should wait, Nell. Give you some time."

"Time's probably the one thing we don't have a lot of," she said soberly. "This sort of killer tends to escalate his activities sooner or later, and the longer he goes without being caught, the more likely he is to do that. He could kill again in two months — or tomorrow." She hesitated. "But if you need to get back to the ranch —"

"No, that isn't a problem. I have a good foreman and a good crew, so the work'll get done whether I'm there or not. But I still think you should rest for a while before we head out to Patterson's place."

Nell was about to argue when she felt the telltale twinge in her left temple that warned of an approaching blackout. *Damn . . . damn . . . damn . . .* She knew only too well that Max would insist on staying and watching over her if he knew, and that was something she wasn't prepared for. Not here. Not now.

So all she said, mildly, was, "I guess this afternoon will be soon enough. There are things I need to do here anyway, and no matter what you say I'm sure you should probably at least check in at the ranch. Can you come back around three or so?"

"Yeah, but —"

Before he could finish that, she added, "And you don't have to come in and check all the windows and doors. What you said about the killer possibly seeing me as a threat made sense, so I'm taking precautions. My partner's sticking close."

"I haven't seen anybody."

"You weren't supposed to." She smiled slightly to remove the sting, then dismounted and handed him the pinto's reins. "But he's close, believe me."

Max glanced toward the house as if to try and spot someone lurking about, then looked down at her, his mouth twisting. "And I'm still not supposed to ask who *he* is?"

"You can ask. I won't answer. I told you, Max — undercover is under cover."

"I could say something nasty, but I won't."

"I appreciate that."

He lifted the reins and began to turn the horses, but paused. He looked away from her and then, as if he couldn't help himself, said roughly, "I got over you."

Nell forced herself to speak steadily, to act as if it didn't matter. "I never expected anything else."

"Didn't you?"

"No."

Still looking away from her, his voice still rough, he said, "I'll be back here about three." He turned the horses and rode off through the woods.

She watched until he was out of sight, then walked slowly to the house. Even before she opened the back door, she knew she wasn't alone so wasn't surprised to find her partner in the kitchen drinking her coffee.

"So you aren't the only one who knows which emotional buttons to push," he observed. And when she stared at him, he added apologetically, "The window is open. Voices carry out here, you know."

"And your hearing is too damned good."

"Sorry about that. In this work it's usually considered a plus."

She poured herself a cup of coffee and sipped, then frowned as another twinge in her temple reminded her she would soon have to find something soft to fall on. "Never mind that now. I have some stuff to tell you and a photograph to show you. And I don't have much time."

"Blackout coming?"

"Yeah."

"A little close to the last one, isn't it?"

"A little."

"Because the visions are more intense than usual? Or because you're home?"

"Christ, who knows." Nell flexed her shoulders, but more in an attempt to ease tension than anything else. "Maybe both. Home isn't exactly a relaxing place to be right now. Anyway, I only have a few minutes."

"And if Tanner gets back here before you come out of it?"

"They never last more than an hour."

"You mean they haven't so far."

Nell got the manila envelope holding Shelby's photo and negative, then joined her partner at the table. "You and Max have a lot in common. You should sit down and talk someday."

"I'll make a note." He accepted the envelope and opened it. "What's this?"

"This may be a problem."

He slid the photo out and stared at it for a moment, then looked at Nell grimly. "There's no *may be* about it. This is one hell of a problem."

"Yeah. I was afraid of that."

Justin searched George Caldwell's apartment twice from top to bottom. He checked out the closets, tapped walls, tried to pull up the corners of the carpet — all in an effort to find a secret hiding place, which, if it existed, insisted on remaining secret.

"Shit."

"We've already done this, you know."

He looked up with a start to find one of his fellow CID detectives, Kelly Rankin, standing in the open doorway with a quizzical smile on her face. Very conscious of the black notebook in his pocket, he managed a rueful shrug.

"Yeah, but I was hoping I'd find something this time."

"Any luck?"

"Not unless you count the bad kind." He shrugged again.

Kelly nodded. "I keep thinking we've missed something. You too?"

"Hell, I don't know. We must have, right? Otherwise we'd be closer to solving this thing."

"Maybe. Or maybe not, that's what I tell myself. Some crimes never get solved, you know."

Justin took a last look around and then joined her out in the hallway. Closing and locking the apartment door behind them, he said, "And I thought *I* was feeling down."

"Not down exactly. Just discouraged. We're just spinning our wheels, not getting anywhere. People are beginning to look at us like we're the Keystone Kops or something."

"It's not that bad. We're not making fools of ourselves."

"We're not making our boss very happy either. I don't know if you noticed, but the sheriff is sort of losing his cool about all this."

"He does seem a mite testy."

She grinned at him as they walked down the stairs to leave the building. "Stop trying to sound Southern. It isn't your best voice."

"Yeah, I was afraid of that. But I have noticed that Sheriff Cole has been more than a little tense. Not surprising, you know. Until this series of murders, he had a nice, quiet little town on his hands. No fuss, no bother."

"Being a detective was pretty boring, I hear. Before you and I were hired, they just had the one, Matthew, and he was mostly used as the sheriff's spy."

Justin gave her a look and she grimaced. "You know it's true. Cole keeps tabs on just about everybody in his town, and Matthew came in handy for that. Probably one reason Matthew doesn't seem to have a clue how to investigate one murder, let alone four of them."

"He's doing his share," Justin protested.

"He's doing what he's told, period. Hardly any initiative there. And not much more from any of the deputies either. You and I are the ones out all hours sifting through every bit of info we have and digging for more."

"Well, since we haven't so far dug up much that's proved helpful . . ."

Kelly shrugged. "Still. Look, Justin, we're both outsiders, new to this town and these people, so maybe we can be a bit more objective than they can. Maybe we can see things a little clearer. All I'm saying is that we should keep our eyes open and maybe not take anything at face value. And watch our backs."

They were standing in the foyer of the apartment building by then, and Justin frowned slightly as he looked at her. "You think the perp is a cop."

"I think too many members of the Lacombe Parish sheriff's department haven't been as . . . helpful as they might have been. Nothing more than that." She didn't wait for his response, but added, "I'm parked out back. See you later, Justin."

He stood there gazing after her, still frowning. It didn't really surprise him that Kelly had noticed something odd about the investigation, because he was reasonably sure any good cop would have — and she was a good cop. What surprised him was that she had chosen to share that concern.

With him.

Was it only because they were the most recent hires in the department, the least likely to be involved in either the murders themselves or any cover-up in the investigation? Or did Kelly somehow know — or guess — that Justin wasn't quite what he appeared to be?

"Shit," he muttered.

He wasted a minute or two thinking about it, then shrugged and headed out the front door. No good worrying, he supposed. No matter what, Kelly's advice was good — keep his eyes open, and watch his back.

But it wasn't guarding his back he was focused on when he reached his car. It was the stunning redhead sitting on the hood who greeted him with a smile that made him, at least for the moment, forget his unrequited love for Lauren Champagne.

"Hey, Justin. Remember me?"

He cleared his throat. "Hey, Shelby. What's up?"

"Funny you should ask."

CHAPTER
TEN

It was a little before three o'clock when Max approached the Gallagher house, this time much more quietly than he had hours before. He didn't want to admit to himself that he hoped to catch Nell's partner lurking about, but that would have been at least partially true.

The rest of the truth was simply that he was feeling more than a little unsettled, worried about what Nell was risking by being here and doing what she was doing, and angry with himself for the earlier leave-taking that had demonstrated another truth all too clearly.

If he really had gotten over her, he wouldn't have felt the need to convince her that he had.

He never had been able to pretend disinterest with Nell. From that first summer, his awareness of her had been immediate and absolute, an intense tangle of complex needs and emotions that had bordered on obsession. He had been able to hide his

226

feelings from others, if only because she had been so insistent that their growing closeness remain as private as possible. But between the two of them, there had been no uncertainty, no hesitation.

They had belonged together, and both of them knew it as surely as though that truth had been stamped in the very molecules of their bodies.

Max had no way of really knowing what Nell's life might have been like since she left Silence and him, and he didn't know why she had run away all those years ago without so much as a note left behind to explain her reasons. But he knew what he still felt, and even trying to pretend he didn't feel it was going to be next to impossible.

So, naturally, he was mad as hell about it.

He dismounted and tied the horses at the edge of the woods, then walked across the small backyard to the kitchen door. It was open, only the flimsy screen door providing any kind of barrier against whoever or whatever might want in, and he swore under his breath as he stepped into the tiny mudroom directly off the kitchen.

He could see her through the doorway, sitting at the kitchen table talking on a cell phone, and she watched, unsurprised, as he stepped into the room.

"Yeah, I know that," she was saying in her half of the phone conversation. "Maybe it'll be a wild-goose chase. Probably will, as a matter of fact. But we should at least get started and see if anything turns up."

She fell silent, and even though he couldn't make out the words, Max could hear the distinctive rumble of a strong male voice on the other end of the connection. It was something he had noticed with some cell phones and some voices.

"No, we're going to check out the Patterson house next," she said. "Yeah. I will." A frown crossed her face as the man on the other end spoke at length, and then she said, "Well, we knew he would sooner or later, right? I'll just have to be careful what I tell him. So when — if — he shows up, I guess I'll play it by ear. Right."

She broke the connection and then slid the little phone into the pocket of the jacket hanging over the back of her chair.

Immediately, Max said, "Precautions, huh? The door's standing wide open, Nell."

"I just opened it a few minutes ago," she said. "I knew you were coming. The coffee's still hot, if you want some."

Since she was obviously not going to refer to anything he had said earlier in the day, he was more than willing to follow suit. At least for now. He nodded and went to fix himself a cup of coffee, saying, "Was that your boss?"

"Yeah."

"What might be a wild-goose chase?"

"Looking for Hailey. Bishop will have somebody back at Quantico try to track her down."

A bit surprised, he said, "Because she was involved with Luke Ferrier?"

"Reason enough to try to find her. Ask what she knows."

"You really haven't been in touch with her at all?"

Nell shook her head. "Keever said my father had received some kind of message from her a week or so after she left, saying she was never coming back and telling him not to bother looking for her. That's when he wrote her out of the will, so maybe it said something else that made him even madder, I don't know. I didn't even know she was gone until I talked to Keever after my father died."

"How did he know where you were?"

"He didn't. I called him."

"Why?"

Nell drew a short breath and said softly, "I knew my father was dead. I felt it. Can we change the subject now, please?"

Max was feeling too rawly exposed himself to be able to back away when he knew damned well how important this was, and so said persistently, "You said you hated him, so why did you care he was dead?"

"I didn't say I cared. I said I felt it."

"Felt what? Felt him die?"

"Felt . . . the absence of him. Max —"

"You sound as if you'd been connected to him all these years."

"In a way, I was. Blood ties, Max. No matter what, we can't escape them."

"What about your grandmother? Did you feel the absence of her too?"

"No," she replied with obvious reluctance.

"Just your father?"

"Just him."

"Then it was more than blood ties. You said he didn't share the Gallagher curse, that he wasn't psychic."

"He wasn't."

"But you felt it when he died?"

After a pause, as if to very deliberately stop the forceful rhythm of his questions, she said, "We're not going to do this, Max. Not now. I came back here to do a job, and that's what I have to concentrate on, because people's lives are at stake. If you want to help me, fine. If not, get the hell out of my house, and stay out of my way."

Her resistance didn't do much to soothe Max's temper, and his voice showed the strain of his effort to sound calm about it. "I see. Well, tell me one thing at least, will you, Nell?"

"I'll have to hear it first."

"Tell me we will do *this* before you run away again. That you'll be willing to answer a few reasonable questions. I think you owe me that much."

"I think I owe you . . . an explanation, yes. And you'll get it, Max. Before I leave Silence. Good enough?"

"I guess it'll have to be."

Nell didn't question the grudging acceptance, merely nodded.

Max drew a breath and tried again to keep his voice calm. "So who're you expecting to show up?"

"Ethan."

"Ethan? Why?"

"The Gallagher curse." She smiled wryly as he finally joined her at the table. "Ethan doesn't believe in it, but we always knew he might get desperate enough to come to me for help. Always assuming he's not the killer. If he is . . . coming to me could still be a good idea. To find out what I know."

"So what makes your boss think he'll show up?"

"It's a logical assumption."

Max had a feeling it was more than that, but he decided not to question.

Nell said, "I haven't asked you before, but do you think Ethan would be capable of killing?"

"Killing — yes. These murders — no," Max answered.

"Why not?"

"To be honest, I think Ethan lacks the imagination for something like this. He's very straightforward and pretty obvious in his likes and dislikes — as I know better than anyone. Subtlety is not one of his strong suits. Plus, if you and your boss are right about some long-buried secret being at the heart of this, I'd be very surprised to find one in Ethan's past."

"Assuming it isn't him," Nell said, "do you think he realizes it might be a cop?"

"I don't know. But there is one thing I'm pretty sure of. When it comes to digging for the truth, he doesn't stop until he finds it. No matter who gets in his way."

Bishop frowned at the scanned photograph that had just come out of their color printer, and said softly, "Shit."

Tony came to peer over his shoulder at the shot of Nell walking down the steps of what appeared to be a courthouse, with a man in the background watching her, and in the foreground . . . "That isn't a ghost, is it?"

"No."

"Then what the hell is it?"

Bishop handed him the photo, his face grim. "Evil."

Tony went around to the other side of the conference table and sat down, staring at the photo with a slight frown. "Really? In what sense? A force? A presence?"

"Probably both."

"Was Nell aware of it?"

"No. And that really worries me."

"Who took the picture?"

"A friend of hers. A friend who thought it unusual enough to take it to Nell."

"A psychic friend?"

"Nell says not. So the camera captured something that was physically there, even if not visible to the naked eye."

Tony put the photograph on the table and leaned back, frowning more heavily now. "Nell's sensitive to events, taps into the energy signature left in rooms and other places by extreme emotions, right?"

"Right."

"How about the spider sense?"

Bishop nodded. "She can enhance her other senses by concentrating. So it's difficult for anything or anyone to sneak up on her, if that's what you're asking."

"Yeah. But this . . . presence . . . snuck up on her. Is looming over her, as a matter of fact, and not in what I'd call a friendly manner." Tony tapped the photo with a finger. "Is that how you knew it wasn't a ghost?"

"Partly. Disembodied spirits in the traditional sense, those without a physical self, have a distinct emotional signature, and it's likely Nell would pick up on that."

Tony frowned. "So she'd know if there was a ghost around, even though she isn't a medium?"

"Probably. Her ability is unique as far as we can tell, but we have developed a few theories — most of them untested as yet. The chances are pretty good that the energy signature of ghosts and other disembodied spirits is close enough to what her mind naturally taps into that she'd at least be sensitive to it. Unable to communicate with a spirit the way a medium can, but definitely aware of a presence."

"But she didn't sense this presence. Because it didn't have the right energy signature?"

"Because it wasn't a ghost or a spirit, and because its physical self existed elsewhere. Astral projection, Tony. Out-of-body."

"You mean this is the spiritual energy of somebody who's alive and well and right there in Silence?"

Bishop nodded. "*Alive* at least. *Well* is arguable."

Tony considered that a few moments, then said, "You believe it's also a force. What makes you think so?"

"Look at its shape, how elongated and distorted it is. It's barely recognizable as anything even remotely human. A normal astral projection that's visible at all assumes the perceptible shape of the body it knows best, the physical body it normally occupies. In other words, what you saw would look like the person it represented."

"This," Tony murmured, "looks like a monster."

"Exactly. That is the physical manifestation of a very disturbed mind. But, even more, look at the size of it, the threatening posture. The sheer mental energy required to project something of that magnitude over any distance at all indicates an extremely powerful, extremely dark intellect."

"And it wouldn't be something innate to or trapped in this area, this building, right?"

"Right."

"Then . . . it was following Nell. Watching her."

"That's what it looks like."

"And we didn't know about it."

"We," Bishop said grimly, "didn't know about it."

Tony winced. "Shit. I guess we can assume the likelihood that this is also the killer they're trying to find down there?"

"We can assume there's a damned good possibility it is. I love a good coincidence, but I seriously doubt there are two separate evils at work in Silence at the same time and that the one we *aren't* after would be focused on Nell."

"Yeah." Tony drew a deep breath and let it out slowly. "And I guess it's unrealistic to think this . . . thing was following her around just because she looks good in jeans."

"Probably. So the question is — why was it following her? Has her cover been blown, at least where the killer is concerned? Or is

. . . it . . . interested in her for some other reason?"

"Is there any way for her to find out? Safely, I mean, without giving away to the killer what she's doing."

Bishop shook his head. "I can't think of a way. She can stay alert and try to keep her senses wide open, but that's dangerous as hell. Even without being a true medium, if she taps directly into something this dark it could leave her vulnerable to attack — psychic and physical. At the very least, he'd know who and what she really is and that she's looking for him."

"And at worst?"

"At worst . . . if he's as powerful psychically as I believe he is and Nell opens up her mind to him . . . if this photo is evidence of true, controlled astral projection and not just a one-time, nightmarish event . . . if Nell has become a focus for his attention, for whatever reason . . . then she's in danger. And not the kind of danger that can be held at bay with bullets or a badge."

"Lots of ifs," Tony noted after a moment.

"I know. Problem is, I think they could all be the truth of what's happening down there."

"So we've got a very dark and twisted

killer who's a cop and who is also psychic. Am I being paranoid, or does the universe seem to delight in stacking the deck against us these days?"

"You're being paranoid. But that doesn't mean you aren't also right." Bishop ran restless fingers through his hair and frowned. "You know, by its very definition, evil is something beyond normal, or at least what most people consider normal. Maybe we should just expect the bastards we hunt to be psychic in some sense until proved otherwise."

"It'd probably save time," Tony agreed wryly.

"Yeah. And in the meantime . . . there's what's happening in Silence. I'm about a breath away from pulling Nell out."

"Given that she now believes this killer may have started his nasty little habits last year by murdering her father, do you really think she'd be willing to be pulled out?"

"No. Dammit."

"And she's already there and involved, connected to what's happening. If she's meant to be a part of it —"

"I'll make the situation immeasurably worse by pulling her out of there. By pulling any of them out of there. Yeah, I know. I know."

"Nell is aware of what this . . . thing . . . could be, right? Knows to be on her guard?"

"For all the good it'll do her, yes. But it's going to be difficult if not impossible for her to protect herself in any meaningful sense when she can't be sure why this bastard is paying this kind of attention to her."

Tony thought about it, then said, "Can anybody else shield her? Psychically?"

Bishop shook his head. "Remember what happens with Miranda when she shields her own mind? When I do? All the extra senses get muffled, even cut off, and we end up psychically blind. We can protect ourselves, or we can use our abilities to reach out and probe — but not both at the same time. Nell needs the advantage of her psychic abilities to get to the bottom of what's happening in Silence, so she can't afford to mute them in any way. She can try to focus and concentrate on specific places at specific times, but that's the only control she has."

"That isn't much protection," Tony noted.

"That isn't any protection."

After a moment, Tony said, "She chose to do this, boss. You didn't order her to.

You never order any of us to."

"Do you think that matters, Tony?" Bishop's voice was very quiet.

He started to reply, but in the end Tony realized there was nothing he could say. Nothing that would help.

Nothing at all.

The house where Randal Patterson had lived was somewhat large for a single person, though certainly not a mansion. And given his apparent personal habits, Nell wasn't surprised to find it also rather isolated from the other houses around it. There was nothing so defined as a neighborhood in this rural area, merely houses scattered along country roads; the Patterson house sat squarely in the middle of at least eighty acres and back from the road so that it wasn't visible to passersby.

"I guess privacy was an issue," Max said wryly as they left their horses to the rear of the Mediterranean-style house and approached across a neatly manicured backyard.

"I guess. Nobody to hear the screams coming from the basement. Are you sure nobody lives here? The place is awfully spiffy."

"Randal contracted the yard work by the

season, and he'd already paid for this year." Max shrugged when Nell looked at him inquiringly. "Same crew does the yard work at the ranch, and they told me. As for the house, it's still pretty much as it was when Randal died, since he owned it outright. The only relative is a cousin living out on the West Coast, and word has it he's interested only in whatever money is left when the estate is settled."

Nell paused on the very nice flagstone veranda to say wryly, "What's really amazing about all this is that someone actually found a few secrets to get angry about. For the most part, secrets don't seem to stay secret very long in Silence."

"What can I say? Wade Keever was Randal's lawyer."

"Of course he was." Nell produced her small tool case and got to work on the door.

Watching her, Max said, "Are you sure this is a good idea?"

"Why not? If the breaking and entering bugs you, wait out here."

"That isn't what I mean. It didn't seem to bother you out at the bayou, but Randal died in this house, and only a couple of months ago. Plus, there are all the painful little games he apparently played in the basement. If you tap into that —"

"I'm not an empath, Max. I don't feel other people's pain — or the leftover impressions of it. For me, having a vision is like watching scenes from a movie. I'm just an observer."

"You said you sensed what your father was feeling when you saw him."

"Sensed, yes. But it's a knowledge — awareness and understanding without sharing the feelings."

That relieved Max, but not entirely. "Still, the visions take a lot out of you."

"It takes concentration and focus, just like any other physical or mental effort."

A slight edge to her voice made Max decide to change the subject. "When it comes to scene-of-the-crime access, this is as far as I can take you — at least via horseback and unobserved. Peter Lynch's wife still lives in the house where he died, and George Caldwell had an apartment in town; we couldn't get near either place without being observed or falling over a cop."

"Well, if the sheriff does ask for my help, I'll suggest we start with those two places."

Max waited until she unlocked the door and straightened, then said, "You say *if* but you mean *when*, don't you? You know he'll

242

come to you for help."

"I didn't know it when I got here."

"Which is at least part of the reason why you asked me for help. Yeah, I figured that out. And now that you know Ethan will show up?"

Nell kept her gaze on him as she pushed open the door. "He can get me access to the other crime scenes. He may even share details of the investigation, details that could help me find the killer sooner."

Her measured words more or less took the teeth out of any argument he might have made against the idea, and Max was sure it had been deliberate. Just as deliberate as it was when she added a quiet statement.

"Whatever your differences with Ethan Cole, the fact remains that he is the sheriff here, and he can help me do the job I came to do."

"You mean if he isn't the killer."

"Changed your mind about that?"

Max hesitated. "I don't believe — can't believe — he's killed four men. Five if we're counting your father. But that doesn't mean he isn't a dangerous man, Nell."

"I'll try to remember that." She walked into Randal Patterson's house.

Max followed, all too aware that he had no right to question her or protest any action she intended to take, whether it be using her psychic abilities to hunt a murderer or walk down Main Street on the arm of Ethan Cole. Max had his own ideas as to why she was so determinedly aloof, convinced it was only partly due to a desire to keep him at a distance so that whatever was between them wouldn't interfere with her job here.

The problem was, she had made it very clear she was not yet ready to discuss the past, and until she was, there was little Max could do to close that distance, let alone hope to have any influence at all over any of her decisions. If he pushed too often or too hard, she was very capable of, at the very least, calling her boss or her invisible partner and having Max put on ice somewhere while she went on working.

The girl twelve years ago couldn't have done that, but this woman certainly could. And would.

When they stood in the foyer of what was obviously a professionally decorated house, Nell said, "I want to check the master bedroom and bath first, since that's where he died. Not that I really expect to get anything of value."

"Why not?" Max asked as they walked down the hallway of the bedroom wing of the house.

"Because he was electrocuted. Any unusual surge of electricity in an area tends to disrupt whatever other energy signatures there might have been."

"Makes sense, I guess." He stood just inside the doorway and watched her move around the very elegant but peculiarly impersonal bedroom. Despite her dismissal of the likelihood she'd tap into anything in this room, he was alert to the slightest change in her face and spoke up immediately when a faint frown came and went. "What?"

To herself more than to him, Nell said, "That weird feeling again. Like everything's at a distance."

"Again? It isn't because of the electricity?"

She looked at him and frowned once more as she headed for the doorway of the master bath. "Not unless there was some kind of electricity out at the bayou where Ferrier drowned. I felt it there too."

Max didn't have to completely understand her abilities to be wary of anything Nell considered out of the ordinary, and he came farther into the room so he could

245

watch her while she went into the bathroom. "Then what could be causing it?"

"I don't know." Nell looked at the neat vanity, the designer towels hung just so, and candles and several decorative jars and bottles placed around the sunken tub. She picked up one jar, studying the sea-salt crystals within for a moment, then put it down and went to open the linen cabinet. "Patterson wasn't married, right?" she asked after a moment.

From the doorway, Max replied, "Right. He had been, once, years ago, but the divorce was final back when I was in college, and she moved out of town right after. Why?"

"Did he date? Openly, I mean."

"His public socializing was limited to church events," Max said. "One of the reasons why his little game room in the basement was such a shock to people."

Nell reached into the linen cabinet and withdrew a half-empty bottle of lavender bath salts. "I don't suppose you noticed if he ever smelled like lavender?"

Lifting one eyebrow, Max answered, "Sorry, no."

If she was amused by the response, Nell didn't let it show. Her voice was grave when she said, "It isn't what you'd call a traditional fragrance for a man."

"I wouldn't have thought so. But given what was found in the basement, it seems obvious he had women in the house from time to time."

Still frowning slightly, Nell returned the bath salts to the cabinet and shut it. "Yeah. It is obvious, isn't it?"

Max backed into the bedroom as she came out to join him, saying, "But nobody knows who they were, is that what's bothering you?"

"He was killed back in January, Max. And this is a small town. If Randal Patterson had a string of willing partners over the years, surely at least one of them would have been identified by now."

"I don't know, Nell. Even in these supposedly modern times, there are some things people would do their best to keep private, and I'd think sadomasochistic games would rank high on the list. Maybe the women are too embarrassed or too scared of the consequences to come forward."

"Yeah, maybe."

"Or maybe there was only one woman, Randal's regular Saturday night date for years. Relationships have lasted longer with less than a common sexual need binding two people together. And a single partner would sure as hell be less likely to be noticed and a lot harder to find."

Nell nodded. "It makes sense."

Max heard himself add, "I mean, Jesus, how many women in Silence could there be who're into that sort of thing?"

"You tell me."

He shook his head, wishing he could convince himself she was implying a purely personal interest. "I have no idea, not being into it myself. But I'd be very surprised if there were many."

"So would I. But we're making an assumption, you know."

"What assumption?"

"That his playmate was a woman."

After a moment Max said, "I guess it is an assumption."

"Yeah; which way is the basement?"

"Since I've never been here before, I don't have a clue." He knew he sounded disgruntled and made a mental note to try harder to rein in his emotions. Or at least stop making them so damned obvious.

Nell sent him a glance he couldn't interpret to save his life, then led the way from the bedroom, saying, "There's usually a stairway somewhere near the kitchen, I think."

She found it very easily, in a small hallway off the laundry room, and indicated with a silent gesture the keyed dead bolt that promised whatever lay beyond the door would remain private even within a private house.

"Is it locked?"

"Shouldn't be, since the police have been here." It wasn't, and Nell didn't hesitate to open the door, flip the light switch, and head down the stairs.

This was not something Max had looked forward to, for a variety of reasons but mostly because of the sexual nature of what he knew they'd find in the basement. He was not a man who was easily embarrassed, nor was he in any sense a prude, but he was far too conscious of Nell and what they had once had together to be able to stand beside her and view with impersonal detachment the carnal playroom of another man.

Especially when it reeked of sex.

That was the first thing he noticed, the strong yet faintly musty odors of sweat and other secretions mixed with the sharp smells of leather and rubber. Even before they reached the bottom of the stairs, he was trying to brace himself to face what they would find.

But bracing himself didn't help at all.

CHAPTER
ELEVEN

"Jesus Christ." His own voice sounded strange to Max, and he wasn't surprised.

Harsh fluorescent lights made it as bright as day despite the absence of windows, and everything was clearly visible. The basement was unfinished, the floor concrete and the walls unpainted cinder blocks, with heating ducts and plumbing pipes and wiring exposed overhead.

The hot-water heater and furnace as well as what looked like a chest-type Deepfreeze were in the far corner, half hidden behind an incongruous Oriental screen. In the near corner, what looked like a very expensive Oriental rug provided a cushioned "room" in which sat a beautiful mahogany sleigh bed complete with luxurious bedding in rich, dark colors. There was even a nightstand with a lovely, shaded lamp atop it beside the bed.

Underneath the stairs and against one wall was an enclosed space that obviously contained a bathroom or half bath, Max couldn't tell which for sure from where they stood. In any case, it was a far less . . . interesting space than the remainder of the basement.

Another richly colored Oriental rug occupied the center of the huge room, its size providing plenty of space for the equipment and tools placed there.

There were things Max didn't want to even try to identify in that space; appliances and devices hung on a pegboard on the far wall, many made up of or decorated with silver-studded black leather. There were large wooden . . . instruments holding various fastenings for wrists and ankles to contort a body into awkward, degrading, and painful positions; one of them was a large, upright X-shaped frame, while another looked like nothing so much as medieval stocks — and a third was a kind of wooden horse, complete with a saddle.

And there were others, apparatuses whose purpose was obvious in their shape, and those more enigmatic in design and function. But there were also tools and "toys" on shelves beside the pegboard that were easily recognizable, from multicolored dildos graphically shaped like penises of varying sizes and coiled leather whips with braided handles to wide leather paddles and black silk blindfolds.

All too conscious of his shaken exclamation, Max didn't dare look at Nell.

"Well," she said rather dryly, "at least he didn't do it in the street and frighten the horses."

A laugh was surprised out of Max. "So that's your attitude? Live and let live?" He looked at her finally to see a faint, wry smile curving her mouth.

"Why not?" she answered. "I've hunted too many rabid animals who destroyed other lives for their own sick reasons to worry much about what consenting adults do in private."

"And if they weren't all consenting?"

"That would be different." Nell looked around, her smile fading. "But I don't believe anything was done down here that the participants didn't want done."

"You don't believe? Don't tell me there's no energy signature in a place like this to tap into."

She hesitated and sent him a quick glance before answering. "I don't know yet. I've been practicing a kind of shield as one more way of trying to control the abilities."

"So you won't get blindsided."

"Exactly." She stepped away from the

foot of the stairs until she stood upon the edge of the rug placed in the center of the basement. "However . . ."

Max took a couple of steps himself so that he could see her face as she closed her eyes and concentrated. He was becoming a little more familiar by now with her visions, so he wasn't surprised to see when she opened her eyes that they wore that fixed, glazed look of peering into some dark distance he could never himself perceive.

As always, he had a strong urge to touch her, hold her somehow, driven by the uneasy feeling that she could drift away from him without an anchor. It was so overwhelming a belief that he actually took another step toward her and began to reach out his hand to grasp her arm.

He hesitated only because she turned her head then, looking through him rather than at him, a disconcerting experience made even more so because her eyes were so dark it was like gazing into the seemingly bottomless depths of a shaded mountain lake. Seconds passed. Her expression was puzzled at first, uncertain, as though she was looking for something she wasn't entirely sure she wanted to find.

She turned her head again, scanning the

room, more seconds passing, then gasped suddenly, her cheeks flooding with color that quickly receded to leave her even more pale than she had been before. Whatever she saw, it was clearly a distinct and unwelcome shock.

Max's fingers closed on her arm. "Nell?"

Like that first time in the woods, she didn't immediately respond to him. She was unnaturally still, and her unblinking eyes seemed to grow even darker and more distant.

A minute passed.

Two.

"Nell?" He caught her other arm and turned her fully toward him. She allowed herself to be moved as though she were a puppet, boneless and unprotesting, with an obliviousness to any possible danger. It scared the hell out of him.

"Goddammit, Nell —" He shook her.

She blinked, looked up at him in bewilderment as her eyes slowly lightened and resumed their normal green color. But she looked confused, and her face remained pale. Too pale. "Max? What —"

"Are you all right?"

"Of course I'm all right —" The words were barely out of her mouth when she winced and gasped, clearly in pain. She reached for her left temple, fingers massaging in an automatic motion. "No," she half whispered.

"Nell, what's wrong?"

"It doesn't happen like this, it's not supposed to happen like this —"

"Nell —"

"Not without warning," she murmured. She looked at him with the strangest mixture of anger and helplessness, then closed her eyes, gave a little sigh, and went totally limp in his arms.

Nate McCurry wasn't at all sure he had done the right thing, but he didn't see that he had much choice. He had to protect himself, didn't he? And what else could he do?

It hadn't taken him long at all to decide that he couldn't take what he knew to the sheriff. If Nate's suspicions in that quarter were right, Ethan Cole knew just as much as he did and was keeping quiet about it because he was scared too.

Which was sobering on several counts, but mostly because it was well known Ethan wasn't scared of much.

So Nate had carefully considered the remaining members of the sheriff's department and arranged a quiet meeting with the one cop he thought he could trust, the boyhood pal with whom he'd sneaked cigarettes under the bleachers in the gym during pep rallies and committed Halloween pranks that had very nearly gotten them both arrested.

That had been a long time ago, but they had remained casual acquaintances in the years since, and Nate thought if there was anybody who'd understand his fright and not condemn him for it, it was an old pal who had puked on his shoes when they'd both inadvertently witnessed, to their fascinated horror, two of their teachers passionately making out in a coat closet at school.

Nate had been about twelve at the time.

He still had nightmares about that one, and was half convinced that the sight of old Mr. Hensen's pale, freckled hands groping beneath the rucked-up skirt of Mrs. Gamble and pawing her exposed, fleshy breasts had made his own sex life as an adult something of a problem.

Not that he mentioned that, of course, even to his childhood friend.

"I know what I'm talking about," he said insistently, trying not to glance nervously around even though they were alone here in the alley behind the drugstore. "I've thought and thought, and it's the only thing we all have in common. I mean, I'm not sure about George, but the other three for damned sure. And me."

"You're wrong, Nate. You have to be. She left a long time ago."

"Did she? Or did she just leave Silence but stay close by to have her revenge on us? Peter Lynch died last summer, remember? Not so long after she supposedly left, and he'd treated her like shit, she told me so. Luke Ferrier had too, and as for Randal Patterson, she said he went way over the line, really hurt her when all she expected were a few games."

"So what'd she expect from you, Nate?"

Nate grimaced. "A good time, far as I could tell. But she was just weird, you know? Intense one minute and laughing like a hyena the next. Really something between the sheets, I'll give her that, but . . . She was more than I could handle, and I don't mind admitting it."

"So you dumped her."

"It wasn't like that. I just told her she wanted more than I could give her. And she *laughed* when I told her that. Laughed and tossed her head and said I'd be sorry. She *said* that, actually said I'd be sorry."

"And I guess you are, Nate."

"Oh, Christ, am I ever. And it makes sense, right? That it's her? That she came back to get even and now she's after all of us?"

"Nate —"

"Don't give me that pitying look, goddammit. I know it's her, and one of you cops should know it too. I know everybody says this is about punishing men for their secrets and sins, and I'm saying it's the sin of being with her and then treating her like dirt that we're all supposed to pay for. She's making damned sure we do."

"Do you have any proof of that, Nate, or is this just you being paranoid?"

"It's your job to find proof, isn't it? And you can do that now that I've told you where to look. You can find proof, and you can find her, and the whole damned sheriff's department will throw you a big fucking party. Especially Ethan Cole. Hell, he'll probably throw you a fucking *parade*."

"Why would he do that?"

"Because he's probably worried about his own ass. He's been in her bed too."

It was characteristic of the blackouts that Nell woke abruptly, without the drowsy sensation that usually accompanied waking from a true sleep. One moment she was out cold, deep in an utterly dreamless unconsciousness, and the next her eyes were open and she was completely alert.

So when she woke, her first very clear realization was that she was in a strange house.

She was lying on a comfortable bed, fully dressed but for her shoes and jacket, and was covered by a thin blanket. A couple of open windows brought in the light of a dying day as well as a cool breeze. And the muted sounds of voices.

Nell threw back the blanket and slid from the bed. A glance at her watch showed her she'd been out for a little less than an hour, which was usual. It was just after five. She looked around the room, studying the gleaming dark wood furniture, the beautiful old rug covering much of the wood floor. There were no photographs she could see, but several very good oil landscapes lent the room a peaceful, old-world quality.

And, faintly, she could smell Max's cologne.

"Oh, hell," she muttered beneath her breath, more unsettled than she wanted to admit even to herself.

She went to one of the windows, standing to one side to carefully peer through the gauzy curtains. This second-floor room was at the front of the house, so Nell found herself looking down onto the front drive and a neat, well-cared-for yard.

A sheriff's department cruiser was parked in the drive.

The two deputies stood on either side of the car, both facing Max, seemingly relaxed and casual in that deceptively unthreatening posture most cops had when they were intent on not looking as tough as they actually were. And Max stood near the front of the car, not quite blocking their access to the house, arms crossed over his chest in body language that was guarded at best — and hostile at worst.

The murmur of voices was indistinct at first, and Nell concentrated, focusing on sight and hearing so she could channel a bit of extra energy to enhance those senses as she'd been taught to do. Bishop was the best at it, using what Miranda had long ago nicknamed his spider sense, but he had taught most of his agents to use a form of the same ability. And it did come in handy at times. Like now.

". . . so we're not picking on you, Max," Deputy Venable was saying matter-of-factly. "Sheriff's got us checking on everybody in the area."

His partner, the gorgeous Lauren Champagne, added in the same tone, "The whole town is jumpy, you know that. So we're providing the most visible police presence we can muster."

"And visiting every house individually?" Max demanded skeptically.

"The outlying ones, sure." It was Lauren who answered, smiling faintly. But her dark eyes were watchful. "And we're asking everyone to report anything they consider odd, no matter how insignificant it seems."

"Most of us are pulling double shifts so we have more patrols out at all times," Kyle Venable added. "Just give us a call, and we can be here within minutes."

"Okay. I'll do that. If I notice anything odd."

Nell grimaced, recognizing a dismissal that couldn't have been more blunt unless he'd told them flatly to get the hell off his property. The two deputies exchanged glances again, then shrugged in tandem and got back into their cruiser.

Without waiting to watch them leave, Nell went into the adjoining bathroom to splash water on her face and finger-comb her hair into its usual unfussy style. She wanted to avoid even glancing into the mirror over the vanity, but in the end stared somewhat grimly at her reflection. She was aware that she was too pale but was far more disturbed by the faint purple shadows beneath her eyes.

They hadn't been there yesterday.

And today, for the first time ever, she had blacked out twice, the second time with a warning of only a minute or two instead of the twenty or so minutes she was accustomed to.

What was happening to her?

Like most of the other psychics she knew, Nell lived with the knowledge that the very sensitivity to and ability to interpret electrical energies and magnetic fields that was genetically hardwired into her brain might eventually damage that brain. Especially if she pushed herself and those abilities, used them too often, or for too long at a time.

No one really knew what might happen, but the possibilities were scary.

And for the psychic members of the SCU, there was also the awareness that the very work they had chosen to do could well increase their risk of, as Nell had flippantly put it to Max, waking up one day with their brains fried. Unlike psychics not involved in law enforcement, they didn't have the luxury of allowing their abilities to control *them,* of waiting around passively and merely allowing the abilities to come when they would.

No, the SCU psychics struggled always to master and use every ability they possessed, often under extremely stressful and dangerous situations and frequently pushing themselves to their limits — and beyond — because that effort could mean the difference between catching the monsters they hunted and allowing those animals another day, or week, or year of freedom in which to destroy more innocent lives.

For some of the psychics, it was likely there would be a heavy price demanded sooner or later. Certain psychic abilities required a great deal of physical stamina, for instance, while others appeared to actually create increasingly powerful electromagnetic fields within the brain itself.

Nell belonged to the latter group.

She had been matter-of-fact and cool about the risks to Max, but the truth was that Bishop kept an unusually close eye on her simply because her abilities were unique even in his considerable experience of the paranormal, and nobody could even hazard a guess as to how much sheer electrical energy her brain was capable of producing — and capable of surviving.

It was beginning to look like she was closer to her limits than she had ever been before.

Nell watched the haunted-looking woman in the mirror bite her lip, then turned away with a muttered curse. Worrying about it, she knew, wouldn't change a damned thing. All she could do was try to get to the bottom of these murders as quickly as she possibly could.

She found her shoes and put them on, then picked up her jacket and fished her cell phone out of the pocket.

"Yeah." His voice was, as always, calm and curiously implacable, like something deeply rooted and utterly certain of itself and its place in the universe.

She envied him that.

"It's me. Are you nearby?"

"About a hundred yards from the house. Close as I could get without being seen. I was going to give it another fifteen minutes and then come in after you. Are you all right?"

"I'm fine. Just woke up."

"Two blackouts in one day is not fine, Nell."

"Okay, maybe I overstated that." She tried to make her voice amused and unconcerned. "But I'm up and functional."

"I don't like this."

"I'm not crazy about it either. But it's the only game in town and you know it."

"Yeah, well, there's something else I know. Word from on high is we'd better all watch our backs. That shadow on the photograph is just what we thought it was."

"Shit. I was hoping we were wrong." Nell tried to ignore the chill crawling up and down her spine. It was becoming a familiar sensation.

"No such luck. He's watching you, Nell, or at least was that once. And we have no way of knowing why."

"But we have to assume he's on to me somehow."

"That's the general consensus. He either knows who and what you are or else doesn't know but perceives you as a threat. Maybe because he's psychic. If you've encountered him casually since you got here, he could have gotten some sense of your abilities and realized you might be able to stop him."

She drew a deep breath. "Okay. Then I have to move faster."

"Faster means you could get careless."

"And slower means I could get dead."

He swore.

265

Nell didn't wait for him to offer more objections, just said, "Any luck finding Hailey?"

"Not yet. You did say she'd be likely to change her name whether or not she married Sabella, and maybe change other stuff as well."

"Yeah."

"That'll make it harder."

"I know. But we need to find her."

"Another tie to her in the Patterson house?" he guessed.

"You could say that."

He didn't ask for details, just said, "Then I'll light a fire under the boys at Quantico. And in the meantime?"

She knew what he was asking. "In the meantime . . . I have to think of something to tell Max."

"How about the truth?"

"Which one?" she demanded ruefully.

"The only one he's interested in, I'd say. He carried you back here, you know. Held you across his lap the whole way. On horseback yet. Impressed the hell out of me."

It impressed Nell too, but she wasn't willing to admit that. "He's always been a natural horseman."

"And a white knight?"

"Some men are like that."

"I wouldn't know. Look, a couple of deputies showed up a few minutes ago."

"Yeah, I saw them."

"I hear they're patrolling all over the parish to keep a close eye on citizens and paying particular attention to the more out-of-the-way places, like this ranch. And your place. If they go by there and find you gone even though your Jeep's in the drive, they might start asking awkward questions."

"I'll say I went riding with Max. Nobody will be surprised."

"He didn't tell them you were here."

"Nobody would be surprised by that either."

He chuckled suddenly. "You know, if this situation weren't such a deadly one, I'd love to sit peacefully on the sidelines and watch you two figure out your relationship."

"You've never sat peacefully on the sidelines in your life."

"Always a first time." His voice sobered. "The blackouts are a warning, Nell, you know that. You can't go on pushing yourself and expect to keep getting away with it."

"I know."

"So *be careful.*"

"I'll do my best."

"Why doesn't that reassure me?" Without waiting for a response, he broke the connection.

Nell slowly returned the phone to her pocket. Under her breath, she murmured, "Probably for the same reason it doesn't reassure me. Because I'm running out of time."

Ethan Cole had brooded about it all day. He wanted to blame Shelby for putting the idea into his head, but the truth was, he'd been thinking for at least a couple of days that maybe he'd see if there was anything Nell Gallagher could tell him about the series of murders in Silence.

Not that he believed in any of that psychic bullshit, of course. And he wasn't anxious to have the town gossips speculating as to his interest in Nell; Shelby had been right about that, damn her.

But he had a feeling Nell could tell him something useful, and he wasn't prepared to examine that feeling too closely. It was all mixed up with other feelings, like the desire to see Nell again, talk to her. Like his growing need to settle with Max and put the past behind them once and for all.

Like the sensation of dread that had been hanging over him and getting stronger with every day that passed.

And like the uneasy sense that what was happening in his town was darker and more twisted than anything he could imagine.

Uglier than anything he could understand.

But he meant to do his job, and doing his job meant he needed to talk to Nell as soon as possible. That was very clear and perfectly reasonable and logical. She was a potential source of information, that was all. To do his job effectively, he really should go and talk to her.

So when the patrol checking things out at the Gallagher place reported in that she wasn't anywhere about even though her Jeep was parked in the driveway, he took advantage of the chance.

"Never mind, Steve," he told Deputy Critcher. "She's probably out walking in the woods." *Or out riding with Max,* he added silently, *the way she used to.* "We can't chase after every citizen in the parish just because they go out to stretch their legs and get some air. I'll send somebody to check on her tomorrow morning or do it myself."

"Okay, Sheriff. You want us to stick around 'til she comes back home?"

"No, that's okay. Continue your patrol."

"Copy that. Over and out."

Ethan absently set his radio's microphone aside and leaned back until his chair creaked, then frowned as he noticed Justin Byers standing in the doorway of the office.

"Didn't want to interrupt," Byers said.

"Nothing to interrupt. Just patrols reporting in. Have you got something to report?"

"I've got a question, Sheriff."

"Oh? And what's that?"

"I was just wondering if you'd know why George Caldwell spent hours at the courthouse just a week or so before he died, studying birth records for Lacombe Parish. I can't find anything at his apartment to explain what he was doing or why."

Ethan stared at the detective. "Birth records?"

"Yeah."

"How do you know he was doing that?"

"Somebody saw him. And according to the clerk, those were the records he asked to see. Birth records. For the last forty years."

"Not work-related?"

"According to what I've been able to find out, no. But more than one person has told me he sometimes dug around in parish and court records, apparently just out of interest."

Ethan grunted. "He was always a nosy bastard."

"Then maybe it was just curiosity."

"The clerk didn't know if he was looking for anything more specific?"

"No. And as far as I can make out, if he copied any of the records he looked at, he didn't have the copies anywhere in his apartment or his office. Unless, of course, the killer took the copies."

Slowly, Ethan said, "That's a pretty big if. You don't know that George found whatever it was he was looking for, or even if he was looking for anything specific, much less if it had anything to do with his death."

"No," Byers admitted. "I don't. But so far, it's the most interesting unanswered question I can find in George Caldwell's immediate past."

"Then I suggest you find an answer to that question, Detective," Ethan said. "And be polite when you ask the clerk for help. Libby Gettys is worse than my old grammar school teacher about manners."

271

Serious as usual, Byers didn't react to the attempt at humor other than with a solemn nod. "I'll check it out. But forty years' worth of birth records will take time to sift through, especially when I don't know what I'm looking for."

"Understood. Do your best. And, Justin? Keep this under your hat for the time being. There's no reason to give the gossips something else to speculate about."

Byers nodded, still solemn, and left.

Ethan stared across the office, feeling that creeping sensation of dread moving even closer.

"Shit," he muttered.

CHAPTER
TWELVE

Nell paused at the bottom of the stairs. Through the front screen door she could see that the sheriff's department cruiser was gone, and Max was nowhere to be seen. But he was nearby, she knew that.

She crossed the foyer to what was clearly Max's office or study and went into the room. The desk lamp and a couple of other lights were on, as well as a PC running a martial-arts-theme screen saver, and a ledger was open on the blotter. She didn't have to use any of her extra senses to figure out that he had been working in here when the deputies arrived.

Probably waiting with all the patience he could scrape together for her to come out of the blackout and tell him what the hell was going on.

Nell hadn't let herself think very much about the trip from Randal Patterson's house, though she wasn't surprised that Max had brought her here rather than take her to a doctor or hospital. He had never understood her abilities or the blackouts, but she had convinced him they were normal for her, and she doubted he would have overreacted to her sudden unconsciousness.

Not Max.

Instead, knowing that she was an FBI agent undercover here and involved in a murder investigation would have made him even more disinclined than usual to trust anyone else, especially with her vulnerable self. As long as he believed she wasn't in any immediate danger medically from the blackout, Max's inclination would be to take her someplace safe and comfortable and wait for her to come out of it.

Nell knew what the blackouts looked like. Like she was asleep, basically. Normal pulse and respiration, no fever, pupil response normal.

Like she was just sleeping, and in no danger at all. And it was something he had seen before, more than once, even if it had been years ago. He would have known she was okay.

So Max had brought her here to his home, on horseback for God's sake, and she had a pretty strong hunch he'd managed to get her into the house without any of his ranch hands even knowing about it.

Shaking her head half-consciously, Nell wandered over to the tall bookcases flanking the fireplace in the room and began absently scanning the titles. But idle interest rapidly became something else as she slowly ran her finger along the spines of the books.

Psychology and parapsychology. Ghosts and hauntings. Telepathy. Precognition. Reincarnation. Telekinesis. Spiritualism. Healing. Astral projection. Remote viewing. Clairvoyance.

His library was wonderfully complete, with books covering everything from the prophecies of Nostradamus and the inexplicable long-ago psychic diagnoses and predictions of Edgar Cayce to the government's own experiments in remote viewing during the Cold War. And the books were obviously well read, most of them with numerous bookmarks or dog-eared pages to mark interesting passages.

Nell felt a pang, wondering how soon after she ran away he had first turned to these books in search of answers. Had it been soon after, when he had tried to open a door only to discover he wasn't able to? Had he learned to hate her then?

"I was out of my mind to come back here," Nell muttered.

"Let's hope not," Max said from the doorway. His voice changed when he added, "Are you all right?"

Nell turned to look at him, nodding slowly. "I'm fine. It was just a blackout, you know that."

"Was it? *Just* a blackout? You said yourself there was something different about it. Or don't you remember telling me that?"

"I remember." She wondered if he remained standing in the doorway to block her retreat; did he expect her to bolt from his house? Probably. Probably. "It was a little sudden, that's all. I usually get more warning."

"I remember. So what does it mean that this time you had no warning at all?"

She forced a smile. "Hell if I know. Like I told you, all this is pretty much theoretical at present. I guess . . . the stress is taking more of a toll than I'd realized."

"The blackout was a warning to stop."

"Maybe. Or slow down. Or maybe it was just a random event that held no meaning at all. I won't run away, Max, if that's why you're still blocking the doorway."

"You ran away once before," he reminded her, his voice suddenly rough again.

"That was different."

"Was it? I know you don't want to talk about this yet, but there's one thing I have to know, Nell. Was it something I did? Was it my fault?"

"Well?" Shelby demanded.

"He doesn't know anything about it," Justin replied, joining her in the car.

"Or says he doesn't."

Justin leaned back and eyed her thoughtfully. "Correct me if I'm wrong, but haven't you known Ethan Cole for most of your life?"

"You're not wrong."

"But you suspect him of . . . what? Knowing more about this series of murders than he's willing to say?"

"At the very least," she replied promptly.

"Why?"

"I told you why."

"You told me why you came to me with the information about George Caldwell and those records he was looking into. Because I'm the most recent hire in the sheriff's department, a virtual stranger to this town and so pretty much off the suspect list, at least in your mind."

He drew a breath. "You haven't told me why any of this concerns you, why you believe anyone in the sheriff's department would be *on* the suspect list in the first place, and you haven't told me why Sheriff Cole seems to be at the top of that list."

"I guess I should answer the first question first."

"I wish you would."

Shelby half shrugged. "It concerns me because this is my town and because I can't not be concerned. It concerns me because I have an inquisitive nature — as anyone will tell you. And it concerns me because I really, *really* don't like murder."

"Okay," he said slowly. "And the rest?"

Shelby hesitated for just long enough to make her seeming reluctance look real. "I think someone in the sheriff's department might be involved because of a few things I've seen and heard. Nothing I could explain to somebody else, more of a feeling than a fact."

"That's pretty thin, Shelby."

"Yeah. But am I wrong?"

Instead of replying to that, he said, "What you still haven't explained is why you believe Sheriff Cole is at the top of your suspect list."

"Because I know him. And I know he's not . . . behaving the way he usually does when he wants to get to the bottom of something."

"And from that you think he's hiding something?"

"That's what got me interested, Justin. It's what made me watch him. And when I did, I went back and checked through all the pictures I'd taken around town in the past year."

"And?"

Shelby reached into her big canvas tote bag and pulled out a manila envelope. "And this is what I found."

Justin opened the envelope and slowly examined each of the photos. "It's hardly conclusive," he said finally.

"No. But it is . . . interesting, isn't it, Justin? It's very, very interesting."

While Nell was still trying to make up her mind how to answer Max, he said abruptly, "Look, it's after six, and I know damned well you haven't eaten since lunchtime — if then. My housekeeper always leaves supper in the oven for me. Why don't we talk while we eat?" In a dry tone, he added, "It'll give you more time to decide how much to tell me."

Nell didn't protest, partly because she knew food would provide her with badly needed fuel; she was inexplicably tired, a disturbing feeling since the blackouts usually left her feeling rested. So all she said was, "I guess a busy rancher needs a housekeeper."

"He does if he hates housework and can't cook," Max responded frankly. "Come on."

Half an hour later, they were sharing a delicious and definitely man-sized chicken pie and salad, sitting opposite each other at a small oak table in a breakfast nook surrounded by windows that probably, in daytime, looked out over his rolling ranch land. The windows were dark now, of course, and since they were curtained only by valances across the tops, the expanse of reflective black glass gave Nell the creepy feeling she was being watched.

At least, she told herself that was the cause of the feeling.

Max kept the conversation low-key and casual while they ate, an abeyance of at least one kind of tension that Nell appreciated, even if she was still conscious of his unanswered question hanging over her like a sword.

What did Max really want to know?

The truth? Which truth? How much of the truth?

And if she was able to offer him the truth he needed, what then? What would change? How would he feel after what he learned, about the past . . . about her?

He poured coffee for them and cleared the table, allowing her even more time to brood, and when he finally returned to the table, he asked her again the question he obviously most wanted the answer to.

"Was it my fault that you left?"

"How could it have been? I didn't even see you that day."

"Was it my fault?" he repeated steadily.

"No."

After a moment, Max settled more firmly into his chair, folding his arms over his chest in an attitude that was so clearly the picture of a man courteously and with inhuman patience waiting for explanations that she had to smile.

"You're about as subtle as neon, Max, you know that?"

"Something that hasn't changed. I don't believe in hiding things, remember?"

She did remember. It had been part of what attracted her to him in the very beginning, that tendency of his to show his feelings openly and without apology, to proclaim with every word and gesture and even the posture of his body exactly what kind of man he was.

Nothing hidden. Nothing deceptive. Nothing secret.

She wondered, not for the first time, if it had been a case of opposites attracting, at least in the beginning. Because in that way she had certainly been as different from him as night was different from day, so much of her hidden beneath the surface or disguised as something else. So much of her unrevealed, contained in silence.

The only friction that had ever occurred between them had been over her absolute insistence that their growing closeness remain private. And secret.

Hoping for at least a slight delay, she said, "One thing seems to be different, at least according to the books in your library. You didn't believe in the paranormal once upon a time."

His broad shoulders lifted and fell in a faint shrug. "Like I said, once you're touched by the paranormal, a lot of things change. A lot of . . . possibilities open up. Or not, as the case may be. I've had plenty of time to think, Nell. Twelve years."

She wanted to apologize for that, or for some of it, but couldn't. Faced with the same situation, she knew she would act in exactly the same way.

All she regretted was the necessity.

Carefully, she said, "Neither of us can go back and alter the past, Max."

"I know that."

"Then why does it matter?"

His mouth tightened. "It matters. What was bothering you so much that week, Nell? If it wasn't me or anything I'd done, then what?"

Nell had made up her mind to tell him, but when it came to the point, she shied away yet again from talking about it. Even from facing it.

Still, she wasn't changing the subject as thoroughly as he might have believed when she said evasively, "Aren't you going to ask me about what I saw in Randal Patterson's basement?"

Max drew a breath and let it out slowly, that neon-obvious attitude of patience still clinging to him. "Okay. What did you see in Randal's basement?"

Nell wrapped both hands around her coffee cup and gazed down at it, frowning. She hadn't been unduly embarrassed by what they'd found in that basement, but the unpleasant details of what she'd seen in her vision were something she had no intention of describing to him. "I saw Hailey again," she replied simply.

"You mean *she* was . . . involved . . . with Randal?"

With a slight grimace she couldn't help,

Nell finally met his gaze. "Completely involved. Intimately involved. And it . . . looked to me as though they were very . . . familiar with each other. I think Hailey was, for at least a while, his regular Saturday night date."

Max leaned back in his chair, staring at her with a frown. "Jesus. I guess you never really know people, do you?"

"I guess not."

"Then why do I get the feeling that although you were shocked by what you saw, you weren't really surprised? You expected to see her there, didn't you?"

Nell barely hesitated. "Yes."

"Why? Because of her connection to Luke Ferrier?"

This time she did hesitate, but only for a moment. "When Bishop was so sure there was something more he was sensing, some elusive fact we didn't yet know tying the murder victims together, I wondered if he was picking something up from me, if it was a kind of . . . secondhand connection, and that was why he couldn't get a fix on it."

"So part of his profile was developed by psychic means?"

"Well, not his official profile. There may be psychic aspects to some of his profiles,

284

but more usually they're based on pure police work, investigative experience, and the psychology of the criminal mind. But he *sensed* something about this killer right from the beginning, even before he sent anyone down here, and I can't think of any other way he could have done that unless he was picking it up through someone connected to this town."

"Which would have had to be you?"

"I think so."

"Why not the mayor? She talked to him before he sent anyone down here."

Nell shook her head. "Even the best telepath can only read a percentage of people he or she encounters. Bishop couldn't read Casey."

"But he can *read* you?"

"Partly. It's difficult to explain, but some psychics have a kind of natural shield just below the level of their conscious thoughts, especially those of us sensitive to some types of electrical energy. If he touches me, Bishop usually knows what I'm thinking, but he wouldn't necessarily be able to sense anything deeper than my own conscious thoughts. I didn't *think* about Hailey being a possible connection between the men, not then, but maybe something inside me deeper than thought wondered, and maybe that's what Bishop could sense but couldn't quite bring into focus."

"If he touches you."

"He's a touch telepath; physical contact is required for him to read most other people." Nell shrugged. "Like I said, he couldn't read Casey. So whatever he was picking up had to be through me. It was when I was on my way down here that I wondered if it might have anything to do with Hailey."

For a moment, it seemed as though Max would continue to focus the conversation on her absent boss, but then he shook his head just barely as if in a silent negation to himself, and said, "So you believe we'll find Hailey somehow connected to the other two men as well?"

"I think it's beginning to look like more of a probability than a possibility."

"You're not saying she killed any of them herself? Your boss says he's sure the killer is a male cop."

"Even the best profiler — and psychic — is wrong from time to time. Especially if he doesn't have all the information he needs or if . . . emotions cloud things. Maybe Bishop is wrong this time. Maybe we're all wrong. Maybe the killer isn't a man, isn't a

cop. None of the murders required unusual strength, after all, so a woman could
have committed them. It would even explain why Luke Ferrier was drugged before
his car was driven into that bayou: because
most women could never have overpow-
ered him if he'd been conscious and able
to struggle."

"Answer the first question, Nell. You're
not saying that Hailey killed any of them
herself, are you?"

Nell dropped her gaze to her coffee cup
once again and frowned. "No, I'm not
saying that. Not that. But I do believe she
would be capable of killing — even four
men — if she had a good enough reason."

"And your father? Could she have killed
him — with a good enough reason?"

She watched her fingers tighten around
the cup and tried consciously to relax
them.

The truth.

"Nell?"

Trying to sound matter-of-fact as though
it were nothing important, she said, "Yes.
With a good enough reason, Hailey could
have killed him too."

"Did she have it? Did she have a good
enough reason?"

The truth.

"Yes," Nell replied finally. "She had a good enough reason."

"I've already searched this place twice myself," Justin said as he and Shelby went into George Caldwell's apartment. It was a fairly typical second-floor apartment, conventionally and professionally decorated, the only anomaly being a conspicuously missing armchair and rug across from the television in the living room.

It was something Shelby noticed. "Is that where . . . ?"

"We have the chair and rug in the evidence room. They were both — well, they were evidence."

Shelby grimaced. "Oh."

"You did want to do this," he reminded her.

"I know, I know. Look, didn't you say you concentrated mostly on some secret hiding place? Because of the blackmail thing?"

"It seemed most likely."

"And didn't find anything. So let's suppose there *is* no secret hiding place because there aren't any secrets. Given that, there has to be something here — probably in plain sight — to prove George wasn't a blackmailer."

"You seem very sure of that."

"I am. George was not a blackmailer."

Justin was still astonished at himself that he had confided in Shelby about the little black notebook, but since her reaction had been instant and definite it had at least served to underline his own increasing doubts. Still, he said, "We have the copies of birth records from the courthouse to go through; maybe they'll tell us something."

"I imagine they will," Shelby said absently as she stood gazing around the apartment with a frown. "There are some people who thought George was just nosy, but he was not a man to waste his time. If he was looking through those records with the intensity Ne— I believe I saw, then it was because he was after something definite."

Justin's eyes narrowed slightly, but he didn't comment on what had sounded like a near slip of the tongue. Instead, he said, "You can take it from me there's nothing even remotely helpful in the bedroom. Unless you find old issues of *Playboy* suspicious."

"How about in here? What's in the desk?" Not a large desk, it was the sort of piece some people used in the more public areas of their homes to contain the seemingly endless paperwork necessary in maintaining a household.

"Mostly private financial information. Checkbook, bank statements, that sort of thing. The serious records he kept at the bank, but there's an investment ledger in the name of his ten-year-old son — Caldwell was building up a college fund, according to his widow — and paperwork concerning a few other personal financial deals. Nothing jumped out."

"Maybe it'll jump out at me," Shelby said, sitting down at the desk and opening a drawer.

Justin watched her for a moment. "This is just an excuse to snoop, right?"

She smiled without looking at him. "Don't be ridiculous. There's a little box of receipts and stuff here; did you go through it?"

"I think Matt Thorton went through that one." He recalled Kelly's warning and felt suddenly uneasy. "But that was early on, so I probably should go through it now just to make sure there's nothing helpful in it."

Shelby handed over the small cardboard box, and Justin carried it to the couch and sat down. What he found when he opened it was, as she had noted, mostly odds and ends. There were several movie and raffle ticket stubs, a few coupons for free car washes and lunch specials, and numerous receipts for the current year that he might have been considering as possible tax deductions.

There was also one small piece of paper obviously torn from a pocket notebook. A handwritten I.O.U. for a hundred dollars — signed by Luke Ferrier.

Had Matt Thorton missed it by accident? Missed the significance of it?

"Shelby?"

"Yeah?" She was frowning down at the ledger open before her on the desk.

"Did Caldwell play poker?"

"Dunno. I'm sure I could find out. Why?"

"If he did, would he have played with Luke Ferrier?"

She looked at him, still frowning. "Well, remember that none of us knew Ferrier had a gambling problem. So I wouldn't be surprised. I doubt George would have made a habit of playing, though; he wasn't much into risking his money."

"How sure are you of that?"

"Pretty sure."

"And if Ferrier had owed him a hundred bucks from some kind of gambling debt?"

Shelby lifted an eyebrow. "You mean would George have tried to get his money back if Ferrier welshed? No, probably not. A hundred bucks wouldn't have meant much to George. But it would have convinced him not to take any more of Ferrier's markers, or probably just not play with him again. He was a fool-me-twice-shame-on-me kind of guy."

It made sense to Justin. He stared at the little piece of paper in his hand, brooding.

So Caldwell had, in all probability, played poker or otherwise gambled with Luke Ferrier at least once; both Peter Lynch and Randal Patterson had been clients at his bank. It wasn't enough of a connection between the four men, Justin thought, to explain the three earlier murders — but what if it explained, at least in part, George Caldwell's murder?

What if the man everyone called too inquisitive for his own good had gotten curious about the three murders, and through his own associations with the dead men either knew or suspected something else that had connected them? And what if his search for the information or verification of his suspicions was what had really gotten him killed?

Lots of what-ifs. And no way for Justin

to know if he was even on the right track, dammit.

"Hey," Shelby said.

"What?"

"That unexplained income of George's. What were the dates of the deposits?"

Justin got out the little black notebook he'd been carrying with him and read off the dates of the supposed blackmail pay-offs listed there.

"Matches," Shelby said. "Every one of them."

"In the ledger? So how're they recorded?"

"Wait a minute, he's got some kind of private code here. . . ." Shelby frowned and rechecked several pages, then nodded. "Oh, I see. It looks like he had transferred some rental property into his son's name about three years ago, and ever since then he was depositing the income into that account as part of the college fund he was putting together."

"Perfectly innocent," Justin said.

"Told you. George was no blackmailer."

Quietly, Justin said, "So why did he have to die?"

Shelby leaned back in the desk chair and looked at him steadily. "If he wasn't a blackmailer, if he didn't have some other deep, dark secret — then he must have been a threat to the murderer. Knew something, maybe. So he had to die. That's the only possibility that makes sense."

"And the murderer would then have been left with a killing he badly needed to connect to the others so we wouldn't start looking for a motive specific to that crime."

Her voice as steady as her eyes, Shelby said, "By fabricating so-called evidence of blackmail. Which is a good argument for a cop being involved. It would have been fairly easy for a cop with at least some access to Caldwell's bank accounts to spot the regular deposits and put together that notebook to make Caldwell's murder fit the pattern."

"Easy enough," Justin agreed.

"And if you couldn't find information on others he might have blackmailed, it wouldn't be all that surprising. Most of the other cops probably wouldn't even have looked very hard to find evidence that George really was a blackmailer. I mean, after all, we're beginning to expect dark secrets to surface after one of these murders. That made it easier for the murderer."

"Which brings us back to the big question," Justin said. "Why did George Caldwell have to die?"

Nate McCurry felt increasingly uneasy as the day wore on, and he wasn't entirely sure why. He had the nagging idea that at some point during the long day he had seen or heard something he hadn't paid enough attention to at the time, something important.

By the time darkness fell, he was literally pacing the floor, checking the security system on his doors and windows repeatedly, and wishing he didn't live alone. And when the phone rang, he nearly jumped out of his skin.

He looked at the instrument for a moment as though it were a viper ready to strike him, then laughed shakily and picked up the receiver. "Hello?"

"You'll pay."

It was a low voice, a whisper really, without identifying characteristics; there was even no sense that told him if he was speaking to a man or a woman.

Nate felt a chill track up his spine with icy claws. "What? Who the hell is this?" he demanded, his voice so shaky it practically wobbled.

"You'll pay."

He drew a breath and tried not to sound terrified out of his mind. "Look, whoever you are — I didn't do anything wrong. I didn't hurt anyone. I *swear.*"

There was an odd, choked laugh, still without identity or gender but with something in it strangely both incredulous and horrified, and then the whisper again. "You'll pay."

The connection was broken with a soft click, and the dial tone buzzed in Nate's ears.

He hung up the receiver slowly and stared at it without seeing or feeling anything but his terror.

"Oh, Jesus," he murmured.

CHAPTER
THIRTEEN

"What reason did she have, Nell?" Max asked steadily. "Why would Hailey have wanted to kill your father?"

"Because she loved him."

Max frowned. "You're going to have to explain that to me."

She knew that, but she had to do it in her own way. "You asked me what happened the night of the prom. One thing that happened was that Hailey told our father I was planning to go with you. A friend of hers worked in the boutique in town where I'd bought my dress. So she knew, had known for days, that I was going. She'd seen you and me out riding one day, so she put two and two together. And, being Hailey, was saving the knowledge to use when it suited her purpose. She'd told me she knew about it a couple of days before the prom, mostly to watch me worry, I think. So that's why I was upset that last day or two, because I knew she'd tell him and ruin everything."

Slowly, Max said, "I knew you two weren't close, but I didn't know there was so much tension between you."

Matter-of-fact, Nell said, "She could never forgive me for being our father's favorite."

"You hated him. Even then, you hated him."

"Yes. I hated him as much as Hailey loved him. Or maybe I loved him as much as she hated him." She shook her head a little. "There are some questions not even . . . time and distance can answer."

Max hesitated, then went on as if forcing himself to say things he'd kept locked inside for a long time. "You never would talk about it, but sometimes I got the feeling you were scared. Scared of him."

"I was."

"He hurt you."

"Not physically. And he never molested us, if that's what you've been thinking." Watching Max steadily, she saw by the flicker in his dark eyes that he had at least suspected her father might have been sick in that way. She shook her head. "No, he never laid a hand on either of us, Hailey and me. We were never even spanked as children. But we were . . . his. Not just his children, his daughters, but his possessions. Like his land and his house and his car — like everything else that belonged to him."

"Nell —"

"No one would ever love us more than he did. That's what he told us, every night of our lives, before we went to sleep. He'd sit on the edge of our beds and tell us. No one would ever love us more. No one would ever take care of us the way he did, protect us, watch over us. He was going to be the only man in our lives. The only man who mattered to us. He'd make sure of that. He would do . . . whatever he had to do to make sure of it. Because we were his. Forever."

"That's sick," Max said at last.

"Of course it's sick. Even more, it's evil. There's been a thread of evil running through my family for a long time, as much a part of us as the Gallagher curse."

"You aren't evil."

Deliberately, she said, "There's a dark place inside me, Max, and you know it as well as I do."

"Maybe what you see as darkness others would see as strength."

"Maybe. But others don't see everything, do they?"

He was silent.

Nell returned to the subject of her father. "A psychologist would probably say my father's . . . needs . . . came from the earliest rejections in his own life. From all accounts, his father actively disliked him, made no secret of it, and had the misfortune to break his neck on the stairs when his son was only a toddler, so that rejection was complete. My grandmother you know about, but what you don't know is that she was afraid of her son."

"Why?"

"She never would tell me. Never told anyone, as far as I know. But I think it was something she saw in one of her visions, a glimpse into the future that terrified her. Whatever it was, it caused her to reject him very early on."

"Is that why you were afraid of him? Because she was?"

Nell hesitated, then shrugged a bit jerkily. "Growing up, I had my own . . . visions. There were scenes I tapped into a few times, things that had happened in the past. I saw the darkness in him, saw how twisted his need for love was, how . . . all-consuming. I knew it was unnatural. Even before I was old enough to understand why, I understood that much."

"You were never close to him?"

"I wish I could say yes, but . . ." She shook her head. "By the time my mother came along in his life, he was determined he wouldn't lose anyone else he loved. So he held on to her as hard as he could. Held on to all of us. My earliest memories are of him . . . watching me. Hovering always nearby. My earliest nightmares were of being trapped, or being lost and knowing there was . . . something . . . stalking me."

"Christ."

Nell blinked, recalled from those cold memories, and summoned a faint smile. "Not especially pleasant to grow up that way. And confusing for a child. Because he never hit me, never threatened, never did anything to me a loving father shouldn't do. Except love me so much I couldn't breathe."

Justin lifted Charlie off his lap and with a final pat set the cat gently on the floor. "You realize, of course, that going through all these parish birth records is going to take us all night," he said.

"That's why I made coffee," Shelby said as she set the tray on the coffee table and joined Justin on the couch. "Plenty of caffeine and snacks to see us through."

Justin had certainly spent worse nights

than sitting on a comfortable couch beside a gorgeous redhead, so he wasn't about to complain. But his innate professionalism demanded he make one last protest. "I'm still not entirely convinced that you should be helping me do this."

"Because it isn't my job?"

"Because it's *my* job. Because you're a civilian and shouldn't be involved in police matters. Because this is a murder investigation and I've got no business putting you in danger."

"I'm not in danger. I'm with you."

"Shelby, odds are we won't be able to stop this guy anytime soon. I mean, unless we find something incredibly revealing in these old records, we are no closer to figuring out who he is. Which means he could kill again. And if he *did* kill George Caldwell because the man knew something, then anybody involved in this investigation could certainly be at risk for that reason alone."

Still cheerful, she said, "In other words, by sticking my nose in I'm in danger of getting it lopped off."

"At the very least."

"I'm willing to risk that."

He stared at her. "I know you are. What I can't figure out is why."

"Didn't buy my fierce devotion to this town, huh?"

Justin blinked. "No. Sorry, but no."

"Or my rabid hatred of murder?"

"Dammit, I just know there's another reason."

Shelby grinned. "There is. Just like there's a reason aside from your job that has you putting in amazingly long hours trying to figure this thing out."

"I'm a cop," he murmured after a startled moment.

"Yeah, that'll be it," she said dryly.

"Shelby —"

"Look, Justin, we both want to find the truth. Isn't that all that matters?" She leaned forward to open the file folder on the coffee table. "Together we can work our way through these copies of birth records in half the time it'd take you to do it alone. I'm perfectly safe here with you. And if anybody does wonder why your car is parked in front of my house all night, well, we're both consenting adults, so whose business is it but ours?"

"In this town? Everybody's business."

Shelby grinned again. "True, but my point is that the killer, if he even notices, will just think you spent the night for carnal purposes. Right?"

"Yeah, probably." Justin only just stopped himself from saying the idea had crossed his own mind more than once in the past few hours.

"Well, then. The killer will have no idea at all that I'm even interested in this investigation, much less that I'm helping you. So there's nothing to worry about."

"I wish I could believe that," Justin said.

"You worry too much."

"And you don't worry enough."

She handed him half the birth records with a smile that had a peculiar effect on his blood pressure. "Maybe not, but I'm smarter than I look and if there's anything I know really well it's this town, so I will help you get to the bottom of this, Justin. Count on it."

Max drew a breath and tried to keep his voice even and unemotional. "So he smothered all of you."

"Smothered. Manipulated. Twisted our feelings. He was a master at using guilt, though I didn't recognize that for a long time. And without making a single direct threat, he had us — or me, at least — convinced that we would never escape him."

Slowly, Max said, "Which is one reason you never told anyone. You didn't see how anyone could have helped you, did you, Nell?"

She knew what he was asking. "No. It was never that I didn't trust you enough to tell you, Max, enough to ask for your help. I was just convinced there was nothing you could have done. Besides, what we had was . . . apart. I wanted to keep it separate from the rest of my life. Secret. It was mine, something I didn't have to share with him. With anyone else. A special . . . place that felt happy and safe. That felt normal."

Max reached across the table and pried one of her hands from around her coffee cup, holding it strongly. "I wish you'd told me, Nell. Maybe I could have done something. We could have left Silence together —"

She gently drew her hand away and sat back, both hands falling to her lap. "A lot of girls aren't very practical at seventeen, but I was, at least in some ways. Your roots were here. Your life was here. The ranch you were working so hard to build, to make a success. Your mother. How could I have borne it if I was the one to take all that away from you?"

"Nell —"

She shook her head to stop him and

shifted the focus back to the strange and painful dynamics of her family. "Where my father was concerned, I felt almost . . . frozen. Unable to act, to take even a step to change things, change what I'd lived with every day since I was small. It just *was*.

"When I was hardly old enough to understand any of it, I can remember my mother pleading with my father. Telling him she couldn't breathe, that every time she turned around he was there, insisting she love him . . . a little bit more. No matter how much he was loved, it was never enough. Hailey adored him, did everything she could think of to please him, but he had this way of . . . smiling sadly whenever he was disappointed. And he was always disappointed. No one could have loved him enough to make him happy."

Max spoke with some difficulty, the words obviously not the ones he wanted most to say. "He was always so angry with other people, so hateful."

"I know. It's like he hated everything and everyone outside his own family. Inside, with the doors closed and the rest of the world shut out, he was very quiet, never raised his voice. But he was utterly relentless. We had to love him all the time. We had to tell him so, again and again, had to prove to him that we loved him. We had to love him so much there'd never be room in us to love anybody else."

Nell shrugged again. "There was no way I could understand any of it then, of course, not when I was a child. When he said he loved me, I thought it was true. I felt bad that I couldn't love him the way he loved me. I was a horrible daughter, I knew that, because I was happiest away from him and wanted to hide my true thoughts and feelings from him. I even believed it was in some way my fault that my mother had left him . . . and broken his heart."

"He told you that?"

"It was a daily litany, repeated with sad eyes and a shaking voice. He had loved her so much, and she had walked away from him. Away from Hailey and me, her own children. She hadn't wanted us. She hadn't loved us at all. Only he loved us."

"Jesus," Max muttered.

"Hailey was older when we lost our mother, but it was a critical age for her, those early teen years when everything matters . . . so much. So I guess it made sense to her that she should try to take the place of our mother in every way she could. She did her best to run the house, cooked and cleaned and minded me despite her jealousy of me — and loved our father with a ferocity he never recognized. That was the irony of it, you know. Hailey was always the one who loved him best, but he could never see it. He was too busy trying to make me love him."

Guessing, Max said, "Hailey looked like him. You looked like your mother."

"That was part of it. But mostly it was because I didn't love him. Just like my mother, I was trying my best to pull away from him. Trying to have room to breathe. Trying to have a life of my own. And he couldn't bear that. So he held on harder. He turned away from Hailey's love, maybe just because he never valued what was freely given — I don't know. I only know that she hated me as ferociously as she loved him."

Max tried to imagine what that must have been like for the sensitive girl Nell had been. Abandoned by her mother, resented by her sister — smothered by her father. Caught between two strong-willed people, Adam pulling her desperately toward him even as Hailey tried just as urgently to push her away. And all Max could see in his mind's eye was how she had been the summer he first noticed her: half shy and half wild, a cauldron of emotions bubbling just beneath the surface of her fey, secretive eyes.

Now it made sense. So much made sense.

In some ways hesitant with him, but hungry as well, tentative about touching or being touched, oddly surprised to discover pleasure. She had been so young, though, and he had assumed it was that.

But he had to wonder now if he had pushed too hard, if his deepening obsession with her, his growing impatience with the secrecy she imposed, had only added to the strain in Nell's young life. Until it became unbearable.

She got to her feet, moving slowly. Too slowly. As if everything ached. "I'm a little tired. Would you mind giving me a ride back to the house?"

Max didn't protest. He could see that she was tired, more than tired, and he didn't like the faint purple shadows beneath her eyes. He had the strong sense that she was nearing a breaking point, whether physically, emotionally, or psychically, and he was wary of doing or saying anything that might push her over that dangerous threshold.

The ride back to the Gallagher house

was silent, and Max didn't try to break that silence. Nor did he bother asking or announcing his intention to search her house and check all the locks on doors and windows before he left her alone there; he simply did it.

She was waiting for him in the front hall when he was done, opening the door with a murmur of thanks, and she sounded so unutterably tired that Max almost left without saying anything else.

But he found himself turning around when he stepped onto the porch and heard himself asking a jerky question. "Nell, did you run away from him? Or did you run away from me?"

For a moment, he didn't think she would answer, but then she sighed and said, "Love, Max. I ran away from love. Good night."

She closed the door, and he heard the lock snap quietly and firmly into place.

From his place not twenty-five yards from the house, Galen watched Tanner's truck retreat slowly up the drive and turn on the main road back toward town.

On the whole, he would have felt better about things if Tanner had stayed the night.

With a slight grimace, Galen reached for his cell phone and placed a call. It was answered on the first ring.

"Yeah."

"I should get hazard pay for this," Galen announced without preamble. "This may be Louisiana in March, but the nights are still pretty chilly. Especially if you spend them in the woods."

"I gather Nell's home for the night."

"Looks like. And alone. Tanner brought her back here and checked out the house, then left. Not looking at all happy, by the way. In fact, if he's a drinking man, I'd say he was heading for the nearest bar."

"He isn't a drinking man."

"Figures." Galen sighed. "You know, I don't feel like much of a watchdog. If the threat to Nell is what we think, there's not a damned thing I can do to protect her from out here."

"There's nothing you could do even inside the house, not against a killer with the ability to project his mind's energy. She has to protect herself from the psychic threat."

Galen brooded for a moment, then said, "Thing is, that's not the only threat, and maybe not even the worst threat. If this bastard *is* watching her, he could see or hear enough to convince him Nell should be next on his hit list and go after her directly."

"Yes, he could. Which is why you're sticking close."

"And you?"

"What about me?"

"You know what I'm asking you, dammit. Would the killer have any reason to suspect you aren't what you appear to be?"

"I don't see how."

"Even so, watch your ass."

"I plan to. And you do the same."

Galen laughed. "Oh, hell, I'm invisible. I'm also not nearly as likely as the rest of you to set off this bastard's psychic alarms."

"No, but you're watching Nell, sticking close. And if he's sticking close as well . . ."

"Yeah, I know. But I'm being careful, and I doubt he's even noticed me."

"Still, don't forget we don't yet know what sort of capabilities we're up against. He might notice more than we could guess."

"There's a whole hell of a lot about this situation we don't yet know, and I don't like it," Galen stated flatly.

"Me either. Because there's one thing I

do know. There's going to be another murder. Soon."

All his senses going into overdrive-alert, Galen stared toward the Gallagher house, keen eyes scanning, searching for any threat. "Do you know who?"

"No. But I know it won't be the last."

SATURDAY, MARCH 25

Nell.

She woke so abruptly that the whisper of her own name was still fading into silence. Her arms were outstretched, reaching for . . . what she needed. What she wanted so badly she ached with it. Her hands were shaking. She felt stiff, so tense her muscles protested with sharp twinges.

It always happened when the nightmares tortured her sleep, this awakening need to reach out for the missing part of herself. Like the phantom pains of a lost limb, something inside her ached to be complete. Because she wasn't whole, hadn't been whole since leaving Silence.

Nell knew that. And knowing didn't make it easier.

Thinking about it didn't either. She began to throw back the covers, turning her head to glance toward the window and the bright morning outside, and it was only then that she saw the doll.

It lay propped against the other pillow of the double bed, its plastic body rigid, its frilly dress yellowing from the passage of more than twenty-five years. But the golden ringlets were still neat, the round face still unmarked, and the wide blue eyes still as bright as they had been on Nell's fourth Christmas.

That familiar, feathery chill brushed up and down Nell's spine.

She reached over and slowly lifted the doll, holding it carefully. So light now, so small, yet then it had been nearly as large as she was herself. A friend who had listened to the whispered secrets no one else had heard.

It smelled faintly of mothballs and dust.

"Eliza. What are you doing here?" She absently smoothed the doll's skirt, frowning.

How had it ended up on her pillow?

The doll had been packed away for so many years Nell had forgotten all about it, and she certainly hadn't dug it out because she didn't like sleeping alone. Even if she had known what trunk or box the doll had been packed in — and she didn't — she'd barely done more than stick her head in the attic so far anyway.

As for the possibility that someone else — some flesh-and-blood someone else — had placed the doll here during the night, how could that be? Galen was outside, and as long as he was, there was nothing coming uninvited either through the doors or windows.

At least nothing he could see.

There were no ghosts in this house, of that Nell was certain, no disembodied Gallaghers who had chosen to stay behind and haunt the place. So if she ruled out a flesh-and-blood visitor and a ghostly one, the only possibility left . . .

She felt another slow, crawling chill.

It wasn't a great jump of her imagination to think about the picture Shelby had taken and the consensus that it represented a highly disturbed mind — in all probability the mind of their killer — and to wonder: That . . . thing . . . had been watching her at least once; had it been watching her here in this house as well? Did that explain her growing uneasiness, the sleep disturbed by more than her dreams?

Was the doll on her pillow meant to freak her out, shake her, or scare her? If so, why? Because the killer knew why she was here? Because the killer knew . . . her?

That was what bothered Nell most of all. Not just the eerie appearance of a doll on her pillow, but the appearance of *this* doll. Because there were lots of toys packed away in the attic, boxes and trunks filled with the things generations of Gallagher kids had outgrown. Lots of dolls. But this one had belonged to Nell twenty-five years ago.

And how had the killer known that?

Unless the killer was Hailey.

Nell didn't know if she would find answers here in the house, but she knew she had to look for them. Especially now. So as soon as she was dressed and had a couple of cups of caffeine in her system, she went upstairs. One of the two bedrooms she had most dreaded even going into, much less clearing out, was the one that had belonged to her mother, literally closed and locked from the day her mother disappeared until her father's death.

She stood at that closed door for at least a minute or two, trying to brace herself emotionally, then turned the knob and stepped into the room.

Though the house had been unoccupied

since her father's death, Nell had arranged through Wade Keever to have a cleaning service come in about a month before her own arrival, so there wasn't nearly as much dust as there would otherwise have been. Still, the upstairs bedroom was eerily still, darkened because the drapes were still drawn the way her father had insisted they remain at all times, and smelled musty.

Nell went immediately to open the drapes and the windows, trying to tell herself the smothering sensation she felt was simply due to dust.

A part of her knew she should keep her guard up and avoid any impulse to stop and try to sense the room and its secrets; she was tired, too tired to fully protect herself, and she knew it. But she knew something else as well. She knew she really didn't have a choice.

Then I have to move faster.

Faster means you could get careless.

And slower means I could get dead.

She was running out of time.

Nell closed her eyes and took a deep breath, then turned away from the window, gazing at the morning-brightened room for the first time since her single brief glance through the door a couple of days before when she'd walked through to see what needed to be done.

Not even Hailey had been able to persuade Adam Gallagher to redecorate this room. It was exactly as their mother had left it more than twenty years before. Silver-backed brushes, dark with tarnish, lay on the dressing table between the two windows, and on a mirrored tray, cut-glass perfume bottles reposed, the stopper lying beside one bottle that had long since lost its contents to evaporation.

The remainder of the room was just as feminine, with delicate French furniture, frilly bedclothes, and soft, faded rugs on the wood floor.

Nell took a step toward the center of the room, drew another deep breath, and closed her eyes in order to concentrate. She had been so careful to keep her guard up in this house during all her waking hours that she'd been surprised only once, in the kitchen with that vision of her father walking through the room. Nothing since. And now it was hard to drop her guard when she was afraid of what she might see here. But what choice did she have? She had to know.

She had to know.

There was, here at least, no sense of everything being held at a distance away from her, no feeling that she was trying to peer through a veil. And almost the instant she forced herself to drop her guard, she felt it, the time-out-of-sync sensation of opening a door into time. Even before she opened her eyes, she heard a voice that scraped across her memories, leaving raw nerves and painful vulnerability behind.

I love you, darling.

Nell opened her eyes with a start.

At the edges of her vision was that softened, almost unfocused aura that always accompanied them, so that her attention was immediately directed to the center, as though to a stage. The bedroom was the same, yet vividly different, a bedside lamp providing the only light because it was night. It was late. And though her parents had slept in different rooms all the years Nell could remember, they were both here now.

Then.

"I love you, Grace." His voice was hoarse, panting, and his face was flushed and beaded with sweat. He was smiling, his gaze fixed on his wife's face. Her averted face.

Nell wanted to look away, desperately wanted to close her eyes, to stop this, but she had to look, had to see. She had to stand there only a few feet away from the bed where her father was raping her mother.

CHAPTER
FOURTEEN

Grace Gallagher was crying, a quiet, broken sound. Wrenching and pitiful. Like a puppy whimpering. Her arms were stretched above her head, her wrists held in the powerful grip of her husband. The covers were half off the bed, as if there had been a struggle, but the room was oddly still now. He was the only thing moving. He held her wrists against the pillow above her head with one hand, and the other hand was braced on the bed beside her.

Grace was wearing her nightgown. It was pink, with white flowers. The hem was raised above her waist, and the bodice was unbuttoned and open, baring her breasts. Her legs were apart, just lying limply on the bed, and he was between them. He wasn't wearing pajamas, just a pair of shorts pushed down around his knees. He kept saying he loved her, over and over, now moaning the words with every thrust of his body.

"I love you, Grace. . . . I love you. . . ."

He was hurting her. She was crying. Her face was wet with the tears, and that whimpering sound she made was so filled with pain. So hurt. As if he stabbed her with a knife. As if he killed something inside her. The bed squeaked rhythmically now, and she bounced like a rag doll, limp beneath him while he hunched and thrust between her legs.

Until he finally groaned and jerked, bearing down on her as if he wanted to push her through the mattress, nail her to the floor beneath. So she couldn't escape him. So she'd never escape him.

Then he collapsed on top of her, panting hoarsely, and for a few minutes all Nell could hear was her mother whimpering and her father breathing as if at the end of a marathon.

She wanted to look away, close her eyes. Why couldn't she stop this? *Why couldn't she stop it?*

Finally, Adam Gallagher raised himself off his wife's limp body and sat back on his heels between her splayed legs, pulling his shorts up. And she immediately turned on her side away from him and drew her legs up, pressed them tightly together as if in a pathetic attempt to stop what had already happened. Shaking fingers pulled the pretty nightgown closed over her breasts and then clenched to hold the material, the buttons beyond her ability to manage. She was curled up like a baby, still crying in that awful way, still moaning the protest, the refusal, that he had ignored.

He put his hand on her hip and sort of rubbed her, smiling down at her as if he saw a sated, contented lover. "I love you, Grace. I love you."

Nell could see her mother shiver and flinch away from his touch, but she didn't open her eyes and, murmuring now, kept saying, "No . . . no . . . no . . ."

"I love you."

"No . . . no . . ."

Sickened, Nell turned away from the bed, trying desperately to fight her way out of the vision and back to a time when the man who had sired her was dead and gone and couldn't hurt anybody ever again. Instead, when she looked toward the half-open door, she saw that she was not the only witness to the brutal marital rape.

Unnoticed by the two in the bed, the little girl stood in the doorway and stared at them, her mouth a silent, trembling O of shock and confusion. She was dressed for bed, her long dark hair mussed, and she stared at her parents as if at two horribly unfamiliar strangers that frightened her.

Hailey.

She was no more than four, Nell thought. Hardly old enough to understand what she had just witnessed — but just old enough for the experience to have a profound effect on her emotional, psychological, and sexual development.

While Nell watched her in numb horror, the visibly trembling little girl backed silently away from the door and retreated out of sight.

Her parents never knew she was there.

"Oh, God," Nell heard herself say shakily.

Her own voice shattered the vision, and she blinked as the light of day seemed to flood into the room. The doorway was empty, and when she turned slowly to look at it, she found the bed equally empty and neatly made, the covers smooth.

She walked to one of the windows and stood gazing out, toward the south trail that led to the ruins of her grandmother's house. Ashes of the past.

Was it all ashes?

Everything out there looked so bright and hard, so . . . stark. None of the edges was blurred, softened, the way they always were in her visions. The present always set itself apart from the past and the future, always wore the clear and distinct stamp of *now*.

Now Adam Gallagher was nearly a year in his grave. *Now* his daughters were at last free of him. Or were they?

Staring out at the hard, bright edges of *now*, Nell thought about the vision. Hailey had looked to be about four, which meant that Nell was born within the next year. Had she just witnessed her own conception? Was she a child of rape, the fruit of a seed planted by force in her mother's flinching womb?

Had her complete rejection of her father been as much instinctive as learned?

Jesus.

Nell leaned her forehead against the cool glass and closed her eyes. Her own pain and revulsion aside, what about poor Hailey? That twisted scene she had witnessed had undoubtedly twisted her as well, giving her an even more cruelly distorted idea of what love was supposed to be.

Was that why she had involved herself with sadistic men, had felt driven to satisfy their kinky needs?

Was that why she had killed them?

When Ethan Cole knocked on Nell's

door late that morning, he wasn't entirely sure what to expect. Or what he felt about it. But since he'd spent more time than he wanted to admit telling himself he was a pro and could handle this interview like a pro, it was disconcerting to discover that the pep talk hadn't done any good at all.

He'd forgotten how those green eyes of hers had the trick of stealing his breath — and of making him feel it was somehow very important that he help her.

"Hello, Ethan." She glanced past him at the deputy leaning against the hood of a sheriff's department cruiser, and added, "Want to come in? Or should we foil all the gossips and talk out there on the porch?"

"Goddammit, Nell," he muttered.

Smiling slightly, she stepped out onto the porch and led the way to the sitting area to the left of the front door — which was in full view of the deputy. There were several pieces of black wrought-iron patio furniture, including a couple of chairs and a small table.

Nell sat down in one of the chairs. "I suppose Hailey must have gotten these. It was wicker in my day."

"There've been a lot of changes since your day," Ethan replied as he sat down.

"Yeah, I've noticed. How've you been, Ethan?"

"I've been all right, Nell. How about you?"

"Can't complain. I hear you got married."

"And divorced. You?"

"Neither. But you knew that."

"Yeah, I ran the plates on your Jeep. Checked you out as far as I could without making it an official request."

"And?"

"And nothing. No police record, not even a traffic ticket, and you pay your bills and taxes on time."

"Nice to know my public record is clean."

"And your private record?"

"Oh, that one's a little more complicated." Nell shrugged. "But isn't that true of us all?"

"I guess so." He nodded, then sighed. "Okay, now that we've got that bullshit out of the way, what say we talk to each other like it matters?"

She was still smiling faintly, but those green eyes were guarded. "Suits me."

"I hear you've been seeing Max again since you came back."

"Some, yeah." She didn't explain or elaborate.

"He tell you about these murders?"

"Several people have told me about them, Ethan. Nobody's talking about much of anything else right now."

"And so?"

"And so . . . that's really lousy for Silence."

He eyed her grimly. "You're going to make me ask, aren't you?"

"Are you kidding? Of course I am." But before he could do more than mutter a curse under his breath, Nell was shaking her head, and said much more seriously, "No, I owe you more than that."

"You don't *owe* me anything, Nell."

"Don't I? You never told Max, did you? About the night I left."

"You asked me not to. I promised I wouldn't. So I didn't."

"And my father?"

"I did what you wanted me to do with him too. Went to him and told him I'd seen you getting on a bus out of town, that I'd found your car parked at the station." Ethan paused briefly. "He thought you left with Max or planned to meet him somewhere, just like you figured he would. Took some time, but I managed to convince him Max was at the ranch and not planning to go anywhere."

Gazing off at nothing, Nell said absently, "I knew he'd be more likely to believe that coming from a cop, even if you were Max's stepbrother."

Ethan said, "Like everybody else, Adam knew there was bad blood between Max and me. He knew I wouldn't lie for Max. Never occurred to him that I might be lying for you."

"Why did you do that, by the way? I've always wondered if it had more to do with hurting Max than helping me."

"If I'd wanted to use it to hurt Max, I would have told him about it a long time ago."

"Maybe. Or maybe just knowing you'd helped his girl to run away was enough. You had to know it would hurt him."

"So did you. I mean, you had to know that turning to me for help in getting away would make running out on him even worse, at least in his eyes."

"Yeah. I knew. So I'm glad you never told him that. And I'm still wondering why you helped me."

He hesitated, waited until she met his gaze, and then said slowly, "The look in your eyes that night. I'd never seen anybody look so . . . desperate. So afraid. I had no business helping you, of course, especially as young as you were. But I was young enough myself that I wasn't thinking in practical terms. Besides, I didn't doubt you were going to leave no matter what I said or did, and it seemed wisest to help you . . . minimize the fallout."

"You did do that. And I'm grateful."

"Not grateful enough to send me a postcard somewhere along the way and let me know how you were doing."

"Sorry about that. It seemed best to . . . cut all my ties to Silence."

"And did you?"

Her smile twisted. "I tried, God knows."

He nodded slowly, his gaze fixed on her. "You must have known you'd have to come back here one day."

"Yeah. I just didn't think it would be so hard."

"Hard because of the dead? Or the living?"

"Both."

"Running away never really solves anything, does it?"

A breath of a laugh escaped Nell. "That depends on what you're trying to solve."

"What were you trying to solve, Nell?"

"It hardly matters now."

"Doesn't it?"

She drew a breath and let it out slowly.

"Girls run away, Ethan. Especially from domineering fathers."

"And boyfriends?"

"He was never domineering. And I told you then it had nothing to do with Max."

"Nothing — except that you were frantic to make sure he was protected from Adam's anger."

"I just didn't want him to blame Max. Or anybody else. My leaving was my decision."

Ethan nodded. "Yeah. Except that you were scared out of your mind that night, Nell. And I've always wondered why. After all those years with Adam, what was the final straw? What happened to make you believe running away was your only option?"

"It's a long story," Nell said after a moment. "Maybe we'll have time for it later. For now, I think we should concentrate on trying to find this murderer. That is why you came out here today, isn't it?"

Ethan accepted the change of subject, though not without a faint grimace. "Just so you know, I don't believe in this psychic bullshit."

"In that case," Nell said deliberately, "there's obviously nothing I can do to help you."

"Look, don't give me a hard time about this, okay? We've hit one wall after another in this investigation, and I'm getting desperate. Hell, at this point I'd be willing to look at chicken entrails. Maybe you can look into your crystal ball instead and tell me something helpful."

"I don't have a crystal ball, Ethan. As for the chicken entrails, I doubt they'd be helpful. And — yuck."

His mouth twitched, but he didn't actually smile. "Well, do whatever the hell it is you're supposed to do. Can you help me, or can't you?"

Nell didn't push it. "I don't know. But I'm willing to try."

He felt a jab of relief and tried to cover it up by not dwelling on the moment. "Great. So what's the first step?"

"I'd like to see where Peter Lynch and George Caldwell died."

"The first victim and the most recent. Why them?"

Nell had a ready answer. "Lynch because I want to see if I can pick up something after all this time; Caldwell because so far no deep, dark secrets have come to light — have they?"

"No."

"Which makes his murder different from

331

the rest, at least according to everything I've read and heard."

"Okay." Ethan looked at his watch. "We can check out George's apartment anytime, but since Terrie Lynch is away for the afternoon and I have the key to the house, we should probably go there first."

Nell stood up, trying not to betray a few twinges from protesting muscles since she didn't want to have to explain why she was so stiff and sore.

Ethan rose as well but eyed her in sudden concern. "You sure you're up to this? If you don't mind me saying so, you're looking a little fragile."

So much for her ability to hide some things.

Nell smiled. "I've started going through the house, sorting and cleaning, and it's something a lot like work. But I'm okay. Let me lock up the house, and then we can go."

She made a couple of very quick calls while she was inside, but didn't linger. Ethan waited for her on the porch, and when she rejoined him a few minutes later, she said, "I'm assuming you don't want it known you came to the local witch for help."

"Is that a question?"

"No. I'm just wondering if it was wise to bring along a deputy."

"I can trust Steve Critcher to keep his mouth shut, or else I never would have brought him along."

"Oh. I thought you might have brought him along to make sure nobody seeing us together could get the idea your interest in me was personal. You're sort of between a rock and a hard place, aren't you? If anybody sees us together, that is. Either they think their sheriff has gone to the local witch for a bit of psychic help in solving these murders, or else they believe they're seeing a fascinating little romantic triangle."

Ethan scowled at her. "And you're so sure I give a shit what people think?"

"People? No. Max — yes. I think that at the end of the day, Max is the last man in the world you want to take on when it really matters. Which is exactly the same way he feels about you."

Ethan stared at her, cleared his throat, and very carefully said, "I've questioned him about these murders, you know."

"I know. I also know you've never seriously suspected him. When are you going to make peace with him, Ethan? Don't you think it's long past time?"

"I think this is something we don't need to talk about right now." Deliberately, he added, "Maybe we'll have time for it later."

"Maybe we will," Nell agreed with a faint, rueful smile.

Galen watched the sheriff's cruiser pull out of Nell's driveway, and said into the phone, "The problem with this whole thing is that there are too many threads we have to weave into place."

"I've noticed that. Any sign of our watcher?"

"Just the thing with the doll. Which, God knows, is creepy enough to keep all of us awake from now on."

"I'll second that. And Nell's beginning to believe it might be Hailey?"

"Well, it makes sense, especially if we admit the possibility she could have inherited the family curse, after all. She's connected to two of the victims for sure, plus Adam Gallagher. If Nell can link her up with Lynch and Caldwell . . ." He sighed. "I checked in with Bishop. He's not backing off the profile."

"Backing off is hardly his style."

"Agreed. Neither is being wrong. But if Hailey is the one we're looking for —"

"Then he's wrong. Wouldn't be the first

time. Won't be the last."

"And here I was thinking he was Super Fed."

"Say that to his face."

Galen grinned, even though he wasn't feeling particularly amused. "Not on your life. Or, more to the point, on mine. Listen, Nell acted very calm about this doll thing, but I think she's seriously freaked by it. She looked like death this morning, and what we found out at her grandmother's place sure as hell didn't improve the situation."

"Did she tell the sheriff?"

"Not yet. I think she means to take him out there later and show him. Maybe Tanner too. I guess she figures it'll explain a few things."

"Doesn't it?"

"Well, it ties up some loose ends in the past. But the present? Damned if I know." He paused. "You said last night there'd be another murder. Anything on that?"

"Officially, no. Not a whisper I've heard anywhere in town."

"But?"

"But I think it happened sometime during the night."

"You don't know who? Where?"

"No. And since it's Saturday, we can't

count on the victim being reported missing because he didn't show up for work. If he lived alone . . . it may be some time before the body is found."

"Shit."

"I'll let you know if I find out anything. In the meantime, keep a close watch on Nell. Aside from everything else, Sheriff Cole is a long way from being in the clear."

"We need to figure out where he stands, and pronto."

"Agreed. If you have any suggestions —"

Galen sighed. "No. Nell seems to think if she spends some time with him she'll know. I'm not so sure. She isn't a telepath, after all. Or a clairvoyant."

"No, but she is able to get a sense of things, of people. Maybe it'll be enough."

"Want to bet her life on that?"

"No. But we may have to."

The Lynch home was an older house that sprawled a bit on its five-acre lot, somewhat isolated in a neighborhood where cultivated fields and pastures tended to separate houses. So as far as Nell could tell, no one in the area took any notice when the sheriff's cruiser pulled up in the drive.

Leaving his silent deputy leaning against

the cruiser, Ethan led the way to the front door. "Just what is it you do?" he asked as he unlocked it. "I mean, if you don't have a crystal ball."

Nell gave him an abbreviated explanation of how she was able to tap into the energy of a place, and she was hardly surprised when he looked disbelieving.

But all he said was, "And that's going to help me . . . how?"

"I might be able to tell you what happened in this house." Nell shrugged. "It's the most intense events I tend to tap into, so if there was any violence here, any threat, that's what I'm likely to see."

"This wasn't a violent murder."

"No, but according to what I've heard, you guys believe poison was put into Lynch's vitamins, right?"

"There is *way* too much gossip in this town," Ethan muttered half under his breath.

"Not much fun when it works against you, is it?" Without giving him a chance to answer, she added, "The poison had to be put into the bottles, which means the killer might have been here in the house. Planning a murder is a fairly intense experience even without the actual killing."

As they stepped into the foyer, Ethan

eyed her with lifted brows. "You spend a lot of time tapping into murders?"

Silently berating herself for slipping up, Nell replied calmly, "It's a bad world. Amazing how many places hold the memories of bad things happening."

It was Ethan's turn to shrug. "Okay. I guess you want to wander around, maybe touch things. Check out the vibes."

"The vibes?"

"I asked you not to give me a hard time about this."

Nell smiled, but as she walked into the living room and began looking around, she said, "Actually, I don't have to touch anything. Where did he die?"

"Master bedroom, upstairs."

"Was he alone when he died?"

"Yeah. Terrie had left earlier for an appointment in town. Peter's usual routine was to down some kind of breakfast drink with his vitamins, make a few calls from the home office across the hall, then work out for an hour or so in the exercise room off the master bedroom. He was in workout clothes when his body was found. Looked like he had been on his way to shower afterward when his heart gave out."

"Not all that uncommon, I guess. A man

his age to have a heart attack after exercising."

"So the doc said. We were satisfied. Until Terrie had a fit and demanded an autopsy."

"Which turned up evidence of poison."

"Yeah. And by then we didn't exactly have what you'd call an uncontaminated crime scene. But we searched the place anyway. And I guess you heard what we found hidden in his closet."

"Porn."

"Very sick porn. Also evidence of the very young mistress he kept in New Orleans."

Without emotion, Nell asked, "Any signs of other abnormal . . . tastes?"

"Just the pedophilia," Ethan replied dryly. He was about to add that he considered that quite enough abnormality for one man when he saw Nell's face change almost imperceptibly. She turned her head slightly, looking toward the front of the house with what Ethan read as uneasiness in her eyes.

Thinking she might be having one of those visions, he said, "What? Do you see something?"

"Not yet." She sighed, and when she met his eyes her own were definitely uneasy.

"Better tell your deputy to let Max come in. He's not likely to stay outside willingly."

Ethan's surprise was brief. "I didn't hear his truck. You sure he's outside?"

"Just turning into the drive."

"A vision?"

"No."

Ethan decided not to try and figure that one out. "So he really is playing watchdog, huh? Or is it because you're with me?"

"Six of one and half a dozen of the other, I'd say."

Ethan couldn't tell how she felt about that. He wasn't sure how he felt about it either. "Okay. And I'm supposed to let him tag along during an official investigation?"

Nell sighed again. "Look, the last thing I want to do is worsen the tension between you two, but we both know how stubborn Max can be. He knows I'll be trying to use my abilities here, and he knows I pay a price for that, so short of arresting him you are not going to be able to keep him out of this."

"Price? What kind of price?"

Nell kept it simple. "Headaches, blackouts. It takes a lot of energy, Ethan, and sometimes my body rebels. Max knows that. He . . . worries." She shook her head.

"It's my risk to take, and I want to help if I can. As for Max sticking close, that's something you don't have to like, but you do have a murder investigation very much at the top of your priority list, so I think we can all be grown-ups about it. Don't you?"

"Think that'll work on Max?"

"It will if you tell your deputy to let him pass before he's stopped at the door and loses his temper."

After a moment, Ethan nodded and reached for the radio clipped to his belt. He issued a brief order to Deputy Critcher to allow Max into the house, then turned the volume back down so they wouldn't be disturbed by radio calls but he could hear it if any were directed specifically at him.

"Thanks," Nell said.

Ethan grunted. "I should have known you'd call him. It was when you went back into the house, right?"

Nell hesitated for only an instant. "I didn't call him."

"Then how did he know we were here? Christ, don't tell me he's watching you that closely?"

She was spared having to answer when they heard the front door open, and a moment later Max came into the living room. Nell knew at once from his guarded but calm expression that Max had made up his mind to keep his temper under control and avoid any confrontation with Ethan, which eased her mind at least a bit.

The last thing she needed was these two at each other's throats.

In lieu of a greeting, she said to Max, "I thought I might be able to offer something useful to Ethan's murder investigation."

Ethan lifted a brow at her in silent appreciation but didn't comment on her version of who called whom for help.

And all Max said, with a brief nod to Ethan, was, "Anything so far?"

"We hadn't had time to get started. Ethan, you said he died upstairs?"

"In the master bedroom."

"Lead the way," Nell said.

CHAPTER
FIFTEEN

Nell wasn't sure she would be able to tap into anything at all with both Ethan and Max so near, the tension between them unexpressed but obvious. And even without that, given her druthers she would have avoided trying to use her abilities again so soon after the trauma of this morning's vision. But she was more conscious than ever of time ticking away, and she knew she couldn't afford to wait.

"So how does this work?" Ethan asked when they had reached the airy, light-filled master bedroom.

Nell stood in the center near the foot of the bed, looking around, and answered absently, "I concentrate and try to tap into whatever energies and memories this room might hold."

"And we stand very still and don't bother you?"

She looked at him and smiled. "Something like that."

Max said, "Are you sure you're up to this, Nell?"

"I'm fine." She didn't give him a chance to question further or protest, but simply closed her eyes and began to concentrate, forcing herself to drop her shields and open herself up, to begin to reach out.

Since Peter Lynch had died in this room more than eight months before, and since his death had been sudden and apparently without warning, Nell really didn't expect to pick up much from that event. She had discovered that she seldom saw anything of an actual death scene, a fact that both relieved and puzzled her.

But she often got something of the minutes before or after, depending on the violence or intensity of emotion involved, and since she was concentrating as specifically as she could on Peter Lynch and his death, she expected to see something of that.

Instead . . .

It was initially difficult to reach out, as if she had to push her way through something, and she was dimly aware of using more energy or energy of a different kind to do that. Finally, she felt that distinctive time-out-of-sync sensation, but veiled again, oddly distant, and she was uneasy about that even before she opened her eyes and found herself in a different room entirely, a living room.

A completely unfamiliar room.

Nell looked around, trying to figure out where she was as well as find something to mark time, something to tell her when this was. An open magazine lay facedown on the coffee table, and when she stepped closer, she saw that it was dated January of the previous year. Most people read magazines the month they arrived, didn't they?

She stood looking around, uneasy. Where was she? And why was she here? What she saw was definitely a vision: The edges were blurred, softened, her attention as always directed to the center. But there was something peculiar about it, about the sensations of it, so much so that Nell felt a chill of real fear. Her first instinct was to try and fight her way out of the vision, but both an innate curiosity and an even deeper need to understand the limits of her own abilities made her hesitate. And in that moment of hesitation, she saw Hailey stalk into the room, obviously upset.

Ethan was right behind her.

"What, I'm not supposed to be pissed about it?" he demanded, grabbing her arm and swinging her around to face him just as they came abreast of Nell.

"No, you're not. You have no right, Ethan, and we both know it."

"No right? I've been in your bed for two months — that doesn't give me the right to get just a mite upset when I find out you've also been sleeping with Peter Lynch?"

"I told you, it's none of your business. We don't have a relationship, Ethan, we fuck." She pronounced the harsh word with complete deliberation, even enjoyment. "Period. You have fun, I have fun, that's it. No strings, expectations, or obligations on either side."

Ethan didn't seem to be buying that; his face was tight, eyes grim. "Not even respect, huh?"

Hailey laughed, and the smile she gave him was incredulous. "Respect? What does respect have to do with anything we do together? If we did it outside in the dirt instead of in a bed, we wouldn't be the slightest bit different from two stray dogs meeting up when one of them's in heat."

"So which one of us was in heat?" he asked roughly. "Which one just had an itch that needed scratching?"

Hailey laughed and jerked her arm free of his grasp. "Me, of course. I'm always in heat, didn't you know? Hadn't you heard? Jesus, Ethan, don't try to pretend you weren't convinced I was a whore long before you came on to me. And what about the scars left by a whip on my back? The cigarette burns? You never even asked about those, did you? Because it's just what you expected to find when you got my clothes off, isn't it?"

"Hailey —"

"Whores are always marked, aren't they, Ethan? Not with a scarlet A, maybe, but we're always marked. So men like you won't feel guilty kicking us out of your beds before dawn."

"Goddammit, I never asked you to leave. Never."

"You didn't have to ask. I knew what you wanted. I always know what men want." She began to turn away from him abruptly, obviously on the point of storming out of the apartment — but then froze.

Nell found herself staring into the widening eyes of her sister and had the sudden, terrifying knowledge that Hailey *saw* her. That she was actually, physically there, in the past.

No longer just a witness.

"Some detective I am," Justin muttered. "I don't even have a clue what I'm supposed to be looking for."

However reluctantly, Shelby had to agree

with him, at least about their fruitless search. "Lots of births in this parish in the last forty years. Listen, are you *sure* there was nothing in George's desk at the bank to explain why he was so interested in these old records?"

Justin leaned forward to drop several pages of birth listings onto the stack on the coffee table, then stretched absently. "There was nothing I could see. Christ, look at the time. Didn't we just have breakfast?"

Shelby heard her stomach rumble and grinned at him. "My stomach says the donuts were hours ago. Why don't we really give the gossips something to talk about and go to the café for lunch?"

"Aren't you tired? We've been poring over these damned records for more hours than I want to think about."

"I'm a natural night owl, and it's not so unusual for me to skip a night's sleep if I get involved in something." She shrugged. "Anyway, since tomorrow's Sunday, we can both sleep as late as we want, so what the hell. You did say this is your weekend off, right?"

"Officially. Sheriff Cole has us all working overtime, but he's insisted everybody gets at least one weekend a month off

348

the clock, and this one's mine. So unless another body turns up, nobody'll expect to see me at the office."

"Do you want to go home and crash? Or lunch at the café? Maybe we can figure out a way to find some clue as to what George was looking for in these birth records."

Justin had his doubts, but he was also enjoying Shelby's company and was far too wired to even think about sleep, so agreed that lunch sounded like a good idea.

It was fairly busy in town on this Saturday afternoon, but the lunch crowd at the café was already thinning out and they had no difficulty getting a somewhat secluded booth near the back.

Shelby, perfectly aware of several covert glances, managed not to laugh, but did say to Justin when the waitress had left with their order, "Life in a fishbowl, that's Silence."

Casual, Justin said, "Is it the fact that you're with me they're interested in, or the fact that I'm with you?"

"Both, I'd guess. You're a very visible part of the investigation, so everybody's naturally interested in what you do. As for me, well, let's just say I seldom have lunch with handsome men."

"That's a surprise. And thank you."

She laughed half under her breath. "Since I'm usually wandering around town with my cameras and probably see a lot of stuff I wouldn't otherwise see, I know most of the men in Silence very well. Too well, I guess. Makes it difficult for me to think of any of them as boyfriends or bed partners."

"Because your candid camera caught them being themselves?" Justin guessed shrewdly.

"Something like that. It's amazing how many people seem to imagine themselves in a bubble of privacy even when they're out in public."

Justin didn't ask for any of the details of what she'd seen, but he did wonder if even one of the hopeful suitors Shelby had undoubtedly turned away had the slightest idea why she found them unacceptable. But before he could say anything, she was cheerfully supplying some of the details he would just as soon not have had.

"I mean, it's hard to blame anybody for scratching an itch even in public, or dealing with a wedgie — because you really *have* to, after all — but nose-picking and cleaning out one's ears really crosses the line, you know? And I actually watched one guy clipping his nose hairs with one of those little battery-powered clippers. I found it extremely unsettling. And not at all attractive."

Justin laughed. "Obviously you're going to have to lower your standards."

"Or put away my cameras," she agreed ruefully. "Not that I'm prepared to do either. Which makes it a good thing that I don't at all mind being alone most of the time."

"Well, for God's sake, tell me if I do anything disgusting, okay?"

Shelby grinned at him. "I don't think you will."

He eyed her uncertainly for a moment while Emily poured coffee for them, and when the waitress had gone again he said, "You have pictures of me, don't you? Candid shots?"

"Just a few."

"Jesus." He tried to remember if he had done anything that he, if not she, would consider embarrassing, but found it all but impossible to recall movements or gestures that probably were unconscious anyway.

In a more serious tone, Shelby said, "One of the reasons I decided to approach you about the investigation was that I had watched you on and off these last weeks. It's obvious you're committed to your job and that you do it well. You've always been very intent, very focused on what you're doing at any given moment, and yet you always pay attention to the people around you."

"I didn't see you and your cameras," he pointed out wryly.

"That's because I didn't want you to see me. Not that I was spying on you or anything like that, it's just that I've developed the knack of watching people without their awareness."

"The way you watched Sheriff Cole," Justin said, deciding to turn the conversation in a less personal direction.

Shelby followed agreeably. "Exactly. Remember, I've been watching Ethan Cole for years, so when I paid closer attention to him after the first murder, I could see he was behaving differently. For a long time, there was nothing I could put my finger on, but when I grouped all the photographs of him together, that's when I found what I showed you. These."

In her enthusiasm, Shelby reached into the big canvas tote bag she always carried and pulled out the manila envelope she had showed Justin the day before.

"These pictures mean something, Justin, and we both know it."

Alarmed, he glanced quickly around the café and found, as he expected to, that several people had noted Shelby's actions. To make matters worse, before he could stop her she opened the envelope and drew out the photos, handing them across the table to him.

"Take another look at them," she invited him.

Justin knew that making a big fuss would only draw more attention to them, but as he bent his head and looked at the pictures, he said under his breath, "I really wish you hadn't pulled these out, Shelby. Not here and now."

"Why not? Everybody in this town has seen me showing off my pictures, so there's nothing odd about it. They'll probably assume I'm just showing you pictures I took of you."

"Yeah, but if the wrong person is watching — or even hears about it — it could make him suspicious. Might make him think your candid camera caught him doing something he really, really doesn't want the law to know about."

After a moment, Shelby said, "Okay, dumb of me. But the damage, if there is any, is done, so you might as well look at them."

Unwilling to betray any undue interest to those watching eyes, Justin leafed through the photos quickly and then handed them back to her with a faint smile for the benefit of the observers. "I agree they could be important. But the sheriff talks to lots of people in this town every day; odds are he would have talked to each of the murdered men as well."

Shelby put the photographs away once again in her bag and tried to keep her expression neutral. She wasn't really afraid, but Nell had warned her to be very, very careful, and she was pretty sure Justin was right about this being a mistake. Still, since it was done, there was nothing to do but push on. "Yeah, but if you'd checked out the back of each of the photos, you would have found a date penciled in. I pulled all the negatives and checked each shot."

"And?"

"And Ethan talked to each of the murdered men the day before that man was murdered. What are the odds of that happening, Justin?"

"Long," he said slowly. "Very long."

"Oh, my God," Hailey whispered, for once clearly shocked. Seeing the image of her sister — and Nell had no idea how she appeared but guessed she looked ghostly — watching what was an intimate and disturbing argument between Hailey and a lover had to be a deeply unsettling experience, especially since Nell had been gone more than ten years at that time.

What could Hailey have thought then? That she was experiencing something fairly common in the annals of the paranormal, a visitation from a recently deceased family member? Had she thought Nell had come to her at the moment of her death, to say good-bye?

Part of Nell wanted to try to say something to Hailey, to assure her that she was not dead, merely — what? Merely visiting from the future?

It lasted only a moment, because even in her hesitation Nell was too shocked not to instinctively draw back, to fight to get herself out of the vision and back to the present. What she saw dimmed almost immediately, Hailey's shocked face vanishing in a darkening haze that grew darker and darker, and for a scary, seemingly infinite period of time Nell felt herself swallowed up by something black and immense.

Something that wasn't as empty as it should have been, because she wasn't alone there. Someone . . . something . . .

was nearby, watching, nearly touching her
. . . reaching for her. . . .

Desperate, driven by an overwhelming
certainty that if it touched her she would
die, Nell fought to wrench herself free of
the smothering darkness. It seemed to take
every ounce of will and energy she possessed, the way an extreme physical effort
demanded that the very fibers of muscles
tear themselves apart in the struggle to do
what was demanded of them.

And then she was free of the darkness,
the past, back in the present with a suddenness that was almost as frightening as
the vision itself had been. A blinding pain
exploded in her head and she heard herself
cry out.

She had never in her life had a headache
like this one. The pain was incredible, as if
something was trying to bore its way into
her brain or out of it, something hot and
ominous —

"Nell."

"Evil," she murmured as she opened her
eyes. At first, all she saw was darkness, but
it lightened rapidly until she was staring at
a dark blue shirt and black leather jacket.

"Nell, for Christ's sake —"

She could dimly feel Max's hands gripping her upper arms, and when she looked

up at him she saw that he was pale and grim-eyed. It wasn't until he reached to grasp her wrists that she realized both her own hands were pressed to either side of her face, hard, almost as if she were trying to . . . keep something in.

"It's not a blackout this time, is it?" Max asked, gently pulling her hands away from her face.

"Umm . . . no," she said finally, her voice hardly more than a whisper, because anything louder hurt. "Dizzy. I think . . . I think I'd better sit down for a minute."

Max guided her a few steps to a bench at the foot of the Lynches' bed. It was only then that she saw Ethan, leaning back against the dresser with his arms crossed over his chest. He was expressionless, but he was also a bit pale, just as Max was.

Nell managed a shaky laugh. "I guess I put on quite a show, huh?" She kept her voice quiet.

"Well, you could use some glitter or neon lights to jazz things up, but the dead silence and thousand-yard stare were pretty goddamned effective." Ethan looked at his watch. "Twenty minutes you were a zombie."

"What?"

Max sat down beside her. "I've been

357

trying for the last ten to bring you out of it."

"I suggested a slap," Ethan offered, "but Max said no."

"Why were you in so deep?" Max asked Nell, ignoring the other man's comment.

The dizziness had passed, but Nell's head still hurt and it was difficult to think clearly. "It . . . I . . . I wasn't here."

"Funny, it looked like you were."

"Ethan, shut the hell up, will you please? Nell, what are you talking about? If you weren't here, then where?"

"Yeah, tell us where," Ethan invited.

If she had been granted a few minutes of peace and quiet in which to think, Nell might have made a different choice. But with Max's insistence and Ethan's rather mocking attitude added to the throbbing pain in her head, she acted on impulse.

"I'll be happy to tell you where," she said, staring straight at the sheriff. "As soon as you tell us how long your affair with Hailey lasted."

The silence was acute and went on for several beats, with Ethan staring back at her without a blink. Then finally, slowly, he said, "She told you."

"I haven't communicated in any way with my sister for nearly twelve years,

Ethan. And nobody else knew, did they? Hailey insisted on secrecy."

"I sure as hell didn't know," Max murmured.

Ethan glanced at him, then returned his gaze to Nell. "Yeah, she insisted on secrecy. Never would tell me why. No reason for us to hide it, after all. We were both over twenty-one and free. My marriage was over by then, and she wasn't seeing anybody else. At least not publicly. And it only lasted a couple of months."

"So how did you find out about her and Peter Lynch?" Nell asked. At first, she didn't think he was going to answer, but finally he did.

"I think she wanted me to find out. We were at my place and she needed something from her purse, I forget what. Asked me to get it for her. The purse had a zippered inner pocket that was open, with a photograph sticking up out of it. It was a shot of her and Peter." His face twisted slightly. "They were playing some kind of sex game. She was dressed up to look like — a schoolgirl. I guess because he liked them young."

Nell had seen too much of Hailey's sexual exploits by now to be much shocked, but she did feel a jab of pain for her sister. Something about the way Ethan spoke of her said it could have been a serious relationship with him, maybe even a lasting relationship. Nell wondered if Hailey had known that, if she had deliberately destroyed what might have been.

And if so, why? Because she felt undeserving? Because by that point there had already been far too many scars on her body and soul from the games of sadistic men? Or because she had known that any real relationship was impossible while Adam Gallagher lived?

Steadily, Nell said to Ethan, "How long have you known that Hailey is the common factor in these murders?"

"I don't know it's true even now," he said immediately. "As far as I know, she was never involved with George Caldwell."

"But the others? Lynch, Ferrier, Patterson. You knew she had been involved with each of them."

He hesitated. "Like I said, I found out about Lynch long before he was killed. Long before Hailey left. As for the other two . . . Ferrier got drunk and bragged to me once that he'd had a few enjoyable nights with Hailey over the years. Not an affair, apparently, just sex now and then, whenever neither of them was involved with anybody else."

"And Patterson?"

Ethan shrugged. "Once I saw all that shit in his basement, I knew Hailey had probably been involved with him."

"Because of her scars? The whip marks, the cigarette burns?"

He flinched. "Yeah."

Even with her head pounding, Nell was focused very intently on the sheriff, trying to get a sense of him that would tell her, once and for all, if she could trust him, could eliminate him as a suspect. His involvement with Hailey made him even more of a suspect, at least on the face of it and assuming Hailey was indeed the common factor in the murders, but Nell had a hunch it was a lot more complicated than that.

She didn't like exposing his private life to others, even to Max — who, for all his anger and the long-standing bitterness between him and Ethan, would never pass judgment on his stepbrother's life or choices — but she didn't feel she could back off, not now. She had to know.

"You never asked her about the scars. Why?"

"How the hell did you know that?"

"Because I saw it, Ethan. I saw the fight you had with Hailey more than a year ago. Was it January? February? In a living room, I'm guessing your apartment. You had obviously just found out about her relationship with Lynch, and you were upset. Hailey was . . . pretty brutal in what she said to you. But she made a point of saying you'd never questioned her about the scars. She obviously thought she knew the reason why, but I'm guessing she was wrong. Wasn't she?"

For the first time, Ethan was clearly shaken. "Jesus. You talk like you were there."

"I was. Just now, I was. Answer the question, Ethan. Why did you never ask Hailey about the scars?"

"Because I thought I knew how she got them."

"You thought it was our father."

He nodded, the movement as jerky as his voice was. "It made sense, at least to me. Both your mother and you running off like that, so obviously scared of him, Hailey's scars . . . even the way she talked about Adam, as if she worshiped him — and hated his guts at the same time. It was all just so goddamned extreme. None of the scars was recent as far as I could tell, and I thought — I believed — she had been abused as a child. I tried to get her to talk about her childhood, but she wouldn't. Got touchy as hell. She wouldn't talk about her life at all to me and made it plain that if I pushed I'd be pushing her right out the door. So I stopped trying."

Max stirred slightly but said nothing, and when Nell glanced at him she realized that since he knew neither of the Gallagher girls had been sexually abused by their father, he was wondering about the visit to the Patterson basement and what Nell had seen there.

She looked back at Ethan, hesitated, then abruptly made up her mind about him. Every instinct and every sense she could lay claim to told her that Ethan Cole was not a murderer, and if she couldn't trust those instincts and senses then she needed to find a new line of work. Quietly, she said, "Our father never abused us that way. Hailey got the scars from Patterson. She was — very young when she was first involved with him."

"How young?" Max asked, obviously still recalling Nell's shock in that basement.

Reluctantly, she said, "It looked like — twelve or thirteen. No older than that. Just about the time we lost our mother."

Ethan looked a little sick, but he was enough of a cop to catch the significance of what Nell said. "Looked like? You saw that too?"

"Yeah. I . . . paid a quiet little visit to the Patterson house."

"And saw the basement."

Nell nodded. "What I tapped into there showed me their . . . relationship."

After a moment and with no conviction in his voice, Ethan said, "It's all bullshit. You couldn't possibly have seen that any more than you could have seen Hailey with me."

"I couldn't possibly. Except that I did."

"It doesn't even make sense," he protested, his voice rising. "You told me yourself that what you see are the memories of a place. I was never with Hailey here, so how could you — what the hell did you call it? — *tap into* any scene between her and me?"

"It's a good question," Max noted quietly.

"And I wish I had a good answer." Nell sighed. "I don't know how I was able to do that, Ethan. Maybe because I was concentrating on Peter Lynch and you were here — and I followed that link to a scene between you and Hailey when you were discussing Lynch."

"Oh, yeah, that makes a lot of sense," Ethan snapped.

"Look, I'm sorry I can't tie it all up nice and neat for you. But the truth is that we're only just beginning to understand how psychic ability works, and there are still a hell of a lot more questions than answers. I can't explain how I was able to see what I saw — I only know that I *saw* it. That I was there, in the past, a witness to that scene between you and Hailey."

"Which," Max pointed out, still quiet, "is something new for you. Right? That the memory you tapped into belonged to a different place?"

She nodded. "It felt different right from the beginning. I had to . . . push harder, use my energy in a different way. Maybe I pushed myself too far somehow."

"And right into Ethan's memories?" Max offered.

Ethan swore. "Well, if that isn't creepy as hell, I don't know what is. Even if it were possible. Which it *isn't*."

Remembering her sister's shocked gaze, Nell was tempted to explain to them both just how different this "vision" had been. But her head was pounding and she was tired — and there was still one more thing she had to do today.

She got to her feet, not protesting Max's help or objecting to the grasp he maintained on her arm. And when the wave of dizziness passed, she said, "Ethan, you'll have to lose the deputy. There's something I have to show you." She looked up at Max. "Something I have to show both of you."

CHAPTER
SIXTEEN

The house that had belonged to Pearl
Gallagher was never much to shout about,
just a little four-room, tin-roofed shack the
old lady had insisted on not updating because she liked things simple. The only
modern amenity it had ever boasted was in-
door plumbing, and that was only because
Adam Gallagher had insisted anything less
just wasn't sanitary.

Still, it had served Pearl well as a sanc-
tuary, and it perhaps wasn't surprising that
the house had not long survived her.

There wasn't much left. The cinder-
block foundation was really the only thing
left standing, surrounding the charred remains of wooden studs and beams that had
collapsed inward, and twisted tin, and the
bits and pieces that had survived oddly intact — like a kitchen sink that sat perfectly
level and surprisingly clean within a mostly
burned-out butcher-block counter. And
the old brass headboard that reared up in
what had been the bedroom, surrounded

now by the incinerated remains of the roof that had fallen in.

"Why am I here?" Ethan demanded, hands on his hips as he surveyed the ruins. Neither he nor Max appeared to notice that the place had been somewhat disturbed recently, and if either had, they doubtless would have assumed vandalism.

"So I only have to tell this once." Nell forced a smile, small though it was. She gently pulled her arm free of Max's grasp and moved to face both men. "The night of the prom, I came out here to Gran's house to show her my dress. She didn't answer when I knocked, so I let myself in. I could hear the shower, and I decided to wait a few minutes, until she came out. I really wanted her to see my dress."

Nell fell silent, and even though she thought she was expressionless, there must have been something in her face, because Max stepped toward her.

"Nell?" His voice was low, worried.

She forced herself to go on, to speak as calmly as she knew how. "I'd had visions before, but they'd been quick, fleeting things mostly. Scenes I could easily recognize and had learned to accept as part of my life. Part of the Gallagher curse. Nothing especially dramatic or tragic, just unsettling. But that night . . . I saw something unlike anything I'd ever seen before."

"What?" Ethan demanded, fascinated despite himself.

"I saw the scene of a murder." In a voice steady with hard-won detachment, she described what she'd seen, the blood and signs of a violent struggle, the body lying so twisted she wasn't able to see the face.

"So you don't know who it was?" Ethan said.

"Yes. Yes, I know. I knew then."

"How, if you couldn't see the face?" Max asked.

"There was a locket. A silver locket I recognized." Nell turned and led the way around to the rear of the ruins, where many years before, an old-fashioned root cellar had been dug out of the ground just a few yards from the back door. "I knew the body must have been buried or hidden nearby. I wasn't sure where to start looking, especially after all these years — and after that vision I had out in the woods." She glanced at Max, and he nodded.

"You saw someone carrying the body of a woman. So that's why you weren't concerned that it might be a future death; you

369

knew it had already happened."

"I was pretty sure it had. But in that vision, the body was being carried toward this house on a stormy night, and I knew she — she had been killed here, inside. I thought he might have been planning to bury the body somewhere else but couldn't because of the storm. So he brought her back here."

Ethan stared down at the warped and splintered old doors of the root cellar. "You're telling us there's a body down there?"

"I came out here this morning to look around. I'd forgotten the root cellar; it was virtually hidden by an old toolshed most of my childhood and never used. But after I'd poked around inside the house for a while, I remembered. The doors were padlocked, but I got rid of the lock."

Max and Ethan exchanged glances, then both bent to open the slanted doors to reveal the stone steps leading downward into darkness. A dank and musty smell immediately wafted out.

"I left a couple of battery lanterns inside," Nell said, starting down the steps. The men followed. At the bottom, she got the small lanterns from a rickety old shelf placed to one side and turned them on.

Then she walked forward just a few steps, the lanterns illuminating a dirt-walled space barely ten by eight feet and less than six feet high.

Ducking slightly, as Max was, Ethan said, "So where —" He didn't have to finish the question.

At Nell's feet lay an open grave. Freshly dug earth was piled on either side of the shallow pit. And inside lay a skeleton that had been only partially uncovered.

Nell set one of the lanterns at the foot of the grave, then walked around the mounded dirt to the other side and placed the second lantern just above the dully gleaming skull.

"Jesus," Ethan murmured. "Who is it?"

"My mother." Nell knelt where she was and leaned forward to point out a tarnished silver locket on a chain now resting among bones and dirt. "The locket has pictures of Hailey and me. She always wore it."

Max drew a breath and let it out slowly. "She never left."

"She never left. Lying here all these years, much closer than I ever —" Nell shook her head. The lantern shining upward lent her face a haunted expression. Or maybe it wasn't just the light. "She didn't leave her husband. Didn't abandon her children. She was here. All the time, she was here."

"What killed her?" Ethan asked.

"Love killed her," Nell murmured. "My father killed her."

By the end of their lunch, Justin and Shelby had not come up with any fresh ideas as to how to find out what made George Caldwell so interested in old parish birth records. Which wasn't to say they had not enjoyed trying. Or maybe they had just enjoyed each other's company.

Justin was wary of asking himself which it was.

The lunch crowd in the café had almost entirely cleared out by the time they finished their meal and prepared to leave, but Justin was uneasily aware that several off-duty cops as well as more than one curious citizen had noted and expressed a covert interest in him and his companion.

What he didn't know was whether that would prove dangerous to Shelby.

"I think you worry too much," she said as they got into his car. "And, anyway, you need my help."

He put the keys in the ignition and

paused, eyeing her. "I do, huh?"

"You do. Two heads are better than one."

"Well, if that's your only reason —"

"Come on, who else can you trust? Is there anybody in the sheriff's department you're *absolutely* sure of?"

"No, but — Shelby, if we're right about this, George Caldwell was probably murdered because he found out something that threatened the killer. No other reason. No high-minded motive like a search for truth, justice, or the American way. He died because he knew something he shouldn't have. Because he had the potential to get in the killer's way. Right?"

"Right."

"So don't you think he wouldn't hesitate to get rid of anyone else who offered even a potential threat? Even a curious redhead who just might have pointed her cameras in the wrong direction once or twice?"

"If I were a threat, he'd have gotten rid of me long ago."

"It might not have occurred to him that you were a threat. Until he saw you with me. Until he saw you showing me a bunch of photographs."

"Which I do all the time. Even if he was suspicious, he has to know I'm acting exactly the way I always act, so why would that raise alarms?"

"As far as we can tell, George Caldwell didn't do much either — just go through parish birth records."

Shelby frowned suddenly. "You know, that's a good point. How would the killer know George was a threat to him? Even if he was camped out at the courthouse and saw George going through the records, there was nothing unusual about that. I mean, it was something George did fairly often. So where was the threat?"

Distracted, Justin frowned. "I thought about that. Whatever it was he found . . . he must have told someone about it. Maybe even the killer."

"Because he didn't realize it was a threat?"

"Probably. To George, it might well have been just some interesting tidbit of knowledge. But to the killer . . ."

"A threat." Shelby shook her head. "Birth records. You don't think he found out some fine, upstanding citizen was a bastard or something like that, do you? Because I wouldn't have thought that would matter in this day and age. Certainly not to the point of murder."

Justin brooded for a moment, absently

starting the car at last. "Unless there was a legal issue. Maybe some kind of inheritance that hinged on legitimacy."

"And again I say — in this day and age?"

"There are some really old laws still on the books, Shelby, some of them arcane. And it might not be as much a matter of illegitimacy as it is of something else — say a family business or the disposition of property with a legal tie to a particular family line. It's possible, at least. Or the threat could be even simpler — a family secret the killer really didn't want exposed, for whatever reason."

"Yet another puzzle." Shelby sighed. "I guess we don't have a hope of figuring out who it was he might have told about whatever it was he found in the birth records."

"The guy was a banker. He talked to people all day long. And as far as I can determine, he was pretty friendly outside the bank as well."

"So we start with the whole town and try to narrow it down?"

It was Justin's turn to sigh. "Now you begin to see why we haven't had any luck in solving his murder."

A sudden rap on Justin's window made them both jump, and they looked out to see several grinning deputies standing beside the car. Justin rolled down the window.

"No parking on Main Street," Deputy Steve Critcher chided in a severe tone.

"Actually, there is," Shelby pointed out cheerfully, leaning forward to look past Justin.

"I meant parking of a certain kind," the deputy said, "as you well know. And in broad daylight too."

Ignoring the reference, Justin said, "Don't you guys have anything better to do than harass fellow cops who're off the clock?"

"Not really," Lauren Champagne replied, smiling.

"Not at the moment, anyway," her partner, Kyle Venable, chimed in. "Quiet Saturday, mostly. And we're just coming off our lunch hour."

"So we were just strolling — I mean *patrolling* — the mean streets of Silence, doing our best to keep evil at bay." Steve sobered suddenly. "Or discussing it, anyway. Scuttlebutt says the sheriff is about to call in the feds. Doesn't really have a choice, we hear."

Justin said, "I imagine Sheriff Cole always has a choice."

"Maybe up to now he did, but the town

council is making a lot of noise. They held an emergency meeting last night, you know."

"No," Justin said, "I didn't know. So they're pushing Cole to bring in outsiders?"

"Sounds like." Steve smiled. "Though I personally think he's looking for help a little closer to home. Psychic help." He sounded the *do-do-do-do* first notes of the theme from *The Twilight Zone*.

"You can't know that, Steve," Lauren objected mildly.

"No, I can't know that. But I'd like to know another reason why the sheriff would take Nell Gallagher out to visit the Lynch house. When Terrie Lynch wasn't there, by the way."

"Surely you don't think Sheriff Cole believes in that stuff?" Lauren asked.

"I would have said not. Then again, maybe he really is getting desperate."

"Or," Justin suggested, "maybe he's just exploring every possible avenue. She is supposed to be gifted, isn't she?"

"So they say," Kyle responded laconically.

"It's all bullshit," Steve insisted. "If trained cops can't find out who's doing these killings, then no pretend psychic is going to. If you ask me, the sheriff is going to have to call in the feds, and sooner rather than later."

Kyle said, "We've got a betting pool going. So far, the odds are just about even that we'll be up to our hats in condescending feds by the middle of next week."

"Oh, joy," Justin murmured.

Steve offered an exaggerated shrug. "Hell, maybe we should just admit we're out of our depth and roll out the welcome mat. At least then they could take some of the flak."

Shelby asked, "Are you getting flak?"

He grimaced. "Let's just say I've been asked more than once how it is that *we* have allowed fine upstanding citizens to be murdered."

Dryly, Shelby said, "Fine upstanding citizens with S and M playrooms in their basements?"

"That point is conveniently forgotten, just like gambling, embezzlement, and collections of porn."

Kyle said, "Why don't you say it a little louder, Steve, so all of Main Street can hear? There might be one or two who don't yet know all the facts."

Unrepentant, Steve retorted, "If you think there's a soul over the age of fourteen in all of Lacombe Parish who doesn't know exactly what's going on, you're nuts."

"What I think is that the sheriff is going to can all of us if he finds out we're talking about this like it's no more important than what we had for lunch. Use your head, Steve."

Whatever response Steve might have made was lost when the radios on the belts of all the deputies as well as the one Justin had in his car suddenly and loudly squawked for attention.

Max looked at Nell sharply but said nothing.

Ethan hunkered down and stared grimly at the skeleton. "Adam killed her? Are you sure about that?"

"Who else could it have been? He's the one who claimed she left, that she ran away. He had access to her things and could have packed up and disposed of some of them so it looked like she had taken clothing and personal effects with her. Nobody else could have done that. And he was so openly angry and bitter about her having run away that nobody stopped to wonder if she really had."

Ethan sighed, still gazing down at what

379

was left of Grace Gallagher. "Probably won't be able to tell how she was killed after all this time."

"In the vision, I saw — I remember — there were stab wounds. Lots of them. But I don't think any of them were fatal. Maybe he dropped the knife during the struggle, I don't know. I do know there was a struggle, a violent one; the whole room was trashed." Nell's voice was steady. "In any case, I'm pretty sure her neck's broken. A forensic pathologist should be able to determine that."

Ethan looked at her, brows lifting. "And what else are you pretty sure of?"

"That the body was uncovered for a long period, then finally buried in this very shallow grave. You can see there are only shreds of clothing left, but as much torn as rotted, and there are some fine marks on some of the bones. Teeth marks, I think. Probably rats." Her voice remained composed, matter-of-fact. "I'm thinking he didn't have time to bury her right away, so he just left her down here, covered with an old tarp or something. The rats got to her, maybe even other animals. By the time he could bury her, there wasn't much left."

"That's what you think?"

"That's what I think."

Frowning, Ethan said, "Why do I get the feeling you sort of know what you're talking about?"

Nell didn't hesitate. She reached into the pocket of her jacket and produced a small leather I.D. folder, tossing it across to him. "Because I sort of do."

Ethan opened the folder, and then sat back on his heels, staring down at the FBI badge and identification. "Christ almighty."

Nell had to smile, albeit faintly, at his incredulity. "Never know how people are going to turn out, do we?"

"You're telling me you're a cop? A federal cop?"

"That's what I'm telling you."

Ethan looked up at Max. "You know about this?"

"I found out a couple of days ago."

Rising slowly to his feet, still holding Nell's I.D. open in his hands, Ethan frowned down at it, then closed it and tossed it back to her. "Tell me it's a coincidence that you came to settle your family's estate just when we're in the middle of a murder investigation."

"Afraid not."

His jaw tightened. "You're here officially. And I wasn't consulted or even informed.

Want to tell me why?"

Nell chose her words carefully. "There was a request made through official channels for an FBI profile of the killer operating here in Silence. The initial profile indicated there was a high probability the killer was a cop."

Ethan turned around and left the cellar.

"Think he's upset?" Nell murmured.

"Did you doubt he would be?"

Nell sighed and got to her feet. "No. I just hope he won't blow a fuse."

"We've both learned to handle our tempers a bit better than we used to."

"I noticed that."

Max half smiled, but said, "Nell . . . your mother. I'm sorry. But at least you can be sure she didn't willingly abandon you."

"Yes. I just wish I'd known it a long time ago." Clearly unwilling to further discuss those issues, she added, "We'll leave the lanterns down here for now. I'm hoping Ethan will okay sending the remains to the FBI lab for analysis."

"And if he doesn't?"

"I think he will. No matter how he feels about the possibility that one of his people is a killer, keeping the discovery of these remains quiet is in his best interests, at least for now. This town doesn't need to deal with another murder, even one more than twenty years old. Especially one more than twenty years old."

"What about you?"

"What about me?"

"Don't you need to deal with it?"

"I've dealt with it." Nell walked around the grave without sparing it another glance, then went up the steps and out of the root cellar.

More than a little grim, Max followed.

They found Ethan once more surveying the burned-out hulk of a house but obviously thinking of something else. His face was decidedly dark. As soon as they joined him, he said flatly, "Just how sure is this profiler of yours that it's a cop?"

"Pretty sure. At least, he was when I came down here."

Ethan turned his head to eye her sharply. "And now?"

"I think he's still sure. But I've had a few doubts." Nell shrugged. "I'm not a profiler, even though I have spent some time in Behavioral Science. I could easily be wrong."

"But?"

"But . . . there's Hailey."

"You don't seriously believe Hailey could have killed four men in cold blood?"

"What I believe is that, so far, we haven't found a better connection between the men. They all had secrets, fairly nasty ones, and one of those secrets was that they all had a sexual relationship with Hailey at some point."

"I told you I don't believe George Caldwell had any kind of relationship with Hailey."

"Then maybe," Max offered, "he was killed for a different reason. Because he knew something, found out something. Because he was a threat. Maybe the reason why your people haven't found any secrets in his life is because he didn't have any."

"Believe it or not, that had occurred to me," Ethan snapped. "I know my job, Max."

"I never said you didn't."

"Funny, that's what I heard you say."

"You're imagining things."

Nell wasn't so tired that she didn't recognize signs of rising tension between the two men. Max was upset with her because he thought she was refusing to "deal" with discovering the truth about her mother, and Ethan was mad because the FBI had been right here under his nose without his knowledge or consent. Both of them wanted to let off steam.

The way her head was hurting, Nell was afraid that if they did that, she'd shoot both of them.

"The point," she said before an argument could really get started, "is that for three out of four of the murders, we can tie the victims to Hailey. Each of them had a secret sexual relationship with her. And each of them, according to the profile, was killed as punishment for his sins. Was killed because the murderer was unable to get justice for what were in all likelihood personal injuries."

"You're saying Hailey could have killed them because they all hurt her?" Ethan demanded.

"I'm saying it's possible."

"Yeah? Then explain to me why Patterson was killed more than twenty years after he played his sadistic little games with Hailey in his basement. If, that is, you're right about how old she was when it first happened."

"We don't *know* their relationship ended when Hailey was a child," Nell pointed out.

Ethan wasn't as shaken by that possibility as he might have been the day before. "Okay. But the question stands."

Remembering the morning's vision of

Hailey as a child witnessing a brutal marital rape, Nell said, "It was probably a cumulative thing. Not being hurt just once, but again and again. The years passed, the hurts piled up, and finally Hailey couldn't take it anymore."

"She *left*," Ethan said. "Maybe she did get fed up, but her response was to leave Silence. What, you think she's been hiding out somewhere nearby for the past eight months, slowly killing off the men who treated her like shit? And nobody's seen her, not even a glimpse of her?"

Without answering his questions, Nell said, "There's one more factor that makes me feel sure Hailey is involved."

"And that is?"

"The first man to die last year was our father."

"Wait a minute. You think Adam was murdered too?"

"Yes. I think —"

Nell.

After a startled instant, Nell reached up to rub her temples soothingly. It was just the headache, that was all. Just this strange, pounding headache. There was nobody whispering in her ear.

Nobody.

"Are you all right?" Max asked.

"I'm fine. Ethan, I know he was supposed to have died of a heart attack, but I think it's at least possible that —"

You're wrong. You're wrong about all of it.

"Nell?"

She stared at Ethan for a moment, then shook her head. "Sorry. I'm . . . sorry. I'm having a little trouble concentrating."

"You need to rest," Max said in a voice that could best be described as determined. "If a blackout is coming —"

"It isn't. At least, I don't think so. I just have a headache, that's all." Nell sighed. "But I think I probably do need to rest. Ethan, I can arrange to have the remains taken to the FBI lab for analysis, if that's okay with you. It'll be quickest, and quietest, so nobody in town has to know until you're ready to tell them."

Ethan swore under his breath, but said, "If Hailey's behind this rather than a cop, keeping quiet won't matter. But just in case your profiler is right, I think it would be best not to have any of my people deal with this."

"Then I'll arrange it."

He nodded. "Far as I know, FBI agents seldom work alone. You have a partner here, don't you?"

Nell didn't hesitate. "As you say, we

seldom work alone. But sometimes we do have to work very quietly, behind the scenes. Even undercover."

"And I'm not supposed to ask, I guess."

"I'd appreciate it if you didn't." Nell smiled. "Please don't think of us as spies, Ethan. We're doing our jobs, just like you. Trying to do the right thing, just like you. Trying to catch a killer — just like you."

"Okay, point taken." Ethan settled his shoulders with the air of a man accepting, however reluctantly, something he didn't like but really couldn't fight. "Do you still want to see George Caldwell's place today?"

Nell didn't wait for Max to object. "Maybe later this afternoon, if I'm up to it."

"I still want to hear all this about Adam's death," Ethan said. "And sooner rather than later."

"I know."

"But for now, I need to get back to town, and you apparently need to rest." Ethan eyed Max. "I gather you're staying?"

"You gather correctly."

All Nell said was, "We should close the cellar doors just in case some kid wanders past, but there'll be someone here to collect the remains within an hour. With any luck at all, we should have at least preliminary results by sometime tomorrow."

"Fast work," Ethan grunted. He went over to close the cellar doors, then rejoined the other two, and they walked back through the woods to the Gallagher house. Ethan had dropped his deputy off in town before joining Nell and Max here earlier, so his cruiser was waiting for him.

"Let me know later if you feel up to seeing the Caldwell apartment," Ethan told Nell. He added flatly, "And I expect to be kept informed from here on out about the activities and conclusions of the FBI."

"You will be."

Ethan's radio muttered quietly but imperatively, and he reached for it to turn up the volume and respond to the summons. They all heard his dispatcher's urgent announcement.

"Sheriff, we've got another one. Another murder."

CHAPTER
SEVENTEEN

"You didn't have to stay," Nell said.

Max debated silently but decided there was no benefit in arguing about it, at least not at the moment. So he ignored the question. "Is your partner taking care of the . . . remains?"

"More or less. Supervising the removal."

"He can hardly watch you from way out there. Some guardian."

Nell smiled faintly. "He knows you're here." She sipped her coffee, keeping her gaze fixed on the dark fireplace. This living room wasn't her favorite part of the house, particularly since even throwing open the heavy drapes did little to brighten it, but the sofa was comfortable and it was infinitely preferable to resting in bed — which Max would otherwise have insisted on.

"You weren't surprised about this latest murder," he observed.

"No. I was . . . warned there had probably been another one. And for it to be so soon after the last one is a bad sign. A very bad sign. We're running out of time."

From his chair near the fireplace, where he could watch her, Max said, "You can only do what you can do. Nobody expects more of you than that."

"Yeah. I know."

"Headache gone?"

"Well, there's still a faint throb," she admitted. "But it's not nearly so bad as it was. And at least . . ."

"At least what?"

"At least this one didn't herald a blackout."

Max frowned. "That isn't what you were going to say."

"You read minds now?"

Max leaned forward to set his cup on the coffee table, and said coolly, "Yours sometimes, yeah. But you knew that."

Nell looked at him finally, expressionless.

"You knew it," he said as though she'd argued with him. "Even though you've done everything in your power to shut me out since you came home, you've known all along that you haven't been able to. Not completely."

"That door is closed."

"Yeah. You closed it. And all these years, you've refused to open it again, except for those moments when your guard slipped, when you were too tired, or too upset, or sometimes when you were dreaming. Then it opened, just a little. Then I could catch a glimpse of your life, a flash of your feelings."

"I never meant —"

"To shut me out? Or to let me in in the first place?" He paused, but when she didn't answer, he said almost mildly, "Do you have any idea how frustrating it was for me to know that door was there — and not be able to open it myself?"

Nell drew a breath and let it out slowly, not looking away, an expression in her eyes that was both wary and numb, as though she expected a blow of some kind. "Yes. I do know. I'm sorry."

"You could have cut me loose."

She flinched. "I didn't want — I tried. I couldn't."

"And now?"

She wavered visibly, then just as obviously shied away from answering that question. With a glance at her watch, she said, "It's been nearly an hour since Ethan left. I wonder if —"

"Don't change the subject, Nell."

"Look, don't you think another murder takes precedence over —"

"No. I don't. Not this time. Ethan made it clear he wouldn't grant you access to this latest crime scene until his people did their jobs, both to avoid alerting the killer if it *is* a cop and to keep your undercover status solid as long as possible. So it'll be hours at least before there's anything new for you to consider."

"Even so —"

"Even so, you'd rather talk about anything else. Anything but us."

"There is no us." Nell put her cup on the coffee table and got up, moving to stand before the fireplace. "It's been twelve years, Max. We've both moved on. You said that. You said you got over me."

"And you believed me?" He laughed without amusement as he rose to his feet. "Did you really think there could be anybody else for me? Really believe I'd settle for something . . . ordinary? Something that could never be half of what we had? Could you? *Did* you?"

"You know I didn't."

"Just like you know I didn't."

Nell fiddled with a decorative gold box on the mantel, then straightened a black-framed picture of her family that looked to be more than thirty-five years old. "Even so, twelve years is a long time —"

"I know it's a long time. Christ, I know. And I won't say I didn't try to forget you, Nell. Because I did. I didn't want to admit even to myself that no one else could take your place, could mean as much to me as you did. But I finally had to admit it. Because no one could. No one even came close."

"Maybe you just didn't give it a chance." She stared at the photograph, wishing she could shut out his voice, his insistence. Wishing her head would stop hurting.

"Twelve years of chances. Twelve years of telling myself you weren't coming back. That you hadn't cared enough even to send me a Christmas card somewhere along the way and let me know you gave me a thought now and then. Twelve years of telling myself I was a fool. Then I walk down Main Street last week and there you are."

"I'm sorry." Nell stared at the old photograph, vaguely bothered by something. But her head hurt. It hurt almost as much as it had at the Lynch house.

"Nell, I understand now why you ran away." His voice was closer now, just behind her. "After that vision the night of the prom, you had to be scared to death. Believing your father had murdered your mother, that he would never willingly let any of you go —"

"I tried to tell Hailey," she murmured, blinking because her vision seemed to be blurring. "But she wouldn't believe me. She said he'd never do anything like that, never hurt us. She was — There was no way I could convince her. We never had gotten along, and by then we were like strangers. So I ran."

"Away from love. When you said that, I thought — But it was his love you ran from, wasn't it? A love so possessive, so jealous, that it killed what it loved rather than allow it freedom."

"I knew he was capable of doing it again. Of killing one of us if we tried to leave. Or killing someone else we — I knew he could do that. And even though she said she didn't believe me, deep down Hailey must have known it too, because she kept all her relationships secret from him. Even the one with Ethan."

"Nell —"

"I guess Glen Sabella was the first one she cared enough about to run away for." Nell reached out to touch the photograph, her puzzlement increasing. "Who is —"

Red-hot pain pierced her skull as though someone had driven a spike into it, and before Nell could even draw breath to cry out, everything went black.

The body of Nate McCurry lay sprawled across his bed, a butcher knife from his own kitchen protruding from his chest. He was wearing only a pair of shorts, but from the tumbled condition of the bed, the fact that he lay atop the covers, and the estimated time of death, it appeared he had at least managed to get out of bed that morning before being killed.

"Nice wake-up call," Ethan muttered.

"Yeah." Justin stood near the sheriff, both of them watching as the two lone forensic specialists the Lacombe Parish sheriff's department could boast did their thing, one photographing the body exhaustively and the other carefully dusting every possible surface in the room for fingerprints.

"Speaking of which, he got a call same as the others?"

Justin nodded. "Last night. According to his caller I.D. it was from one of the pay phones in town."

"But we haven't found evidence of a secret life. So far."

"So far," Justin agreed. "No hidden rooms or compartments, no false floor in any of the closets, no concealed safe. Paperwork here looks normal, just personal bills and records, and if Kelly had found anything unusual at his office, she would have called. From all the evidence we've found so far, he was a perfectly normal insurance salesman — if there is such a thing."

Ethan offered a faint smile at the weak joke, but all he said was, "This time, the killer got very, very close; you can't get much more hands-on than stabbing a man in the chest. Unless he means to strangle his next victim."

"You think there'll be another victim?"

"Don't you?"

With a sigh, Justin said, "We're sure as hell not stopping him, I know that. And for him to kill again so quickly —"

"Is a bad sign. Yeah, I know. Either he's been spooked into moving faster, he's deliberately escalating for some reason we don't yet know, or he's escalating because whatever restraints there might have been once are no longer holding him back. And we have no way of knowing why that is."

Justin eyed the sheriff thoughtfully. "Look, I'm pretty damned sure that George Caldwell didn't have a nasty secret he was trying to hide. I think we all are. Right?"

Ethan nodded. "I think we would have found it by now if it existed."

"Okay. But we're at least sixty percent sure he was killed by the same man."

"The same killer anyway," Ethan muttered.

Justin didn't miss the inference, but said only, "Which has to mean that Caldwell was a threat to the killer or somehow got in the killer's way, made himself a target."

"Odds are."

"Remember I asked you why Caldwell would have been searching through old parish birth records?"

"Yeah. I haven't had a chance to ask you if you found anything."

"Well, I haven't found anything. Or, at least, I haven't found anything that *looks* like anything. But it's still the only unexplained thing Caldwell was doing in the weeks before his murder. So he must have found something, some kind of information, and either passed it on to the killer in all innocence or accidentally. Information the killer considered a threat."

"And George was killed to shut his mouth."

"Nothing else makes sense, at least not to me."

Ethan brooded for a moment. "But how do we find out whatever it was? You said it was more than forty years of parish birth records, right?"

"Right. Lots of babies born in the last forty years, I can tell you that much. And we don't even know if it's the births or something else. Place of birth, parents' names, stillborn children or kids that died young, witnesses to a birth, the doctors who delivered the babies — God knows what we're looking for. I sure as hell didn't see anything worth killing over."

"You're new to the area," Ethan noted, "so you might not have noticed what someone born and raised here might have seen."

"True enough," Justin said after a slight hesitation, still wary of saying anything about Shelby's involvement.

"Do you have the copies of the records?"

"Locked in the trunk of my car."

"When we get back to the office, bring them to me. If there's something odd there, I'm willing to bet I'd spot it as quick or quicker than anybody else would."

"George Caldwell may have been killed for spotting it," Justin reminded him.

Ethan didn't like to think that one of his deputies or detectives might be a traitor, and he was almost equally unhappy to think that one of them might be an FBI agent operating undercover, but one thing he was sure of was that he couldn't afford to play guessing games or second-guess his own instincts. So he continued to talk to Justin Byers as if the shadow of neither possibility had ever crossed his mind.

"George had trouble keeping his mouth shut," he told Justin. "I don't. Plus, it's entirely possible that he didn't realize what he knew was a threat. I'll definitely know."

"If you find something."

"Yeah. If I find something."

"And if you don't?"

"Then we're no worse off than we are now." Ethan shrugged. "At this point, I'm willing to try most anything."

"Including the paranormal? Like, maybe, talking to an avowed psychic?"

Grim, Ethan said, "Either Steve Critcher is less discreet than I thought, or somebody else saw me talking to Nell Gallagher."

Without answering that directly, Justin merely said, "It's a small town. Hard to do anything without being noticed."

"You mean unless you're keeping a nasty secret?"

Justin smiled wryly. "Yeah, I haven't

quite figured that out yet. As for you talking to Nell Gallagher — was she able to tell you anything helpful?"

This time, Ethan did hesitate. "Maybe. I'd rather not say anything until we thoroughly check out Nate McCurry. And I mean thoroughly, Justin. I want to know who he talked to, who his pals were, who he dated in the last ten years, and who cleaned his teeth."

"Matt's out now with a couple of deputies gathering that information. What is it you're hoping they'll find?"

"A secret," Ethan said. "One secret all these men had in common."

"You mean they all had the same secret? Apart from all these nasty little bad habits we've discovered?"

"I think so. All except George, so far. I want to know if Nate did as well."

"It might help if I knew —"

"I know, but I'd rather not . . . contaminate your judgment when I have nothing solid, no evidence I could take to court, to support this . . . theory."

"Just information supplied by a psychic?"

With a grimace, Ethan nodded. "Exactly. Which, by the way, you don't seem too bothered by."

"I don't care if we find the answers in tea leaves, as long as we find them," Justin said frankly. "I've seen enough weird things in my life not to discount anything out of hand. Maybe it's possible for some people to see things the rest of us can't. Maybe it's just another rare but natural human ability. Who am I to say it can't be real?"

"Well, I'm not quite so untroubled about the possibility, but I'm also a lot less certain of my certainties than I was yesterday." Ethan sighed. "I guess we'll see. I'm going back to the office. I've got a shitload of reports and calls to handle. Stay here and get this wrapped up, will you? And do what you can to transport the body out of here quietly."

"I'll do my best." Justin watched the sheriff leave, then returned his gaze to the two technicians still working silently. He didn't suspect either of them of being something other than they appeared, but it certainly did no harm to oversee every possible aspect of the investigation just to make damned sure nothing fell through the cracks.

It didn't surprise him that Ethan Cole hadn't wanted to tell everything he knew; Justin hadn't exactly been either completely forthcoming or entirely truthful himself. He wondered if that reticence would come back to haunt both of them, then dismissed the thought.

Nothing he could do about that at the moment.

He was just about to ask the photographer if he was done yet when Brad spoke first.

"Hey, Justin? You guys see this?"

"See what?" Justin joined the photographer beside the bed.

"My zoom lens caught it," Brad explained. "See that little piece of material sticking out past the hem of his shorts?"

Justin bent closer and looked, frowning. "Yeah. So?"

"So I don't think it's part of his shorts. He's wearing regular cotton boxers, and that little bit of material is silk. Colorful silk, as a matter of fact."

"Some kind of lining, maybe?"

"Not unless it's homemade. I use that brand, and they're just cotton. No lining at all."

He'd investigated too many murders to have any squeamishness left, so Justin didn't hesitate to bend even closer and grasp the small bit of material. He pulled gently, carefully, beginning to draw it from inside the dead man's shorts.

"Looks like a scarf," Brad murmured, watching intently as more of the silky blue material became visible. "A lady's scarf. You can see little flowers — hey. What the hell?"

Encountering a sudden resistance, Justin stopped pulling and shifted position so he could gingerly lift the waistband of the shorts far enough to see inside them. "Christ."

"What?"

Justin hesitated, glanced up at Nate McCurry's open, sightless eyes, and murmured, "Sorry to do this to you, buddy, but I have to."

"Have to what?" Brad demanded.

"Help me pull the shorts down. You'll have to get a picture of this."

Brad opened his mouth, then closed it and rather gingerly helped Justin pull the dead man's shorts down around his knees. When the genitals were exposed, the photographer muttered something under his breath, then silently began snapping pictures.

The fingerprint technician, whose name, improbably, was Dolly Sims, came to the foot of the bed, studied the corpse for a moment, then said to Justin, "You guys ever consider you might be after a woman?"

"Not until now," Justin said.

She nodded. "Well, I'd say the odds are pretty good this was done by a woman. Maybe a woman scorned. Or just one who was *real* pissed off."

"Yeah," Justin murmured, looking down at what had been done to Nate McCurry. "Real pissed off."

The colorful silk scarf had been tied in a jaunty bow around his penis and testicles.

Being out in a rural area had its advantages; Galen had the satisfaction of knowing that the remains he and Nell had that morning uncovered were removed and taken to the FBI lab by a very efficient team who had arrived and departed unnoticed by any of the locals.

At least, he was pretty sure they had.

It wasn't yet dark when Galen settled back into place to watch the Gallagher house. Since Tanner's truck was still parked out front, he knew Nell wasn't alone, but as he studied the house he felt oddly uneasy. Something was different, and he didn't know what it was.

Something he saw?

Something he felt?

When his cell phone rang, he was definitely relieved to see the call came from Nell.

"Tanner giving you a hard time?" he asked in lieu of a hello.

"Not yet," Max Tanner replied imperturbably. "At the moment, Nell is out cold — and I want to talk to you. Face-to-face."

Galen's hesitation was momentary. "Is Nell okay?"

"I don't know."

"How long's she been out?"

"More than an hour."

This time, Galen didn't hesitate. "I'll be right there."

It required no more than two minutes for him to reach the front door, where he found a very grim Max Tanner waiting for him. Galen had been in this situation before, "meeting" for the first time someone he had watched unseen long enough to feel he knew fairly well, but he didn't blame Max for the wariness that was plain to see.

"I'm Galen." He stepped into the house, offering no more than the brief introduction.

"Max." His lips twisted as though Max appreciated the absurdity of introducing himself to this man, but he merely turned and led the way to the living room. "Nell's upstairs, in bed," he added.

"You say she's been out for more than an hour?"

"Yeah. I tried to wake her just before I called you, but couldn't get any kind of response. Pulse and respiration are normal, and her color's good. Better than it was when she collapsed, as a matter of fact."

"Collapsed? It wasn't the usual sort of blackout? There was no warning?"

Facing the other man as they both stood before the cold fireplace, Max said, "No warning at all. We were talking, and she went out literally in the middle of a sentence. I have never seen her go out so fast or hard."

"It's been getting worse," Galen noted slowly. "More blackouts more often. Stronger pain. And I don't think she's been sleeping well at night."

"So I'm right in thinking this isn't normal for her."

Galen looked at him. "We've only worked together a few times, but from what I've been told, no, it isn't normal. Until she returned to Silence, Nell averaged a blackout no more often than every few months. She's been here less than a week, and this makes at least the fourth blackout."

"Is it because she's been using her abilities too often? Pushing herself too hard?"

"I don't know."

"You damned well should know," Max said in a harsh tone just this side of violent. "I know she feels this special unit you all belong to is something that made her life better, but that doesn't give you people the right to push her so goddamned hard — to use her up, burn her out, until she ends up in a coma with her brain fried."

Mildly, Galen said, "In case you hadn't realized it, nobody pushes Nell harder than she pushes herself. And just so you know, it's not really company policy to use up field agents and then throw them away. Plays hell with the payroll, to say nothing of recruitment."

Max drew a breath and made a visible effort to control his temper and his anxiety. "Maybe not, but even Nell admitted that some psychics risk more than a bullet doing this work. She's obviously one of them."

"True enough. It's also true that we don't know what price Nell might ultimately pay for using her abilities in her work. But she knows the risks. And accepts them."

"Because she's got a fucking death wish."

"Is that what you think?"

Max hesitated, then said, "I think part of her does, yeah. She's convinced she comes from something evil and that her family is cursed. That *she's* cursed. Doomed to live her life alone in any meaningful sense. Unable to let anybody get close because she's afraid this so-called darkness inside her will hurt whoever she cares about."

Max shook his head. "Coming home just made it worse, since she found the evidence that Adam did kill his wife — and that Hailey was not only involved with sadistic men but might actually be killing them. Some family tree."

Galen debated silently, then said, "Before we came down here, Bishop — you know who Bishop is, right, Chief of the Special Crimes Unit? He told me privately that he was convinced Nell's blackouts were only indirectly caused by her abilities. He believes they have something to do with her past."

"In what way?"

"Well, that's the question. It could be some trauma she's suppressed all these years, some knowledge she hasn't been able to face directly. Probably something that is connected to her abilities, since using them seems quite often to trigger a blackout, though there's no way to be sure until we find out the truth. But the thing is, Bishop said that if he was right about that, and if this investigation somehow made Nell begin to face her past, to examine her roots here, then it would be likely that the blackouts would become more frequent or more severe — as she got closer to whatever it is causing them."

Max was frowning. "Have you reported back about her blackouts coming more often?"

"Yeah. Bishop said to consider whatever she's saying or doing when the blackouts hit. Is there some commonality? A particular place? A certain line of the investigation? Anything to indicate there's something in particular her mind is resisting."

Still frowning, Max said, "I know she blacked out the day she arrived, probably here in the house. She was here today when she blacked out. But she also blacked out at the Patterson house, after one of her visions."

"The first blackout might have been as much stress as anything else," Galen suggested. "Coming home had to be incredibly difficult, especially when she knew one of the things she'd have to do was look for her mother's remains."

"No kidding." Max glanced at his watch. "She's been out an hour and a half now. That's too long."

"We'll give it another half hour. If she's not awake by then and we aren't able to wake her, there is one thing we can try. Another psychic, a telepath, can try to contact her mind directly."

"Would that be you?"

"I'm not a telepath. But we do have another team member here undercover who is." Somewhat dryly, Galen added, "Or you could try. Have you, by the way?"

"I'm not even psychic."

"No, but you're linked to her. Have you tried to use that?"

Max looked both startled and a bit annoyed, and avoided Galen's eyes when he said, "She won't let me in. Won't even let me get close. Sometimes her guard drops and I catch a glimpse, the flicker of a thought, but then — Anyway, how the hell do you know about that?"

"Sorry, but there aren't many secrets among a team of psychics, especially when so many of them are telepaths. Bishop knew she was linked to someone else and had been for quite a while. We guessed it was you."

"Bishop," Max muttered.

Not really surprised by the reaction, Galen said lightly, "I know, he can be a pain in the ass. Very irritating to have to deal with somebody who isn't often wrong. But in case you weren't sure about it, Nell isn't in love with him. He just inspires an incredible brand of loyalty from his agents. I've never seen anything like it, actually. Probably has a lot to do with the fact that he pretty much single-handedly changed their lives."

Max glanced at him, then cleared his throat and changed the subject. "You said we should consider whatever Nell might have been doing or saying when she collapsed, right?"

"It might give us a piece of the puzzle, yeah."

"Okay. Do you happen to know if the earlier blackouts here at the house came with any warning?"

"I'm pretty sure both of them did. I know the second one did, because I talked to her just before, and she warned me one was coming."

"Just the usual blackouts, the sort of thing she's experienced most of her life."

"Right."

"But when she went out at the Patterson

house, and again when she went out here today, it was without the kind of warning she was accustomed to. I know she came out of the vision today with a bad headache, but she insisted it wasn't one warning of a blackout. Still, it was bad enough that she was pale and afterward more than once seemed to lose the thread of the conversation." He didn't add that she had also been less guarded, a vulnerability he had taken advantage of by pressing her to talk to him about their relationship. "She seemed . . . distracted, almost as if she was trying to listen to something."

"What did she see at the Patterson house?"

"A very intense vision in which Hailey, as a young girl, was . . . involved . . . with a man who liked to play sadomasochistic games."

Galen nodded. "Today she was with you and the sheriff at the Lynch house. A vision, but no blackout, at least not immediately. All she told me when she filed her so-called report after you guys got back here was that she had a vision apparently unrelated to Lynch's death. A vision that told her Hailey and Sheriff Cole had been involved at one time. She said the vision was odd, that it felt different, but she didn't explain just how."

"The commonality seems to be Hailey," Max said slowly. "Hailey and her relationships."

"You sound doubtful."

"It doesn't feel right somehow. I can barely accept the possibility that Hailey might be hiding somewhere nearby taking out the men who treated her like dirt. But that doesn't explain Nell's blackouts. Both times she went out with little or no warning, the visions she had recently experienced were unusual in some way: the intensity of the vision in the Patterson house, and then — what was odd about this latest vision — seeing Ethan and Hailey in a completely different place."

"So you think it's not so much what she saw as how she saw it that might have triggered the blackouts?"

"All I know is that Nell is experiencing things she never has before. It's not just a case of the blackouts getting more frequent and more intense, it's also that the visions themselves are changing. But even that doesn't make a lot of sense. Sometimes it seems her abilities are getting more and more powerful, and at other times they seem almost weakened . . . muffled."

"As if there's some outside influence at work? Someone or something blocking her at least part of the time?"

"Is that possible? I've read a lot about the paranormal, but the research on anything like that is sketchy —"

"The official research, yeah. Luckily, we have our own. And, yes, it is definitely possible for a psychic to be blocked or influenced by another psychic. And we do have reason to believe that this killer, whether it's Hailey or someone else, is a pretty powerful psychic."

Max stared at him for a long moment, then said, "Then maybe that's it. Look, what if we're all — even Nell — looking at this whole thing the wrong way? What if we're only seeing what somebody wants us to see? What if Nell is so certain it's Hailey because that's what the real killer wants her to believe?"

Slowly, Galen said, "The original profile said the killer was likely to be a cop. Mix investigative knowledge and savvy with a psychic's ability to manipulate, and —"

"And you've got a killer leading you around by the nose," Max finished grimly.

CHAPTER
EIGHTEEN

Nell.

She wanted to ignore the summons. The pain wasn't so bad here where it was dark and peaceful and she wasn't worried about anything. Not about killers or her own evil bloodline, or even whether it was possible for her to walk away from Max this time. None of that bothered her. Everything was fine.

You have to wake up, Nell.

A stab of pain sliced through her mind like a burning knife, and Nell winced, tried to retreat further into the darkness. If that whisper would just go away and leave her alone . . .

There isn't much time left.

She could feel herself being pulled, drawn relentlessly from the peaceful darkness toward the cold uncertainty of consciousness, and she resisted as hard as she could.

You need —

Nell opened her eyes and sat up in the

same motion. Her head throbbed immediately, but at least it was a dull ache, soreness rather than pain. Her entire body felt sore, now that she thought about it. The question was, why?

Rubbing her temples gingerly, Nell murmured, "What the hell happened?"

She was in her lamplit room, on her bed. Covered by a quilt, still dressed except for her shoes. When she managed to bring her watch into focus, it told her only that she had been out for at least an hour and possibly longer.

Probably longer.

Jeez, what had set her off this time? She had been downstairs talking to Max, hadn't she? Sitting drinking coffee. Or had they been standing? He'd insisted they talk about them, about their relationship, and her head had really been hurting then, and — and what?

Another of these weird and sudden blackouts, apparently. Either she was simply more tired than she had realized — or her brain was getting seriously fatigued from the too-frequent use of her abilities.

The latter possibility was more than a little frightening, but Nell shoved it grimly aside. There was nothing she could do about that now. Nothing.

Nothing?

The whisper was so soft she was almost certain she hadn't really heard it. Almost certain. Still, she listened intently for several moments, and all she heard now was, faintly, the murmur of voices downstairs, male voices. She didn't really have much extra energy to enhance her hearing, but what little she could use allowed her to be fairly sure that Max was talking to someone.

Galen.

"Oh, great." Not exactly the last two men in the world she'd want discussing the situation — and, undoubtedly, her — but close enough.

Nell pushed the quilt away and slid carefully from the bed. A shower, that's what she needed. A long, hot shower to wash away the cobwebs and soreness. Maybe then she could at least start to figure out what was wrong with her.

Then again, maybe she already knew.

"She's awake," Max said.

Galen nodded, then listened for a moment. "In the shower. You know her better than I do, but I'd say she won't be too happy to find us down here talking."

418

"She'll be prickly as hell," Max agreed. "But I think we both agree it's time to put at least some of our cards on the table. Especially if there's even the possibility that Nell's being influenced by someone else."

"That's the part she's going to hate."

"Yeah. I know." Max shook his head. "The question is, who's doing the influencing? Even with the profile . . . is it more or less likely that it could be Hailey rather than a stranger?"

"On the face of it, more likely. The kind of influence and control we're talking about is rare even among psychics, seldom possible except between mates or blood siblings."

"But?"

"But, aside from the fact that Nell's certain Hailey was never psychic, over the years we've encountered more than a few predators whose psychic abilities were seemingly enhanced by the sheer twisted evil of their minds. They were capable of some incredible things — including forms of mind control."

"It makes sense. And I guess the killer began trying to influence Nell because he became suspicious of her. But what would have given her away?"

"There's no way to be sure about that."

Galen hesitated, then added, "But we've known almost from day one that the killer was watching Nell, or was at least once." He explained about the photo Shelby had taken and the consensus as to its probable meaning.

"Jesus." Incredulous, Max added, "You're telling me this maniac has been waltzing in and out of Nell's mind —"

"No, not in the sense of direct communication. Nell would have known if that happened. Watching her, at least from time to time, certainly. As for how he's been blocking her, maybe even influencing her, my guess is that he made contact while she was unconscious or asleep, while all her guards were down, then planted a kind of posthypnotic suggestion deep in her mind set to trigger the headaches, maybe even the blackouts, whenever she got too close to whatever he's trying to protect."

"I had no idea that was even possible."

"Like I said, we've come across some seriously disturbed psychics. If we've learned anything, it's that where the will of the human mind is concerned, nothing is impossible."

"How the hell is she supposed to protect herself against that kind of thing?"

"She can't," Galen answered matter-of-factly. "Oh, she could throw up a shield around her mind, but she's not a telepath, so it's never been anything she had to learn in order to protect herself. Odds are, it wouldn't be a solid enough shield to shut out someone as powerful as this guy seems to be, especially given the fact that Nell's resources aren't exactly at their peak right now. Blocking a link is one thing; keeping out a determined psychopath who doesn't give a shit about kicking a door in is something else entirely."

"You said there was another agent here, a telepath —"

"Yeah, but helping Nell shore up her mental shields isn't something just any telepath can do. Psychics are oddly isolated in their abilities, unable to link up to help each other or increase their strength. There's only one exception I know of."

"Which is?"

"Mates. It seems to demand a very special sort of trust, and a lot more intimacy than most of us could stand, to allow two psychics to bond deeply enough to share their abilities."

After a moment, Max said, "And if one of the . . . mates isn't psychic? What kind of bond can there be then?"

"You'd know that better than I would."

Galen waited until Max met his gaze, then added, "But from what I've been told, the bond between lovers when only one is psychic is different from couple to couple. It depends on how strong the psychic is. And how strong the physical and emotional connections between the lovers are. Sometimes there's an actual telepathic or empathic link, sometimes not."

"Not an area that's been intensively researched, I guess."

"Not even by us. Like I said, it's difficult to keep secrets among a group of psychics, but even so, some things are more private than others."

"Yeah." Max almost visibly pushed the subject aside, at least for the moment. "Listen, before Nell gets down here, there's one more thing." He turned to the mantel and picked up a framed photograph, handing it to Galen.

Studying it, Galen saw an old family photo that appeared to be professionally done. It had been taken from the front of the house, with Adam Gallagher, his young wife, and his mother standing on the steps, and two other women in the background near the front door. Grace Gallagher looked both unhappy and several months pregnant, and the two women in the back-

422

ground appeared, from their aprons and position in the photo, to be family servants.

"What am I supposed to be seeing?" Galen asked.

"Just before she blacked out, Nell was fiddling with this picture. Sort of looking at it, but not really." Max shrugged. "We were — let's just say the discussion was a bit tense."

"Okay. And so?"

"And so, all of a sudden, she frowned at the picture, started to ask who someone was — and went out like a light. I checked the back of the photo, and from the date I'd say it was taken a few months before Hailey was born."

"Nell would know her parents, of course. Her grandmother. So it must have been one of these other women who caught her attention."

"That's what I thought. As I recall, there were times when Adam Gallagher did well enough with his investments that the family had quite a bit of household help, especially in those early years. Not live-in servants, but certainly a housekeeper and cook who came in daily."

Galen nodded. "Wasn't this something Nell knew? I mean, even if this was taken before she was born, wouldn't she just assume these other women were employees? It's fairly obvious from the pose and their clothing that they are. Weird that they'd be included in a family photo, but —"

"Not weird if you knew Adam Gallagher. He liked to see himself as the benevolent patriarch and lord of all he surveyed; having the household help visible in a family photo just enhanced his image of himself."

Galen lifted an eyebrow, but said only, "Then I'd think Nell's natural assumption would be that these women were servants. So why her interest in one or both of them?"

"What bothered me was that she wasn't even able to finish the question. It was like . . . like as soon as she paid attention to the photo, she was put out of commission."

"Because she maybe got too close to whatever our psychic killer is trying to protect. Or . . . the timing could be completely coincidental."

Max nodded. "Or it could be coincidental. Problem is, the only way I can think of to test that theory is to have Nell look at the photo again."

"And maybe be put out of commission for a couple of hours again — or something more permanent."

"Exactly. Not a risk I want to take. So I was thinking maybe you could look into it. Tap some of those FBI sources and see if you can put names to the faces. Look, it's probably nothing. But maybe there's a reason Nell isn't supposed to ask questions about one or both of those women."

Galen nodded and turned the frame over so he could open the back and get the photo out. "I can use Nell's laptop, scan this in, and modem it to Quantico. But unless one of these women has a criminal record or has come up missing or murdered, we aren't likely to find them in FBI files. This is a professional shot, probably taken by what is — or was — a local photographer; that's not really the kind of thing you tend to find in federal computer databases. You know anybody local who could check it out discreetly?"

Max hesitated, then said, "Maybe."

Galen smiled faintly. "You could always get Justin Byers to do it. After all — he is your man in Silence. Isn't he?"

"I just don't know why you didn't tell me sooner."

"Because I wasn't supposed to." Shelby frowned at Justin. "Nell told me not to say

anything unless and until there was an-
other murder." Her frown deepened.
"Come to think of it, she said *when*, not if.
I think she was expecting this. Poor Nate."

"If she's an FBI agent, of course she was
expecting it. You say they developed a profile, so they knew damned well there was
likely to be another murder." Justin
sounded more than a little put upon.

"I think it was more than that." Shelby
shook her head. "Never mind. The point is
that Nell asked me to . . . um . . . suggest
this line of investigation to you. The birth
records. It wasn't something she could
openly do herself and still be undercover,
and she knew you could be trusted."

Justin eyed her somewhat grimly. "And
she knew this how?"

"She just knew. Seemed completely sure.
Hey, she's psychic. I figured she'd know if
anybody would. Would you like a cup of
coffee?"

"No. Thank you. I just stopped by to ask
if you knew anything useful about Nate
McCurry. And to tell you Sheriff Cole
wants to go over the birth records himself."

"Don't know much about Nate, at least
not anything likely to help solve his
murder. As for Ethan, you don't seem too

bothered by his interest in those records." She smiled suddenly. "You got word you could trust him, right?"

Justin silently counted to ten, but even so his voice was somewhat tight when he said, "And how long have you known that?"

"Um . . . a while."

"Something else you weren't supposed to tell me?"

Shelby grimaced slightly in apology. "I'm sorry, Justin, but I promised Nell I'd do exactly what she told me to. It was almost like she . . . knew things had to happen in a certain order, that it was important they did. Or maybe it's less a psychic thing and more FBI investigative techniques. Either way, I promised I'd follow her instructions to the letter."

"Uh-huh. So how long did it take you to find those photographs that *seemingly* implicated Cole?"

"Not all that long," Shelby responded brightly. "He does talk to just about everybody, you know, and I have pictures of him going back years, so it wasn't hard. Of course, I did have to fudge the dates a little bit to make it look like he'd talked to the murdered men just before they were killed, but —"

"Jesus, Shelby."

"Well, you wouldn't have let me tag along if I hadn't given you good reason to distrust Ethan even more than you did. And the profile *did* indicate the killer could be a cop, so Nell didn't want to take the chance you might confide in the wrong coworker. Much better for you to talk to me, especially since I had to not only find out what you knew and suspected but also nudge you toward those birth records."

"Jesus," he repeated.

She looked him straight in the eye, smiling just a little. "Was I the only one lying?"

"I could charge you with obstruction of justice, do you realize that?" he snapped, unprepared to give in just yet.

"I imagine you could. And what could you be charged with? I mean, *is* there something a licensed private investigator could be charged with when he goes undercover and gets a job with the local police? Or would that not be illegal but just something your fellow officers would be really, really pissed about?"

Justin leaned forward on Shelby's sofa, put his elbows on his knees, and rubbed his face slowly with both hands. "Christ," he muttered. "Secrets really don't stay secret for long in this town."

"A more-or-less established fact. Whoever named this town had a wonderful sense of irony."

"You're telling me Nell knew all along that I've been working for Max?"

"Apparently so. I guess she didn't tell him she knew, huh? Maybe because he wasn't honest about it himself."

Justin drew a breath and let it out slowly as he sat up straight again. "Oh what a tangled web we weave. I knew somebody was going to get tripped up by it."

"Mixing your metaphors. I think. Look, if it makes you feel any better, Nell really is good at this stuff, Justin. And she was always secretive even before she got that federal badge. Plus, they were pretty sure the killer was a cop, so everybody had to be undercover and had to be careful who told who what, so —"

"Everybody?"

"Yeah, well, I think there are others. Don't know for sure, because Nell wouldn't say, but I don't think she's down here alone."

"Does Sheriff Cole know this?"

"He does now, I expect. Nell was planning to tell him today. She left a message on my voice mail, and I got it when you brought me back here after lunch."

"That would have been before we got the call about Nate McCurry."

"That she told Ethan? Yeah, I think so. Why?"

"Another fluent liar," Justin said with a sigh. "He admitted that he had talked to Nell but made out that it was just to get her psychic take on the investigation."

"Probably true enough, at least as to his motives before she told him who she really was."

Justin frowned. "If she told him who and what she was, then she must have told him the FBI profile pointed to a cop being the killer."

"That was the plan."

"He didn't act like he suspected me. Because he's a good actor, or because Nell told him about me?"

"I wouldn't have said he's a good actor, but he's always been capable of keeping his thoughts to himself. Want me to call Nell and ask?"

"No. Not right now, anyway. I talked to Max about an hour ago, and he said Nell was sleeping."

"Sleeping? This early?"

"A blackout."

"Nell has blackouts? Why?"

With faint mockery, Justin said, "You mean there's actually something you *don't* know?"

"Just explain about the blackouts, will you, please?"

He did, keeping it brief, then added, "She's been under a lot of strain, obviously. Coming home after so many years and being undercover here. And, apparently, using her abilities takes a lot out of her just on a normal day. Which she probably hasn't had since she got here. Max is worried about her."

"I'm worried about her," Shelby admitted. "When I was out at her place yesterday morning, she looked awfully tired. And worried. And if the killer suspects her —"

"Hold on." Justin stared at her. "I know Max has been concerned about that too, but you make it sound like more of a certainty than a possibility. Why would the killer suspect Nell? I don't mean to brag, but if I didn't guess she was a federal cop, I doubt anyone else has."

Shelby explained about the photograph she had taken and what it was likely to mean.

"Shit. You mean we not only have a killer who's probably a cop but is also psychic?"

"That seems to be the prevailing opinion, yeah."

"Can this get any more complicated?"

"I'm just wondering if it can get any more creepy." Shelby sighed. "That picture shook Nell, and I don't blame her for being spooked. If you'll pardon the pun. It must be awful to know some evil killer could be hanging around in the ether watching you. Invisibly, yet. How can she possibly know when he's watching and when he isn't?"

Justin leaned back and frowned. "He. After what was done to Nate McCurry, I was at least half convinced we should be looking for a woman."

"A female cop? There are only half a dozen or so in Silence, aren't there?"

"About that."

"Any likely suspects?"

Justin thought fleetingly of Kelly Rankin and her sober warning to him to watch his back. Just one good cop warning another, or something more? "I don't know any of them well enough to even guess. But this latest murder . . . leaving McCurry like that . . ."

"A spiteful gesture?"

"Or a furious one."

"Or," Shelby suggested, "meant to look

that way. You know, if I was a male killer trying to throw off the police, I might try something like that."

"To throw us off track?"

"Well, think about it. The first three murders, everything goes exactly as he plans. The men die, their nasty secrets come spilling out, and all you cops are very focused on that aspect of the crimes. Just the way he wants you to be. Then George Caldwell apparently pokes his nose into things and becomes a victim, and because the killer can't make him fit the pattern as well, suddenly that murder stands out from the rest. You're looking at it differently, more closely. Now the killer's got a potential problem. You're not looking at what he wants you to, so there's a greater chance of you finding out things he doesn't want you to know. So he kills again, much more quickly than before, and at this murder scene he leaves a big, bold clue for you to find."

With a rueful smile, she added, "Five will get you ten you find out that scarf belonged to a particular woman."

"And we get led down another garden path," Justin said.

They stared at each other for a moment, then Shelby said, "You know, I think maybe you should call Max, and I should call Nell. I think it's time we pooled all our information."

"Past time," Justin said, and reached for his cell phone.

Ethan was on the phone with the mayor when Justin came by his office sometime after six to drop off the copies of the birth records, so all he did was cover the receiver with his hand and say briefly, "Thanks. Isn't this supposed to be your weekend off? Go home and get some sleep. You look like hell."

"That scarf we found with McCurry —"

"We're trying to run it down, but Saturday isn't the best time to get anything like that done fast. If we make any progress, I'll call you. Go home."

Justin hesitated, then nodded and left the office.

Ethan took his hand away from the receiver. "Casey, I'm not pissed you called them in. Well, not very pissed. But how you could have even imagined it might be me —"

"I just couldn't take the chance, Ethan, you know that. We had to have a completely impartial investigation by people unconnected to your office, and it had to be done fast and quietly. I didn't want to bring in the state police, so the FBI was the best answer. Meeting Nell seemed providential."

"I wonder if she'd agree," Ethan murmured.

Mayor Lattimore sighed. "I know it's been rough on her, coming back here. But at least maybe she'll get some sense of closure out of it."

"Yeah. Maybe. Look, Casey, I have a new murder on my plate and a desk piled with work. I'll talk to you tomorrow."

"All right. And I'll do my best to keep the town council from doing anything rash."

"Like firing me? I appreciate that."

"They're scared, Ethan."

"Yeah, I know. We'll talk tomorrow, Casey. 'Bye."

"Good night, Ethan."

He hung up the phone and for several minutes stared broodingly at the far wall of his office. Nate McCurry. Jesus Christ. Nobody else knew yet — or at least he didn't think anyone did — but Nate was yet another of Hailey's onetime lovers.

Ethan wouldn't have known about it except that Nate had seen him and Hailey leaving a motel out on the highway and had later warned Ethan that Hailey was "nothing but trouble."

Ethan hadn't taken too kindly to the warning.

Still, he'd managed to convince Nate to mind his own business and keep his mouth shut about the business of others, and he hadn't thought much about the other man since.

Until today.

He hadn't yet seen the crime-scene photos, but Justin had reported what he and the photographer uncovered — so to speak. That scarf tied in a way that seemed an obvious intent to mock and humiliate the dead man.

It sounded like something a woman would do.

It sounded like something Hailey would do.

He hadn't intended to fall in love with her. Hadn't wanted to. When it started between them, he had believed what she obviously believed, that it was just sex, just a good time between a couple of people who had known each other for most of their lives and were comfortable together.

His marriage had broken up by then, and Hailey had seemed just what he needed — an undemanding bed partner uninterested in anything else. A bed partner, moreover, who was so skilled and uninhibited that she gave him quite a few heated, mind-blowing memories he knew he'd have for the rest of his life.

Then, somehow, as the weeks passed, he realized he was bothered by her insistence on secrecy. Bothered by the faded scars on her otherwise beautiful body. Bothered by her refusal to talk about her life outside the bed they shared for a few hours every week. Bothered by the look in her eyes whenever he had tried, awkwardly, to ask for more from her than sex.

What bothered him now was the certainty that it had been Hailey who had precipitated that final argument. He had been pushing, trying to get closer to her, and even though the sex had continued to be explosive and she had seemed to at least need that, she had chosen to walk away rather than allow him to deepen the relationship.

It wasn't her style to end a relationship quietly; she preferred or needed drama, needed to be able to control the breakup, as she controlled everything else in her life. Needed to be able to pretend it didn't matter to her.

Ethan wondered if he wasn't pretending

himself when he believed it had mattered to her. That he had mattered to her. But he'd been angry and baffled, and it had seemed best then not to protest when she said it was over. Time, he'd thought, they just needed time, *she* needed time. Time to herself, time without him pushing and prodding. So he'd waited a few weeks.

The scene Nell had "seen" had actually taken place in early February; Ethan hadn't tried to approach Hailey again until nearly the end of March. He had found her chilly and elusive and had told himself he had to be patient.

But only a few weeks later, with nothing settled between them, Hailey had shocked the town by running off with Glen Sabella, a married father of two.

As far as Ethan knew, no one in Silence had seen her since. Except, possibly, five murdered men.

"Is it you, Hailey?" he murmured. "Are you doing this? And if you are . . . why haven't you come after me?"

CHAPTER
NINETEEN

Nell poured what must have been her third cup of coffee from the pot on the dining room table, then leaned back and thought absently that the formal dining room of this old house had certainly never before hosted a gathering like this one.

Two FBI agents, a cop-turned-private-investigator-turned-cop-again, a rancher with a political science degree, and a photographer who looked more like a fashion model.

None of them quite what they appeared to be.

And all of them wary — except for Shelby, of course.

"Anybody else want the last of the sesame chicken?" Shelby waited for the others to shake their heads, then drew the paper carton toward her and dug in happily. "Now I wish we'd brought some of those sugary pastries as well," she told Justin.

"Where do you put it all?" he asked, mildly fascinated.

"I burn, I don't store. Calories, I mean." She waved her chopsticks in Nell's general direction. "Hey, I meant to ask earlier how you knew Justin was one of the good guys. Psychic stuff?"

Nell smiled faintly. "We ran background checks on everybody in the sheriff's department, of course. Justin stood out initially because he hadn't been here very long, because he'd moved here from Atlanta, and because he had no family here. Plus, shifting from cop to private investigator and back to cop again definitely seemed . . . interesting."

"I thought I'd covered that base," Justin murmured.

"You nearly did," Nell assured him. "But we dig deeper than prospective employers — which is why we found the private investigator's license when Ethan Cole didn't."

"So how'd you know he was working for Max?" Shelby asked.

"When we checked more closely, we found that he and Max had been roommates in college. Also that Max had called him several times just before Justin moved to Silence, yet the two of them were never seen together publicly once Justin lived here. So it just made sense."

"In our world, anyway," Galen murmured, sipping his coffee.

"I think it's all fascinating," Shelby said unnecessarily. "I mean, I know it's a murder investigation and that men are dead, but finding out about all this stuff that's been going on behind the scenes is definitely fascinating."

"But is it helpful?" Nell reached out and tapped a file folder lying on the table. "You and Justin didn't find anything suspicious in these birth records at all?"

"Nothing that looked suspicious to us. Maybe Ethan will find something."

Justin said, "I didn't tell him I made copies of the copies or that I was bringing a set here tonight. Matter of fact, I didn't tell him I was coming here at all. He thinks I'm at home."

Since he sounded slightly guilty, Nell said, "It's more important for Ethan to go over those birth records than to be here listening to a rehash of information. So far, we have nothing new to tell him, at least not in the way of solid evidence or a new lead. Besides which, finding out how the birth records come into it would just put him off. He's had about all he can take of psychic abilities, at least for now."

Max stirred slightly and said to Nell, "I

441

know you went to the courthouse a few days ago. Was that when you found a reason to believe the records might be important?"

She nodded. "Being here to settle my family's estate gave me a good reason to go there at least once, but I wasn't really looking for anything to help investigate the murders. Then, while I was there, I got a quick image of George Caldwell, and I knew he'd found something he hadn't expected to find while he was looking through old parish birth records. I couldn't tell what it was, but I felt sure it was what got him killed."

Justin was watching her steadily. "And you still believe Hailey could be the killer?"

Nell answered carefully, just as she always did when faced with that question. "I believe Hailey is a common denominator in the first three murders. So far, I haven't heard of any connection with George Caldwell, but since I believe he was killed for a different reason, I don't expect to find one."

"And Nate McCurry?"

"Too early to know anything for certain. But judging by what you said about the way that scarf was tied, it's at least possible he was killed by a woman."

"And Shelby's idea that it could have been something done to mislead us?"

"That is also possible." Nell sighed. "When I checked my e-mail a little while ago, there was a note from Quantico that they haven't had any luck tracking down either her or Glen Sabella, so one or both of them could be nearby."

"But how likely is that?" Max objected. "Nearby all these months yet not seen by anyone? Besides which, everyone seems agreed that this killer is psychic in an unusually powerful way, and you're positive Hailey never has been."

"You think it's a coincidence that the first three victims were all her past lovers?"

"I think the term *lover* is stretching the truth a mile, but, no, I don't think it's a coincidence. I just don't think Hailey killed those men."

"Then they were killed because of her." The moment the words were out of her mouth, Nell realized with an odd little chill that it was the truth. "Because of her," she repeated slowly.

Max was frowning. "We know Patterson played his masochistic little games with Hailey in his basement when she was just a kid, and according to Ethan, Lynch dressed her up like a little girl for his sexual kicks. What about Ferrier? You said they were involved, but you didn't say he hurt her."

"I don't think he did." Nell shook her head slowly. "At least not in a way that Hailey didn't somehow enjoy."

"Yuck," Shelby murmured.

Nell agreed with a grimace. "It isn't what most women would enjoy, but Hailey . . . seemed to enjoy it, even revel in it, at least judging by what I saw. Still, that doesn't mean he didn't abuse her in some way."

Galen said, "Maybe from the perspective of an outsider, he did. Maybe all these men — at least aside from Caldwell — are being killed to punish them for what they did to Hailey."

"Because they hurt her?" Shelby said.

"Maybe," Nell said. "Or because they . . . corrupted her. This killer, whoever he is, could have blamed the men rather than Hailey for her lifestyle. He sees or somehow knows about the secretive, sexually brutal relationships, and he believes those men defiled her."

"Because he's in love with her?" Galen suggested.

"Could be. Hate and jealousy combined

444

can be powerful motivators."

"Why start killing them when he did?" Max asked, then answered his own question. "Because she left. She ran away with another man, got disinherited by her own father, so it wasn't likely she'd come back, and the killer blamed all the men in her life for taking her away from him."

"It tracks," Justin said. "And making it harder for us, the killer himself might never have had any direct contact with Hailey; plenty of scorned lovers are scorned only in their imaginations and fantasy lives."

Intently, Shelby said, "So he might have built up this whole relationship with Hailey in his mind, put her on a pedestal, fantasized about her — and then he began to find out about these other men. But instead of her falling off the pedestal, he saw her as a victim and blamed the men who had victimized her."

"It was probably the only way he could allow himself to go on loving her," Nell said. "Self-deception is one of our strongest defense mechanisms."

Shelby reached over to tap the file of birth records. "So what do these have to do with it?"

Nell tried to remember the flash she'd

gotten at the courthouse, but it had been more a fleeting image and sense of knowledge than an actual vision. "I don't know. Maybe nothing, directly. I mean, it might have nothing to do with Hailey at all, just some bit of information the killer didn't want exposed. Maybe something that linked him to one or all of the first three murders."

"Oh, great," Justin muttered. "Let's widen the range of possibilities even more. Why is it that each time we find out or figure out something new, it does nothing except give us too much to think about?"

"Murphy's law," Shelby offered.

"The question is," Galen said, "what's our next step?" He was looking at Nell.

Rather than answer that directly, she said, "Justin, Ethan was planning to go over the birth records tonight, wasn't he?"

"Yeah, from what he said. The last few weeks, he's pretty much worked 'til long after midnight and then sacked out on the couch in his office for a few hours. I'd expect more of the same tonight, especially after another murder. And Shelby and I can vouch for the fact that it'd take one person hours and hours to go over all these records."

"I'm certainly not likely to see anything

446

you two missed," Nell said. "You're a good cop, and Shelby knows this town and its people. So as far as these records go, we'll just have to see if Ethan notices anything."

Max said, "It's too late for you to check out Caldwell's apartment or Nate Mc-Curry's house tonight, even if you were up to it. And considering the possibility that the killer is somehow influencing you when you do try to use your abilities —"

"I'm still not sure that's possible," Nell objected, as she had when Galen and Max had brought up the subject earlier.

"You know it's possible," Galen said.

"Yeah, I know it's *technically* possible for a strong enough psychic to influence another's mind. I just don't believe I could be influenced and not know it. Not feel it somehow."

"If he's only able to reach you while you're asleep or in a blackout," Max pointed out, "how would you know? Nell, you've been blacking out too often, and it always seems to be either immediately after a vision or when you've pushed yourself too hard. Who's to say he hasn't found a way to make damned sure if you get too close to figuring out who he is you'll black out?"

"Even if that's true, I can't stop looking for him," Nell said. "It's my job, the reason I'm here."

"Yeah, we know that. I know that. But you won't solve this if you're out cold or worse. All I'm saying is that it might not be such a good idea for you to try to use your abilities again, at least not anytime soon."

"In the meantime," Galen said after checking his watch, "it's nearly ten, and I think we'll all agree it's been a very long day. What say we start fresh in the morning?"

Nell was conscious of an uneasy sense of time ticking away, but told herself it was only because things were finally starting to come together now. That was all.

"Suits me," she said firmly.

It was after eight when Ethan finally managed to settle down at his desk with the copies of parish birth records, and he was so tired by then he was afraid he wouldn't see something important if it reared up and bit him on the nose. Still, he grimly drank black coffee, turned his office television to CNN with the volume down low, and began going through the records.

It must have been at least a couple of hours and several cups of coffee later that one of the records caught his attention and made him concentrate harder. He'd already found the birth records for several of his deputies and most of the thirty-five-to-forty-year-olds he knew in town without seeing anything odd, but something about this record nagged at him.

Why?

Place, time, father's name, mother's name —

Mother's name.

Ethan Cole knew the history and people of Silence very well indeed. He'd made it his business to know, and for a good many years. So he was pretty current in terms of who was getting divorced or married, who was expecting a baby, who might be in trouble financially, who had drinking problems, and who was cheating on a spouse.

But that was now. Facts dealing with events in his earliest life and even before his birth were not things that had particularly interested him. Like most kids, he had accepted things at face value, so if a childhood acquaintance had mentioned at some point that his mother — his real mother — had died years before, Ethan wouldn't have questioned or doubted. He'd probably felt no more than a quick rush of fellowship for another semi-orphan and may even have complained himself that his own father's remarriage to Max Tanner's mother had landed him with a new mother and younger sibling who were demanding all the time and attention his father could spare after endless ranch work.

A moment of camaraderie with a casual friend, hardly a blip in Ethan's life.

Until now.

He picked up a pencil and circled the name he'd found. "She raised him," he murmured. "Her name is here as his birth mother. So why did he say his real mother was dead?"

"You haven't said a word about me contacting Galen."

Nell didn't look up from the copies of the birth records she was studying. "What was there to say? You made a judgment call, probably the right one. We had reached the point where it was undoubtedly best to meet and compare notes." She paused, then added wryly, "Though it taught us both a valuable lesson in being undercover. Next time, we'll make damned sure our cell phones don't allow just anyone to access the menu or redial options."

"I thought that might have been overlooked."

"Yeah. Well, we live and learn."

"If we live."

Nell hadn't been surprised that Max had — without comment or explanation — remained behind when the others had left. He had helped Shelby clear away the remains of the Chinese takeout she and Justin brought along for everyone, giving Nell the chance to speak quickly and privately to Galen, and then had made a fresh pot of coffee while the others said their good-byes to Nell.

The coffee told her he expected to be here awhile.

He had been watching her more or less steadily most of the evening, and she had been highly conscious of it. He hadn't said much about the blackout, beyond asking her if she felt better, and since Galen had been present and Justin and Shelby had arrived very soon afterward, there had been no opportunity for them to continue the discussion that the blackout had interrupted.

Something for which Nell had been deeply grateful.

He and Galen had appeared to be perfectly comfortable with each other, which hadn't surprised her; Galen could make himself agreeable when he wanted to, and since he wasn't the type to play macho games with other men, Max had undoubtedly found him both informative and easy to talk to.

Informative. Nell hadn't yet had the nerve to ask exactly what the two men talked about while she was out cold upstairs, but the possibilities worried her.

Still, Max had seemed calm. Surprisingly so, really, given how much her blackouts seemed to upset him. Even the revelation that Nell had known from the beginning that Justin Byers was working for him hadn't seemed to bother Max too much, though Shelby's participation had startled him, at least initially.

But Nell didn't have to look at him now to read his increasing tension; she could hear it in his voice.

"You and Ethan seemed to get along fairly well today, all things considered," she noted, ignoring his comment. "When are you two going to make peace?"

"Whenever he's ready. I've been more than willing for years. But then, I'm not the one who felt wronged."

Nell did look up then, gazing across the table at Max with lifting brows. "It was hardly your fault or even your choice that his father left you the ranch. Besides which, Ethan would have made a lousy rancher, everybody knows that. Even Ethan knows it."

"I gather it's the principle of the thing. Or a question of fairness. The ranch was in the Cole family for three generations."

"And he would have sold it if he had inherited it. Anyway, his father did leave him other properties and holdings. The estate was fairly divided between the two of you."

"I was the stepson, yet I inherited what his father loved most. It bothers him. There's nothing I can do about that."

"So the peace is his to make." Nell sighed.

"Would you make peace with Hailey if she was standing here in front of you?"

"I don't know," Nell answered honestly. "I'd like to ask her why she made some of the choices she made in her life. If she got involved with all those abusive men because in some twisted way she thought it was punishing our father for not loving her. Or punishing herself for being unworthy of his love."

"Is that what you think?"

"It makes sense. Maybe I'm wrong, maybe Patterson seduced her or lured her into that basement playroom of his when she was a kid, starting her down a path she has to follow for the rest of her life."

"But?"

"But I don't think it was that simple. In fact, I wouldn't be at all surprised if it was her seducing Patterson rather than the other way around."

"Seriously? That young?"

Nell hesitated, then said, "When she was even younger, she . . . saw things in our house. Things that would have given her a very twisted idea of how relationships between men and women are supposed to be."

Max was silent for a moment, then said, "What about you, Nell? How did living in that house affect the way you look at relationships?"

"I got away."

"When you were seventeen. But any psychologist will tell you that most of our attitudes and ideas are formed before we reach adulthood. So how twisted are your ideas of relationships between men and women?"

Nell knew he was deliberately goading her — but she also knew it was a real and honest question, and she did her best to answer it honestly.

"I lived in my own little world, Max, you know that. Even at a young age, I knew there was something wrong with my father, something unnatural in how he treated all of us. So while Hailey was watching avidly and trying her best to be what he wanted or what she thought he wanted, I was trying to pull away."

"And me?"

"What about you?"

"Why were you drawn to me? Why was I able to get close to you when no one else could?"

Nell dropped her gaze finally to the records on the table in front of her. "I don't know. I don't even remember knowing you until — until you came home from college that summer."

"The summer before. When you were sixteen."

She nodded. "By then I stayed out of the house as much as I could. During the summer, that meant riding a lot. Exploring the fields and trails, the woods. I'd creep out of bed early every morning and throw a couple of pieces of fruit and a sandwich in a paper bag, then bridle my horse and ride away. Most days I didn't come home until sunset."

"It didn't bother your father that you'd stay gone all day?"

"He didn't like it. But by then I had

made it such a habit there wasn't much he could say about it. When I was younger, sometimes I'd be out riding and hear something — and there he'd be, in his car or on another of the horses, watching me."

Max drew a breath and let it out slowly. "Which explains why you were always so tense and nervous even miles away from this house."

"By the time I was sixteen, he'd stopped following me so often. I guess he'd learned that I was always alone and never doing anything he could have objected to. But every once in a while, he'd still turn up without warning, checking on me. So I knew he could. I knew I couldn't let my guard down for long."

"Jesus." Max shook his head. "Do you realize it's a goddamned *miracle* you let yourself get involved with me?"

"Is it?"

"Well, from my point of view. Maybe from yours it's more like the one huge mistake you made in your life."

Nell flinched slightly. "I never said that."

"No. You just ran out of my life without a backward glance. And after —" He drew another breath and, again, let it out slowly. But his voice was still strained when he finished, "— and after we'd made love for the first time that very day. We'd made love, and while I was still trying to cope with the unexpected . . . aftershocks of that, you were gone."

"I told you why."

"Twelve years later, you told me why. Then . . . all I knew was that you were gone. You were seventeen years old and, as far as I knew, completely alone in the world. I can't begin to tell you how many nights I woke up in a cold sweat, terrified that you were lost somewhere with nobody to help you, maybe even pregnant, having to do God knew what just to stay alive."

"I'm sorry. I'm sorry I didn't say good-bye, that I didn't let you know I was all right. I'm sorry I was too much of a coward to come back in all the years since. But as long as my father was alive, I —"

"You didn't have to come back to let me know you were all right. You didn't even have to pick up a phone or mail a post-card." Max's voice was slow, deliberate. "All you had to do was let me in just long enough. What would it have cost you to open that door just for a minute, Nell?"

She pushed her chair back away from the table and left the room without a word.

Max followed her, not surprised when they ended up in what was arguably the most coldly formal room in the house, the living room. There were only a couple of lamps burning, so it was dim and cool and quiet. Nell stood as she had earlier that day before the dark fireplace and didn't seem to notice the missing family photo that had been on the mantel.

"Is it cold enough for a fire, do you think? No, never mind, it's so late anyway —"

"Not this time," Max said grimly. He grasped her shoulders and turned her to face him. "This time we'll finish it if it kills both of us."

"Max —"

"I want to know, Nell. I want to know why you chose to let me think you could be dead or starving somewhere rather than open yourself up to me."

"You knew I wasn't dead." She didn't try to escape his grip, just stood there looking at him with unreadable eyes.

He let out a laugh that was no more than a breath of sound. "Yeah. I knew that much. That was almost the worst of it, *is* almost the worst of it, this constant sense of you. In the quietest moments I can almost hear you breathe. Always there with me. And yet not. A flash of your mood, like quicksilver. A whisper of a thought. The flicker of a dream. Then you slip away from me again. Cool, distant, just out of reach — a part of me I can't even touch."

"I'm sorry."

"I used to think you were doing it deliberately, to punish me."

"Punish you for what?"

"For loving you. For getting too close. For doing whatever it was that drove you away."

"I never meant — I'm sorry."

He shook her briefly. "Stop saying that, dammit. You didn't know it would happen, did you? You didn't know that making love with me would cost you that little piece of yourself, would open a door you could never quite close again, at least not for good."

"No. I didn't know it would happen."

"And if you had known?"

"What do you want me to say? That I wouldn't have done it if I'd known? Even if somebody had told me, had warned me, I wouldn't have understood what it would mean. And I . . . probably wouldn't have cared even if I had understood. Not then. I loved you, Max. I wanted to belong to you. And I don't think it would have stopped me if I'd known it would be forever."

One of his hands lifted and touched her

cheek. "Then why are you shutting me out now?"

"It's been twelve years."

"That isn't it. I want the truth, Nell. What is it you don't want me to know?"

"Max —"

"What is it you don't want me to see?"

"You're very quiet," Shelby noted as they approached downtown Silence. She was driving, since they were in her car, and Justin hadn't had a lot to say.

"Just thinking about the investigation. All the questions."

She glanced toward his shadowed face. "Sure it's not that you're still mad at me?"

He sighed. "I was never mad, Shelby. But this is a dangerous situation, and Nell had no business pulling you into it."

"She didn't pull. She asked if I was interested. *And* made sure I'd be with a cop, in case you forgot that."

"You can't be with me twenty-four hours a day until this thing is over."

"I can't?"

He glanced at her but said nothing.

"You're just tired," Shelby said. "Look, if it'll make you feel better about me being involved with this, why don't you stay at my place tonight? I have a very comfortable guest room."

After a long moment, Justin said, "I'm not that tired."

Shelby took the turn that would take them to her house and said calmly, "Well, the master bedroom is very nice too, if you'd prefer that. Though I will warn you that I sleep with the windows open even in winter."

Justin waited until the car turned into her driveway before saying, "If this is in the nature of an apology, you really don't have to go that far."

Unoffended, Shelby laughed. "No, I wouldn't do that. But if you don't like the woman doing the asking, just say so."

"I'm flattered."

"Are you?"

"And puzzled."

Shelby shut off the engine, turned to her passenger, and then leaned across the console to kiss him. A moment or two later, she drew back far enough to murmur, "Still puzzled?"

His arms tightened around her. "No."

"Good. Let's go inside."

CHAPTER
TWENTY

"What is it, Nell? What is it you don't want me to see?"

"I've told you before." There was tension in every line of her body as she stared up at him. "You didn't believe me, but it's true. There's evil in my family, a darkness more than bone deep. And it's in me too."

"You've never done an evil thing in your life."

"You can't be sure of that."

"Yes, I can." His hands tightened on her shoulders. "I can."

"I wake up from nightmares, Max, horrible dreams filled with blood and violence. Every night since I got home, but even before, even years ago. You know that. You've caught glimpses, haven't you?"

"They're just dreams, Nell. We all have them, even the dark and violent ones."

"No, not like these dreams. I know abnormal, believe me. I've seen it in the flesh more times than I like to remember. And one thing I'm sure of is that my dreams are coming straight from hell."

"So what? Nell, your life has *been* hell. Surviving this family, what happened in this house, then running away when you were no more than a kid, having to build a life for yourself all alone. Living with abilities you barely understood. And then becoming a cop investigating the worst sort of crimes, the most evil, vicious killers alive. Of course you have nightmares. Without that outlet, you'd probably have suffered a breakdown a long time ago. Or turned out like Hailey, so damaged by your father that a normal relationship isn't even possible."

"What makes you think it is?"

"Let's find out." Pulling her closer, he kissed her.

A part of Nell had expected it to be different this time, but it wasn't. Just like on that warm spring day twelve years before, the instant his mouth touched hers and his arms closed around her, all she was conscious of was an overwhelming sense of being exactly where she was supposed to be.

She belonged with Max. She always had.

It was like recognizing an elemental truth, knowing that. Even with all the years and distance between them, some part of her had always known she could never be whole without Max, and realizing it now gave her a feeling of certainty and freedom unlike anything she'd ever known before.

"I think it's very possible," Max said.

Nell couldn't say much of anything because he was kissing her again and she was kissing him and feeling things she hadn't felt, hadn't allowed herself to feel, since the last time he had held her like this. It all washed over her in a tide of emotions and sensations, and she nearly cried out because it was such simple, uncomplicated pleasure.

"Let me in, Nell."

"No . . . you'll see. . . ."

"I want to see." He kissed her again and again, deep, drugging kisses so insistent that everything inside her demanded she give him whatever he needed from her. "I have to see."

Nell was never sure afterward if she would have protested again given a moment or two to think about it. Max didn't give her that moment or two. She felt him lift her up into his arms and carry her from the cool living room and up the stairs, conscious of a tiny shock that he could do that so easily and that she could enjoy it so much.

Then sensations rushed in and pushed everything else aside. Clothing falling away, sliding against her skin. His hands on her, warm and hard and urgent. The feeling of his powerful body under her own searching fingers. Her heart hammering against her ribs and her breath coming quick and shallow. Then the bed beneath her, disconcertingly soft and not at all like a thin woolen blanket that had barely protected them from the cold spring ground.

It was a dizzying reminder that a dozen years had passed, and her own body insisted she understand that. She was no virginal girl now, shy and half terrified of what she wanted, and Max was no longer that gentle, careful young man so intent on not hurting her that it hadn't occurred to him there might be another price demanded of them for those few minutes of incredible closeness.

"Nell . . ."

He was a little rougher now, more direct, more insistent, his hunger for her so fierce that it was a caress all its own, touching her deepest instincts, igniting a response as involuntary as the beating of her heart.

She reached out for him blindly, needing him to be as close as he could possibly be. Her arms held him, and it wasn't close enough. Her body held him, and it wasn't close enough. She needed him closer.

Closer.

It had shocked Max, the first time it happened. Shaken him. Nothing in his life had prepared him for the incredibly intimate closeness Nell had offered. No — demanded. Passion and need had seared away everything but instinct, and in joining physically with the man she loved, Nell's instinct had driven her to mate in the deepest possible way.

This time, he was ready for it.

Max caught his breath just as she did, staring into her eyes as her senses blended with his, her thoughts, her emotions. It was something deeper than sharing, something more elemental and absolute. Their hearts beat with precisely the same rhythm, their breathing was perfectly in sync, their bodies moved with a single will.

They were one.

Ethan set aside the birth record that puzzled him and continued through the stack of copies. But as the clock on his credenza ticked away the minutes and he read record after record, he began to feel restless, uneasy. He got up once and wandered through the building, not so much checking on his people as needing the exercise in order to think.

When he finally returned to his desk, the question in his mind was no less answerable for being clear.

It couldn't be that, could it? So simple a thing?

My real mother's dead. She died when I was born.

A boy's inexplicable lie? Or something else?

It was nearly midnight when Ethan sat back, over half the birth records still unread, and picked up the one that bothered him. This late on a Saturday night, there was no way he could check this out — unless he simply asked.

A good idea, or a bad one?

Take someone with him, or go alone?

He opened his desk drawer and pulled out the schedule to see who was supposed to be working this weekend, but even as he studied it he knew from his stroll through the building that most of the deputies were either still on the clock or else were gathered here in the lounge, playing poker or just quietly talking. Some of the married ones would have gone home to their families, but most would hang around just as they had been doing for weeks.

Waiting.

Ethan put the schedule away, still undecided. He picked up the birth record again, staring at the circled name of the birth mother. Supposed birth mother.

He was cop enough to know that people found the oddest, most inexplicable reasons and rationalizations for murder, but he couldn't think of any reason why this name on a birth record could have gotten George Caldwell killed.

My real mother's dead.

Did it mean something?

Ethan briefly considered calling out to the Gallagher house, but dismissed the idea almost as soon as it occurred to him. No. Despite his reassuring words to the mayor, he was not at all happy that the FBI had been called in behind his back, and he'd be damned if he'd run along behind Nell now, touching his hat and saying yes, ma'am, and no, ma'am, while she and her invisible partners solved the case.

Besides, she seemed way too convinced the killer could be Hailey, and the more Ethan considered that possibility the less likely he thought it was. Not that Nell had yet explained what she'd meant about Adam Gallagher's death, but Ethan couldn't see any reason why that death,

468

even if it hadn't been natural, could point to Hailey. She'd been gone by then, disinherited by an openly furious father, so why come back just long enough to put him in the ground?

No, Hailey being the killer just didn't track.

As for this birth record . . .

Making up his mind abruptly, Ethan folded the report and tucked it into a pocket, then got his gun out of the desk drawer and clipped it to his belt. He shrugged into his jacket and went out into the bullpen.

With several patrols out, there were only a couple of deputies in the big room, and one of them was on the phone. Ethan stopped beside the other one, who was sitting on the corner of a desk and contemplating a dartboard hanging on the wall nearby.

"Hey, Kyle. Where's Lauren?"

"Went home to take a shower. We aren't officially on the clock, but —"

"Yeah, I know." Ethan looked over to see that Steve Critcher was still on the phone, then said to Kyle, "Interested in taking a little ride with me?"

"Sure. Where we going?"

"Out to Matt Thorton's place. There's something I need to ask him about."

★ ★ ★

"You were afraid," Max said. "That was part of it, wasn't it? Part of why you kept the door closed as much as you possibly could all these years. Part of why you shut me out so fiercely when you came back here. I could hardly get through at all."

"I was afraid," Nell admitted, the lamplit peace of the bedroom allowing her to say what she might have resisted saying anywhere else.

"Because of how I reacted the first time."

She hesitated, then sighed. "I didn't blame you for that. What happened shocked me, so I knew it would be hard for you to deal with it. You were . . . a little freaked."

"A lot freaked. But fascinated too, Nell, you had to know that."

"I knew. I also knew it made you wary. Made you wonder if you would lose all your privacy. People need a quiet place inside them where they can be alone, and you were afraid you wouldn't have that anymore."

"That's why you shut the door so quickly, almost as soon as . . . as soon as we could both think again."

"It wasn't just your reaction I was afraid

of, Max. The . . . power of it scared me. I'd never been close to anyone, really, and then to so suddenly find myself that close to you . . ."

Max shifted his weight so he could look down at her. "And now? The door is almost closed again. Not slammed this time, just eased to during the last few minutes."

Nell didn't have to share his thoughts to know he was disturbed by that. "Max . . ." She shook her head. "I'm not a telepath, and neither are you. This connection we have, this doorway — I don't think it's supposed to be wide open all the time."

"Is that a rule?"

"Don't get angry. I'm not trying to shut you out because I don't want you. You know better than that, we both do. But I . . . there *are* things I don't want to share with you, things I don't want you to see."

"The nightmares. The visions."

She managed a smile. "No reason why both of us should risk a short-circuited brain."

"So I can share the pleasure, the joy, but never the pain or fear?"

Nell reached up to touch his face, her fingertips tracing the straight line of his grim mouth, trying vainly to soften it. "Would that be so bad?"

Max caught her hand and held it. "I love you, Nell. I've loved you since you were sixteen years old. And in all the years after you ran away, the only thing that made being without you even bearable was that tiny, distant connection with you. Sometimes I couldn't sense anything for months on end, but then out of nowhere I'd know how you were feeling, if you were upset or happy or worried — or afraid. I'd catch a glimpse of a nightmare or wake from one of my own dreams certain I had felt you lying beside me, heard you breathing."

"I know," she murmured. "I felt that too."

"And you felt it whenever I'd start thinking about trying to find you. Because almost as soon as I'd think about it, I'd know you didn't want me to. That's all, just that strong negative, that refusal. *Stay away.* Sometimes I thought I was just imagining it, yet part of me knew I wasn't."

"Max —"

"You could warn me off, deliberately, but you couldn't tell me why you'd run away, or where you were, or even if you were building a happy life for yourself. And I couldn't tell, not from the little that got through. But I knew there were hurts and worries and fears. And I knew you were alone."

"Sometimes it's best to be alone."

Max nodded as if he'd expected the answer. "That's really it, isn't it, Nell? You have to be alone, have to keep that door between us closed as much as you can, because you're convinced the Gallagher curse really is a curse, something unnatural, dark, even evil. You're convinced that sooner or later it *will* drive you insane."

Nell drew a breath and released it on a little laugh that held no amusement whatsoever. "Why should I be the exception? It drove the rest of them mad, so why not me?"

Quietly, Max said, "I know the stories. After you left, I did a little research. So I know most of the Gallaghers who claimed psychic abilities ended up . . . under medical supervision."

"You mean ended up in padded cells screaming their guts out," she corrected. "All of them did, as a matter of fact. Sooner or later. Some, like my grandmother, lived to old age with their wits reasonably intact, so they were only called eccentric by their families and neighbors. I understand she was fairly rational right up until the last few months of her life. By then she had to be restrained."

"Nell —"

"She was a Gallagher cousin, you know, as well as marrying my grandfather. Her father died in a lunatic asylum. Going back two hundred years, long before they settled in Silence, the Gallaghers lost at least one in every generation to stark raving insanity. And they all had the curse. Of course, they didn't call it that back then. They actually called it a gift. Even a blessing. In whispers. 'She has a gift.' 'He has the sight.' And it drove every one of them out of their minds."

"It won't happen to you."

"No? How do you know that, Max, when nobody else can offer me a guarantee? I told you once that not even the doctors can be sure what's going on inside my brain, but most of them agree that all that electrical energy they can see on their various tests doesn't really bode well."

"I know it won't happen to you because I've been inside that brain of yours, Nell." His hands slid underneath her shoulders, holding her as if he feared she would try to escape him. "I've felt the strength and power of it, and I've felt that cool, confident reason at the center of your mind. Christ, you're the sanest person I know."

"Maybe now. But what happens later? Do you realize that there isn't even a name for what I can do? I see into time. Literally into time."

"Places have memories, that's what you said."

"Yes. And tapping into those memories at least has a rational explanation, one I partly understand and can accept as reasonable. But I can't explain how I can see something that hasn't happened yet. And I can't explain how I could find myself in Ethan's home watching him have an argument with Hailey that took place more than a year ago. And I sure as hell can't explain how I was able to be there, actually *there* in the past. She saw me, Max. Hailey turned around and saw me there."

His arms tightened around her. "You're sure?"

"Positive. I was there, physically there in the past." She forced a laugh. "Still think I'm not losing my mind?"

"Is that why you said . . . When you came out of that vision, the first word you said was *evil*. Was that why? Because your abilities worked in a way they never had before and you were convinced it was something evil?"

"I don't remember saying that, but probably. It's what I feel. What I've always felt. And it's stronger now, so much stronger. Max . . . you can't deny you've felt it too. That darkness in me. The blackouts coming more often and more suddenly. I think . . . I'm afraid it's just the beginning of the end."

"I don't accept that." He was tempted to repeat what Galen had told him about Bishop's private concerns, that Nell's blackouts could be at least partly due to something she was unconsciously repressing, but he was afraid it would do more harm than good. The human brain tended to repress information or experiences only for very good reasons, and the only thing he was sure of was that forcing her to face anything like that before she was ready to was a very bad idea.

"I know you don't accept it." Nell smiled faintly. "Hey, I hope you're right."

"But just in case I'm not, the door stays closed."

"Most of the time." Her arms slipped up around his neck. "But not all the time. You asked me earlier today if I could have settled for something ordinary, something that wasn't half of what we had together. I couldn't. Max, this is the one good thing that ever came of the Gallagher curse. And whatever the price is, I'll pay it."

"Jesus, Nell —"

She kissed him, inviting him closer. Closer. Opening the door.

Galen had long ago perfected the knack of napping like a cat, all his senses alert, at least half his mind completely aware of his surroundings even as the other half rested. A twenty-minute nap now and then, and he could function at top efficiency for weeks. He could also respond instantly to a threat or any summons.

Which is why when a call came though his cell phone, set to vibrate rather than ring, he was answering it while his eyes were still opening.

"Yeah."

"Anything to report?"

"Nothing to speak of. I told you what went on at the powwow after it broke up. Byers and Shelby Theriot are long gone, probably back at her place."

"Yeah?"

"Yeah. They had that look."

"What about Nell and Max Tanner?"

"Well, he hasn't left yet." Galen checked his watch. "After midnight. I'd say he's there for the duration. There are still lights on downstairs, but the lamp in Nell's bedroom went out a few minutes ago."

"You don't see or hear anything that troubles you?"

"Looks and sounds like a peaceful night. I hear bullfrogs and crickets, even an owl. Not a thing suspicious stirring out here in these woods. And since our killer struck so recently, I'd say it would take something seriously threatening to set him off again so soon."

"So you're feeling unnecessary as a watchdog?"

"Pretty much. Tanner's hardly let her out of his sight, and I'd back him no matter what the fight was about, so she's in good hands."

"Then maybe this would be a good time for us to meet."

"Isn't that taking a chance?"

"Yeah, but I've got a few things I want to show you, and I can't stay out of touch too long. Better if we meet up closer to town."

"And we're less visible in the middle of the night. Okay. Say where."

SUNDAY, MARCH 26

Doing his meditation thing was a bit harder than usual, not because he was particularly

478

tired but because he was keyed up. So he had to calm himself first, really meditate and get centered and balanced.

That was all bullshit, of course.

What he really had to do was take that leap of faith that was required whenever one left one's body. He had wondered idly more than once what would happen if somebody found his body while he was out of it. He'd used a camcorder to tape himself once, curious to see what his body looked like when he was gone, and had been disappointed to find that he'd merely looked like he was dozing.

But what if somebody tried to wake him? Would that jerk him back into his body? Or would touching him at all break the fragile connection that kept him tied to that husk of muscle and bone?

He hadn't yet put it to the test, choosing his meditation times carefully to make very sure no one would disturb his body in any way. That had limited him severely, and he hadn't been able to visit Nell as often as he'd wanted to.

So he had made every visit count.

It was really late by the time he visited her on Saturday night. Actually, it was Sunday morning, well after midnight. He got to her quickly, as usual, going straight to her bedroom.

She wasn't alone.

They were lying close together, almost tangled together, under the covers but obviously naked, and it caused him the most profound shock to see them that way.

To see her that way.

Ruined.

Ruined just like Hailey.

He wanted to cry, to scream and destroy things in his grief. How could she do this to him? How could she give herself to this . . . this cowboy with cow shit under his fingernails?

And this was just the beginning, he knew that. There'd be another man and another and another, all of them using her, dumping their seed in her and then moving on to the next broken spirit, the next spoiled angel. . . .

"Nell," he whispered, agonized. "How could you? I didn't want to have to punish you. I never wanted that. Never." He drifted closer, knowing that tears would have been flowing down his face if he'd had his body with him.

"Look what you're making me do. . . ."

It wasn't exactly a nightmare, but Nell didn't like this dream.

She dreamed she was in a very dark place, and someone was whispering to her, telling her to do something. She wanted to move closer to Max, to feel his arms tighten around her even in sleep, holding her safely, but the whisper nagged at her.

And worried her. An instinct deeper than thought told her that Max was in danger, that she had to keep the door between their minds and souls firmly closed and needed to move away from him physically.

She hated that. Hated leaving him. But she had to.

She dreamed that she gently eased away from him and slipped from the bed. There was moonlight now, streaming in the windows, so she could easily see to find her clothes.

The whisper urged her on, and she obeyed it, dressing warmly, finding shoes and a jacket. In utter silence, she got ready to go out, and then left the bedroom.

There were lights on downstairs, which vaguely surprised her. Why hadn't anyone turned them off? Not that it really mattered, but still.

She unlocked the front door and opened it, went outside onto the porch. Keys. She didn't have her car keys. No matter. The voice wanted her to walk. It wasn't very far, through the woods, that's what the whisper said.

Nell dreamed it was a cold night for March, but the moon was almost full, and it was easy for her to see her way. As she walked, the whisper explained carefully where she was to go, made her repeat it, then urged her a final time to hurry.

She walked faster.

Not far, that's what he'd said. Not far at all, and when she got there she'd be happy because an old friend would be waiting for her.

An old friend.

For the first time, her steps faltered. An old friend. But —

Nell.

But she didn't have any old friends in Silence, not really. Did she? She'd run away from them all a long time ago.

Nell, snap out of it.

She was even less happy about the dream now, because her feet were cold and this voice wasn't a soothing whisper, it was sharp and insistent and somehow grated on her nerves.

Nell!

She was about to yell back at the voice to leave her the hell alone when a disconcert-

482

ingly solid slap literally stopped her in her tracks.

And woke her up.

She stood there, bewildered, finding herself in a moonlit clearing in the woods with no idea how she had gotten there. Her hand lifted to her stinging cheek automatically, and a second shock went through her when she saw who had delivered the slap.

"The traditional remedies," Hailey said rather grimly, "always work best."

CHAPTER
TWENTY-ONE

"Jesus, did you have to hit me so hard?" Nell demanded, rubbing her still-stinging cheek.

"You're lucky I didn't knock you on your ass. Yelling at you sure as hell wasn't working. Boy, when you're out, you're *out*."

"Well, you still didn't have to —" Nell cut herself off and stared at her sister. "What are you doing here? Have you been in Silence the whole time?"

"Just since you got back."

"So — you didn't kill those men?"

"Of course I didn't kill them. Why on earth would I have done that?"

"Oh, I don't know. Maybe because they treated you like shit?"

Hailey laughed. "I know it's not everybody's cup of tea, baby sister, but I liked the way they treated me."

"Yuck."

"That's not the best word for it."

"Hailey —"

"Look, we don't have a lot of time for talking here. Come on."

Nell followed as Hailey led the way through the woods, realizing only belatedly that they were continuing to move away from Gallagher land. "Wait a minute, where are we going? For that matter, what the hell am I doing out in the woods in the middle of the night?"

"You don't remember?"

"Well . . . there was a dream. I thought it was a dream. You mean I walked in my sleep?"

"In a manner of speaking. Think about it. Try to remember the dream."

Nell tried, still automatically following her sister. Her mind was oddly fuzzy, and it felt sort of like pushing her way through a thick fog looking for something. But something in Hailey's voice had been too urgent to ignore, so Nell pushed her way through the fog.

She remembered . . . being in bed with Max, both of them falling asleep after incredible lovemaking. So much still unsettled between them, yet so much more understood and accepted. She remembered . . . peaceful sleep that had gradually filled with an uncomfortable, frightening darkness. And then . . . had there been a whisper?

An oddly familiar whisper, telling her to do something?

Her head throbbed suddenly, and she reached up to rub her temple. "Oh, hell. Not another blackout, not now."

"He doesn't want you to think about him when you're awake. Thinking about him gets you closer to what he doesn't want you to remember."

"He? Who is he?"

Hailey stopped and turned to face her. A shaft of moonlight found its way through the trees and shone on her face, illuminating her wry, mocking smile.

"He's our brother, Nell."

Galen used his pencil flashlight and studied the police file. "This is a hell of a thing to find out at this late stage," he noted grimly.

"Yeah."

"So how'd we find it at all?"

"These murders seemed so obviously confined to Silence, so clearly the product of a local, that we just didn't look outside the parish. But when we connected the first three murders with Hailey, I started to wonder about that. As secretive as she'd been, so careful to keep her sexual relationships quiet locally, there was every chance she'd been involved with at least one man outside Silence. So I checked

VICAP for similar crimes in the region. And bingo."

"Four other men murdered in the last five years," Galen said. "All of them left behind family and friends just surprised as hell to find those nice respectable men had at least one nasty secret, usually sexual. Different parishes, so none of the cops put it together they were looking for one killer. Somebody's even serving time for the first murder."

"Yeah. I'm guessing he's innocent."

"Sounds like. Does this help us narrow the field?"

"I think so. I cross-checked the time sheets for every deputy and detective who's been in the sheriff's department at least five years against the approximate time of death for each of these murders. Here in Silence, the killer could well have been on-duty and still carried out a murder, but I figured for those outside the parish he was far more likely to have been off-duty or even on vacation."

"And?"

"And I came up with only two names of men who were either off-duty or otherwise unaccounted for during every one of these murders. One is Sheriff Cole."

"Who we are reasonably sure is in the

clear. And the other?"

"Kyle Venable."

"Jesus," Galen said.

"Yeah. How about that."

"You're not serious," Nell said, lifting her other hand so she could rub both temples. The fog was even thicker now, and that plus the throbbing pain made it even more difficult for her to concentrate.

"Oh, yes, I am. Kyle Venable is our brother. Half-brother, anyway. Our father's son by another woman." Hailey turned and continued walking.

Nell followed, tried to think, to understand. "What woman? And when did this happen?"

"You make it sound like a car crash."

"Hailey, I don't —" She felt dizzy, sick.

"Listen to me," Hailey snapped, her voice intense. "Listen to my voice, Nell. Concentrate on that."

"My head —"

"I know. But you have to push through the pain, stay in control. You can't let him block you this time."

"Block me?"

"He's been in your head for years."

Nell stopped, her stomach heaving so strongly that she nearly threw up. "What?"

"You shared something, Nell. Something besides our father's blood. The Gallagher curse. Come on, keep walking. We don't have much time."

Nell obeyed almost blindly. "But what — how —"

"It happened, baby sister, before either one of us was born. As you may or may not remember, our parents had a few . . . difficulties in sharing the same bed. Apparently, those difficulties went all the way back to the start of their relationship. So dear old Dad had himself a nice piece on the side. Several, in fact, in those early years. Household help, usually."

"Oh, Christ," Nell murmured.

"Yeah, disgusting, isn't it? For what it's worth, I think most of them were willing. Seduced probably, but not coerced. He could be very charming when he wanted something, and he wanted sex often. He usually picked older women, widows or divorcées. You know — the type who were likely to enjoy sex but didn't have a regular man in their beds. And he liked variety, which is why our cooks and housekeepers never seemed to last very long."

"Are you saying he slept with other women under his own roof?"

"At least a few times he did," Hailey responded coolly. "I saw him. Don't slow down now, we have to hurry."

Nell followed, so numb she wasn't sure if she could feel anything at all now, except the pounding in her head. "And when he got her pregnant? Kyle Venable's mother? What then?"

"Well, to do him justice, he didn't know he had. See, she was different from the others. Never married and sexually inexperienced. Younger, prettier. Looked a bit like Mom, as a matter of fact. He got sort of obsessed with her, started trying to control her the way he tried to control us. She got spooked and quit, left the parish."

"Pregnant."

"Yep. I guess she was too scared of him to ask him for any help, or maybe just too scared, period. Being pregnant without a husband was still a scandal in those days, at least in most places. She was Catholic, formerly a good girl, so abortion wouldn't have been possible even if she'd known how to find a doctor willing to do it."

Nell was still fighting to think clearly, and there were so many questions in her mind she couldn't even choose one, so she just listened.

"Her sister, who was a young widow, lived near New Orleans. That's where she

490

went. Told her sister the story but made her promise that if anything happened, the sister wouldn't try to contact Adam Gallagher in any way or ever let him know there was a child. When it was time, and as the sisters had agreed, she checked herself into the hospital using the sister's married name. Maybe she had a touch of the sight herself, because she died in childbirth.

"So the sister, who'd been left fairly well off when her husband died, found herself with a child to raise. I don't know why she brought Kyle back here to live. Maybe she thought he needed to be near his father. Maybe she was just curious. Or maybe she thought she might need to contact him someday. But she didn't."

"A son," Nell murmured.

"A firstborn son; he was born a month before I was."

"Without the Gallagher name."

"But with the Gallagher curse. He knew he was different from the time he was just a kid. Started having experiences he couldn't really explain. Scared the hell out of his mother, and she finally told him who his father was. Big mistake, and in so many ways."

"What happened?"

"He was a voyeur as a kid. Liked to

watch people without them knowing. He started watching Dad. Peeking in the windows, hiding behind trees. He saw him controlling us like we were puppets or dolls. Saw him always hovering around Mom, touching her, stroking her in that way he did, as if she were a favorite pet. He saw him screwing the help like some medieval lord of the manor, treating women other than us as if they were no more than a handy handkerchief to jack off in."

"How do you know —"

"And then Kyle saw something else." Hailey stopped and turned to stare at her sister. "He saw Dad kill Mom."

Nell was dimly aware that they had reached the edge of the woods and that across a cultivated field was a house with several lighted windows, but she didn't take her eyes off her sister. "I tried to tell you."

"I know. I even believed you, I think. I just couldn't admit it. But it did happen. And there was a witness."

"He was watching?"

"Yeah. Peering in the window. He heard them argue, heard Mom saying she was leaving — and taking us with her. Dad accused her of having a lover, said she'd ruined herself, that she'd let another man spoil her. He started beating her."

With brutal suddenness, Nell saw a flashing image of a fair woman cowering, crying, a big dark man swinging big fists. She could hear a harsh voice yelling the same word over and over. *Whore. Whore. Whore.* Heard the blows, dull and wet, pounding like her head was pounding, splitting flesh, breaking bone, hurting her.

Killing her.

Grief washed over her, and the pain was so intense her knees nearly buckled.

"Nell."

She opened eyes she hadn't realized she had closed and stared into her sister's curiously impassive face. "I . . . I saw. *I* saw him kill her."

"Tell me something," Galen requested dryly. "Tell me what good psychic ability does an investigator when it so seldom even picks up on what's right under your nose?"

"He has shields. Not unusual, especially in a small town. There was nothing to indicate his shields were in any way different from anyone else's in Silence."

"You sound defensive."

493

"Well, I'm no more happy I missed it than you are."

"I thought psychics were supposed to recognize each other."

"Not always. That would make it too easy, wouldn't it? The universe would be giving us a gift. It doesn't do that, as a rule."

"Uh-huh. And is that little shortcoming included in the Special Crimes Unit literature? Because I don't remember reading it when I signed on."

"We try to keep it quiet. It tends to unsettle the new recruits."

"I guess it would. Look, do you think we should — Hey. What is it? Did you see something?"

"No. I didn't see anything. Get back to Nell's."

"What are you going to do?"

"Call out the troops."

"I saw him kill her," Nell repeated.

Hailey nodded. "Kyle found you later, when he went back to . . . nose around the crime scene. You were hiding in a closet, where you'd been playing with a litter of kittens before the violence started. You were pretty much in shock. Maybe he felt sorry for you. Or maybe our father's views had already begun to twist his thinking and he didn't want your pure little mind corrupted by watching your mother being punished for whoring around."

"He touched me," Nell remembered. "Put his hands on either side of my head. Told me it would be all right. That I'd . . . never have bad dreams."

"To his credit, he did try to make sure of that. But he was only thirteen himself, and his abilities weren't entirely under his control. He didn't really have the skill to do what he tried to do. He couldn't take the memory away from you, but he did manage to hide it from you, lock it in the smallest, darkest corner of your mind. Without even knowing what he was doing, he placed a block there as well, so that anytime you got close to remembering, you'd black out."

"It wasn't the visions?"

Hailey shook her head. "The only reason you so often blacked out after having a vision is that the visions use a part of your mind close to the block. Or maybe it's the same kind of electrical energy, since both the visions and the block come from the Gallagher curse. From our family, our blood."

Nell was silent for a moment, trying to

take that in. "Hailey, how do you know all this?"

"Does that matter?"

"I think it does."

Hailey turned her head and gazed off across the field at the lighted house, then looked back at Nell and said, "There's no time. Listen to me, Nell. That darkness you've been afraid of all these years? It isn't you. It was never you. It's Kyle. When he touched your mind, Kyle messed up, he left something of himself there by mistake, some of his energy, I guess, his essence. You were both so young, neither of you able to protect yourselves from that kind of energy, and he went so deep. . . . It's how he was able to make contact again when you came home."

"He's . . . connected to me? Linked to my mind?"

"Not the way Max is. He can't read your thoughts, never knows what you're thinking or feeling — and if you'll think about it, you'll realize you've never had a sense of him. As another mind, I mean, another person. But he has been able to influence you, even control you, when you were sleeping or unconscious. That was the whisper you heard sometimes. The whisper you've been hearing in your dreams ever since you came back to Silence."

Nell drew a breath and let it out slowly. The fog in her mind seemed to be clearing, but it was still difficult for her to absorb all this. "He's the killer. Kyle is the killer. And he killed all those men . . . because of you."

With a grimace, Hailey said, "Like father, like son, I guess. Only two kinds of women in the world, according to them. And I turned out to be the wrong kind. He couldn't stand it that someone of his blood had been . . . tarnished. Spoiled. But for the longest time, he couldn't bring himself to blame me. It was them. Those men. They had corrupted me, and they had to pay for what they'd done to me. So he made sure they did."

"We can stop him, Hailey. We can put him in a cage where he'll never hurt anybody else again."

"Yeah, that'll be great. But we have to catch him first. And I'd rather we did that before he kills Ethan."

Nell was conscious of a chill. "What?"

"That house across the field is Ethan's. Kyle has him inside, and he's planning to kill him. He's just waiting for you."

"Me? That's why he called me out here?

To see him kill Ethan?"

"You'll have to ask him why, but I know he's waiting for you. And if you don't reach the house in the next couple of minutes, he'll know something is wrong, and he'll try to get inside your head again. We can't let him do that."

"He will *not* get inside my head again," Nell said fiercely.

Hailey smiled. "No, he won't. Remembering what he didn't want you to destroyed the block, Nell. And his way in. But if he realizes that before we're ready, we'll lose the element of surprise. That's what they call it, isn't it, in all the detective books? The element of surprise?"

"This isn't a book, dammit."

"Yes, I know. The guns are real." Hailey reached inside her jacket and produced a pistol, holding it rather gingerly as she handed it to Nell. "He didn't let you bring yours, so here. I think the FBI agent should always get the gun, don't you?"

"The FBI — How did you know about that?"

"Never mind now. The point is that you have to get your ass in there, and armed is probably better than not."

Nell automatically checked to make sure the gun was loaded and the safety on, then said, "Why the hell didn't you tell me all the important stuff sooner, so I could call out the troops? I'm at least two miles away from a phone I could use, from any backup. Kyle has a marksman's medal — I remember that from the background check — so even if he does believe I'm under his control, it won't give me much of an edge."

"Just stall him, keep him from killing Ethan. I'm going after that partner of yours."

"Galen is —"

"Not him. The other one."

Nell blinked. "I still want Galen. He's a pit bull when he's pissed. Or even when he isn't."

"I'll see what I can do. In the meantime, you might try calling Max."

"Calling —"

"Oh, hell, you could always call him, even before you two carved your initials in that tree. Call him. You might be surprised how he can help you now that Kyle can't get in."

Nell would have said something to that, but Hailey gave her a somewhat mocking salute and hurried off through the woods back the way they'd come, leaving Nell to mutter to herself.

Hailey had always been able to do this, dammit. Answer only the questions she chose to, manipulate people into doing what she wanted without bothering to explain herself. So damned typical.

Even with the tensions and strains between them, she'd had the knack of carrying Nell along in a rush, overwhelming any objections or protests, do this, do that, hurry now — and Nell always found herself in trouble at the end of it.

There was entirely too much about the situation Nell found bewildering, but as she hurried cautiously across the cultivated field toward the lighted house, the last of the fog cleared from her mind and both her training and instincts finally kicked in.

The situation was definitely not a good one. She was one agent alone, and even if she was well trained and experienced, it would require more than surprise for her to get the upper hand against a psychotic killer who just happened to be not only a cop but also a half-brother.

And psychic.

She needed help.

Maybe Hailey could get the cavalry here quickly enough and maybe not. Nell had to assume the latter and make her plans accordingly, that's what her training and experience told her. She was alone, and —

Was she alone? She thought about that as she crept closer to one of the lighted windows and very cautiously peered through the narrow opening of the curtains and into the house.

The first window showed her nothing but an empty room, what looked like a den. But the second, the living room, was definitely occupied. Ethan was sitting in a dining room chair, his hands cuffed behind him. His head lolled, and Nell could see blood on the side of his face, though from her angle she couldn't tell how bad his injuries were.

Kyle Venable was also in the room. He was at the doorway of the room, leaning against the door frame. There was a length of rope in his hands. He was knotting a noose.

Was that what he intended for Ethan, suicide? If he set it up right, it could certainly make sense. The FBI could provide their profile indicating the killer was a cop, and there was, after all, no solid evidence clearing Ethan. Just Nell's certainty, and if Kyle had brought her here to witness this death, it was unlikely he meant to allow her to live long enough to testify on Ethan's behalf.

A body found with a note, the motives for murder and suicide painfully apparent, and who would question? The sheriff, last of Hailey's lovers still in Silence, killing himself after murdering all the men who had corrupted his love.

Nell saw Kyle look at his watch and frown, and she immediately drew back from the window and began making her way around the house to the front door. She checked the gun again, then stuck it down inside the waistband of her jeans at the small of her back, hidden under the tail of her jacket.

She knew she could get her hands on it fast, but would it be fast enough?

Useless to pretend she wasn't terrified, both because she was about to face a killer and because it was at least possible Hailey had been right, that Kyle had lurked in her mind all these years like a cancerous growth, stealing her very consciousness, twisting her own self-image. Nell hadn't had time enough to take in all Hailey had told her, all she had realized for herself, but that was clear, that possibility. It was terrifying, that something alien could have been with her all this time.

But it also offered a hope Nell clung to.

That the only evil in her had been him.

She had to know. She had to.

Nell stepped up to the front door and put her hand on the knob, then closed her eyes briefly.

Max. I need you.

She opened the door and went into the house, looking around with a frown, blinking in the light of the foyer, trying to give the appearance of someone waking up out of a deep sleep.

"Hey, Nell. Come on in."

Galen didn't bother to reclaim his watching post in the woods, because as soon as he neared the house he could see the front door standing open. His gut twisted, and he was drawing his gun before his foot hit the first step.

"She's gone." Max met him just inside the door, dressed but obviously in haste and pulling on his jacket even as he spoke. "Ethan's place."

Galen didn't ask any questions until they were in Max's truck barreling down the driveway, and then all he said was, "Is she telling you anything now?"

"A little, but I'm not getting everything. Bits and pieces. Something about Hailey being here, about Venable holding Ethan and getting ready to kill him. And about

503

Venable being her brother. Christ, how did he get her out of the house past both of us?"

"I haven't been outside for the last hour," Galen said. "We didn't think he'd move again so soon, and we knew you were in the house with her."

Max didn't waste time with condemnation of either his own obliviousness to the danger Nell had been in or Galen's absence. He just gripped the steering wheel harder and floored the accelerator as soon as the truck reached the highway.

"A brother?" Galen said, getting out his phone and beginning to punch in a number.

"Yeah."

"We've got to get some new psychics. The ones we have keep missing some pretty important stuff."

"I would have preferred to wait a bit longer before punishing Ethan," Kyle said, gesturing with his gun to indicate Nell take a seat on the couch at right angles to Ethan's chair and his own position near the doorway. "Let all my fellow cops stumble around in the dark a while longer searching for Nate McCurry's secret sins while Ethan looked like an ass. But what the hell. Might as well finish it."

Nell sat down but on the outer half of the cushion, making sure she could get to her gun. If she got the chance. "I don't understand any of this." It wasn't difficult to sound bewildered about it.

"Don't you?"

"No." She sneaked a glance at Ethan. His head still lolled forward and his eyes were closed, but she had a hunch he was at least half conscious. "I really don't."

"Oh, it's quite simple, Nell. I had to take care of you and Hailey. I had to protect you. That's what big brothers do."

"We don't have a brother," she said, not so much stalling for time as following her instincts.

"I know we were never properly introduced, which is a shame." He was smiling, relaxed. "We grew up in different homes and with different mothers, after all. But Adam Gallagher was my father too. He didn't know about me, you see. He didn't know until I told him. Last May."

"May? You mean — just before he died?"

"Well, that wasn't the plan. I knew he was upset, losing both his girls. You'd been gone for years, then Hailey. I thought he needed to know about me, that it would

505

make him happy. I even offered to change my name, to make sure the Gallagher name would go on."

"And the Gallagher curse?" Nell asked.

Kyle's smile widened, but his eyes were curiously flat. "I thought that would please him most of all."

"It didn't, did it?"

"No. It didn't. He threw me out of the house, can you believe that? Actually knocked me down the steps."

Intently focused on Kyle's face, Nell was surprised when she got a strong flash, a harsh voice yelling. "He called you a liar. He . . . called your mother a whore."

"He never should have done that," Kyle said reasonably but with an edge to his voice. "I had to punish him for that. Because my mother wasn't a whore."

"Was that when you killed him?"

"I had to. You see that, don't you, Nell? That I had to kill him?"

CHAPTER
TWENTY-TWO

Nell drew a breath and nodded slowly. "I guess you did. But how? Everyone thought it was a heart attack."

"It wasn't difficult to cause a heart attack in a man who'd been on the verge of having one naturally for years. As a matter of fact, I used digitoxia. And I had to be there, of course, because I didn't want him calling for help."

"You watched him die?"

"I enjoyed watching him die."

As much as she had hated her father, Nell realized in that moment that she would not have enjoyed watching him die. Even knowing he had beaten her mother to death —

Beaten?

"I knew he had disowned Hailey," Kyle continued calmly. "That you'd been left everything. I honestly didn't think you'd come back here. So I did some discreet checking just to see if there was any way I could inherit — without having to prove paternity, of course."

"Because you couldn't?" Nell concentrated on the conversation, on him. There would be time later, she hoped, to solve any lingering puzzles.

"Because he hadn't acknowledged me. Maybe I could have got the name legally, but so what? And I didn't need his property. If you hadn't come back, I might have done something about that. But you did come back." His face darkened suddenly.

Nell, realizing abruptly what he must have "seen" when he summoned her to come to him tonight, said slowly, "I'm here tonight because you wanted me to be. Because you . . . came to me. You saw, didn't you? You saw Max with me."

"In your bed. Did he even bother to scrape the cow shit out from under his fingernails first?"

She chose her words carefully. "He didn't corrupt me, Kyle. He didn't spoil me."

"Of course he did."

"No. I love Max. And he loves me."

"That's not love," Kyle said scornfully. "Wrestling between the sheets? Rutting like a couple of animals? Have you ever watched, Nell? Seen what it looks like when two naked, hairy bodies do that? It's

508

ugly. Unspeakably ugly. At least I didn't have to watch you do it. But Hailey . . ."

"You followed her. You watched her."

"I had to. She was sick, from the time she was a child. Sick. Randal Patterson infected her with his own sickness. Down in that basement of his, when she was just a little girl." His mouth twisted. "I wanted to kill him then. But I was just a kid myself, so I couldn't."

He shrugged and frowned down at the gun he still held with seeming negligence in one hand, and Nell took the opportunity to glance quickly at Ethan. She saw his eyelid flicker, his head move just a bit, and knew he was fully conscious now.

But it wasn't time. Not yet. Not yet.

She said the first thing she could think of to Kyle to keep the conversation going. "There were other men after Patterson. How could you keep blaming them rather than her?"

"She didn't know what she was doing," Kyle said, spacing every word carefully for emphasis. "But they did. They took advantage of her. I know she was upset when your mother went away, but —"

"Our mother didn't go away, Kyle. He killed her. You saw him do it."

Kyle looked at her for an unblinking moment, then smiled. "So did you."

"And you made me forget."

"I had to. With her whorish blood in you, I knew all it would take would be a trigger. Seeing her being punished, hearing her cry and plead and tell him she was really good when it was so obvious she was lying through her whoring teeth — that might have been enough."

Nell felt her stomach heave and fought desperately not to show the reaction. "Why didn't you . . . try that with Hailey? Why didn't you try to . . . to cure her sickness that way?"

"She never had the Gallagher gift. Oh, I tried, more than once. To reach her, to touch her mind. Even to go visit her while she was sleeping, the way I could visit you. But it never worked with her. I guess she was already ruined then, even though I didn't want to admit it."

"You visited me? While I was sleeping?"

Kyle smiled again. "All the time, before you ran away from Silence. When you ran away . . . I don't know. I lost you somehow. I wasn't even sure I could do it again when you came back, but it was really easy. Maybe because I knew you were there in the house. That must have been it, don't you think? That I knew where you were?"

"I . . . guess so."

"I had no idea I could make you do things. Started small, at first, telling you to turn over in bed. To get up and brush your hair for a while. To go up into the attic and find your doll."

"I wondered how she got onto my pillow," Nell said, forcing her voice to remain calm even though her very skin was crawling.

"You didn't figure it out, honestly? You had no idea it was me?"

Nell shifted her weight slightly, putting both hands on the cushion on either side of her hips as if to brace herself. Quietly, she said, "How could I guess? I didn't know about you. I didn't know I had a brother. And you wouldn't let me remember what you had done for me."

"There was no reason for you to remember." Kyle frowned. "I wonder if that's why you let Max Tanner into your bed, because you remembered you had the blood of a whore in your veins. Was that it?"

She ignored the question. "What was the final straw with Hailey? Why did you begin . . . punishing the men she'd had sex with? Was it because she ran off with Glen Sabella?"

Kyle laughed. "She never would have run off with him, Nell. She didn't care any more about him than she had any of the others. He just fed her sickness, don't you understand? After Grandmother died, Hailey used her house as a meeting place so they could rut. But that's all she wanted from him."

"You watched them."

"Sure. That last day, they had a fight about something. And he hit her. She just laughed, but . . . I didn't like it. I didn't like it at all. She always got dressed and left first, so I waited for that. And as soon as she'd gone, I went in. I had my nightstick. He was strong, but I caught him by surprise."

"You —"

"I hadn't really meant to kill him. Just punish him. But he wouldn't stop moving, wouldn't shut up and stop groaning. So I kept hitting him." He sighed. "Hailey had come back for something, I don't know what. She saw me. Saw what I'd done to him. That was when she ran."

"What . . . did you do with Sabella?"

"Buried him. And it was so easy, so simple. I thought it would feel different, killing someone I knew, but it didn't. It was just the same. Like swatting a fly."

"If he looks out one of the windows," Galen said in a voice hardly above a whisper, "we're screwed. With that huge moon, it's bright as day out here."

"He's not looking," Max said, keeping his voice just as low. "Nell's keeping him talking."

"That direct line you've got is coming in handy," Kelly Rankin said, double-checking her weapon for the third time. "Somebody want to explain that to me?"

"Later," Justin told her. "Max, how much longer can Nell keep him occupied?"

"I don't know. A few minutes, maybe." The past quarter of an hour had provided Max with ample understanding of just why the door Nell had flung open might be better closed most of the time; it was incredibly difficult for him to concentrate on two places at one time, let alone sort through the jumble of thoughts and emotions that were both his and hers.

Nell was trying to help him and he knew it. She was concentrating intently on Kyle Venable and what he was saying, not allowing herself to think too much about what that psychopath was telling her. And she kept her emotions damped down, refusing to give in to the horror and revulsion his revelations created in her.

But it was still distracting and not a little confusing for Max. He expected he'd get better with practice, and he was damned glad that door was open now with Nell in there confronting an insane killer, but he had to admit this could easily be more of a hindrance than a help.

"Just the two doors." Lauren Champagne eased up beside the others where they crouched in the shadows of some farm equipment at the edge of the field. "But there's a window I think I can get open on the other side of the house. That'll give us three ways in. Three chances."

Even with his attention split, Max looked at her and said, "That's your partner in there."

"If you're wondering if I can kill him if I have to, stop wondering." Even in the shadows of the equipment, there was enough light to show that her lovely face was utterly composed. "I have no problem disposing of rabid animals."

"And she's a crack shot," Justin murmured.

Lauren looked at him, one brow rising.

"The shooting range," he explained. "I saw you practicing a few weeks ago."

"Ah."

Galen said, "Max, you're the only one here who isn't a cop. If you've got Nell's gun, hand it over."

"Forget it."

"Max —"

"I'm also a crack shot."

"I don't give a shit," Galen told him politely. "This is potentially messy enough without having a civilian involved in a shoot-out."

"There isn't going to be a shoot-out," Max said. He swore under his breath. "Nell's in there. Do you really think I want bullets flying?"

"We're running out of time," Lauren said.

"And time is the issue," Galen added. "Or timing is. We'll only have one chance to get this right."

Max went still for an instant. "We have to move," he said. "Now."

"Killing . . . someone you knew? You mean Sabella wasn't the first?"

Kyle shrugged. "He was the first local. But Hailey had gone out of town sometimes, and I couldn't let those filthy bastards off scot-free, could I? They all had to pay. They infected her with more and more sickness, and they had to pay."

Nell, conscious of the clock ticking in her head, shifted slightly on the couch and said, "Which, I guess, brings us to Ethan. Why kill him, Kyle?"

"He's no different from the rest."

"Isn't he?"

"No. He just used her and tossed her aside like the others did. He fed her sickness. I have to punish him, just like I did the others."

"And what about me, Kyle? What did I do?" She kept her gaze steady on his face.

"You let Tanner into your bed. You're infected too, Nell. I thought the Gallagher gift would save you, but it hasn't. Don't you see that the infection is everywhere? I've tried and tried to cure it, and I think — I think the only way to do it is to cut it out."

"You mean to kill me."

"I have to cut out the infection," Kyle said, his tone chillingly reasonable.

"You'll kill me without giving me a chance to . . . repent? To change?"

For the first time, Kyle looked hesitant. "I don't want to."

"Then don't." Nell rose to her feet, careful to make no sudden movement that might startle him into using the gun he still held in one hand. She managed to turn just far enough so that the fingers of her left hand would be visible to Ethan without Kyle being able to see them move slightly.

Beginning with a fist, she began to very slowly extend one finger after the other, pausing briefly between each. Counting to five. She only hoped Ethan saw it, and got it, because she hadn't been able to think of any other way to warn him.

"If you kill the only family you have left here in Silence, you'll be all alone," she reminded him. "Is that really what you want?"

Kyle shook his head, more in reproach than negation, and his free hand reached for the rope he had set aside on a nearby table when Nell had arrived. "All I want is —"

Nell caught the flicker of movement in the foyer beyond Kyle in the same instant that she reached the count of five. She felt as well as heard Ethan wrench his chair sideways even as she went for her gun.

"Drop it, Venable!" Galen's voice rang out.

Maybe it was training or instinct that told Nell that Kyle would not obey the command. Or maybe it was simply the Gallagher blood or the Gallagher curse they shared that told her what he would do.

She saw him start to turn, to swing the gun toward her. Even saw, in one of those peculiar telescopic views one often saw in critical moments, his finger tighten on the trigger and his mouth curve in a smile.

It was as if time had slowed to a crawl. She was moving, leveling the gun Hailey had given her, throwing herself toward a chair that was the only possible cover nearby. She saw Kyle jerk before she heard the gun's report, saw scarlet bloom on his uniform shirt, then saw a second bullet hit him and wrench him around so that he was ironically in a better position to fire at her. Her gun bucked in her hand just as she saw the recoil of his own gun.

And then something slammed into her with the force of a train, and everything went black.

As soon as Nell opened her eyes, she knew that time had passed. A lot of time. She had that heavy, sandpapery-eyes sensation that told her she had slept for hours, yet felt remarkably well for all of that. At least until she moved.

"Ouch. Dammit."

"Serves you right. Don't move and it

won't hurt so much."

She turned her head cautiously to see Max sitting beside her bed. Her hospital bed. Her head throbbed a bit, and she was conscious of a restricted sensation in the region of her left shoulder and arm. "What happened?" she wondered.

"You don't remember?"

Nell thought about it and, slowly, everything came back to her. Or most everything, anyway. "Is Kyle dead?"

"Yes." Max grimaced. "Even though it took a bullet from almost every gun we had to bring him down. And even then, he still managed to shoot you."

Which explained the constriction she felt in her arm and shoulder. Heavy bandages, from the feel of them. Nell fumbled with her right hand until she found the bed's controls, then used them to raise the head a few inches.

"Ouch," she said again as her shoulder began to throb in concert with her head. "The bullet didn't hit anything vital, did it?"

"Amazingly enough, no. Passed right through. The doc says most of the heavy bandages can come off by tomorrow, and then you'll wear a sling for a week or so. He says you heal fast."

Nell eyed him, perfectly aware that his level and unemotional tone was about as stable as nitro. The psychic door between them was securely closed; she had slammed it shut the second she had realized Kyle would probably shoot her, knowing too well that Max would have shared her pain — and possibly more than that. But even without the direct communication, she knew Max Tanner pretty well. "I feel fine," she told him. "Rested, in fact. How long have I been out?"

"It's nearly five. Sunday afternoon."

She blinked. "What? I slept all day?"

"The doc also said you seemed to need rest — the body's way of healing itself. Galen informed me that you'd been shot before and had slept for hours that time too."

"Is that what this is about?"

"What?"

"You're upset because I was shot before?"

Max drew a breath and let it out slowly, the picture of a man holding on to his temper or his patience. "I'm upset you were shot at all. Either time. Both times. You'll have to forgive me. Seeing you lying there bleeding is not destined to be one of my favorite memories."

"It doesn't happen often. Most agents go through their entire careers hardly drawing their guns, much less getting shot."

"It's happened to you twice. And how long have you been an agent?"

Nell smiled at him. "I'm fine, Max. Really."

He stared at her for a moment, then reached over and took her free hand in his. "Don't do that to me again. Ever."

"I'll certainly try not to. It wasn't much fun."

"Is that why you slammed the door shut? So I wouldn't be able to feel what happened to you?"

"I didn't want to shut you out. But I had to then. Feeling what I felt could have incapacitated you just when you needed to move or react."

Max hesitated, then spoke slowly. "Look, last night showed me pretty clearly both the benefits and the drawbacks of sharing a connection with you. So I understand better now why you'd prefer to keep the door closed most of the time."

"But?"

"But . . . all through those years without you, knowing that door was there, always there, and I couldn't do a damned thing to open it myself, was . . ."

"Frustrating? Maddening?"

"Painful."

She held his gaze steadily. "Another drawback of hitching your fate to a psychic's. I'm sorry, Max, but I don't know any way to change that, to give you any kind of control over it. I think — all that reading you did over the years, you must have been searching for an answer. Right?"

"Yeah, more or less."

"You didn't find one."

A breath of a laugh escaped him. "Hell, I didn't find anything that even came close to explaining what had happened between us, let alone offered a suggestion of how I could become an active rather than a passive participant."

Nell chose her words carefully, all too aware that, despite love, Max could well decide in the end that hitching his fate to a psychic was not a future he wanted. "Is that what you want? To be psychic yourself? Or is it more a matter of control, really?"

"It's a matter of sharing, Nell. I don't have to be psychic myself, not if you're willing — truly willing — to open yourself up to me. In the bad times as well as the good ones."

"If the door had been open when I got

shot, you would have felt that, Max. I told you, it could have —"

"It could have gotten me hurt, yeah. But if it's a choice of hurts, then I choose sharing yours and risking whatever happens afterward. Because even with the distractions and potential problems of keeping that door open, every time you close it in my face I feel like you're pushing me out of your life. Every time. And that hurts."

"I don't mean to shut you out. I never wanted to do that."

"You're shutting me out now." He shook his head. "I got enough last night to realize that you're pretty sure that the darkness you've felt in yourself all these years was Kyle somehow. His evil, not yours. That's true, isn't it?"

"I . . . think so. I can't be sure, of course, but I knew as soon as I woke up that there was a lightness in me I'd never felt before. As if a weight had lifted. But there's no guarantee, Max. Nothing to say my abilities won't eventually . . . break my mind in some way."

"I'm willing to risk it. I've had twelve years of being without you, Nell, and the one thing I know absolutely is that being with you is what I want."

"And my work? It's important to me."

"I know it is," he said immediately. "I would never ask you to give that up."

"Your ranch is here. Your life is here."

"We'll find a way to make it work, Nell. All you have to do is say it's what you want too."

"You make it sound so simple," she murmured.

"That part of it is. Tell me you love me and want to spend the rest of your life with me. Everything else will take care of itself in time."

"Max —"

"It really is that simple, you know. All the rest is just a question of discussion and practice."

She had to laugh, albeit unsteadily. "Our future, boiled down to two sentences?"

"Well, we'll build on it."

Nell instinctively shifted to move toward him and winced as her shoulder throbbed a protest. "Maybe I'd better postpone any rash decisions until I have the use of both arms again."

Max lifted an eyebrow at her. "You're stalling."

"No, I'm not."

"That's what it looks like from where I'm standing."

Nell laughed again, this time with more amusement. She was grateful that Max was backing off a bit, because despite his confident words she knew there was a lot for both of them to think about. "Maybe you should change positions," she suggested.

Max's fingers tightened around hers and he began to move toward her, but then Ethan walked into the room, looking very tired and rather interesting with a square bandage over one temple.

"So you're awake," he said to Nell. "Good. The doctors were about to sedate Max."

"Funny," Max said.

Nell smiled at Ethan. "You don't look bad, all things considered."

"I feel like a fool," he said frankly. "Trotting off cheerfully with the killer. Oh, yeah, some cop I am."

"Where were you supposed to be going with him?"

"I'd asked him to ride with me out to Matt Thorton's place. I had found something that bugged me in those birth records and wanted to ask him about it. I thought I was being smart in not going alone. Picked the wrong goddamned deputy to ride shotgun."

"You thought Thorton might be the killer?"

"I just wanted to know why he'd told me when he was a kid that his real mother had died, when she hadn't."

"And why had he?"

Ethan grimaced. "He was pissed at her. She wouldn't let him go on some stupid field trip, so he decided she wasn't his real mother at all. Which would have been fine, except that he had to tell me his fantasy."

Nell frowned. "Okay, but — what set off Kyle? I mean, why did he decide to kill you last night?"

"I made the second mistake of telling him that I was going through the birth records. Looking for whatever got George Caldwell killed."

"Notice I'm saying nothing," Max said.

"You're saying it loudly."

"Boys." Nell shook her head. "So, did he happen to mention what *did* get Caldwell killed?"

"He didn't, but I intend to find whatever it was. Eventually."

"In the meantime," Nell said, "where are the others?"

"Back at the office," Ethan answered. "Now that everybody's out in the open, so to speak, working together to do all the reports and collect evidence seemed best."

"And," Max said, "you might as well use FBI agents while you've got them, right?"

"Right."

"What about Hailey?" Nell asked. "She wasn't one of the storm troopers out at your place last night, was she, Ethan? Because I know she couldn't shoot, and she always punched like a girl."

He moved around to the other side of her bed and frowned down at her. "No, Hailey wasn't there. What made you think she would be?"

"She's the one who told me Kyle had you and was going to kill you. After she slapped me out of that sleepwalking stupor he'd put me in." Nell frowned at him, then at Max. "She went for help. Didn't she find you guys?"

An odd expression on his face, Max said, "Nell, Hailey wasn't there last night. She couldn't have been."

"What do you mean? I saw her, Max. I talked to her. She was there."

"Nell," Ethan said, after exchanging a glance with Max, "your boss got in touch a couple of hours ago. The . . . remains you uncovered out at your grandmother's place? The FBI lab was able to use dental records to make a match, a positive I.D.

527

But it wasn't your mother."

"It's Hailey," Max finished slowly. "Their estimate is that she's been dead ever since she supposedly left Silence. Almost a year."

EPILOGUE

Max was hardly a two-finger typist, but it wasn't his best skill and getting his rather lengthy statement on paper was taking longer than he'd planned.

"Why am I typing this?" he asked Ethan. "Isn't one of your bright boys or girls supposed to do it?"

"They're busy," Ethan told him.

"Busy? Two-thirds of them are off-duty."

"After using up my overtime budget for the entire year, everybody's going to be taking vacation and sick days for a while. It's a statement, Max, you know how to write one up."

"Well, stop hovering, then."

"I'm not hovering. I just thought you might be interested in knowing that Nell's boss is here."

Max stopped typing. "Bishop?"

"Yep."

"What's he doing here?"

"Apparently just finished up another investigation in Chicago."

"So what's he doing here?"

Ethan grinned. "I'm trying to make out whether you consider him a rival or just somebody who's going to spirit Nell back to Virginia."

Max refused to give him the satisfaction, and said only, "Answer my question. What's he doing here?"

"Tying up a few loose ends. Supplying some necessary paperwork, like that original FBI profile. Lending his expertise while we try to find answers for the few remaining questions. Gathering up his people."

"Where's Nell?"

"Talking to him in the conference room."

Max pushed his chair back and got up.

"Statement finished?" Ethan asked politely.

"Do not make me tell you what to do with your statement. I'll finish it later."

Ethan laughed, but didn't protest when Max left the office he'd been using and made his way through the mostly deserted sheriff's department to the conference room.

Despite Ethan's goading, Max didn't really consider Bishop a threat to his relationship with Nell, but he was intensely curious to meet the man. He paused in the doorway, noting that Galen was there — very relaxed with his feet propped up as he thumbed through the town newspaper. Justin and Shelby were also there, sitting at the far end of the conference table.

Two other people were in the room. Nell was casual in jeans and a sweater, only the sling holding her left arm immobile a sign of the bullet wound in her shoulder. Yesterday's shock over discovering that Hailey was dead — and had, apparently, appeared with amazing corporeality to help Nell — had not lingered very long; Nell was far more sanguine about such things than most people would have been.

Her only wry comment had been that she should have known Hailey would try to control things to her liking even from beyond the grave.

Now, composed as always, she was talking intently to the man half sitting on the conference table as they faced each other.

He was a big man, probably somewhere in his late thirties, dressed as casually as the others, in dark pants and a black leather jacket. Obviously powerful, he had an athletic build and a way of holding himself that said he was very comfortable in his own skin.

He was also good-looking in the dark, hawklike way that women seemed to love. Jet-black hair. The kind of tan that hadn't come from a sunlamp. Movie-star good-looking, Max thought, eyeing that perfect profile with unease. Then Bishop turned his head suddenly, and Max felt a shock.

The scar marking his left cheek was more distinctive than disfiguring and, added to the dramatic widow's peak and the narrow streak of pure white hair just above his left temple, lent him an appearance as striking as it was unusual.

This was one FBI agent, Max thought, who would rarely find it possible to work undercover.

Max moved into the room to be introduced to Noah Bishop, and as they shook hands he noted that the handsome face was still and that the steady eyes probably seemed chilly due to their pale silvery color.

Or maybe not.

"Glad to finally meet you," Bishop said, his voice deep and not quite as cool as those eyes.

Max decided not to question that statement, merely saying, "An interesting unit you've put together, Agent Bishop. Nell told me you're a telepath? A touch telepath, I think she said."

Hard mouth curving slightly, Bishop said, "That's right."

"Which means . . . what? That you can read someone's mind when you touch them?" He tried not to feel wary over the fact that he had just shaken hands with the man.

Bishop shrugged, still smiling faintly. "About sixty to seventy percent of the time, yeah."

Shelby said, "Who would have thunk it? Psychic FBI agents."

"What *will* they think of next," Justin murmured.

Max, who was determined not to ask if he fell into the percentage of people Bishop could read, met Nell's steady, amused gaze and wondered suddenly if he was so transparent that a blind man could have read him, never mind a psychic.

Galen spoke up then to say, "Not all of us are psychic, you know."

Bishop looked at him, brows lifting. "Well, technically you are."

"Only by your definition. And you'll never make me believe that you didn't add a footnote to the SCU manual just to make sure I'd have the qualifications for the job."

"There's a manual?" Shelby looked from one to the other with brightly interested eyes.

Max, who was more curious to know just how Galen fit into the SCU, opened his mouth to ask, but then forgot to when he saw Bishop look toward the door suddenly, his face changing rather dramatically.

The agent began smiling — a real smile this time — and those chilly eyes warmed up about forty degrees, transforming him from a cool professional to a man who was very happy and didn't give a damn who knew it. He moved past Max toward the doorway, and Max turned just in time to see the gorgeous, smiling Lauren Champagne come into the room and get lifted off her feet in a welcoming hug.

Somewhat blankly, Justin said, "I take it they know each other."

"You could say that." Nell grinned. "You could also say they're married."

Max stared at her. "You never mentioned Bishop was married."

"No. I didn't, did I?"

Galen chuckled and said, "It's hell when she knows where all your buttons are, isn't it?"

"Quit stirring up trouble," Nell told her partner.

"Who, me?"

"You thrive on it. Look, why don't we all sit down?"

"Is your shoulder bothering you?" Max asked her.

"Buttons, buttons everywhere," Galen murmured.

Nell sent him a threatening look and said to Max, "No, I'm fine. But since we're all trying to finish up reports and statements today, there are probably some things we need to talk about."

"I wouldn't say there were many questions left," Galen said somewhat lazily.

"A few loose ends," Bishop said as he and his wife joined the others at the conference table.

Justin, noting that Lauren Champagne's formerly dark eyes were now an electric blue, said slowly, "Contact lenses."

She smiled at him. "It's amazing how just a couple of simple things can make you look different. Brown contact lenses, a bottle tan, a slightly different accent. I'm Miranda, by the way."

"Why use a false name?" Max wondered.

"It isn't a false name, it just isn't mine." She shrugged. "Sometimes it's quicker and easier to borrow the name and background of a real person — which is why we've built and maintain a list of cops and other useful people around the country who're willing to give up their identities temporarily. The real Lauren Champagne is a cop who wanted to take a few months off from her job in Virginia and drive across the country."

"Every investigation we get involved in is different," Bishop said. "In this case, we had Nell, who had a perfect cover because she had a legitimate reason for coming to Silence. But we needed someone inside the sheriff's department as well, someone who could move among and observe the other cops, check the files and other paperwork, that sort of thing."

"It took time," Miranda continued. "So I came down here first and settled in, a couple of months before we knew Adam Gallagher's estate would be through probate and Nell could be expected to arrive."

"By the time I got here," Nell continued, "Miranda had eliminated most of the cops from suspicion, but there were several we couldn't be sure about. And then there was you, Justin." She smiled faintly. "We were sure Max had brought you in because Ethan was making noises about arresting him for the murders and he knew he needed someone solidly on his side involved in the investigation. But even if we'd been wrong about that, you were eliminated from suspicion because you hadn't been in Silence long enough."

"You knew I could be trusted. Which is why you aimed Shelby at me."

Shelby started laughing.

Nell grinned. "Well, yeah. I knew the answer to why George Caldwell had been killed lay in those birth records, and I couldn't really check into them myself."

"What *was* in those records?" Shelby demanded. "Nobody ever told me."

"Kyle had done what he called some 'discreet' checking to find out if he could inherit my father's — our father's estate," Nell said. "He wasn't about to go to Wade Keever, given his reputation for indiscretion *and* the fact that he was the lawyer for the Gallagher family, so Kyle went to another lawyer in Silence, one who wouldn't ask too many questions."

Nell sighed. "That lawyer's golfing partner happened to be George Caldwell, to whom he casually mentioned Kyle's questions. Curious, Caldwell started digging. The irony from our point of view is that there was nothing there to find.

Nothing at all in Kyle's birth record that was in the least bit suspicious."

"All those hours reading birth records," Shelby moaned.

"I know. Sorry about that. What actually happened, as far as we can tell, is that when he couldn't find anything in the records, Caldwell just casually asked Kyle if he was related to the Gallaghers. By then, word was spreading — thanks to Wade Keever — that I was coming home. Kyle was afraid Caldwell would ask me the same question, and since he wanted the timing of introducing himself to me as my brother to be his rather than someone else's, he decided to get Caldwell out of the way. Another murder didn't mean anything to him, after all. It was just like swatting a troublesome fly. Putting together the blackmail scheme was just a fun bonus."

"What about the other lawyer?" Justin asked. "Didn't he pose a bigger threat to Kyle?"

"No, because Caldwell never got the chance to tell Kyle what it was that had made him curious. But we were afraid Wade Keever might pose a threat, not because we were sure he knew anything to threaten the killer, but because we were certain if he *did* know anything he certainly wouldn't be able to keep his mouth shut about it." Nell frowned suddenly and looked at Miranda. "I guess we can let him come home now."

"I've already called the safe house and ordered his release." Miranda chuckled. "He'd stopped threatening a lawsuit and was playing poker with the agent watching him. So now he really does have some information worth sharing."

"You mean you kidnapped Wade Keever?" Shelby exclaimed, grinning.

"Not at all," Miranda said. "I just suggested he might want to relocate until we identified the killer."

"Suggested at gunpoint," Bishop murmured. "At night, underneath a streetlight."

"Like you wouldn't have done the same thing."

Bishop started to deny it, then paused, considered, and suddenly smiled. "You're right. I would have."

"Not finished yet?" Nell asked, coming into the small office where Max was typing his statement.

"Almost. I think Ethan gave me that list of questions just to keep me here all day."

"Now, would he do that?" Nell asked,

perching on a corner of the desk Max was using.

"I won't even dignify that with an answer."

"Good to see you two playing nice again."

"Is that what you'd call it?"

Nell grinned. "Well, yeah. For you two."

Max sighed. "We'll see. Listen, I meant to ask sooner if you'd decided to keep looking for where Adam buried your mother."

"Ethan says his people will. Now that we know Hailey's was the murder I saw in my vision and that Kyle was the one who killed her, finding my mother's remains is really the only thing left to do. For closure, I mean."

"Do you think Kyle deliberately buried her locket with Hailey to throw you off in case you ever came back?"

"Maybe. Or maybe he was just getting rid of all he had of his other sister — me. We'll never know now, I guess."

"Unless Hailey comes back again?"

Nell smiled. "I don't think she will. She took care of her unfinished business in one night."

"And now she's at peace?"

"I hope so. Bishop says that sort of visitation only happens when a spirit is ready to move on."

Max pushed his chair back from the desk a bit and eyed her somewhat hesitantly. "Didn't Bishop also say the plan was for the team to leave first thing tomorrow?"

"Yeah, but he and Miranda have already gone." Nell smiled. "Considering how long she had to be down here and the fact that they were barely able to see each other the whole time, I think they intend a little R and R on their way back to Quantico."

"I don't know where he's spent the past weeks, but I'd say she's certainly earned some time off."

Nell nodded. "They work together as much as possible, but sometimes they have to be on different cases. It's tough on them, I think."

Max braced himself. "I imagine it's easier because they love each other. Or harder."

"It's something they've had to deal with."

"Which they've clearly done. Dealt with the problems and figured out a way to make it work."

Nell drew a breath and let it out slowly. "Speaking of which."

"Yeah." Max wondered if he looked as

tense as he felt. "I've tried not to push, Nell. Tried to give you time to think things over."

"I know you have. Thank you."

She was so grave that Max felt a chill of real fear. "You aren't — You won't leave in the morning. Will you?"

"Max, are you sure? Really sure?"

It was his turn to draw in a breath and let it out. "If you have any doubts, open that goddamned door. I love you, Nell. I want to spend the rest of my life with you."

Still grave, she said, "Even if it would mean my traveling sometimes for my job? Bishop says there's no reason why the SCU can't base agents in other areas of the country, especially since we travel so much anyway. I could work out of the Baton Rouge field office. Could you deal with that?"

"Yes. Happily."

"My work is dangerous sometimes, you know that. And I can't afford to be distracted at the wrong moment. So if the door stays open, we'll both have to learn how to handle it."

"We will."

"Are you sure?"

"Open the door, Nell."

She looked at him for a long, steady moment, then opened the door. His thoughts flowed into hers, his emotions. His utter certainty. She caught her breath, stared into his dark eyes.

"I love you," he said. "We've always been forever, Nell. Didn't you know?"

"I know now," she said.

Careful not to jar her wounded shoulder, Max reached up and pulled her into his arms, and again Nell had that sense of coming home. But this time, there was no fear, no reluctance, nothing inside her insisting she hide any part of herself from him.

This time, it didn't take a physical act to drive Nell to open her mind and heart to him. And this time, not even she had the ability to close that door. Not any longer.

"I love you, Max."

"It's about damned time," he said, and kissed her.